> "Karen Ranney writes with power,
> passion, and dramatic flair."
> *New York Times* bestselling author
> Stephanie Laurens

A LORD NOT MEANT TO MARRY

Hamish MacRae, a changed man, returned to his beloved Scotland intending to turn his back on the world. The proud, brooding lord wants nothing more than to be left alone, but an unwanted visitor to his lonely castle has defied his wishes. While it is true that this healer, Mary Gilly, is a beauty beyond compare, it will take more than her miraculous potions to soothe his wounded spirit. But Mary's tender heart is slowly melting Hamish's frozen one . . . and awakening a burning need to keep her with him—forever.

A LADY WHO DARES NOT LOVE

Never before has Mary felt such an attraction to a man! The mysterious Hamish MacRae is strong and commanding, with a face and form so handsome it makes Mary tremble with wanting him. Yet, already shadowy forces are coming closer, heartless whispers and cruel rumors abound, and it will take a love more pure and powerful than any other to divine the truth—and promise a future neither had dreamed possible.

KAREN RANNEY

TO LOVE A SCOTTISH LORD
BOOK FOUR OF THE HIGHLAND LORDS

An Avon Romantic Treasure

AVON BOOKS
An Imprint of HarperCollinsPublishers

This is a work of fiction. Names, characters, places, and incidents are products of the author's imagination or are used fictitiously and are not to be construed as real. Any resemblance to actual events, locales, organizations, or persons, living or dead, is entirely coincidental.

AVON BOOKS
An Imprint of HarperCollins*Publishers*
10 East 53rd Street
New York, New York 10022-5299

Copyright © 2003 by Karen Ranney
ISBN: 0-380-82106-0
www.avonromance.com

First Avon Books paperback printing: August 2003

Avon Trademark Reg. U.S. Pat. Off. and in Other Countries, Marca Registrada, Hecho en U.S.A.
HarperCollins® is a registered trademark of HarperCollins Publishers Inc.

Printed in the U.S.A.

10 9 8 7 6 5 4 3 2 1

With grateful appreciation to
Suzie Housley,
who named Book Four

Prologue

September 1782

Scotland welcomed Hamish MacRae back to her shores with fists of black clouds looming on the horizon. Weak sunlight left the day overcast and gray, and the wind whistled out of the north, chilling him to the bone.

He anticipated the coming storm, the pulsing, pounding fury of it. He wanted to experience a Highland tempest in all its rage. He'd stand in the middle of it, arms outstretched to the heavens, and command the thunder, invite the lightning. Perhaps God would finally strike him dead for all his sins.

"There," he said, pointing to where the land sat humped like a dragon's back. Atop the last mound was a castle, a place he'd remembered from a previous visit to Scotland. A desolate-looking sentinel on a rocky islet, it was connected by a small stone causeway to the mainland.

1

"It's a ruin," his brother Brendan said at his side.

"I've lived in worse."

From the Orient to India, they'd each spent time in palaces and hovels. Even their own ancestral home, Gilmuir, might be considered a ruin. His older brother had it in his mind to rebuild the castle. Hamish had no doubt that Alisdair would have accomplished miracles since he'd seen the place three years ago.

"Set me down here," Hamish said, wishing that his throat didn't feel scraped raw. He'd have to learn to deal with the new sound of his voice as well as other reminders of his time in India.

Brendan moved to stand a little ahead of Hamish on the bow, as if that foot or so distance would gain him a better vantage point over what he studied now.

"No man could survive there."

"Which is not exactly a deterrent," Hamish said, allowing a small smile to curve his lips.

"Don't joke about such things."

Brendan had lost his humor in the past three months while Hamish had, oddly enough, gained a sense of the ridiculous.

"Very well. Let's discuss my life. I have to live it somewhere."

"You could remain at sea."

Hamish smiled again and tipped his head in acknowledgment of Brendan's words. "Of course I could. I'm a captain who's not only lost his crew and his ship but also the use of his arm. Who wouldn't wish to sail with me?"

Brendan's silence didn't surprise him. Even his brother couldn't conjure up a remedy for the wreck he'd become.

His smile was too difficult to hold, so Hamish let it slip away. "You'll get what I need, then?"

"You know I will," Brendan answered. "What will I tell the others?"

By the others, Brendan meant his two older brothers, Alisdair and James. Hamish loved his brothers, but he didn't want their companionship or their understanding. Nor did he need their pity.

"Tell them whatever you wish, Brendan. Something, hopefully, that will keep them far from here. Tell them the truth, if you must."

"What is the truth, Hamish? You've been sparing with it ever since India."

Hamish turned and looked at his younger brother. What did Brendan want from him, a litany of his capture? If so, he was doomed to be disappointed. Some things Hamish would never tell anyone.

He directed his attention to the castle.

The shoreline was rocky, and farther in, the black boulders gave way to multicolored stones in hues of gray, black, and brown. Beyond the bridge was a strip of pines curving around to the road like a green ruff adorning a crone's neck.

In his mind he'd named it Aonaranach, the Gaelic for lonely. The place was obviously deserted, as were so many other dwellings in the Highlands. Once Hamish might have been curious about why it had been abandoned. Now, however, he couldn't summon up a thought or a degree of empathy for the long-vanished inhabitants. All he cared about was that it was empty and a refuge of sorts for him.

"If you're going to ground, Hamish, at least choose a half-decent burrow."

Hamish glanced over at his brother, frowning. "It will do for my use. It's deserted and far away from any settlement."

"I don't like this."

"I know your sentiments, Brendan. You've been very clear about them."

"But it doesn't matter, does it? You're set on this, Hamish?"

He nodded, staring at the castle. "I'll not return to Gilmuir." He'd been too ill to countermand Brendan's instructions when they'd left India. Now, however, he was grateful his brother hadn't decided to go home to Nova Scotia. He could well imagine what the sight of him would do to his parents. Yet he wasn't prepared to sail farther north for Gilmuir, either.

"Dying won't make them come back," Brendan said.

Hamish didn't bother explaining that he had more guilt to bear than the loss of his crew. He only smiled, touched despite himself by his brother's fierce devotion. Brendan had always been loyal. Why had he expected this situation to be any different?

Ever since they were young, he and Brendan had been the closest of the MacRae brothers. They'd goaded and pushed each other, each always achieving more with that extra bit of competition. They'd planned their voyages to meet in far-off cities, and sometimes the two MacRae ships would take the same trade route.

Now, however, he wished that Brendan would simply let him be.

"I won't die, Brendan," he said. "I have an unquenchable, irrational, desperate desire to live." The fact that he was standing there proved that.

Brendan didn't say anything else, only moved away, no doubt to give orders to his men.

Hamish stood at the bow and listened to the sounds behind him, playing a game in his mind about what the crew would be doing. The scrape of metal against metal was the sound of the anchor being lowered. Its drag would slow the forward momentum of the ship. Iron against wood signaled that the heavy sails were being drawn in, the huff of canvas as wind clung and then reluctantly surrendered its hold.

Slowing a ship was noisy business, but speech was needed only to relate orders. There was no good-natured ribbing or laughter, or supposition about the shore leave soon to come. A pall had fallen over the ship ever since India.

The first mate came and stood beside him. Hamish knew the man well from previous voyages. Sandy, they called him, not because of the color of his hair but because of his first adventure at sea. He'd stranded a longboat on a sand bar and had been ridiculed by his crewmates, the teasing resulting in the name he had carried for twenty years.

"I'll have my trunk," Hamish said, and gave the order for the other possessions he wanted. He'd have enough provisions to last him until Brendan came back. His brother had reluctantly agreed to bring supplies to the castle, at least until Hamish decided what to do with his life . . . or until death itself claimed him.

The first mate nodded, but unlike his brother, he didn't try to talk Hamish out of his decision. Perhaps Sandy, and the others, couldn't wait for him to leave the ship. Sailors were a notoriously superstitious group, and his presence aboard was no doubt seen as a bad omen.

Less than an hour later, he was being rowed to shore. Brendan sat opposite him in the boat, frowning at him.

"You've done all that you can and more," Hamish told his brother, trying to assuage any misplaced guilt Brendan might be feeling.

"Why do you talk as if you're dying, Hamish?" Brendan said sharply. "Is that what you're going to do, will yourself to die?"

"The process of attrition?" Hamish asked, genuinely amused. He would simply forget to eat or drink, not make the effort to tap a cask or remove a piece of hardtack or jerky from its crate. He would simply not hunt or prepare a fire. Without his lifting a hand, death might come to him. It was a frighteningly seductive thought.

To die, and not to feel. To die and no longer hear the tortured screams of his crew. To die and not awake sweating and racked with guilt. But he didn't die easily. Hadn't he already proven that?

The boat hit the shore, and Hamish stood, grabbing one end of his trunk with his good hand.

"You only need time," Brendan said, reaching for the other handle. "You still haven't completely healed from your wounds."

Hamish only smiled. He was completely healed, but he'd never again be whole.

Chapter 1

"**T**ell me about my patient," Mary Gilly said.

"When we were boys, I called him Hammer," Brendan said, glancing over at her and then away as if afraid to witness her response to his words.

"Hammer?" Mary asked. "A rather fearsome name."

Brendan smiled, an appealing expression she'd thought when she'd first viewed it. Now, however, she was well aware that the man was actively attempting to charm her.

"As a boy he had a head as hard as iron. He used to butt me in the stomach whenever he didn't like what I had to say, which was most of the time. I started calling him Hammer then."

"I'm more interested in him as a man," she said.

"I no longer call him Hammer, of course. It would be foolish to call a man over thirty by his boyhood name. Yet I've been known to do something daft now and then." He glanced at her again, and Mary couldn't help but wonder

7

if he was thinking that bringing her here was one of those foolish acts.

She was having the same doubts.

He was the brother of Alisdair MacRae of Gilmuir, a long-time customer of her husband's. Had it not been for the fact that she'd known Alisdair and his wife, Iseabal, a number of years, she wouldn't have considered leaving Inverness with Brendan. Now, however, she doubted the wisdom of that decision.

Mary stared straight ahead, deliberately concentrating on the mane between her horse's ears. She and her long-suffering mare were both feeling the effects of this journey. They'd been pelted by rains all day. At first, the roads were not only passable, but very good. In the afternoon, however, they'd turned off the main thoroughfare and were now following a meandering course beside the loch. This path was rutted and muddy, their pace slow to allow the full wagon behind them to catch up from time to time.

"Don't be surprised by his appearance, Angel."

She glanced at him, irritated. "Please, do not call me by that name."

"It's what everyone in Inverness calls you." There was that charming smile again.

"Not everyone," she countered.

"Enough."

"Just because people repeat something doesn't mean it's right or proper." She looked at him, willing him to understand. "I do not want you to think that I'm capable of miracles. I can't guarantee to help your brother," she said, compelled to offer him the truth. "His injuries may be too far advanced for my limited skills."

"He may be too far for anyone's," Brendan said glumly.

"It's been nearly a month since you've last seen him?"

Another question trembled on her lips. Finally, she forced herself to speak it. "Are you certain he's still alive?"

"Of course he is." But his lips thinned, and his expression made her wonder if he were as optimistic as he sounded.

The farther west they traveled, the more barren and desolate the landscape became. To their left was the loch and beyond, the sea. On the right were stark mountains even now dusted with snow. The lowering skies tinted everything somber and gray, the color of sadness.

She smoothed her hand over the medicine case on the saddle in front of her. The case was a talisman of sorts, and her stroking a habit. The leather was worn smooth where her fingers had caressed it beneath the handle so many times before when she was nervous or simply waiting.

Patience was a requirement in healing, she'd discovered. She must wait for a patient to improve, for a medicine to work, for a fever to break. Sometimes, the outlook was good. At other times, it was not, and Death swooped in, black garbed and cackling, to steal the ill from her grasp.

"You mustn't be surprised at his appearance," Brendan said. It was the second time he'd made the comment, as if he were afraid she'd exclaim aloud or recoil in aversion upon meeting her new patient.

Otherwise, he'd been remarkably reticent about his brother's injuries. She, in her pride and foolishness, had been in a rush to be of assistance, not asking all the questions she should have prior to leaving Inverness.

"I've seen many grievous things, Brendan," she assured him quietly.

"India changed him. He's not as he was."

"People who've always been healthy often react with

anger to sudden illness. They don't expect their bodies to betray them."

"He's not angry," he said and then looked away, as if uncertain whether to continue. "Perhaps resigned," he added after a moment. "He seems to simply accept whatever happens to him, almost as if he's ready for the worst. It's not like Hamish."

"It could be a symptom of his illness," she told him, familiar with such behavior in her patients. "Even the healthiest man will have the doldrums if he's been laid low."

He nodded but said nothing further.

Her hands were chilled beneath her leather gloves, and Mary felt as though she had never been warm or dry. The wind whistled out of the north, flattening the horse's mane. A gust traveled beneath her voluminous red cloak, lingering at her ankles. She held herself tight, elbows pressed against her sides, chin erect.

"We'll be there shortly," Mary said. It was not a question, rather a hope voiced in a statement. Brendan, however, did not dispute it, remaining silent.

He reminded her, oddly, of her late husband's apprentice, Charles. Brendan was a more attractive man, with an open countenance and a face that encouraged an answering smile. His hazel eyes were earnest; his brown hair had a habit of falling over his brow boyishly.

Charles had a narrow face and an even narrower mind. Over the past few months, he'd been irritatingly possessive of her, so much so that she'd seen this new patient as an escape, of sorts.

The two men were alike, however, in their single-mindedness. At dawn they'd left Inverness and had begun their trek west, never halting despite the weather. She had the feeling that no obstacle would stop Brendan until they reached his brother.

She'd never been this far from home, and during this interminable day told herself that the adventure of this journey would be worth the minor discomforts of it. When other people mentioned their travels from now on, she would be able to say that she, too, had traveled beyond Inverness. Even if the only sights she saw were snow-capped peaks and a gray, finger-shaped lake that pointed to the sea.

Brendan slowed his horse, pointing ahead. "There it is, Castle Gloom."

"Castle Gloom?"

"That's what I thought when I first saw the place," he said, staring ahead.

Peering through the trees that lined the road, she saw her destination. She'd never expected an isolated castle dominated by a tall tower. Of dark red brick and stone, it seemed a blot on the landscape. Almost a wound. The thought was as disconcerting as the flock of seabirds suddenly circling overhead. With a rush of wings, they flew swiftly away in the other direction, almost as if in warning.

They heard the explosion first. Brendan's face paled, but before she could understand what he was about to do, let alone prevent it, he lunged at her, launching himself off his saddle and into her with such force that she was catapulted to the ground. A moment later, she was on her back in the grass beside the road with him atop her. Before she could push him away or demand to know what insanity had overcome him, a projectile crashed into the tree to their left.

"He's firing at us! The damn fool is firing at us!"

"Who is?"

"Hamish!" he said angrily.

She pushed at Brendan's shoulder. He moved off her, but neither of them made an effort to rise.

"What sort of man shoots at his own brother?"

Brendan didn't have an answer to her question, and she didn't press the matter. In a moment, she sat up. He stood and helped her stand.

Her knee hurt and her left shoulder ached from where she'd hit the ground too hard. However, she didn't mention those minor inconveniences. They paled in significance to being blown away by a cannonball.

Behind them, the trees sparkled. In the grayness of the day, the sight was eerie, as if she'd chanced upon a magical forest. Mary bent and picked up a piece of the shot and held the warm, glittery metal in her gloved palm.

Before she could comment on it, Brendan reached out and plucked it from her hand.

"What is it?" she asked.

"A piece of bronze."

He met her eyes. In his gaze was the same confusion she felt.

"Why is he shooting at us?"

"I don't know, Angel," he said.

This time, however, she didn't correct him.

If he'd only lowered the sight two inches, he might have been able to hit the top of the tall pine. Hamish jotted down the coordinates, using a piece of charcoal wrapped in a rag. He was nearly out of paper. He hoped Brendan arrived before the rest of his supplies were as depleted.

The tower room in which he sat was drafty. He'd stuffed straw in some of the archer's slits to cut down on the wind, but he'd left the lone window open, folding back the shutters. Now the barrel of the cannon rested on the stone sill.

On one of his early explorations of the ruins of his borrowed home, he'd discovered the cannon sitting there in the tower. It hadn't been difficult to figure out why such armament had been laboriously carried up the four flights of curving stairs. Resting just within the curtain wall that followed the irregular shape of the island, the tower commanded a view of the countryside and was in the perfect defensible position. If he stood at the window and looked left he'd have a view of the loch and beyond, the sea. To his right was a narrow strip of woods and the road that led to civilization.

The bridge, however, was flooded at every high tide, protecting him from any possible intrusion.

He pulled the cannon back on squeaking wheels and loaded it again, using bits of metal and stone as shot. As for powder, there was plenty of that. The defenders of Aonaranach had left a small magazine behind, buried beneath a pile of straw.

Reaching for his tinder box, he lit it and then the fuse, stepping back a few feet while the cannon belched its contents in a deep-throated roar.

There, he'd hit the pine tree exactly.

A shout made him straighten and approach the window. With one hand braced against the sill, he leaned out to his right. A scrap of red material tied to a long branch was emerging from the grove of trees. At the end of it was a very angry Brendan.

Hamish understood immediately. He'd been firing at a tree only a short distance from where his brother stood. He waved his arm to signal that he'd seen the makeshift flag. Brendan, in turn, frowned up at him, and then staked the branch in the ground, standing there with feet planted apart and arms folded in front of him.

A woman stepped out from behind a tree to join him. She wore a bright red wool skirt and cloak, but her kerchief was missing. Brendan's flag, he thought.

Hamish pulled back but she didn't move, her face tilted up to the window. He wondered if she'd seen him and then thought not. If she had, she wouldn't have continued to watch with such a calm expression on her face. Nor would her smile, small though it was, have remained so firmly moored on those full lips.

Her hair was brown, with hints of gold glinting in it even on this gray and somber day. Her eyes were dark, but she was too far away for him to discern the color. Her waist was narrow and her bosom ample. Only her slender neck and delicate wrists showed, and glimpses of her ankles as she walked. The vision he instantly had of her naked reminded him how long it had been since he'd been with a woman.

A wife? Three weeks was too little time for even his fast-acting brother to secure a bride.

"I'll be married come the spring," he'd said in India. "I have a yen to settle with one woman."

"Where would you put this bride of yours?" Hamish had asked.

Brendan's ship was large, one of the first vessels built at Gilmuir. Even so, his accommodations and captain's quarters were too small for a family.

"I'm thinking in Scotland," Brendan said. "Or maybe Nova Scotia. Either is as close to a man of the sea."

"Do you think that's fair? You'd be away for years at a time, and she might actually be lonely for you. If, that is, you manage to find the one woman in the world who would miss that ugly face of yours."

Brendan had only smirked at him, secure in his ability to attract females.

No, she couldn't be a wife. Even Brendan couldn't be that fortunate.

Brendan turned toward her, saying something that made her smile fade. She tilted her head back and regarded the tower once more.

Hamish left the window and stood in the middle of the circular room. If it had been only Brendan, he wouldn't have felt any hesitation in descending the stairs and opening the oak-banded door he'd repaired. But he was curiously reluctant to show himself now. He'd not been in close quarters with a woman since he'd been captured.

He wished, for the first time since he'd left Brendan's ship, that he'd thought to bring a mirror. After he stared into it, he'd be able to gauge the depth of her revulsion. How would she act? Would she gasp or shudder, or give in to tears?

There was nothing to do but let them in. Bending beneath the lintel, he descended the stairs. Once on the ground floor, he removed the bar and opened the door, taking the precaution of retreating to the steps again to stand in the shadows.

Brendan came first, looking around the tower. He marched to the bottom of the steps, and catching sight of Hamish, placed his fists on his hips and glared.

"It's taken you long enough, brother," Hamish said.

"Is that how you repay me for my tardiness, Hamish? By trying to kill me? Why the hell were you shooting at us?" Brendan's shouts echoed through the tower. Where once there'd been no sound at all in the castle, now there was abruptly too much.

"I was not," Hamish said stiffly, all too conscious of the arrival of the woman behind his brother. "I was simply amusing myself. If I'd known you were there, I would have pointed the cannon in the opposite direction."

"Where did you get a cannon, Hamish? I would have thought this godawful place would only boast spiders and bats."

There had been enough of those, but he felt a curious protectiveness for his hermitage and only said, "A legacy from a former owner, no doubt. Someone once wished to defend it."

"I can't see why."

Brendan stepped aside, leaving Hamish an unobstructed view of the woman in crimson.

Her eyes were brown; an unremarkable color that nonetheless now seemed deep, dark, and almost mysterious.

"Who are you?" he asked in a voice sharper than he'd intended.

Brendan frowned up at him, almost protectively.

"Angel, this surly creature is my brother. Hamish, allow me to introduce Mrs. Mary Gilly. A healer of some repute."

He told himself that he was enraged because Brendan had overstepped his authority, not because of the way his brother's hand rested on the woman's shoulder. Nor did his sudden foul mood have anything to do with the soft and winsome smile she gave him in return.

"A healer? All I wanted was for you to bring the provisions I asked for, Brendan," he said curtly.

She took a few steps forward, and Hamish took another step back, wishing that he had the power to banish her with the blink of an eye or a commanding gesture of one finger pointed toward the door. He held up his hand, palm toward her as if to ward her off.

"I am sorry you've come all this way for nothing," he said. A perfectly rational sentence uttered in a remarkably civil tone. Considering that he'd not talked to another human being in three weeks, he should be congratulated not only for the restraint of his utterance, but also for the clarity of it.

Abruptly, he turned on his heel and left them.

Chapter 2

Brendan entered Hamish's room without knocking, but then, Hamish expected it. Brendan could be exceptionally charming when he wished, but now was not one of those occasions.

His brother halted at the threshold, staring at the cannon still sitting by the window. "You'd have more room in here if you moved that thing outside."

"Ah, but then I wouldn't have been able to amuse myself by lopping off the tops of trees."

"Is that what you were doing?" Brendan frowned. "A waste of your talents, Hamish."

"Who is she?" Hamish asked, changing the topic of this conversation.

"A woman of Inverness," Brendan answered. "As I told you, a healer with a great reputation."

"Why do you call her Angel?"

"She evidently saved a little boy on his deathbed. At least that's the story Iseabal related. She knows of Mary's talents because of her husband, a goldsmith. Evidently, she and Alisdair commissioned him to make several objects for Gilmuir."

"She's married?"

"No longer. Her husband died some time ago, I believe."

"So you fetched her from Inverness because of Iseabal's recommendation?"

"Can you think of a better reason?"

In all honesty, he could not. Hamish had the greatest admiration for his sister-in-law. The problem was that he didn't want a healer there.

"Mrs. Gilly sounds like she will be sorely missed in Inverness. Perhaps you should take her back there with all possible speed."

"Don't you want to get better?"

Hamish couldn't help but laugh at that question. "I am as good as I will get." He turned, finally, and faced Brendan, standing unflinching before his brother's inspection. He spread one hand out while the other remained at his side, useless. "This is all that I am. This is what I look like healed. If she can give me back the whole of my body, I would take it. Gratefully. But she cannot."

"Perhaps she can, especially if she's as gifted as they say."

"I need no miracle worker, Brendan. God Himself would have to erase these scars."

"They'll heal in time, Hamish, and not be as noticeable as now."

"But they'll always be there. Take her back to Inverness, Brendan."

"I don't think Mary will go," he said.

Hamish turned and faced the window again. "Then you must convince her."

Brendan had been there less than ten minutes and had already made his presence felt in the old castle. Through the window, Hamish could see a wagon piled high with boxes and crates on the bridge, being unloaded by two more strangers.

Mary Gilly was striding across the courtyard toward the castle. The least Brendan could have done was to bring him a healer who was advanced in years, someone with age and wisdom, and missing a few teeth, perhaps. Or a physician, if no old wise woman was available.

A beautiful woman had power of her own. Was that how she healed her male patients? Did she simply will them to health? He wasn't immune to such blandishments. As the Atavasi had learned, he was all too human.

Had she charmed Brendan? Was that why he'd brought her there?

The twilight graced her with loveliness, the shadows falling over her like an ethereal blanket. She seemed a part of this place, a ghost returning to its home.

"Who are the others?"

"A cook and a carpenter."

"All I wanted was a few supplies, Brendan. I don't need a cook, a carpenter, and most especially a healer."

"I've never seen a man who needed one more."

Hamish sent a swift look to his brother, and Brendan only smiled in response.

Hamish MacRae might be her patient, but it was only too obvious that she wasn't wanted. After Brendan followed his brother up the sloping stairs, Mary remained where she was, feeling like a parcel Brendan had forgotten.

The ground floor was sparsely furnished. A settle made of planked pine sat to the side of an arched fireplace. Two chairs and a table on the other side of the room comprised the remainder of the furniture.

Long moments passed, but Brendan didn't return. She could hear the sound of voices, and it disturbed her to be an accidental eavesdropper on their conversation. Turning, she left the tower.

She stood in the middle of the courtyard on a grassy patch of ground with the wind pressing her skirt against her legs and tossing her hair askew. She was an Inverness woman, born and raised within the city. True, there were grand sights to be seen there, and places to go that caused her breath to hitch in wonder or sheer pleasure. However, nothing she'd ever seen before incited her imagination as much as Castle Gloom did now.

Where were the men in arms who'd once patrolled these walls? Where had the cook and all her helpers gone, and the lord of the manor? What had happened to the lady, and any children born here? They'd simply vanished, and she couldn't help but wonder what had happened to them all.

She turned slowly, thinking that the castle didn't look nearly as forlorn or forbidding as it had appeared from the road. To her left was a long, rectangular building backing up to the wall for shelter. To her right was the tower, midpoint in the long, curving wall. Behind her was a glorified lean-to that had evidently been used to house the animals, and where she and Brendan had put their own mounts.

Crossing the courtyard, she knelt at the wide stone lip of the well and lowered the bucket, delighted to discover that the water was crystal clear and cold. Placing the dipper back in the bucket, she followed her inclination and headed for the main building.

If she were to stay there, at least for a few days, she

must find a place to call hers, a little corner of Castle Gloom where she could command some privacy, arrange her medicines, and treat Hamish. She wondered if Brendan would be able to convince his brother that she could be of assistance.

A stubborn man couldn't be reasoned into changing his mind. He must be led to it by example. More easily done in Inverness, where there were a host of cures and enough tales of her successes to bolster a patient's confidence in her. But here, in this remote castle, how did she convince Hamish MacRae to trust her?

She pushed open an oak door, surprised that it swung ajar easily. A short hallway gave way to a large room, surprisingly well lit. She tilted her head back to see the windows aligned high in the wall. As if heaven approved of her curiosity, the sun suddenly speared through a cloud, further illuminating the chamber.

The room was barren, but without much imagining, she could almost see the shields on the walls and the banners hanging across the ceiling. This place held the memory of its own history, even if none of its inhabitants was there to speak of it.

The wooden door was heavily notched in places, as if someone had leaned against the frame and nicked at it with his knife in boredom. The stone floor beneath her feet was pocked and smooth, made that way by generations of well-shod feet. Yet, for all the emptiness of this place, it wasn't a sad room. Instead, it felt merely waiting, as if it were a sentient being and knew, somehow, that its time had not quite passed.

She turned and walked through the hall to a short door set into the wall to her left. This chamber was filled with shadows, and she didn't enter it completely, merely stood at the threshold looking inside. Evidently, the room had once been used for lodging, judging by the number of cots stacked against one wall. She couldn't help but wonder if the castle had been used to garrison troops, since a belt buckle and a powder horn sat against the wall near the door.

On the other side of the Great Hall was another room. Inside, a long wooden table stretched the length of the space. Dozens of shelves lined the walls, but they were all empty. Not one pot or pan remained in the kitchen. Not a butter churn or a knife, bucket or bowl. Not a jar. The emptiness of the larder buttressed her idea that the exodus from Castle Gloom had been a deliberate one accomplished over time.

As in the Great Hall, windows high in the white walls illuminated the space. Shafts of sunlight struck the floor in squares, intersecting with each other to form a crisscross pattern. The ceiling was arched, and whitewashed as well, except for a dark spot over the massive fireplace discolored by years of fires. There were no clues to the absence of the inhabitants of Castle Gloom, but she'd solved one problem. If she could find no other room, she'd use the kitchen.

That is, if she was allowed to stay.

Charles Talbot couldn't believe Mary had left him to run the shop alone. For hours after she'd closed the door behind her, he waited for her to return. When she hadn't, he'd finally understood that a stranger had taken precedence over him.

His surprise at her desertion had begun to change to anger.

Today, he'd finished his commission for one of the

wealthy matrons of Inverness and had carried the tureen to her home himself, needing to get out of the shop for a little while. When he'd returned, he found two customers standing on his doorstep, neither one of them amenable to waiting, and each wanting to be served at the same time. If Mary were there, such a situation would not have occurred.

Mary was much more suited to welcoming their customers than she was to traipsing all over Inverness and beyond. But she never saw that it was a more worthwhile use of her time to cultivate those who could afford their wares instead of spending so much time trying to heal those with no way to pay for their treatment. He'd told her that sickness would always be with them, and so would the poor, but she'd only laughed in response, as if he'd made a jest.

She was two years younger than Charles despite the fact she'd been married to a man twice her age for a decade. Still, she'd have to learn, once she married him, that he wasn't as easily swayed as Gordon.

After Gordon's death, he'd said nothing, allowing her to mourn for a year like a good wife should. For twelve months, he'd hidden his feelings, only to have her say goodbye to him without a backward glance, taking herself off with no thought to her reputation or his concerns.

Charles closed up the shop, taking care to muffle the bell attached to the latch. At night, sometimes a draft would make it sound, and he'd be roused from sleep in his room in the back, thinking that a customer was demanding entrance.

He looked around the shop, pleased that it all but belonged to him now. The mahogany counters with their etched glass stood at right angles, displaying a few samples of his wares. A scarred bench sat in front of a sloping table. Here, Gordon had sat hunched over until his shoulders were permanently stooped. A magnifying glass and an eyepiece he had habitually worn around his neck now sat in a drawer beneath the table. The wooden floor was gouged in spots but otherwise well polished.

Gordon hadn't left him title to the place, but Charles felt he'd earned the ownership of the goldsmith's shop. He deserved it because of twelve years of diligent labor. None of the good residents of Inverness understood that yet, perhaps because Gordon had treated Charles as if he'd had no talent. Not once had the older man ever given him credit for his work.

Charles frowned at the memories, extinguishing the lanterns and moving toward the stairs.

Toward the end, when Gordon had been too ill to sit at his bench, he'd finally given Charles some of his commissions, critiquing every movement of Charles's chisel and pointed awl from a chair arranged in the corner. When Gordon gave his grudging approval, Charles knew he'd done his best work. The McPherson christening cup was one such piece. He'd delivered it himself that evening.

McPherson had approved of it with a great glowing smile, but he'd talked more of Gordon's design than Charles's execution of the work.

"An artist. A genius. How will we ever do without him? And Mary? Is she coping with her loss?"

Charles had smiled, rubbing the tips of his fingers together in a gesture he'd borrowed from Gordon. "She's doing as well as can be expected. She misses him each day, I'm certain. Although it's better for both of us if we don't speak of Gordon, he's in our thoughts always." He hadn't mentioned, however, that Mary was feeling so much better that she'd taken off for the Highlands.

He stood at the bottom of the stairs, listening for noises above him. Both Cook and the maid, Betty, were asleep in their room. Their accommodations were almost luxurious compared to what he'd had as a young apprentice.

Gordon had cleared out the storeroom for him, and it was there he still slept. A few years ago, however, he'd installed a latch on the door, a lock that Gordon surprisingly respected. Perhaps age or marriage to Mary had mellowed him. Gordon had been happy toward the end of his life, which was more than many men could say. He had the respect of his peers and wealth, along with the love of a beautiful woman. What else could a man want?

Charles opened his door with the key on his watch fob. Despite the fact that the shop was empty, he locked the door as a precaution. He went to his bed and sat on the side of it, reaching into the bedside drawer for one of his most prized possessions. A lad with talent in his fingers had sketched Mary's picture one day at the Inverness market, and Charles had taken it from Gordon's room when he was ill. Here it rested, in a place no one ever came, waiting for him. Every night he pulled it from its hiding place.

Mary was his muse and his inspiration, but now the words he spoke were fueled by anger.

"You need to realize, Mary, that your time of wandering around Inverness is over. You must heed those who say that you take too much upon yourself. But most of all, you must realize that Gordon was lax with you. I'll be more attentive to your behavior."

She continued to smile back at him in her sweet and somber way, her eyes sparkling at him as if laughter was trapped in their depths.

He placed the picture back in the drawer, moving something aside so that it fit more easily. He palmed the vial, smiling down at it. The container was another item he'd taken from Gordon's room when the older man had been too ill to protest.

If Mary balked at his instruction, or his plans, he had another idea. One that would force her to comply.

Chapter 3

Mary returned to the gate to find Micah unloading the wagon. Hester labored beside him, the couple working in silent tandem.

They'd met at dawn and spent only a few moments together throughout the day, but Mary found the other woman pleasant and helpful. Hester was a tall woman, her frame nothing more than jutting bones draped by sagging skin. Her complexion was bronzed, her face etched and lined like the ruts of the road they'd traveled to Castle Gloom. Hands that picked up a cask of ale were knurled and scarred. Her hair was laced with strands of silver. Only her eyes were young, bright blue, clear and accepting; they measured others with interest and intelligence.

Micah was as old, but the years had treated him with more grace. His hair was a thick brown, his blue eyes were deep-set in his face, and wrinkles stretched outward from his mouth to meet those around his eyes, resulting in a merry expression. He looked as if he'd been caught too long in a smile.

Brendan came out of the tower and began to help them unload the wagon in silence. They each carried their individual burdens up the eighteen shallow steps to the gate.

Going to the back of the wagon, Mary withdrew a small cask and tucked it beneath her arm, resting it against her hip.

"I'll carry that," Brendan said a few minutes later.

"Nonsense," she said. "There are other, heavier items that you can carry. Allow me to help where I can."

He grinned at her, the expression making her wonder if his brother had ever been so affable.

"Are we going to be allowed to stay after all?"

He nodded once.

"Without being fired upon, I trust?"

"You mustn't mind Hamish, Mary. He seems a lot fiercer than he truly is."

Turning, she smiled at Brendan, genuinely amused. "He doesn't frighten me."

She would've been wiser to be frightened, wouldn't she, instead of having this strange feeling that she'd embarked upon an adventure. How foolish of her.

At the top of the steps, she added the cask to the small pile of crates stacked in the middle of the grassy area.

"I found a larder in the castle area," she said. "And a kitchen."

"It's not in ruins?" Brendan lowered the crate he carried, glancing toward the main building.

"Not at all."

She led the way, the three of them following.

"It's a wonder," Hester said, tilting her head back to

study the arches of the kitchen ceiling. "But it's a good thing we brought dishes and pots and pans with us."

Hester was a pleasant woman but didn't speak often. When she did, however, her words gave Mary the impression that she'd listened intently to the opinions of others before forming her own.

"Have you known them long?" Mary asked as she and Brendan went to retrieve more crates from the wagon.

"Only about a week. But they come well recommended by my brother and his wife. As you did."

She smiled, remembering Alisdair and Iseabal MacRae well. She recalled her husband Gordon's descriptions of their home, Gilmuir. A place that seemed romantic and dramatic, somewhere she'd longed to see. Now it seemed she'd gotten her wish in a way, since she was in her own isolated fortress in the Highlands.

The extent of Brendan's foresightedness was evident during the next hour when Mary helped Hester unpack some of the crates and barrels. He'd purchased candles, spoons, pots, pans, and large mixing bowls, everything that might be needed to set up housekeeping. He evidently expected Hamish to reside at Castle Gloom for a long time.

Hester inspected the kitchen fire, peering into the chimney and pronouncing it free of birds' nests or debris.

"I cannot help but wonder where your brother has been cooking his meals, sir," she said to Brendan when he and Micah delivered a heavy cask of ale to the larder.

"If I know Hamish, he has a brazier and wok. He learned the Oriental way of cooking years ago and sometimes subscribes to it."

Hester looked interested, but rather than ask him any questions, turned her attention to the lack of firewood. A moment later, both men were dispatched to the line of woods to fell a tree.

"It's strange how large the place is," Hester said, planting her hands on her hips and looking about her. "It looks like a ruin from the road. Even more curious is that there's no sign of life."

"I wonder why they left," Mary said.

Or why a man like Hamish MacRae would take up residence here.

After their meal was prepared and eaten, and darkness had fallen over Castle Gloom, they began to make preparations for sleep. Since the tower was deemed to be the most hospitable place at Castle Gloom, Micah and Brendan began to move a few cots they'd found up to those rooms. Micah and Hester surprised her, though, by choosing to sleep in the main part of the castle.

"There's a corner of the Great Hall we can make cozy-like," Hester said, and she slanted a glance toward her husband that Mary envied. In that look was fondness, and the hint of a promise.

"Hamish occupies the top floor," Brendan said as they left the kitchen. "Which do you want, Mary? The first or the second?"

"The first," she said quickly. The fewer stairs she had to mount, the better.

He nodded.

"Does he never leave the tower?" Mary asked, looking across the courtyard. He'd remained there all evening, never once emerging. Brendan had carried a dinner tray to him, returning without comment.

"He doesn't like the company of strangers," Brendan said.

"Has he always been that way?"

He shrugged. Brendan could be very irritating occasionally. Sometimes he divulged too much information and sometimes not enough.

"You should tell me what I need to know if you want me to help him."

She glanced upward to where the lone window was open, seeing the flicker of a candle. Did he watch them from his aerie?

"Do you know anything about India?" Brendan asked.

She shook her head. "Only where it is, and that, I confess, is only an idea."

"The British East India Company has been making inroads there for the past thirty years. That's not to say that they've been welcomed at every turn." His expression grew somber. "There are those who would be just as pleased if the British turned tail and left their country. Among them are the Atavasi, the native people of India. They've been rebelling against the British incursion for the past five years. They captured Hamish's ship, killing his crew. Hamish was their prisoner for a year."

"A year?" she asked faintly.

They were at the tower now, and Brendan hesitated outside the narrow doorway. "A few months ago, he and two other men—Englishmen captured by the Atavasi—managed to overpower their guards and make their way overland. He was the only one to finish the journey."

Brendan put his hand on the door but didn't make a move to open it. "We'd given up any hope of him being alive after the rebellion was put down." Brendan looked directly at her, but she couldn't see his expression in the darkness. "I didn't recognize him at first. His eyes were the same color, and his features were the same. There's a scar on his knee from where he'd fallen from a tree as a boy, and a mark on the base of his thumb from a MacRae blood oath. But everything else was different. He didn't talk the same, and he doesn't act the same."

"Perhaps he blames himself for the loss of his crew. But that doesn't explain why he's a hermit."

Opening the door, he stood aside for her to precede him. Once inside the tower, he looked heavenward as if he were restrained in his comments by the man who was the subject of them.

She waited as he lit a candle, grateful for the light to study his face. Brendan's gaze on her was intent, but she would not have expected his next words under any circumstances.

"He was tortured."

She stared at him. "Tortured?" Her voice was low, but the stone walls sent the word back to her jeeringly. She shivered, feeling a coldness creep through her as she looked up at the winding stairs.

"He needs you, Angel," Brendan said.

"You promised," she said, shaking her head at him, "not to call me that name."

"Was it a promise? I thought I said I would try. My wits must be slipping."

It was truly difficult to remain angry at him. He had such an engaging grin. Nor could she help but admire him. Take this mission, for example. He'd been determined to obtain medical care for his brother, however much Hamish refused it. Such brotherly devotion was to be commended.

But despite his lively smile and cheerful hazel eyes and the goodness of his character, Brendan wasn't the MacRae who interested her.

He was tortured.

She glanced up the stairs again and shivered.

Chapter 4

❧❧❧

Brendan grabbed her valise and a candle, leaving Mary to follow. She gripped her medicine case with her left hand, flattening her right against the wall for added support as she mounted the steps. If she were careful not to look to her left or above her, she'd be free of that strange disorientation she always experienced when climbing stairs.

How easy it was to identify her flaws. She wished it were as simple to eliminate them. She had an intense dislike of heights and darkness.

And death.

Perhaps that's why she waged a war so single-mindedly against illness and disease. Death had seemed to be a constant presence in her life, perching on her shoulder and cackling wildly when she was happy or carefree. In addition to her husband, death had taken her three-year-old brother after he had contracted measles, and her sister at age nine from influenza, the same disease that had taken her parents a few months apart, not long after her seventeenth birthday.

At the landing, she looked around her. To her right, the stairs continued upward. To the left was an opened door.

Mary realized that remaining in this desolate castle might be a trial, indeed. But no act was completely wasted. Being forced to climb the stairs might make it easier for her to continue to do so.

Brendan entered the room, and she followed, unsurprised to find that the chamber was nearly empty. A small brazier sat in one corner, along with a large trunk and a few empty crates. The only furniture, besides the cot Brendan and Micah had brought in earlier, was a chair, similar in style to the two below.

Brendan put the candle on the chair and placed her valise on the floor next to it.

"I'm sorry it doesn't look better," he said, looking around the room.

A broom had not been taken to this floor for years, it seemed. Dust filtered through the air so thickly that she could reach out her hand and grab it.

She waved away his apologies. "It's better than some accommodations I've been offered," she said.

"Then I'll leave you," he said awkwardly. "Unless you need something else?"

She shook her head, and then smiled. "I'm fine, truly."

When he was gone, she placed her medicine case on the lid of the trunk and readied her small chamber as well as she could, making the bed, unpacking her valise, hanging her clothing on the pegs beside the door. Standing in front of one of the archer slits, she wished she had something to close the opening. The Highland wind carried a bite to it although it was only autumn. The sky presaged snow, and both the loch and the sea seemed silvery in the dusk. She shivered, turning back to the room.

She was considered a wealthy widow, but she'd never appreciated Gordon's fortune as much as now, as she lit one of the thick beeswax candles she'd brought with her from Inverness. Money accomplished little in life other than to purchase comfort. It didn't bring her happiness or an end to the loneliness she felt in the long hours between dusk and dawn. But neither would she choose to be destitute. She'd seen, firsthand, what poverty could do to a person.

Cupping her fingers around the flickering flame, she wondered how the inhabitants of Castle Gloom had managed to survive the winters. Perhaps they did so wearing furs and wool, or they simply had become used to the blustery wind.

Above her was the sound of footsteps on the wooden floor, and she wondered if Brendan was settling down in his tiny chamber.

She looked around the room again and wondered what Gordon would think of her presence there. He would have counseled against it, but then he'd never known of her secret yearnings. How could she confess to her husband that she'd dreamed of faraway places? Or that she always felt that something was missing in her life? Those were not thoughts to be confided to anyone, let alone a husband, and certainly not to Gordon in those final years.

Moving to the trunk, she laid her medicine case down flat. The fitted case and the vials inside it had been a gift from Gordon, one of the last he'd given her.

"It's a small thing I give you, Mary, in comparison to what you've brought to my life." She felt tears mist her eyes at the thought of his kindness. He'd been such a dear man.

Gordon, a friend of her father, had offered aid and comfort when her aged parents had died within months of each other. When he'd asked her to marry him, she'd unhesitatingly agreed.

He'd been the most gallant of husbands. Those who knew his talent as a goldsmith often remarked that he could have made his fortune in Edinburgh. Gordon had only smiled and said that he'd made enough money for his needs and a little more, and wasn't that enough?

Theirs had been exactly the kind of marriage she'd thought it might be, coupled with a few surprises. She'd expected him to treat her in a fatherly fashion, and he'd been both a guide and a teacher. Gordon's passion for her, however, had been unforeseen, surprising the innocent she'd been. But he'd always been the first to encourage her in her interests. When she expressed an interest in medicine, he'd encouraged that as well.

She sat on the edge of the bed and slowly unfastened her braid. Every night as she did so, she thought of her husband. Gordon had liked to watch her brush her hair in the evening.

"It is, my love, a sight to warm even an old man's bones."

For a few moments, her smile was fond, remembering the love and affection he'd so effortlessly brought into her life. Then, just as she did each night, her thoughts slid a little, as she remembered the later years when Gordon changed and love didn't seem to matter.

Sometimes, it wasn't wise to recall the past.

After readying herself for bed, she tucked herself in, wedging the blanket around her. With her back against the wall, she sat and stared at the shadows around the trunk and the doorway, wishing that they didn't look like crouching animals. How foolish she could be at times. But she was feeling absurdly lonely in this deserted castle and adrift as she hadn't felt in months. Was it because she was away from Inverness, apart from her friends? The world felt like an unfriendly place at the moment, and her presence in it small and insignificant.

The moon was too pale to illuminate the room. As her eyes became accustomed to the darkness, she could see the archer's slits around the curved walls, framing long, rectangular patches of dark gray sky.

Sitting alone in the blackness of night didn't make her more comfortable with it. She raised her knees and wrapped her arms around them. How odd that she should be so tired and her mind still be active. She couldn't help but think of Hamish MacRae, in the room two floors above her. His imprisonment might account for his aloofness now, but even former prisoners had friends, welcomed family. Why did Hamish shun even his brother?

He was tortured.

What had they done to him? And why wouldn't he allow her to treat him?

She couldn't make a person change his behavior simply because she wished it. She'd learned that lesson from Gordon well enough.

One day, on returning home from treating a sick child, she'd been greeted by Charles's frowns and unspoken censure. "Gordon is ill."

"Ill?" She'd hung up her cloak and stared at her husband's apprentice.

"He often becomes ill, Mary, but he doesn't want you to know."

She'd rushed to Gordon's side, sitting on the edge of her husband's bed to feel his forehead. It had been clammy and pale, almost waxen, and his lips had been bluish.

"I promise I won't leave you again, Gordon." Guilt had prompted her vow.

He opened his eyes, his clear blue gaze looking distant, almost as if he had begun to physically leave her.

"You mustn't say such things, Mary," he said weakly. "Of course you'll go. If they're sick, they need you. I'm only one man, and the whole of Inverness could use your healing talents."

"It's not the whole of Inverness, my dearest," she'd said, smiling a little. "Just a patient here and there."

"Promise me," he said, "that you'll not stay home for my sake." He gripped her hand tightly, and she'd been concerned at how cold his fingers felt.

She nodded, and it seemed to assuage him.

For two months he'd been ill, but refused to stay in his bed. Every night, she prepared a dose for him, something to settle his stomach, but it hadn't made him well. Nothing she'd done had made any difference. When Gordon had died, the world she'd known, safe and secure, had sadly changed.

"What would you think of him, Gordon?" she asked, addressing the ceiling, and then wondering why she sought her husband's counsel. Gordon had disapproved of adventure. He'd always said that a man was born to a role in life and should adhere to it.

He'd been a goldsmith, apprenticed, just as Charles had been, as a young man. He'd spent his life developing his talent for working in fine metals, and had been supremely content in his vocation. People from as far away as Edinburgh had come to their small shop to purchase Gordon's works of art, goblets with rampant lions and gryphons etched along the rim, or small silver boxes adorned with embossed thistles.

Gordon had wanted Charles to take over the shop, but the two of them had never made the final legal arrangements. He'd left Charles some of his tools and inventory, but the rest of the contents of the shop belonged to Mary, along with Gordon's lockbox of gold and silver ingots.

In short, she was wealthier than she'd ever dreamed of being, and alone for the first time in a dozen years. Alone and wakeful in a strange, deserted castle on the edge of the world.

Sleep was difficult for Hamish. Tonight, it was made doubly so with the addition of Brendan's party to Aonaranach. Hamish found himself pacing his small round room, walking in circles like a tethered bear.

These last few weeks had been the first time in his life he'd been completely and totally alone. At first, he'd missed the sound of voices, so much that he had wandered through his new home talking to himself. Yet he was now nearly desperate to banish the first people he'd seen in almost a month.

Leaning against the edge of the window, he stared out into the cold night. A sliver of moon only occasionally viewed through rapidly moving clouds was the only illumination. The sea was a giant black creature licking at the shore and breathing heavily in gentle swells of waves. A night bird called in a lonely, plaintive cry, and was left unanswered.

He was no stranger to this view, having learned it well over the past weeks. Tonight, however, he could smell the cook fire, and the odor of ale from a cask, scents that hadn't been there before and meant habitation, civilization, and strangers.

He couldn't fault the meal he'd been served. That, at least, was a change from the past weeks.

Glancing at his cot, he made no move toward it. However much his body needed sleep, his mind counseled against attempting it. Tonight would no doubt be the same as it had been for weeks. He'd fall into a restless slumber, only to be awakened by strange, misshapen nightmares as if he were drugged on opium. Men he'd known all his life paraded before him, reciting their names as if he didn't know them as well as his own. Samuel, Brian, Alex, William, twenty-seven of them in total.

Those who'd sailed with him had done so not because he was a MacRae or because he'd made a fortune for his crew three times over since first given command of his own ship. Men sailed with him because they believed he had the right mix of daring and wisdom. In short, men signed on with him because they respected his abilities.

One man was no match for a mob of fifty, and at least that many had swarmed over the side of his ship. He'd watched in numbed horror as they'd killed his crew and then set his ship ablaze until only a burned husk was left above the water line. Finally, it, too, tipped over and sank to the bottom of the ocean.

The nightmares followed the same litany each night. When the roll call of his men was done, he was propelled back to the encampment at the hands of the Atavasi, his dreams mimicking the reality of his imprisonment. He was being dragged along from village to village, from waterfall to mountain, from valley to riverbank. Each scene was marked by another interlude of pain. Just when he'd begun to pray for an end, his captors had allowed him to regain some strength, the better to prolong their torture.

Hamish returned to the cot and sat on the edge to remove his boots. Standing, he stripped off his clothing and stood naked in the night air.

He knew his body well, acknowledged the tensile strength of each bone, the tolerance of each muscle and nerve. He'd been both captive within it and separated from it, part of himself and yet not. He felt about his body the way he had his ship, an extension of himself, simply a vessel in which he lived.

The Atavasi had done their best to make him a walking corpse. The fact that they'd not succeeded was due to his indefatigability, a quality he'd never known he possessed until India.

All during that time, his mind had refused to believe what was happening to him. He'd distanced himself from what they'd done to him by disappearing into his thoughts, transporting himself back in time with his memory or forward into wishes. He'd clung to a tiny vestige of hope that still remained despite the circumstances and the torture they'd inflicted on him.

Toward the end, he'd felt himself separate, as if the creature known as Hamish MacRae had to divide itself in order to survive. The physical body had been given up for lost; the mind controlled the pain by fleeing from it, his spiritual nature was muted by pain and a sense of horror.

Gradually, after his escape, he'd begun to heal as much as he could, given what they'd done to him. His mind was still troubled and would no doubt remain so for the rest of his life. Only lately had his soul emerged from its cocoon to announce its presence, just when he no longer needed God.

As he lay on his bed, staring off into the darkness, Hamish thought of Mary Gilly, the healer with the omnipotent touch. Unbidden, his thoughts shifted to the sight of her striding across the courtyard, her loose limbed gait hinting at long legs and curving hips. He'd not been with a woman for years, and his body was suddenly very aware of that fact.

Deliberately, he lay uncovered, allowing himself to be chilled by the night air. The blanket, the sheet would be too abrasive. He rested his good arm under his head, stared up at the ceiling, and felt himself harden at the thought of being healed. Not in the way she imagined, perhaps, but with the only touch he craved.

A widow. Was she as lonely as he? Or was that word even correct? Could he even be lonely anymore with the ghost that inhabited his thoughts?

He resolutely pushed that idea away and stood, knowing that sleep wouldn't come tonight.

Mary cupped her hands around her elbows. The wind howling through the three archer's slits sounded mournful and condemnatory. A gust blew out the candle on the bedside table, leaving her in total darkness.

Standing, Mary grabbed her dress from the peg by the door and donned it over her nightgown. Without her stays she wasn't exactly proper, but she doubted anyone else was awake, as late as it was. She wrapped her shawl around her shoulders and opened the door.

Gordon had had the most beautiful dressing gown made for her that last year, something he'd commissioned from the dressmaker as a surprise. Countless hours had gone into embroidering the yoke and shoulders of the beige silk with crimson thread, to form a trail of prim-

roses. Each time she donned it, she ran her fingers over
the tiny, delicate stitches. Gordon created masterpieces in
gold, but these talented women had done the same with
their needles. Because it was one of her most cherished
articles of clothing, she hadn't brought it on this journey.
Now she missed its warmth as the wind swirled out the
door, as if gleeful to escape.

Mary flattened herself against the curved wall of the
tower and dared herself to go either up or down, anything
but stand there frightened of the dark.

A sound from below captured her attention. Moving to
the top of the stairs, she realized that deep shadows flick-
ered along the wall. Someone had lit a fire on the main
floor of the tower and was standing before it.

She would have liked to call it courage, but Mary was
only too aware that it was her curiosity that propelled her
down the staircase.

Halfway down, she saw him.

He turned at a sound, looking up at her. She stopped, a
hand pressed flat against her chest to calm the sudden
skipping beat of her heart.

Brendan should have warned her. Instead of telling her
that his brother had a fearsome name or describing him as
a boy, he should have stated that Hamish was arresting,
that a woman's heart might stutter when first viewing him.
He should have told her that he was a tall man with broad
shoulders, and possessed of a warrior's body.

His face, however, drew her attention, his jaw jutting
out pugnaciously at the world, his lips oddly squared. His
cheekbones were high, and his nose was broad. A half
dozen or so irregular circles marred his face, each pitted
and dark as if long healed. They kept him from being

called handsome, but they could not take away the impression of strength.

"Go back upstairs, Mrs. Gilly." His voice was raspy, more than a whisper but less than a normal speaking voice.

"I couldn't sleep," she said, in defense of her curiosity.

He said nothing, only turned and stared at the fire, his arms folded in front of him. A pose of dismissal all the more potent for its silence.

She descended the stairs, wrapping the ends of the shawl around her hands. Now was not the time for reticence. She walked closer, moved to stand in front of him, and before losing her courage, reached up with one hand and placed her fingers against the worst of the scars on his face.

"What happened to you?"

Pain was etched on his face, and a flatness of expression she'd never seen before except in the old or terminally ill.

Gently, he pulled her hand away, his thumb and forefinger easily encompassing her wrist.

"I need no healer, Mrs. Gilly. Brendan exceeded his authority. I'm sorry for the loss of your time and for your trouble."

She stood with his hand still around her wrist. She could have easily shaken free, but she remained where she was, bound by his restraint.

"Won't you tell me what happened?"

Her question was left unanswered.

In the silence, she reached up with her other hand and placed it flat on his chest, surprised when he flinched. He dropped her hand and stepped back, putting a little distance between them.

He didn't like her touching him. She tucked that information away. Before ever beginning to treat her patients, she studied them, getting to know as much as she could about the way they lived and their general condition.

Hamish MacRae might be surprised by what she'd already deduced.

"I suspect you're not as healed as you wish me to think, Mr. MacRae. I also think, despite your words, that you do need me."

"I've been without a woman for nearly two years, madam. That's the only need I have."

His crudeness was deliberate. There was a look in his eyes, however, that cautioned her to be wary. She took a deep breath and brazened it out.

"I've treated a number of male patients," she said, not adding that they were mostly infants or the elderly. None of them had been remotely like Hamish MacRae. However, she continued with her bravado. "I'm used to the ways of men, as well as the workings of their bodies. Nothing you could do or say has the ability to shock me. Shall we not play that game between us?"

"I didn't say what I did to distress you, Mrs. Gilly," he said, "but to give you fair warning."

"Most men in your condition would have other things on their minds."

"In my condition?" One corner of his lip curved upward in a sardonic smile.

He stepped back, but she noted that he kept his fingers resting in the placket of his shirt, as if that was the only way he could support his arm.

"Why can't you move your arm, Mr. MacRae?"

"Go back to Inverness," he said, and this time, his voice sounded as if it could cut glass.

"Your brother paid me to treat you, and treat you I will."

"I will pay you to go back to where you came from."

"I can't do that," she said, smiling gently at him.

"God save me from interfering women."

She didn't know quite how to answer that comment. Granted, she was not always welcome by the entire household when she was summoned to a patient's bedside. Most of the time, however, the patient wanted her there.

"You need me," she said, refusing to back down. "The sooner you agree to my treating you, the sooner I will be gone."

"You'll be gone in the morning."

He turned and walked away. But she was not so easily dismissed.

Resolutely, she followed him to the stairs.

"At least let me see your arm."

He turned and stared at her, the look on his face not at all friendly. "My brother says you're a miracle worker of sorts. Do you intend to work your miracles on me, Angel?"

"Do not call me by that silly name," she said crossly. "I have neither the temperament nor the holiness to be addressed as an inhabitant from heaven. I am only too human."

"But you don't deny that you have the power of miracles at your fingertips."

"On the contrary," she said, irritated. "I'm a student of Matthew Marshall's, and have read everything he's written on medicine. If there are any miracles in the work that I perform, it is because of his education and his discoveries."

"A squirrel tail, severed at midnight? Rat's whiskers added to three dashes of pepper from the Spice Islands?"

"Are you reciting a recipe?" she asked, frowning up at him.

"I am devising one, rather. Something less miraculous and more suitable to witches, I confess."

He really was the most annoying man.

"Nor am I a witch, Mr. MacRae. My treatments have nothing to do with snails or beaks or other questionable ingredients. Instead, I believe that washing my hands will do a great deal more to protect a patient than any potions I might give them or any ground up toad infusions."

His half smile didn't waver.

"I ask that my patients bathe often, that they adopt a simple diet, and that they take a bracing walk each day. I am here to help facilitate wellness, but the patient is the author of his own health."

"So you don't believe in bloodletting?"

"I do not," she said firmly. "Nor does Mr. Marshall. The medicines I prescribe are simple and easily understood, with ingredients long held to be beneficial. I also believe in cold water, hot poultices, and herb teas."

She crossed her arms in front of her and continued. "I know of at least nine hundred treatments for two hundred seventy-six named ailments. I would have to examine you first and use my powers of observation before I decide upon a course of treatment."

"I wash often, Mrs. Gilly, and my diet for the last year or so has been painfully simple. I've walked the equivalent of the length of Scotland. Using your measurements, I am facilitating my own wellness."

She tapped her foot on the floor, impatient at his recalcitrance. No one had ever before asked her to prove her skills. "I have at least seventy successful treatments to my credit, from pustule boils to cankerous throats. Would you like me to enumerate them?"

His smile broadened. "I think not."

"Then what would convince you to let me treat you?"

"Why should I?"

She blinked at him, surprised by the question. "Why, to get better, of course."

He surprised her by descending the stairs and returning to the fireplace. Watching her, he asked, "What would you give me for being unable to sleep?"

"Nothing," she said, and could tell that her answer wasn't what he'd expected. "Perhaps you don't need as much sleep as other men. Matthew Marshall believes that a man can sleep too much, that it's better to be abroad at night than to be captive to one's pillow."

"Most physicians would have prescribed a sleeping draught."

"I don't agree with most physicians," she said, wondering if that admission would only strengthen his resolve not to let her treat him. "I only prescribe morphine for dangerous conditions," she explained. "Or for those who are so sick that their condition will likely lead to death. I think your arm should be treated, Mr. MacRae. Otherwise, I doubt your injuries are that serious, however much you might wish them to be."

He looked startled. "Why would you say that?"

She studied him for a moment, realizing that she'd already said too much. There was nothing left but the truth. If he repudiated her, then so be it.

"I think your sleeplessness, Mr. MacRae, comes about not because of your physical condition as much one of the mind. For that I would prescribe a long, thorough discussion with another human being. Someone with whom you could purge your soul. Perhaps your brother?"

She wanted to put her hand on his arm, pat his hand, initiate some physical link between them, but knew that he would pull away if she did so. There were times when that was the greatest help she could give another human being. That was why she sometimes brought a litter of kittens to her elderly, querulous patients. Before the visit was over, the patient was smiling, and like as not, Mary had found a home for one of the kittens.

This man, however, with his palpable aloofness, didn't need a puppy or kitten. But he almost desperately needed the comfort of another human being, that much she knew from the look in his eyes. She could feel his aloneness as if it were the match of her own.

"The passions have a greater influence on health than most people know," she said softly. "Where they hold sway, there's little I or any other person versed in medicine can do."

"You're a poor practitioner," he said, turning and speaking to the fire, "if you aren't attempting to get me to swallow some pill or tonic. How will you make a living at your trade?"

"What would my reputation be if I dispensed pills and tonics with no hope of them working?"

"So you would have me talk to Brendan. What if he doesn't wish to be the recipient of my conscience?"

"Then I will be." The words escaped her before she censured them. But he said nothing to her admission, which emboldened her further. "Why couldn't you sleep tonight?"

"I was thinking of you, Mary Gilly," he said, turning to face her.

"Me?" One hand went to the base of her throat, as if to ease the sudden constriction of her breath.

"I wondered if you were a lonely widow. Are you?"

Other than asking about her health in a general, desultory way, or inquiring if the day was proving to be a good one for her, her patients never asked her personal questions. They never wanted to know what she thought or how she felt about an issue, and not once had anyone asked if she was lonely.

She clasped her hands together tightly and answered him honestly. "So much so that I want to weep with it, sometimes," she admitted. Too much bluntness, perhaps, but it felt as if the night had stripped them both of the decorum normally present between strangers.

He said nothing, just studied her in the firelight. Once more she marveled at his appearance. He wasn't at all attractive, not in the way that a handsome man was. He could have come from any culture or any place on earth and been instantly identified as a warrior, a leader of men. Yet here he was in an isolated tower, eschewing all that was human or companionable.

"And you, Hamish MacRae? Is it loneliness that keeps you awake?"

"No." He took a few steps toward her. She didn't move when he reached out to touch her, straightening her shawl around her shoulders. He let his hand rest there so that she could feel the warmth of his palm through the wool.

"I would be happy to have loneliness as an excuse, Mary Gilly. But it isn't the reason why I can't sleep at night. Or, when I do, why nightmares threaten."

"If you tell me your confidences, Mr. MacRae," she said gently, "they would remain between the two of us. I would never reveal anything to anyone else."

"I'm not ready to divulge my soul any more than I am my wounds."

He bowed slightly and headed for the staircase.

As she watched him climb the steps, exhilaration filled her. She sometimes experienced that sensation when a treatment resulted in a patient's marked improvement. However, she'd never felt this way when embarking upon a case. She suspected it had little to do with medicine and a great deal to do with Hamish MacRae.

Chapter 5

Mary woke feeling rested, grateful that Betty had delayed waking her. An instant later, she blinked open her eyes and stared at the ceiling, realizing that she wasn't home in Inverness but in the tower room at Castle Gloom.

Something had awakened her, and she glanced at the archers' slits in surprise, realizing that the sun was shining brightly in the sky. Dawn had come and gone, and she was still lying in bed like a slug.

She sat up on the edge of the bed, clamping her hand over her mouth as she yawned. Standing, she attended to her morning chores, and then dressed as quickly as she was able in a serviceable dress of brown linen and a scarf of beige at her throat. She untied her braid, brushed her hair quickly before arranging it in a tight bun at the back of her head and topping it with a ruffled white cap.

After straightening the sheets and the coverlet on the cot, she retrieved her case and opened it, spreading it wide on the bed. First, she donned her apron, and then tucked into the pocket the various medicines she thought she might need.

Going down the stairs was as difficult as the ascent. She couldn't imagine doing this day in and day out for the rest of her stay at Castle Gloom.

Even before leaving Inverness, she'd decided that she'd be gone only a week. Otherwise, she'd miss the meeting with Mr. Marshall that had been arranged weeks before. The famed author and minister had actually wished to meet with her and discuss treatments, an honor especially since there were so many demands on his time. It had taken a day to travel here, and the return would take the same amount of time. Therefore, she had five days in which to treat Hamish, and already one had passed.

However, from what she'd witnessed the night before, the man was less in need of her medical skills than of an understanding ear. But his arm was worrisome. What could have caused such lameness? Her mind was on various conditions that might have done so and actually eased her discomfort on the stairs.

The day felt unseasonably warm, the breeze flowing through the iron gate smelling of the sea. The birds in the nearby trees were all singing together in a riotous greeting to the morning, so loudly that she had to raise her voice to be heard when she greeted Brendan.

"Good morning," she said, nodding to him and Micah. The two men were sawing another log. No doubt more firewood at Hester's behest. There was a stack of wood propped up against the outer wall, and a newly felled tree just inside the land gate.

Brendan had taken off his shirt, and his torso gleamed

in the morning sun. From the expanse of tanned shoulders and back, he'd evidently done this often.

"Is your brother planning on remaining here all winter?" she asked, dipping the bucket into the well.

"Why didn't you ask him yourself last night, Angel?"

She felt her face warm, and wondered at her reaction. She was no miss, no maiden to be reduced to blushes. Why, then, was she acting the innocent?

"You heard us?"

"Sound carries in the tower."

"Then you'll know I'm no closer to treating him than I was yesterday."

"Does that mean you're giving up?"

"Of course not," she said in a clipped voice. "You've hired me to treat your brother and treat him I will."

"Even if he doesn't wish it?"

"An ill patient is like quarrelsome child. A parent does not ask the child what he wishes to do. A wise and loving parent simply tells him."

"So you're going to be his mother?" Brendan grinned at her.

She nodded, deliberately not responding to his goad. Nor would it do any good to explain the whole of her treatment plan. Most people didn't understand that medicine was a guessing game. The more experience she had, the more Mary understood that each patient was unique. The treatment that worked with one might not work with another.

Matthew Marshall had understood that. In his book *The Primitive Physick*, he'd explained that good treatments were based on empiricism—experience, and not theory.

"I'm going to treat him," she said firmly. "Even if he does not wish it."

She took the bucket of water to the kitchen, intent on heating it in order to finish her morning toilette. Matthew Marshall subscribed to basic treatments, one of them being the axiom that cleanliness was vital. Mary had discovered that she had fewer infections once she'd begun washing her hands in hot water before visiting a patient. She'd taken other precautions as well, such as dusting her hands with boric powder and wearing a mask when treating noxious wounds.

Hester was smiling, looking as pleased as a child with a new ball. Around her, the kitchen lay spotless. The floor had been scrubbed, as well as the walls. The packing crates had been removed, and every new bowl, plate, and cup had been washed and hung in the built-in cupboard. A wonderful smelling stew was cooking over the fire, and something equally as delicious was cooling on the end of the long table.

"You've been busy this morning," Mary said, looking around at the changes.

Hester nodded. "The place calls for a little loving touch. Plus I found a kitchen garden just outside," she said. "Overgrown, it was, but there's still rosemary and thyme and mint." She placed a plate holding a slice of meat pie from dinner last night on a tray. Beside it was an earthenware jug of ale, and a mug.

Hefting the tray in both hands, Hester headed toward the door.

"Is that tray for Hamish?" Mary asked before the other woman could leave the kitchen.

Hester's look was amused, as if the thought of waiting on either Brendan or her husband was humorous.

"I'll take it," Mary said.

"Brendan was going to deliver it. Not me."

"Maybe he'd welcome me if I come with food," Mary said.

"Is he proving to be stubborn?" Hester asked, surrendering the tray. "Men are, on the whole. Especially when they're feeling poorly."

She wasn't entirely certain it was his health that had Hamish MacRae acting so obstinate.

Mary crossed the courtyard, nodding at Brendan, who took one look at the tray in her hands and began smiling. She frowned at him but it did no good; he was still wearing that silly grin as if he anticipated the confrontation to come.

After last night, perhaps she should have been wiser. Hamish had, after all, left no doubt as to his feelings about her presence. His unvoiced vulnerabilities touched her, a fact that would no doubt horrify him if he knew. It was why, she suspected, he wanted her gone from Castle Gloom. A man like Hamish MacRae would deplore any weakness in his character, even that of simply being human.

She climbed the first flight of stairs in the tower feeling as if her heart were booming in her throat. Taking a deep breath, Mary forced herself to calm. All she needed to do was to keep close to the wall and not look down, that was all. It seemed a simple enough task.

Another flight, and she passed the room where Brendan had slept the night before. It was darker here, as if night lingered atop the tower. She made the mistake of glancing down for just a moment. A wave of dizziness swept through her. Instantly, her feet felt sweaty and her stomach weightless.

She hated this weakness. Gordon had once said that she was not meant for parapets or bridges. She'd laughed with him, but now her fear of heights was no laughing matter. It was getting in the way of treating a patient, and that would never do at all.

Finally, after taking the last few steps on feet that felt remarkably weak, she made it to the top landing. Determinedly, she knocked on the banded oak door with one hand while she balanced the tray with the other. She waited for a response, but it didn't come.

"I need assistance, Mr. MacRae," she said a moment later. "The tray is heavy, and there is no place to put it down."

"I don't require that you serve me, Mrs. Gilly. Place it on the floor, if you will."

"I thank you for your suggestion, sir," she said crisply. "But it would be better if I could place it on the table, instead. Surely you have one within that lair of yours."

"It's a sanctuary at the moment, Mrs. Gilly. Not a lair."

His comment brought a smile to her lips. He was a stubborn man, but she was even more obstinate.

"Mr. MacRae, there is nothing you have that I have not seen before at least a hundred times. Unless, perhaps, you have lied to your brother and me all along. Perhaps you're not human at all. Are you a dragon? Are there scales below your shirt, or a tail hidden in your trousers?"

She leaned against the door frame, balancing the tray.

"If that's the case, then I confess I would be surprised, perhaps even alarmed. Scratch against the door with your claw, or allow the tip of your tail to appear beneath the door. Or perhaps grunt in the way dragons roar or belch a little fire. If I'm convinced that you're not truly human,

I'll put the tray down this second, disappear from this tower room, and never come back."

The door opened so quickly that she was startled. The sun was behind him, and for a second that was all she saw, just the bright glare and not his expression or his features.

"I do not want a healer. I do not want anyone in my chamber. I do not want you, especially, Mrs. Gilly."

It shouldn't have hurt. He was simply angry with her, that was all. She thought she might have made some inroads last night, but evidently, he was still obdurate. Despite the moments of oddly pleasing conversation between them, they were strangers. She would be wise to remember that.

She stayed where she was, extending the tray toward him. Instead of taking it, he motioned to a table beside the door. While she waited, he picked up a square board with several small, oddly shaped figurines resting on it. Once the table was cleared, she placed the tray atop it, and then turned to leave.

Without a word, she walked back to the head of the steps, wishing that he would go back into his room and close the door behind him. Instead, he stood and watched her.

"Forgive me. I was rude," he said slowly.

She glanced over at him. A moment passed before she spoke. "Yes, you were. But you've not accomplished what you intended, you know. I may not have convinced you now, but I'll keep trying."

He stepped out of the sunlight and over the threshold of his room. Now there was no doubt of his expression. He was decidedly irritated.

"Why?"

His hair was askew, as if he had threaded his fingers through it, but his clothing was immaculate. His white shirt was loose, and topped with a carefully tied stock. His dark breeches were tucked into boots that were, even here in this deserted castle, highly polished. He might have retreated from civilization, but he had not yet become uncivilized.

"Because I must," she said simply, not expecting him to understand.

"You'll not be done with me until I'm your patient, will you?" he asked, a decided asperity to his tone.

"I'm afraid not." She smiled at him, but he didn't look mollified. Instead, he looked as if he might say something intentionally rude.

She decided to deflect his attention, instead.

"What is that?" she asked, pointing to the board he still held in his hand.

He glanced at it as if he'd forgotten its presence. "Something Brendan brought me, a game they play in India. My brother seems to think I need the diversion."

"Are you good at it?"

"I haven't played in more than a year. Why do you ask?"

"Would you care for a wager? I've never been especially good at games, but I'm willing to learn. If I play against you and win, would you allow me to treat you?"

"And if you lose?"

"I'll go away without a backward glance. Without another word to you."

"That alone is almost worth the wager," he said. But she couldn't feel insulted, because one corner of his mouth turned up in an almost smile. "Have Brendan teach you," he said, holding out the game to her. "That way it would be fair."

"When shall we play?"

"Tonight. If you think that's enough time for you to learn to play."

It wasn't, of course, but she nodded regardless. "In the meantime, perhaps you might give some thought to emerging from your cave," she suggested. "Sunshine and fresh air would do you more good than remaining in your hermitage."

"I didn't stay in this room until you came."

"Then why do you do so now?"

He only frowned at her in response. He was quite good at frowns, she decided.

Taking a deep breath, she placed her left hand on the wall for support. The descent was certain to be less nerve-racking than coming up the stairs with the heavy tray.

She glanced back once to discover him still standing there in the shadows, watching her. She wished he wouldn't do that. Yet asking him to cease studying her so avidly would reveal that his look discomfited her. It did, but not because he was scarred. Nor was she intimidated by his anger. Instead, something about him drew her.

He was less a patient than he was simply a man. For that alone, she should surrender in this battle of wills and ask Brendan to take her back to Inverness. Or find a way alone, if he refused.

Her curiosity about Hamish MacRae overpowered her concern, and what compassion she might have felt as a healer was no match for the interest she felt as a woman.

*　*　*

Matthew Marshall pulled his chair closer and opened the sloping top of his secretary. He flexed his fingers, straightened his shoulders, and took a few deep breaths, all preparatory to beginning his morning work. As a minister, he always began his day with a prayer service but then returned home to his study.

Selecting a quill, he trimmed the nib to the exact point he liked. He smiled as he removed the pewter top of his inkwell. It had been a gift from a congregation in America, something to commemorate his twentieth visit there and engraved with a verse that he especially liked.

Pulling out his manuscript, he worked on the forward of the book soon to be delivered to his publishers. The work was the compilation of his newest studies of medical advances. Only then did he begin to answer his correspondence.

Withdrawing the stack of letters he'd received in the afternoon post the day before, he began to thumb through them in order to decide which to answer first. There were the usual requests for donations. Then, there were the pleas for intercession, as if he, a mortal man, had more influence with God than any other creature. Lastly, there were his two favorite types of letters, those either having to do with new advances in medicine or imploring him to visit.

He began with the requests for donations. He knew only too well how difficult it sometimes was to solicit funds, therefore his answer was as gentle and kind as he could frame them.

I regret, dear sir, that most of my funds go to clinics for the poor throughout England. I will, however, take your situation under consideration. Perhaps there is a congregation who could assist you in some manner?

He wrote the same message for each solicitation.

The implorations to God were answered with prayer, and a two-line message.

Please note that I have no greater power than you in seeking assistance from the Almighty. However, I have added my prayers to yours in the hope that He will visit his kindness and benevolence upon you in your troubles.

Finally, he wrote answers to the requests for his time. His traveling plans were normally arranged a year in advance. He reached into his right desk drawer for his itinerary, disturbed when it wasn't exactly in the place he'd left it.

Order was a necessity. Since this desk traveled with him, he knew its contents well. He frowned down into the drawer, wondering why the information about his electrical machine was located to the left of his replies to his American congregations. None of his correspondence was in order. He often made copies of his letters, especially when it involved his travel arrangements.

Had Maddie looked for something? He sighed at the idea of leaving his wife yet again.

His time was equally divided between England, Scotland, and America. Rarely did he go to the continent, unless it was Amsterdam. He liked the tidiness of the Dutch, but chafed at the stubbornness of the Germans, and deplored French politics. The excesses of royalty had destroyed the country, making it a nation of poor, malnourished creatures. Nor were the French disposed to hearing any criticism of their methods. They would let their own citizens starve rather than take advice from a foreigner.

He sighed, wishing that his dear wife would come with him on his next trip to Scotland. Madeline would not, citing a wish to remain here with her lingering cough. She'd grown weaker in the past months, and had it been any other visit, he would have stayed behind as well.

In addition to meeting with a female healer with the unlikely soubriquet of the Angel of Inverness, there had been some promising correspondence from a young Scottish inventor. They'd been communicating for well over a year, and just last month, the man had sent him the plans on what promised to be some very interesting advancements to his favorite healing machine.

He finally unearthed his itinerary. He would begin his trip tomorrow, traveling to a series of smaller Scottish towns that he'd not visited in more than a decade, and finishing up in Inverness. Along the way perhaps he'd polish up a few oratories not yet given to large crowds. The Scots were a difficult audience; he knew that from his earlier trips.

Despite the lingering worry about leaving his wife behind, he was eager for the journey to begin.

Chapter 6

Mary and Brendan sat at the kitchen table after the noon meal. Hester was baking bread on the other side of the room, while Micah sat opposite her, mending harness. The room had become, in one day, their communal meeting place, since it was the brightest and warmest spot in Castle Gloom.

"It doesn't look appreciably different from chess," Mary said, watching as Brendan laid out the board she had brought down from Hamish's room.

"It's an older version of it, called shatranj, played in India."

"He has a great many things around him that remind him of India, doesn't he?"

"Hamish allowed you into his room?" Brendan asked, surprised.

"I looked inside," Mary said, shrugging. She was trained to notice things quickly.

He glanced at her, but didn't comment. Instead, he showed her the game pieces.

"The layout is similar to that of chess. However, elephants replace bishops, and generals take the place of queens. The board is different as well. You'll notice that the kings and generals are transposed, facing each other."

"On the way here you said that India changed him. What did you mean?" She propped her elbows on the table. "A man is more than his health, just as a patient is more than his disease," she explained in his silence. It was a sentiment espoused by Matthew Marshall. Her words, however, concealed a curiosity that had nothing to do with altruism or medicine.

"There's a reserve to Hamish that was never there before," Brendan said, speaking softly so that Micah and Hester couldn't hear his words. "As if he's on his best behavior around me. I'd much rather he would be himself."

"In what way?"

"Once he had a booming laugh," Brendan said. "And a wry sense of humor. He used to smoke the most godawful pipe, simply to annoy our brothers, I think. He was the brother in the middle, the one most consistent. Hamish was always the same. Always just himself."

Standing, he went to the cask they'd opened the night before, pouring four mugs. He handed Micah and Hester each one before returning to the table. Pushing one across to Mary, he continued. "Sometimes, I'm not even certain I know him anymore."

"Why did you never rescue him?"

He stared at her, and for the first time since she'd met him, Brendan wasn't affable or genial. Instead, anger blazed in his eyes.

"Do you think I didn't try? I scoured every port in India. I wouldn't give up, no matter what evidence I saw or what tales I'd heard. I knew he had to be alive."

She didn't speak, waiting for the rest of the story. The anger she'd seen burn so quickly wasn't, she realized, directed at her.

"I never found him."

"I didn't mean to suggest that you didn't try, Brendan. Please forgive me." She reached across the table and placed her fingertips on his wrist.

He shook his head as if to negate her words. Or perhaps he'd discerned her compassion and refused it as ably as his brother.

"Seven months after the rebellion had been put down, the British authorities showed me a grave. They told me that Hamish was buried in it, that the body had been so badly burned that he was nothing more than scorched bones."

"What happened then?"

"I became a coward," he said, smiling humorlessly. "I couldn't go home and tell my parents, and I didn't want to go to Gilmuir and let Alisdair know. So I remained in India."

"And found him alive, finally."

"He found me," Brendan corrected. "Evidently, he'd crawled out of the desert on his hands and knees, and was in such bad shape that they didn't expect him to live. But he fooled them, recuperating from his ordeal. Still, I almost didn't recognize him."

"Don't you think a year of being imprisoned would have changed a man?" Or did Hamish now hate humanity to such a degree that he would rather hide in an isolated castle than live among people?

Brendan glanced down at the board. "Perhaps. But he's

different. He doesn't talk about that year." Unexpectedly, he smiled. "You'll have to get Hamish to tell you. I don't doubt you will. You got him to play shatranj with you. I must warn you, however. Hamish doesn't play with many people, but when he does, he unfailingly wins."

"You discount any abilities I might have. I used to play chess with my husband when we were first married."

"Did you win?"

"Sometimes," she admitted. "Mostly, I just learned."

"You won't have a chance to just learn with Hamish. He's very competitive, and very skilled."

She smiled but didn't comment. She suspected that Hamish MacRae's civility would come to her rescue. A man with the character to note and to apologize for his churlish behavior despite his own internal struggles would allow her to win. At least she was hoping so. By losing at this wager, he'd be able to concede to her treatment of him while still keeping his dignity.

"Tell me the rules," she said, concentrating on the board.

"The quickest way to learn shatranj is to understand how it's different from chess. In addition to the elephants and the generals replacing the other pieces, there is no initial two-step move. Stalemate is always considered a win. So, too, is a bare king. Lastly, the board is not checkered."

"Otherwise, do the pieces move in a similar direction?"

"Except for the elephant," Brendan said. "It can only move in a diagonal jump."

She listened intently, making mental notes and acquitting herself well enough when they played a few practice games.

The intervening hours passed slowly, as if knowing

how impatient she was for the game. Finally, dinner was finished, and the kitchen put to rights. She said good night to Hester and Micah, and walked with Brendan back to the tower.

Brendan had taken a dinner tray to Hamish earlier, returning deep in thought. She'd not asked why he looked so pensive, or what the two men had discussed. Perhaps Hamish had taken her advice and spoken to Brendan after all. If so, then she'd already won a partial victory.

They both glanced upward to the soft glow of candlelight in the top of the tower. The deserted castle enveloped Hamish, offering refuge. She felt as if they were unwanted there, that Hamish and Castle Gloom suited each other very well.

"Who owns this place?" she asked.

Brendan shrugged. "From what I could discover, the McLarens. But they abandoned the castle a decade ago."

They entered the tower, Brendan lighting the wall-mounted sconces from his candle.

"I'll leave you, then," he said, hesitating at the base of the steps.

"Wish me luck, or your brother will not allow me to treat him."

"Then I wish you success. After all, you've had a great teacher."

He grinned at her, and she smiled in response, wondering why she'd never seen it before. He reminded her of Elspeth. Her friend in Inverness was a few years younger, but the closest friend Mary had. Brendan was similar in temperament and nature.

As he headed up to his room, she went to the fire, building it up with one of the logs the men had cut only that morning. The new wood popped and sizzled, the sound accompanying her thoughts. She should have donned a new dress, or changed her scarf. At the very least, she should have brushed her hair.

He is a patient.

He is a man.

He has been wounded. Tortured.

You have suffered as well, Mary.

That thought drew her up short. What arrogance to think her own sense of loss the equal of his experience. But he suffered from nightmares, and she couldn't sleep without a candle, and the two seemed not unalike. So much so that she couldn't help but wonder if memories and restlessness kept him awake as well.

She knew most of her patients, cared for them as people, as friends. What she didn't know about them she learned, snippets of information that helped her decide how to cure the patient and not just the disease. She used the information to personalize the treatments, give a little comfort where there was only pain or illness. If a man disliked the feel of wool against his skin, she wrapped a poultice in linen, instead. If a woman loved the scent of lavender, she often dropped a few sprigs into the water used for bathing. A child's favorite toy was often used to help alleviate a child's fear.

Illness brought out the worst in people, made them feel vulnerable, angry, and afraid. Often those feelings were directed at her. She had to overcome those emotions before she could be an asset to her patients, before she could begin to cure them of what made them sick.

But she'd never before had the desire she did now, to know everything there was to learn about the man she waited for, to flesh out that missing year, sketch in the details Brendan had told her. She wanted to know about those unknown months, about the time when no one had seen or heard of Hamish. What had happened to him? Where had he been?

Why was he here?

"I should make you come to my room," he said from behind her.

She held herself tight and turned to look at him.

He'd prepared for their meeting as she had not. His shirt was different, a beige linen that looked to be soft to the touch. His trousers were immaculate, and his boots as well polished as before. His brown hair seemed to gleam with golden highlights from the fire.

"I thank you for sparing me the journey," she said.

"You don't like the stairs?" he asked, frowning.

"I don't like heights," she admitted, then clarified. "I feel a strange disorientation on the steps. But I never suffer the same dizziness at a window. I suspect it is a flaw in my balance, but I've not investigated it further."

"Yet you brought my breakfast tray. Are you that desperate for a patient, Mary Gilly?"

"Perhaps I am," she said, smiling at his teasing.

He held out a chair for her, and she sat at the table. The shatranj game had been laid out and she'd not noticed it, being so entranced in her own thoughts.

"I trust Brendan taught you what he could?"

She nodded, feeling absurdly shy. What nonsense. How could she gain his trust if she acted as foolish as a girl? "You don't sound as if you have much faith in Brendan's instructions."

He smiled again, a halfhearted attempt at humor that managed only to be distantly pleasant. As if it were an expression he used to mask what he truly felt.

"I'm just anxious to conclude our wager."

"The sooner you win, the sooner I'm gone?"

He nodded.

She wished the firelight were not so bright, casting an almost festive orange glow over the two of them. She could see him well enough, and the one thing that stopped her from staring unabashedly at Hamish was his own hooded gaze. From time to time, she would look up from the board to find him contemplating her.

He seemed to know the pieces well by touch, his fingers spreading over his portion of the board as if to mark their position with his palm. He was a more aggressive player than Brendan, and much more adventurous than Gordon. Little time elapsed between the end of her move and his.

"Brendan said you were a widow. Did your husband die recently?" An acceptable question, but it nevertheless surprised her. But he'd done that before, evinced an interest in her that was the equal of hers in him.

Not a normal patient.

"A year ago." In September, when the winds howled of winter to come and the rooms were chilled and the shadows lengthened, a time for burrowing into havens and gathering with family. However, other than Charles, who'd been like Gordon's son, she'd no other relatives.

"Do you miss him?"

She glanced up at him, her fingers still resting on a pawn. "Yes, I do. He was so much a part of my life that it would be unusual if I didn't."

"Tell me about him."

She sat back and considered her words. Her fingertips rested on the edge of the table and she examined them.

"My husband was a goldsmith. An artisan of some renown. He was talented, but a good businessman as well. He cared about his customers, and our neighbors. Is that what you want to know?"

"Not really," he said. His voice was abrasive but not his tone. "When did you marry?"

"When I was seventeen."

"Brendan said he was much older than you."

She frowned at him, but her irritation was reserved for Brendan.

"It's true he was an older man, a friend of my parents. My father ran a tavern, and Gordon came often, especially in the winter months. He was a sociable man, for all that he'd never married."

"So, he saw you and decided you should be his new wife, is that it? Was there no one to stay him from marrying a girl so young when he was so old?"

"It was considered a very good marriage for me," she corrected him. "A very prosperous union. Gordon was not only a wealthy man, he was a good one. After my father died, he kept the tavern open to provide income for my mother. When she became ill only weeks later, he took her into our home and was always unfailingly kind and polite to her. Any woman would have felt grateful to have him as a husband."

"Did you nurse your mother?"

She studied him in the candlelight. "Yes," she said finally. "I did."

"And your husband as well?"

"Yes."

"Do you never grow tired of the aged or the infirm?"

What an odd question. His gaze was steady, and she

couldn't discern his thoughts. Had he learned the ability to hide himself in plain sight in India?

"I find great satisfaction in making someone well."

He nodded as if content with her answer.

"Is that why you became a healer?"

Again, he surprised her. "Yes," she said.

"Did your husband make you laugh?"

Now, that was hardly a question he should be asking her. Because it irritated her, she embellished the truth a bit. "He had a wicked sense of humor and could imitate almost anyone who came into our shop. He collected anecdotes the way a child would accumulate pebbles in his pocket." She looked into the fire, thinking that it was better to remember the early years than the difficult times. "So, yes, he made me laugh."

"How did he die?"

"He had a sickness in his stomach. Probably a tumor."

Silence hung between them as thick as the shadows in the corners.

"You have no children, do you?"

She shook her head. "Are you a father, Mr. MacRae?"

"To the best of my knowledge, I'm not. Didn't you wish to have children?"

"Isn't that question presumptuous on your part?"

"Perhaps it is. But no more so than your determination to have me be your patient."

She nodded, unwillingly conceding that point.

"Why are you? Are there no patients in Inverness craving your talents? Or are you here because of Brendan? He holds you in great esteem."

Was his voice a little frosty, or did she simply imagine it?

"He's concerned about you," she said.

"Enough to spend a fortune to hire a healer to come to an isolated castle for the purpose of badgering me."

"It wasn't greed that brought me here," she said, amused. "The money he gave me will go to the free clinic for the poor."

"Then what brought you here?" he asked sardonically.

She didn't tell him that she was beginning to yearn for adventure. But what she did say was perhaps as revealing. "Perhaps the idea of traveling so far outside Inverness was too tempting."

"Have you never left the city before?"

She moved a piece on the board before glancing at him.

"You mustn't sound so contemptuous, Mr. MacRae. Not all of us can be ship captains from birth."

"Did Brendan tell you that?" It was his turn to be amused.

"Most of the journey was spent with him telling me of your family, how they left Scotland many years ago, how your father, despite his dislike of the sea, began a thriving trading company. You have twenty-two ships now in the MacRae fleet, I believe, and each of the brothers has had his turn at being a captain."

"You have an impressive memory."

"It was an exceedingly boring journey."

"What did Brendan tell you about me?"

Had he heard their earlier conversations? "Enough to make me think you need me more than you say."

"As you can see, I'm not the wreck that my brother no doubt portrayed me to be."

"But you can't move your left arm, and I suspect that you're not healing as well as you would like me to believe. A few times now, your right hand has brushed across your chest. Is there a wound there that bothers you?"

He stared at her. "It's disconcerting to be defined by my symptoms."

"How am I to judge you otherwise? We've spent most of our time in conversation with your questioning me."

He nodded once, a concession she accepted.

"Would you consider it a loss, if I don't allow you to treat me? Some celestial battle between good and evil, with a black mark on your side of the score sheet if you fail?"

"Do you think that life is measured so easily? I don't. But I will worry about you, and that's a nuisance."

He smiled fully then, the first time he had truly done so.

"So in order to prevent your worry, I should simply acquiesce and allow you to do what you will? So that I'm not a nuisance, that is."

"I would appreciate it," she said, propping her chin on her hands. "There are so many other people who need my thoughts more than you."

"But if you don't treat me, I'll be at the forefront of them?"

She didn't tell him that she was very much afraid he would be there whether or not she tried to heal him. He was an immensely fascinating man.

He shouldn't be sitting there with her. The firelight accentuated the darkness of her eyes and the subtle sheen of auburn in her hair. There were tiny marks at the corners of her eyes as if she laughed often. But she was young, for all her protestations of wisdom.

Tonight, she smelled of bread and ale, scents that nonetheless managed to accentuate her voluptuousness. Her lips fascinated him, so much so that one part of his mind sat back in bemused wonder, almost ridicule, and watched the mature Hamish act as if he were a lovelorn youth.

Her top lip did not have an indentation, but curved almost like an inverted bottom lip. The effect was curiously pouty, as if she begged for a kiss with every word that began with an "h." He began to watch for it, or for her to say "you."

The Angel of Inverness was an earthbound spirit.

Her mouth wasn't the only feature to attract his attention. Her eyes, soft and brown, were worthy enough in their own right. They were deeply colored, encircled in black, giving them definition and depth. Perhaps that's why they appeared so much darker than his. But then, he had not seen himself in a great many months.

Perhaps he should be thankful for that omission.

She had a way of clasping her hands tightly together, thumbs aligned in military precision. She tapped them against each other in an oddly rhythmic way, or placed one over the other. He wanted to reach across the table and still her hands, but he was so entranced with the movement, and the fact that it betrayed her nervousness, that he did nothing, simply watched her.

Sometimes, she took a deep breath, and the gauzy scarf at her neck lifted by several inches. Such an effect did not hide the fulsomeness of her bodice.

What would she say if he told her that the only treatment he wished was her mouth on his? He wouldn't say it, of course. It was better to wish her gone, however much he might want her. Women like Mary Gilly remained fascinating long beyond their time. He didn't want any additional memories. His were blackened by his nightmares and tinted with regret.

They played in silence for several more minutes, he

content to simply study her. The firelight's glow was diffused only a little by the scattering of candles. She was equally as lovely in daylight, another youthful thought from a man who'd long since put his adolescence behind him.

Perhaps that's why they called her Angel. She didn't offer potions and possets, only a curious kind of forgetfulness. Last night had been the same. For a few minutes he'd forgotten who he was and what he'd done, even finding some measure of rest after leaving her. Perhaps tonight he wouldn't have nightmares, only dreams of a brown-haired woman with warm eyes and a winsome smile who urged him to sleep.

She fascinated him, and that was an even more naïve musing. Last night, she'd startled him with her forthrightness and her candor. This morning, she'd amused him as well. Now, he was too taken with her appearance to wonder at her wit and intelligence.

He moved his piece, then sat back and surveyed her, his gaze once again focusing on her mouth.

She smiled, and he thought that he should warn her that even humor would not save her. The only thing protecting her from his more libidinous impulses was his legacy from the Atavasi. If he revealed himself to her, she'd no doubt run screaming from the tower, choosing the shadows and the night rather than remaining in his presence.

Otherwise, he would have amused himself by slowly removing that scarf from around her neck, letting the fabric gently abrade her throat. Then, he'd unfasten the bodice of her dress until it revealed what it now attempted to so cunningly conceal.

He would lift up her skirts gently, slowly, delicately. She'd raise her arms until he pulled her clothing over her head. There she would stand in shift, stays, and stockings, nearly unveiled for his eyes.

"I've beaten you," she said, her voice abruptly dragging him from his thoughts. She stared at the board in wonder.

"Indeed you have."

Her eyes met his. In that instant, he knew that she'd not been fooled after all. However, she didn't call him on it, or otherwise refuse her win. A wise woman.

"Do you go to any lengths to treat your patients?"

She looked surprised at the question. "I don't think so, no."

"Since you've won," he said, "I'm at your mercy." The impulse to let her win had been a foolish one. Either way, she'd be gone from this place with more speed then she'd planned.

A pity, truly; they might have found some comfort in each other. If she didn't run in horror from him, perhaps he'd give in to his baser impulses after all. Another reason to wish her gone, a last protective impulse that would shield her from the man he'd become, empty and shell-like, lacking heart and possessing only a shriveled soul.

"Would you like to begin tonight?"

"It's rather late," she said. "Perhaps in the morning? Unless you're in pain?"

He shook his head, thinking that he'd be given a respite, then, a few hours of grace before she went back to Inverness with the tale of a hideous hermit crouching in his castle. How strange that he wanted her gone at the same time he wanted the actual moment of her departure to be delayed.

Was she possessed of the intellectual genius of a physician, the wisdom of an old crone, the nurturing spirit of a mother? He could do with all of them, or sim-

ply her understanding, a gentle hand on his arm, an unspoken acceptance.

What a fool he was.

"Is there anyone in Inverness you do not charm?"

She looked amused, her warm brown eyes dancing with
humor.

"I do not charm a great many people," she said. "My
husband's apprentice, for one. Charles is forever impatient with me, telling me that I shouldn't give so much
money to the clinic, or spend so much time among the
poor. I think he believes that poverty is contagious."

"Do you pay any attention to his words? Or do you simply ignore him?"

"You make it sound as if I'm headstrong and spoiled,"
she said. "I simply want my life to mean something. Most
people do, and they find a certain satisfaction in caring for
their families. I have none. What else should I do with my
time? I have no other skills."

"There are women in my family who would tell you
that they have no talent," he said, "but they can create
marvels in stone or weave beautiful cloth. My sister-in-
law Riona can make the desert bloom, I think. What is it
about a woman that makes her so modest?"

Her laughter bubbled free. She sat back and regarded
him with humor. "Perhaps it is the MacRae men," she
said. "Any woman might appear self-effacing next to such
an arrogant group."

"I don't think we're arrogant," he said discomfited by
her words.

"A person's flaw is sometimes like the back of his neck.
Impossible for him to see."

He sat back and regarded her. "So arrogance rarely rec-
ognizes itself?" He wasn't entirely certain that he agreed

with her, especially in view of the fact that he'd let her win the game and the wager.

Standing, he bowed slightly to her. "Then I'll see you in the morning. Here?"

She nodded.

He left her then, grateful to her in a paradoxical way for irritating him. It meant that for tonight she was safe from him, and that his dreams, when they came, would not include her.

Chapter 7

~~~⟲⟳~~~

Mary pressed her hand against her midriff in order to still her rapid breathing. It would never do for a patient to know how anxious she was. *Oh, Mary, do not lie to yourself. Or to God, who must surely hear you.*

Because there were no windows, she propped open the door and allowed sunlight to illuminate the first floor of the tower.

The morning was cool, but the sky was still fair, the weather suited more to summer than autumn. She stood in the doorway, looking toward the sea gate. Birds, wings outspread, coasted on the air currents and then dipped toward the ocean waves.

Suddenly, she heard a sound on the stairs, and he was there.

It wasn't treating him that made her blood race. It was the sight of him standing tall and large at the bottom of the stairs. Or perhaps his half smile, or even the expressionless look in his eyes that made her wonder at his thoughts.

"Good morning," she said brightly, determined to be professional.

He only nodded in return, distant and almost wary, as if they'd never met.

Entering the room again, she busied herself opening her medicine case and arranging her implements on the tray. A quick glance told her that he had changed his shirt again.

"You shave every morning, don't you?" she asked, and then wondered if that was too personal a question. *Silly, Mary, you've talked to your patients of much more intimate subjects.* But none of her other male patients had ever towered above her, or seemed so much like a lord of this castle that she was almost intimidated.

"I do," he said, and it seemed as if his voice reverberated up the stairs and down again, echoing onto itself.

"Does it pain you?"

"Because of the scars?" he asked, rubbing his hand across his face.

She nodded.

"No."

"What did they use to burn you?"

"I wasn't burned," he said. His fingers settled on a few of the marks. "They're scars from copper nails."

She dropped one of the vials, and stared as it bounced on the stone floor. Grateful that it hadn't broken, she retrieved it, inspecting the frosted glass for damage. Each of twelve containers fit into one side of her chest, her implements and a drawer to hold her aprons and other commonly replaced items on the other.

"They pounded nails into your body?" she asked, wiping off the vial and placing it on the table. She tied a fresh cloth around her hair, busying herself to hide the fact that her hands were trembling.

He nodded and came to stand beside her, inspecting her medical case with great care.

"Why?" she asked faintly.

He smiled slightly, and it was almost an expression of pity that she might be so naïve as to ask that question.

"Because they wanted to see how well I screamed," he said matter-of-factly, as if it were a commonplace thing he discussed.

"Did you?" There, she could match his casual tone.

He looked directly at her. "I discovered that I could scream very well. Like a songbird to heaven."

Such revelations were painful, Mary discovered. Not only for him, but for her, having to listen to them, to witness his clear, direct gaze. Her hand replaced his on his face, her fingers resting lightly against the marks on his skin. In that instant she was there with him in that faraway place, feeling the pain he must have endured as the nails were driven into his jaw.

Abruptly, she dropped her hand, turned, and withdrew a cloth from her case, setting it beside the bowl she'd brought from the kitchen. Going to the fire, she withdrew a small iron kettle and poured the steaming water into the bowl.

"Are you going to bathe me?" he asked, smiling.

"I'm going to treat your arm," she answered. She pulled out the chair and stood beside it, waiting for him to be seated. He did so, finally, that enigmatic smile of his appearing again.

"How long has it been since you were able to use your arm?"

"Since I was captured," he said simply.

"I want to see it," she said. "I want to know if we can get it to work again."

"We?"

"A healer is only part of the process, Hamish. The patient must wish to get well."

He looked amused, but didn't comment. She knew, from conversations with Brendan, that he'd objected not only to her presence but also to that of an Arab physician summoned when he was first rescued. It was as if he didn't wish to recover completely from his ordeal. Or simply didn't think it important.

Picking up his left arm, she cradled it between her hands. Slowly, she rolled up the cuff of his shirt. Even though he couldn't use his arm, the muscle had not yet begun to waste away, and the skin was tanned and firm. Those were good signs. Not so the scars illuminated by the sun. She traced their path from his wrist to his elbow to his upper arm.

"They used nails here, too?"

"Exquisitely," he said. "The Atavasi are masters of torture."

"Did they do any damage to your other arm, Hamish? Or your legs?" The question was posed with great calm. She was, after all, a healer. But she'd never before seen such acts of barbarism. The wounds were near joints, calculated to cause the most damage and pain.

"No," he said, his voice as devoid of emotion as hers. "This was something new. I decided to leave before they made it impossible for me to do so."

Holding his arm, she pressed delicately against one scar, to see if the muscle flexed in response.

"You must tell me," she said, "if I cause you any discomfort."

He only smiled again, as if her statement were foolish.

"Does your arm hurt?" she asked, when his muscles remained flaccid.

"From time to time. But nothing unbearable."

"Twinges? Or a pulsating pain? In the cold? Or when there's a chilled breeze?"

"At night, mostly. Did you know that you frown when asking all those questions? You're very earnest, Mary Gilly. Very intent upon your work." Glancing over at the table where she'd laid out her instruments, he picked up her extended tweezers. "What's this used for?"

"For a variety of tasks. To lance a boil, peer down a swollen throat. I've even used it upon occasion to aid in childbirth." He dropped it back on the table, and reached for another.

"Did your husband craft these for you? I've never seen such things made of silver."

"The case was a present from Gordon for our tenth wedding anniversary. He wanted me to have the finest tools, so he created them himself. Some I've never used," she admitted. "He got the idea for them from corresponding with some men in Edinburgh."

"A doting husband."

His tone didn't sound complimentary, even though his words might have been.

Her palm stroked his arm, testing resiliency in the muscle. "Press against my hand," she told him, but there was little resistance in his fingers.

"If you don't use your arm soon, it will begin to wither," she said, the calm tone of her voice hiding the worry she felt.

"How do you propose I do that?"

"Exercise," she told him. "Even if your arm cannot move on its own, it will help to keep it limber."

She laid his arm on her lap, reached over, and selected a

vial. Smoothing the contents onto her palm, she massaged the ointment into his skin using long slow strokes.

"What's in that?" he asked, looking down at her hands. "It feels both hot and cold."

"Cloves, spices, and camphor, in a base of pork fat. Something to stimulate the blood."

Again, that odd half smile.

"I wish I had Mr. Marshall's electrical machine. I do not doubt that it would aid in regenerating the nerves in your arm."

He raised one eyebrow. "Electrical machine?"

She smiled brightly at the cautious look on his face. "I'm very interested in new advances. Mr. Marshall is a proponent of an electrical machine. How it works, I'm not entirely certain. I've never seen one, although I've read everything he's written about it. It gives off a jolt of energy, not unlike lightning itself. I think if we could find such an instrument, we might be able to effect some healing in your arm."

"Shall I extract a promise from you?"

"I won't hurt you," she assured him. "I understand there's only a slight tingling when it's administered."

He laughed, the sound encouraging her smile. "I doubt you could do anything to me that I could feel. No, the promise I want is that you not hold out too much hope. I've grown used to my infirmity."

"You don't seem the type to pity yourself."

He'd looked as if he would like to say something else but restrained himself. A moment later, however, he evidently thought better of that notion and spoke. "I don't pity myself, Mrs. Gilly. But neither am I unrealistic. I have two good legs and one good arm, and although I'm not pleased with that, I can accept it."

"How did you bear being tortured?" It wasn't a question she'd meant to ask, especially so bluntly, but it had come tumbling free in the silence.

For the longest time, she thought he wouldn't answer her, but he finally spoke.

"I am blessed with a hearty constitution," he said wryly. "It enabled me to endure more than I thought."

"Were you angry?"

He looked surprised at her question.

"I would have been," she explained. "Anger would have been the only thing to keep me strong, I think."

"I wasn't," he said, surprisingly. "I learned to distance myself from what was happening. I wasn't angry until I escaped, and then I found it a difficult emotion to control. I needed my energy for survival, and most of it was spent in rage."

"How did you escape?"

"Across the little desert north toward Aleppo and the Mediterranean. I was fortunate to find Brendan in Rhodes."

That wasn't what she meant, and she suspected he knew it well.

Their gazes met and held. Unexpectedly, he smiled at her. A charming man before he'd decided to be a hermit. How many women in how many seaports had thought the very same thing?

She dipped the cloth in the bowl, wrung it out, and laid it over his elbow. A moment later, she removed it, beginning to massage some of the salve from wrist to joint.

"It's very important that you have a massage often," she said. "At least three times a day to keep the muscles active."

"I know why you're such a successful healer," he said. "You're too stubborn to lose a battle with illness."

She smiled in response.

"How did you make the transition from caring for your mother to becoming a healer?"

"I happened upon Matthew Marshall's book *The Primitive Physick*, and began to study. I started with my own notes, and practiced on myself, then took what I'd learned and volunteered to treat the poor."

"You could not have endeared yourself to the physicians of Inverness."

She shook her head. "They didn't care. No one wished to treat someone with little ability to pay. But in my case, I wasn't earning my living as a physician, so I offered my services where I could."

She soaked the cloth again, and placed it above his elbow this time.

"Your hands are very strong."

She smiled at the note of surprise in his voice. "Medicine is for neither the faint of heart nor the weak of limb, Mr. MacRae. I've had to set a dislocated shoulder in a man larger than you, and the task required all my strength."

"How did you become the Angel of Inverness?"

She frowned at that appellation but continued her ministrations. His skin was beginning to warm beneath her palms. "I was called to the home of a prosperous merchant who had a young son. Jack was near death, and the physician who'd been treating him declared his situation hopeless." She met his eyes. "Dr. Grampian was the same man who also refused to treat any of the poor practically on his doorstep."

"And you cured him," he said.

She nodded. "His was not the most desperate case I've seen, but he did need treatment or he would have certainly died. The disease had obstructed his breathing. Once his throat was cleared, he recovered in a few weeks."

"I'm surprised the physician didn't claim credit."

She laughed lightly. "He did, but I preferred not to call him a liar. He has nothing good to say about me, and I choose to ignore him. He will never come to believe that a healthy body and mind act together in concert."

"What treatment would you propose for a burn?"

"Is this a test? I'd advise cold water immediately applied to the affected area."

"What would you prescribe for me, Mrs. Gilly?"

"A massage of your arm three times a day," she said.

"And your electrical machine?"

"If I had use of one," she said, nodding. "But there aren't very many of them in existence."

Mr. Marshall had published an entire book on the treatment, stating that the apparatus could cure all sorts of conditions. He'd taken Richard Lovett's work on treating diseases by electricity, and proven that headache, gout, rheumatism could all be cured. Perhaps when she met with Mr. Marshall, she could ask him about the efficacy of using it under such conditions.

"Do you really think it would work?" he asked, looking down at his arm.

"Perhaps it would," she said matter-of-factly. "But we don't have it, so it doesn't matter. We shall have to work with what we do have."

"Which is?"

"That indomitable will of yours."

Grabbing his wrist with her right hand, she placed her left above his elbow. Slowly, she bent his arm. His only response was to stare at her intently, his brown eyes never veering from hers. She was the one to look away first. When she glanced back at him, his eyes were closed. That was all the indication he gave that what she was doing was painful.

"You must begin to exercise this arm or it will never work again. I don't know how much damage the nails did, but we must work on the premise that what has been injured can be healed. If it cannot work on its own, then we'll help it."

"I was right, you know. You badger disease away."

"I don't care how the result is obtained, Hamish," she said with a smile. "Only that the patient gets better."

"That's twice now," he said.

She glanced at him, waiting.

"You called me Hamish. I suppose such familiarity is to be expected between patient and healer?"

Her face warmed. "Of course not," she said, embarrassed. "I'll address you as Mr. MacRae, if you wish."

"I'd prefer Hamish. And Mary to Mrs. Gilly. Or would you object?"

She shook her head, repeating the movement of his arm. A few moments later, she could feel some faint resistance, as if the muscles were beginning to come to life. Only a reflex action, she suspected. For another quarter hour, she worked on his arm, a careful silence between them. It was easier to concentrate on her task than on his eyes, now open and fixed on her.

"Does it hurt?" she asked, letting his arm rest finally.

"Less so than when you began."

She opened the vial and placed more of the camphor ointment on his skin again, massaging it once more.

"I think I should examine your chest. You flinched when I touched you."

He looked at her for long, solemn moments.

"Will you take off your shirt?" she asked calmly.

Without speaking, he began to unfasten the buttons. When he was finished, she reached over and helped him slide the shirt off his shoulders, then withdrew her hand.

When his chest was revealed, she sat back, biting her lip rather than making a sound.

Chapter 8

His eyes were on her, she knew it. She could feel his gaze, intent and unrelenting. She blessed her training and the experience she'd had in facing a dying patient's family. *Give me strength.* An often uttered prayer, repeated like a never-ending echo now.

What had they done to him?

Welts of blue, green, and vermillion discolored his skin. An even deeper outline of black accentuated the multicolored swirls and lines. The longer she stared, the more she could discern the shape of it. Tattooed on his chest was the figure of a man.

No, not just a man. A bizarre form, depicted dancing, his arms outstretched to wind up to Hamish's arms, his waist disappearing beneath the fabric of Hamish's trousers. As if, she thought wildly, his captors had tried to obliterate Hamish beneath the picture of this stylized figure.

"Who is it?" she asked, placing her fingers on the face, realizing that the drawing was so intricate that it must have taken days, if not weeks, to finish. Each color was deeply inscribed into Hamish's skin as if they'd scored him with a knife to create the design.

"Shiva," he said expressionlessly.

She glanced up at him. "Shiva?"

"A Hindu god of destruction and birth. All things are created by Shiva, and destroyed by Shiva. Good and evil dwelling together."

Slowly, she withdrew her fingers.

"How did they do this?"

His gaze didn't leave hers. "First they cut me," he said calmly, as if reciting the ingredients for a medicine. "Before the scars healed, they were colored with dye. The smaller areas were done with long copper needles, dipped in dye as well as acid. The procedure was enough to be painful but not enough to kill me all at once. As Shiva was coming to life, I was slowly dying."

She felt nauseated. "That's hideous."

He smiled at her, an almost fond smile for all its humor. "Yes."

"Is this why you cannot sleep?"

"No."

Mary stood and walked around to his back. There, the image was as detailed, the reverse of the god in all his splendor. One shoulder was completely tattooed in brilliant colors, the yellows, oranges, and blacks forming the picture of a snarling animal.

"What is this?" she asked, tracing the outline of the animal's head.

"A tiger," he said shortly. "As you can see, I'm a testament to my captors' artistry. They evidently grew tired of Shiva. Or perhaps I was used as practice like a blank canvas. Like their form of torture on my arm and face."

"Why did they do this? Why not simply kill you?"

She wrung out the cloth once more, smoothing it over the marks on his skin. She was so close that her skirts covered the legs of the chair in which he sat. Her sleeve brushed against his bare back. The heat of his body was warmly welcoming, as if he was a brazier and she trembling and chilled.

He shrugged. "They wanted to humiliate an Englishman. What better specimen than the captain of a ship? I was the living embodiment of all they'd come to despise, a stranger invading their country."

"But you aren't English. Why didn't you tell them that?"

His laugh echoed throughout the room.

"We didn't speak the same language, first of all. Everything I learned about Shiva was after the fact, I'm afraid. But even had I told them they'd captured a man born in Nova Scotia, whose family hated the English as much as they, I doubt they would have released me. It would have been easier to simply kill me, and I found that I wasn't quite ready to die yet. Not then. I became the English trophy that they carried from village to village, letting anyone see me, and their handiwork."

She moved to the table, dipped the cloth in the warm water, and wrung it out again. All routine actions. Her gaze was on his face, on the distant look in his eyes, as if he saw into the past rather than a small tower room in Castle Gloom.

"I was their sacrifice to Shiva, the Englishman rendered in his image." His voice held an edge to it. The first time she'd heard him express any emotion about his imprisonment. "They'd captured two other men as well, but I hadn't known of their existence for months."

"Did they mark them as well?"

He smiled. "I was the only one to be honored in such a fashion."

"How were you captured?" she asked, moving around to his back once more, and placing the cloth on the worst of his scars. She could almost feel his pain as they cut him.

He shrugged, dislodging the cloth. She replaced it, smoothing her fingers over his damp skin.

"My ship was attacked and fired. Although we fought them off as well as we could, we were outnumbered and soon overrun. You mentioned my family, Mary, the fact that we were all captains of our own ships. We MacRaes were never reared to believe that we might fail in some venture. It took me weeks to believe it could happen."

She smiled. "Then you have lived a very fortunate life, Hamish MacRae. All of us fail at one time or another."

"Have you?"

He looked at her directly, the force of his gaze a little too curious. She picked up the basin and walked outside, emptying the cooling water near the curving curtain wall. She took advantage of the time to take a deep breath and calm herself before entering the tower again.

Had she failed? A question she'd prefer not to answer.

Brendan and Micah were repairing the lean-to, the horses left to graze in the courtyard. An almost pastoral scene, and one on which she concentrated rather than the tumult of her thoughts. But all too soon the image of what they'd done to Hamish was at the forefront of her mind.

She'd wanted to know, and now she did.

Entering the tower, she walked to the fireplace, folded a cloth several times, and used it as a pad to lift a bucket from the fire. Moving back to the table, she poured the boiling water into the basin. After placing the empty bucket on the floor beside the table, she dropped a linen bundle tightly tied with a string into the water. Instantly, the room was suffused with the scent of rosemary.

"Another potion?"

"Something to ease your muscles," she said.

Dipping another cloth into the boiling water, she held it by the corners to squeeze out the excess moisture. She waved it in the air to cool it a little before placing it on his left shoulder. He didn't even flinch at the heat.

"This should be done at least once a day," she said. "It might not hurt to do the same on the marks on your back. At least for a few weeks."

"Will you be here that long, Mary?"

She hesitated. "No," she admitted reluctantly. "Only a few days. Mr. Marshall is coming to Inverness, and wishes to meet with me. It's a very great honor."

"Your mentor?"

"Hardly that. I'm a student, it's true, but I've never thought to have the opportunity to talk with him."

"When will you be leaving?"

"Soon," she said.

"With an easy conscience, I trust, now that you've treated me."

She nodded, and then realized he couldn't see her, as she was standing behind him. "Yes."

"Perhaps you'll see one of his electrical machines," he said.

"I wish I'd thought to ask if he was bringing it." She dipped the cloth into the water again. "Can I extract your promise to treat your injuries as I would?"

"You can always ask, but will you trust me to honor a promise?"

He was a stranger, a man she'd known for only a little

while, yet she knew that if he gave his word, she could believe in it.

"Yes," she said softly.

"But I cannot give it," he said. For a moment, all she felt was disappointment. "I cannot reach areas of my back, Mary. Not as well as you."

"Brendan can help you. Or Hester."

"Will either of them be my confidant as you have?"

"If you wish them to be."

"I didn't mean to tell anyone what I've told you," he admitted. "But you'd counseled me to do that, didn't you?"

She smiled and moved in front of him.

"Will I sleep better for it?"

"I am surprised that you can sleep at all with the nightmares you must have," she told him honestly.

There was that half smile again.

"Perhaps you'll give me a potion to help me sleep after all."

"Or perhaps you'll find something else to do at night," she suggested. "Read a calming book, sketch a drawing."

His smile broadened, but he didn't comment on her list. She felt her face warm, and moved around to his back again. She asked him to bend forward, and she inspected his scars. The Atavasi had evidently known where to inflict the greatest pain with the least damage. There were no marks near Hamish's spine. Nor were there near any vital organs. But his torturers had left no large muscle untouched.

"You'll miss Brendan," he said unexpectedly.

It wasn't a question as much as a statement.

"Brendan isn't my patient," she said, tracing the deepest of the scars on his back with gentle fingers.

"So speaks Mary the healer. How does Mary the woman feel?"

"I cannot separate the various parts of myself, Hamish. The healer is the woman."

She realized, however, what he was asking. She halted in her explorations and answered him. "I find Brendan to be a very pleasant companion. But he reminds me of a younger brother." There, a confession that the healer shouldn't have made, but the woman felt compelled to tell him.

"A sentiment that would irritate him, should he learn of it."

"I have no intention of telling him," she said calmly. "Do you?"

His silence incited her curiosity. What was he thinking? Where had he learned such restraint? Had it been during his imprisonment, or had he always been this way?

Once again, she submersed the cloth, wringing it nearly dry and cooling it slightly before placing it on his skin. She busied herself with the task of being a healer. Only when she moved in front of him did her composure come close to slipping again.

She placed the cloth on his chest, concentrating on her hands rather than looking into his eyes or seeing that charming half smile.

"Brendan does not smell of flowers, Mary. How can you ask that I trade him for your presence?"

He teased her, she knew. However, his banter had an edge to it. The prettiest rose also bears a hurtful thorn.

"What would your life be like if you'd not found healing to occupy you?"

She hesitated, her hands flat against his chest. Her gaze

met his, and for a second, she thought she could see herself in his eyes. Did he merely think her a pretentious woman? Someone who dabbled in the hobby of treating illness to keep her days full?

"I'd have been content to live my life just as it was. A normal life, an ordinary one."

"I think you would not have been content with that, Mary."

"As you were not?"

"Perhaps," he admitted.

"You're an example of why I shouldn't wish for too much adventure, Hamish." She pressed gently against his chest, as if to emphasize the rendition carved into him by the Atavasi.

He looked surprised at her words, as if he'd expected her to take his barbs and not return one of her own.

They fell silent once again; the only sounds those of the slosh of the water in the basin and the slap of the cloth against his skin.

"Will you play shatranj with me again tonight?"

"I would probably be bored," she said. "Especially if you allow me to win again." She glanced up to find him smiling.

"You weren't surprised," he said.

"Not truly," she admitted. "I'd hoped that you'd concede the game and allow me to treat you. I trusted in your gentlemanly impulses."

"That was a mistake."

She ignored that comment. "Your loss was very skillfully done. Someone who was not as good a player could not have managed it, I think. But then I might have won on my own." She pulled out the neighboring chair and sat.

"Another error on your part, to believe yourself that skilled."

Sitting back with the cloth wadded up in one hand, Mary stared at him in amusement. "You're very arrogant."

"I'm very good. While you have the capability to be a good player, you're not yet a great one."

"But I learned quickly. You have to admit that."

He nodded, smiling.

"As far as improving, perhaps all I need is practice."

"I'll set up the board in my room. Shall we say after dinner?"

She really shouldn't. They both knew that. "Yes," she said. "Will you join us for dinner?"

He shook his head.

"Why not?"

"You've seen me, and you still ask that question?"

"Brendan has seen you as well. But unless you're going to take your shirt off for Micah and Hester, they wouldn't have a comment on your appearance."

True, his back and chest was a frightening scene. But his face wasn't that badly scarred. The small marks would probably fade in time, being no more visible than a milk-maid's pox.

He was far from ugly.

"I think people would notice you, Hamish, but not because you're scarred."

One of his eyebrows lifted, but he said nothing. She felt an unaccustomed blush suffuse her face. She was not used to complimenting a man on his appearance.

"Do I not frighten you, Mary?"

Her gaze flew to his. "Of course not," she said quickly. That first moment she met him half shrouded in darkness, he'd been only a subject of fascination, not revulsion. Even now, with his chest and his back revealed, she could only think one startling thought. He was too much a man for them to kill him.

If he didn't feel rage toward his captors, she did.

He reached out and touched her cheek with his fingers. Mary turned her head, and before she realized what she was doing, held his hand against her face. Worse, she compounded the error of the moment by keeping his hand there long after she should have pulled away.

She should have told him that it was a gesture Gordon had often made, and that she'd been caught up in a moment of memory. But the truth was that she'd not remembered her husband at all. In fact, she would be hard-pressed to remember his face at this moment.

When his fingers moved slightly and touched her lips, she should have pulled away completely and stood, moving to the other side of the room. But in actuality, she wanted him to touch her. It had been so very long since she'd felt tenderness or the slow, heavy pounding of her heart that preceded desire.

Slowly, propriety returning to her in droplets, she stood and skirted the table. Handing him a dry cloth, she watched as he wiped his chest in deliberate strokes. When his skin was dry, she picked up his shirt. The stitches were finely sewn, and she wanted to ask him who'd made this for him. Was it a mother, a sister, a sweetheart?

"Have you ever married?" she asked as she handed the garment to him. There, a normal enough question between almost strangers. A healer and her patient might pass the time learning of each other.

"Never," he said abruptly, the words sounding bitten off.

"Did you never wish to?"

"There never seemed to be the time. Nor did I find the right woman. The sea became my wife, mistress, and sweetheart."

"A watery companion, Hamish," she said, and was rewarded for her teasing with his smile. "You should give some thought to marriage. My married patients live longer and have more contented lives than those who remain single."

"Do you counsel your women patients as well as men?"

"Women rarely need advice about marriage," she said calmly. "They know that the natural order of things is to be joined in life."

"Not all of us are willing to settle for the type of marriage you had, Mary."

Startled, she stared at him.

"What type of marriage do you think I had?"

He shrugged and donned his shirt.

"I shared a great friendship with my husband. And loved him as well."

He looked dubious.

She wiped down her instruments, placed them back in the case, and returned the vials to their positions. One was missing, and she ran her fingers over the hole its absence created. She'd used most of the mixture in the nightly tonic she'd given Gordon and had misplaced the container soon after. Perhaps she'd not yet replaced it as a way to remind her of her own failings, a warning to be humble in the face of disease.

"What would you have in your marriage, if not companionship and friendship, Hamish?"

"Passion. Adoration."

She blinked at him several times. "Passion is fleeting, and adoration is best reserved for God."

"Then you've never truly seen a happy marriage, only one that's a pale shadow."

He stood and smiled down at her.

For her peace of mind, she should limit her acquaintance with Hamish. This fascination she felt about his adventures and tribulations would gradually pass, as would her curiosity. Or if it didn't, she could satisfy it by asking questions of Brendan. But she shouldn't be in Hamish's company any more than was necessary. He made her forget that he was a patient, and she a healer.

"Will you join me tonight?" He hesitated on the stairs, and she looked up at him. Now was the time to offer him an excuse, to be wise and proper.

"Yes," she said, knowing that it was the worst possible answer.

Chapter 9

His tray was brought by Brendan, who didn't badger him to appear at dinner. Brendan understood, more than most people. Still, he didn't know everything, and if Hamish had his way, he never would. There were some secrets meant only for dark nights filled with howling winds, or for nightmares.

Hamish closed the shutters against the night, before lighting a small fire in the brazier set against one wall. He pushed the cannon to the side of the circular chamber before moving the table out into the center, arranging the two chairs, and lighting a succession of candles. Setting up the board, Hamish wondered if she would appear after all, or simply, and wisely, stay away.

He placed his right hand flat on his chest. Beneath his shirt was a design he knew only too well. He'd watched as they'd cut into him, refusing to flinch or show any outward expression. Mary, however, had not looked away. Not once, and he'd been watching her eyes carefully.

She'd appeared interested rather than repulsed, fascinated rather than horror-struck.

The design didn't stop at the waist, but traveled around his buttocks and down his thighs. Even the soles of his feet had been the target of their knives and needles.

A unique method of torture, and one that was perfect in its execution. He could almost admire the venal architect of his pain. He'd never known who it was, had not been able to separate one person from the crowd of captors to blame more than the other. Even in this, they'd been clever. He wasn't able to simply hate one man but was forced to hate a group, a task he'd found more difficult than he'd anticipated.

Each needle was tipped with a painful mixture, each inch of the design tattooed on his body represented thousands of tiny pinpricks. As he was passed from village to village, they'd all had their turn, marking him as if he were no more important than a parcel to be stamped. He'd realized, early on, that the entire process was designed to dehumanize. In that, they'd succeeded. For months, he'd simply existed, a creature who knew he was alive, was hungry, felt pain.

He moved to his bed, rearranged the crimson and gold coverlet atop it. The fabric was a reminder of an earlier time, a better memory than most. A crowded market, an aged vendor, a beautiful length of silk he'd purchased, sent to Brendan's ship for transport back to Nova Scotia. His brother had kept it safe, along with a few other trinkets, never realizing that they would become remnants of a former life.

Could a man be born again? Could he live two lifetimes? Hamish felt as if he'd done it, becoming a different man from the one he'd been reared to be. Certain physical traits were the same, such as the color of his eyes and hair. But his voice was different, a rasp when he spoke too long. A result of screaming for months. He was as tall, but his slenderness was a result of months of near starvation.

The greatest changes were not so easily seen. He no longer possessed the easy optimism of his youth. Nor did he accept that tomorrow was guaranteed. Time itself had become precious to him. His thoughts dwelled not on adventure or the next voyage as much as on his beliefs and what he might expect from himself.

Just like the tattoos on his body, his thoughts had been slowly reshaped, forming a pattern he was still trying to unravel.

He wondered if Mary would come. He needed the company of someone who didn't know him as he had been, someone who could accept him as he was now. His family and friends didn't understand that the changes he'd undergone had been to far more than his appearance. He was, simply put, not the same man.

The sound of her shoes on the steps ended the waiting. She was here. Glancing behind him to ensure that all was in readiness, Hamish opened the door.

She'd changed her dress. This one, in the same modest lines, was dark blue. Instead of a kerchief adorning her bodice, however, only a brooch of gold and silver rested at her neck.

"Did your husband design that?" he asked, reaching out to touch the intricate design of silver thistles.

She nodded, smiling lightly.

Do you wear it to remind yourself that you're a proper widow? A question he decided not to ask. There were some answers he didn't want to hear.

Mary wasn't wearing her kersch. The headdress had

been left behind with the kerchief. She was less modest now, the Widow Gilly, but infinitely more approachable. What would she do if he reached out and took down her bun, uncoiling the braid and spreading her hair over her shoulders? Would she murmur a soft complaint or bat his hands away with a censorious look?

She remained on the threshold, and he waited patiently for her to come inside. She tilted her head, surveying him wordlessly, and then entered with as much caution as a virgin sacrifice. He let the door swing shut of its own volition, only flattening his hand against it when the latch clicked.

The brazier gave off enough heat to render the room comfortable now that the window and the archers' slits had been closed against the wind. He took the candle from her, setting it on a small, curved shelf.

"What is that?" she asked, pointing to a brass statue mounted on a heavy pediment of bronze.

"Shiva."

She looked shocked. "Why would you keep such a thing?"

"Why not?" He fingered the bronze ring that surrounded the figure shown in a stylized dance. "Lord Shiva is the lord of mercy and compassion, representing the supreme reality that dissolves and recreates the universe. He's the third deity in the Hindu triad of Brahma, Vishnu, and Shiva, and considered the most fearsome of the Hindu gods."

He heard his own voice, almost a monotone. He wouldn't tell her that it seemed strangely right to have the replica of the god there; its presence was a solid reminder of battles Hamish had won. There were times, especially in the deep darkness of night, when he needed to recall something good about himself.

"Why is he dancing?" she asked, narrowing her eyes. Shiva's foot was raised, arched to mimic the same angle as his knee. His hands were likewise as bent as if he were in the midst of a dancing to a tune only he could hear.

He smiled. "Because he represents the source of all movement in the universe."

"So if he does a jig in India, a wave crashes on the shore in Scotland?"

He chuckled at the derisive expression on her face. She evidently didn't think much of the Hindu god. "Perhaps."

"I would think you'd want to forget all about India."

He sent her an amused look. "Just because a bee stings you, Mary, is no reason to hate all living things."

She studied him intently. "How can you excuse them?"

"Not easily," he said. "Or even well. If I'm ever going to forget that time, then I must dispense with my hatred."

"Can you?"

"I've had to work at it, for more hours than I care to admit."

"I admire you for that. But I don't think I could."

He didn't respond. What could he say to her? His own sins outweighed what the Atavasi had done to him.

"It's a very cozy place," she said, looking around his room. She deliberately didn't look toward his bed, however. He'd taken a cot and adjusted it for his height, adding a little more width for comfort. What he really wanted was a creation of pillows and soft silk sheets, piled high with furs and surrounded by bed curtains of intricately woven wool. But his cot would have to do.

She stared at him with those soft brown eyes of hers,

blinking slowly at him as if she could not quite understand where she was or why. *This is a dream, Mary Gilly*, he wanted to say. *Anything might happen in this place, in the candlelight, with the sound of the blustery winds just outside the window. What do you require of me?* She might say anything, she with her fingers pressing lightly against her throat as if to measure the pounding of her own blood. Did her heart beat rapidly in her chest? Her breathing was quick, her gaze fluttering from his trunk, to the window, to the table.

She would have been wiser to hide what she felt. Hadn't he learned that it was safer to reveal nothing?

He was a man who'd been pushed beyond his limits. Rules that had once applied to him didn't seem to matter anymore. They might pertain to other men, but suddenly it didn't seem that great a sin to lure her to his room. He'd done worse than he did now, standing here immersed in lust.

"Lie with me," he said softly, reaching out with one hand and brushing his fingers over her cheek. "Let me love you tonight."

She simply blinked at him, as if not quite understanding the words he'd spoken. In case there was any doubt, he repeated them again. "Let me love you tonight."

"I'm not willing to go to any lengths to treat you, Hamish," she said.

An almost humorous rejoinder and one he saluted with his smile. "A pity," he said. "Think of the patients you'd have if you offered the promise of physical comfort. You might dole it out as a reward."

"If you take your medicine, I'll offer a bit of love?"

"It's not love I want from you." There, would she flinch from such directness?

She didn't. She pulled herself up straighter, clasping her hands in front of her. A moment later, she pressed the fingers of both hands inward as if to still her stomach or quiet her breath. She'd passed one trial he'd set for her. Would she pass another?

"I want to feel your skin," he said softly, moving one step closer to her. He bent his head, breathed in the scent of her. Pressing his lips against her temple, he fingered the brooch at her neck. "I want to taste you."

She drew in a deep, shuddering breath. If he were the man he'd once been, Hamish would have done one of two things at that moment. Either enfolded her in his arms to comfort her, or stepped back, apologizing for the crudeness of his words, if not the suggestion. But he did neither, being well past absolution. Instead, he held himself still, listening to the silence interrupted only by their soft breathing.

"Yes."

The word, uttered in a lifetime of waiting, made him breathe deeply for the first time since she'd entered the room. Yes. Mary's assent propelled him into anticipation and eagerness, twin emotions he'd not felt in years.

He lowered his head, placed his lips against her throat. A tender salute to warm flesh, beneath which her pulse beat wildly and strong.

From the moment he had seen her, she'd not done what he expected. And this instant was no different.

"Is this something you truly wish, Hamish?" she softly asked. The words lingered on that lush mouth of hers, her eyes intent on his face as if she sincerely waited for an answer.

He smiled, wondering if she knew that the question had been answered the moment she entered his room.

"Oh, it's something I truly wish," he said, tracing a path up her throat with the sweetest, kindest of kisses, only to hesitate at her chin. He wanted to kiss that mouth, but he wavered, enjoying the feeling of being perched on the knifepoint of longing. He wanted his desires assuaged, but not too easily or swiftly. He wanted to linger with her, measure his own endurance.

He watched her mouth as he grew nearer, anticipating the taste of her lips. But she drew back, reaching up to undo the heavy braid at the back of her head. In a matter of moments, her hair was unbound, pins clutched in her left hand.

Holding his hand out, he waited until she transferred the gold pins to his palm, noting their gleam in the candlelight.

"Another present from Gordon?"

"Yes," she said softly.

Suddenly, he despised her dead, unknown husband.

She bridged the distance between them once again by planting her hand flat on his chest. "I mustn't stay too long. Brendan will know." Her voice was soft, a melodious chastisement.

"Do you think I care?"

She looked startled.

He pulled her closer using his good hand, wishing in that moment that he had two arms that worked well enough to surround her.

She looked up at him, her eyes direct and unflinching. Slowly, as if she knew how much the gesture would inflame him, she licked her lips. Lust suddenly swamped him.

He bent his head and kissed her.

Her lips tasted warm, and then all thoughts disappeared beneath a mindless wonder. He coaxed her lips open with his thumb at the corner of her mouth, and heard her almost inarticulate whisper of protest. His tongue traced the seam of her lips, and then explored further.

His hand cupped her face, his thumb rubbing her cheek softly. He tilted her head, deepened the kiss, feeling starlight behind his lids.

His erection swelled, delight soon transformed to something deeper and more dangerous, a selfish need that ignored everything in its path. He wanted to feel her, smooth his palm over her naked skin, delve into crevices, and hollows. Now. Not five minutes from now or a quarter hour.

He walked her backward until she was pressed against the curving wall, and raised her skirt with one fist. The material was keeping him from touching her and it frustrated him. Images of Mary, unbound and unlaced, arching in wild abandon on his bed made him want to tear the clothes from her. Instead, he burrowed beneath the fabric, restraining himself to no more an animalistic impulse than lifting her shift. Finally, blessedly, absolutely, his fingers trailed over a warm, curving hip. Mary, unfettered at last.

He couldn't breathe. His heart was beating so loudly that the sound of it was like thunder in his ears. His fingers and toes tingled, but all other sensations centered on his erection, gloriously tumescent and demanding in a way he hadn't felt for years.

"Unfasten my shirt," he muttered, unwilling to surrender the prize he'd captured. His hand was on her waist and moving up, popping stitches in her shift. He wanted to feel her breasts overflowing his hand. He continued to kiss her, needing the touch of her mouth on him.

She'd abandoned the pose of sweetly virtuous widow

somewhere in the maelstrom of their kiss and was now surprising him with her skill. Her tongue explored his mouth and stole his breath.

His hips began pressing against her, mimicking the act of possession. The fingers of his good hand cupped one buttock, drawing her closer, grinding against her so that she couldn't help but feel him, hot, hard, and ready. His skin felt tight as if it were suddenly too small for his body. Even his palms felt on fire.

Her bare hands on his chest were all the indication that she'd succeeded in the task he'd given her. Her nails scratched against his skin in thoughtless abandon, making him smile. She'd traded her roles, going blessedly from healer to siren.

He was desperately grateful that she didn't use words as a barrier and hadn't flounced, insulted, from his room. He would worry about the consequences of his actions at a later time. For the moment, he wanted her. Needed her.

Her skirt unfastened, he disposed of her outer clothing soon enough. But the stays required her assistance. He drew back, and she bent her head, pulling at the lacing herself. Her hair fell in glorious disarray around her shoulders. When she lifted her head, finally, and stared at him, her face was flushed, her lips were swollen, and her eyes had a glittery brightness to them that came from passion, not remorse.

He stretched out his hand and with teasing fingers pulled out the untied laces one by one until her stays fell to the floor.

"Why do women wear so many garments?" he asked, surprised that he'd spoken the thought aloud.

"To protect their virtue?"

He fervently hoped that this was not going to be an intellectual discussion of whether she should continue upon this course. Thankfully, she said nothing further, only bent to lift up the hem of her shift to remove one garter and roll down one stocking. She used him as support as she pulled it from her toe. Repeating the procedure with the second stocking and garter, she finally stood in front of him clad only in her lace trimmed shift.

The man he'd once been had a well-defined sense of honor. He would have ignored the heat of his own desperation and questioned her further. *Is this what you want, Mary?* The ghost of that man whispered the words but he ignored them.

Afterward. He'd ask her afterward. At some other occasion, he'd ask her, perhaps at breakfast. Or tomorrow at dinner. But not now, not when she was nearly naked and standing, trembling, in front of him.

With as little shame as she'd demonstrated, but with perhaps more inward reluctance, he shed his own clothing. She was beautiful; he was ugly.

She said nothing as her eyes traced the colored lines from his waist to his feet and back again. However, it was with grateful amusement that he noted her gaze barely skimmed the grotesque shadings and drawings they'd made on his flesh. Instead, she seemed fixed and fascinated by his ever growing member.

She took two steps toward him until the tip of his erection touched the linen of her shift, an excruciatingly delicate touch that sent shivers through him. If she cupped him, he'd explode in her hand.

"They didn't touch you here," she said, reaching out and stroking him with one delicate finger. His erection bobbed in response, almost a subservient bow.

"No doubt I would have been made a eunuch in time."

"Is that why you escaped?" A small smile dusted her mouth.

He was almost amused by the question. "Not entirely."

When she would have touched him again, he gently grabbed her wrist. "Please," he said, a word he'd not uttered in all of his imprisonment. He'd screamed to heaven in his agony, but he'd never begged.

She took a step back and removed her shift, standing naked and glorious in front of him. Her nipples were puckered and erect, the hair at the juncture of her thighs thick and pillowy. Her legs were long, her feet delicately arched. His gaze traveled from her ankles up to her shoulders, taking the time to savor the image of Mary, naked. Her hand rested on her waist, fingers dancing over her navel as if she were impatient with his perusal of her.

Suddenly, and blessedly, the bed was there. Somehow, she was lying on it, and he was beside her. She widened her legs as if to welcome him, and he wanted to tell her that if she did that again he would take advantage of her wordless invitation regardless of her readiness for him. He'd invade her in one single thrust, uncaring about anything other than his own release.

However, he'd learned enough of barbarism in his recent past and wouldn't inflict it on another, especially a woman who was blessing him with her sweet acquiescence.

She felt like the softest down pillow, the warmest blanket, a meal to a starving man, a cup of water to a parched throat. She was all manner of comfort and more.

With the tips of his fingers, he traced a path from her lips and down her chin across her jaw to her throat. Grabbing her hand, he brought it to his lips, kissing her knuckles, and wanting to tell her that he'd never seen a more beautiful woman. Unreserved, she stared back at him, her lips solemn, her eyes wide. He wanted to know what she was thinking, yet now was not the time for speech.

He wished again that he had two good arms, so that he could rise up over her. Instead, he lay on his back and pulled her atop him, until she was straddling his thighs. Reaching out, she cradled his erection between her hands, and once again, he thought he might find his release with her fingers.

"You're so large," she said softly.

"Words to please any man." She smoothed her fingers down his length. "If you continue doing that with your hands I will be beyond words and anything else."

"Has it been very long for you?"

Once again, she startled him with her directness.

"Suffice it to say it's been a long time." He would not regale her with his exploits, or quote the exact number of weeks and months. No one else belonged here but the two of them. And yet he heard himself ask the question. "And you?"

"A long time," she replied, smiling softly.

Leaning forward, she placed her hands on either side of his shoulders, her breasts brushing against his chest. He reached up with his good hand, stroked her breast softly, trapping a pert nipple between his fingers.

She kissed him then, trailing a path with her luscious mouth around his face, as if she connected his scars in a sweet and sensuous blessing. Returning to his mouth, she kissed him deeply, making him wonder why he'd never remembered that a kiss could be so powerfully seductive.

Slowly, in a movement that was excruciatingly delicate and almost heavenly, she encircled his erection and slid her hands slowly up and then down, repeating the gentle massage until his hips began to arch up to meet her hands without his conscious volition. She was like a snake charmer in an Indian market, and he was a King Cobra responding to her summons.

He should tell her not to touch him, but he was too immersed in the feeling to protest it.

"You're very skilled," he said, his guttural voice not sounding like his own.

"Do you like what I'm doing?" she asked softly.

"I like it too much."

She was relentless in her ministrations. Finally, he grabbed both of her hands with one of his, jerking her close to him, swallowing her protest in a fierce kiss. He pulled her up until his erection was at the juncture of her legs. He wanted in, now, without finesse or words or teasing or pleading. He wanted her now in a way that was barely human.

He slid into her, experiencing a sensation so perfect that he closed his eyes in an effort to prolong it. Thank God she was ready for him. Thank God he was alive to feel what he did at this moment, the pure rapture of sex.

He was acutely aware of every sensation, the heat of her, the dampness that welcomed him, her sigh as he arched beneath her. He measured the moments in heartbeats, then breaths, prolonging the sensations as he surged deeper. He heard her moan and clenched his teeth, praying to think of anything but what he was feeling, something to make the moments last.

Suddenly, his body erupted, split apart, and scattered. The bliss he experienced in that moment was so perfect and pure that he wanted to cease breathing and thereby preserve the sensation for infinity. Then he was simply adrift in silence, several seconds strung together on a delicate filament and punctuated only by the sounds of his rasping breath and his slowing heartbeat.

His lids felt heavy, his eyelashes weighing a hundred times what they should. Nevertheless, he blinked open his eyes and surveyed Mary. She lay propped up on one arm, her fingers threading through his hair, a proud, benevolent, almost Madonna-like smile playing over her mouth.

It was obvious she'd not yet experienced any pleasure.

He ran his hand down her body, saw her eyes darken and her expression change as he cupped one buttock, and moved slightly within her.

"You can't think I was finished that soon, Mary?"

He reached down until he came to the joining of their bodies, feeling the soft hairs meshed together. Her soft folds were slightly swollen, and he gently inserted his thumb, finding the one spot that would bring her the most pleasure.

He brushed a soft kiss on her sweet pink mouth and smiled as she deepened it. "Perhaps I'll show you what I was taught in India."

She undulated against him, her nipples gently abrading his chest.

"Sit up," he said, breathing the instruction against her cheek. She shook her head again, stubborn Mary, but placated him with a kiss.

"Sit up," he repeated. "I want to kiss your breasts."

This time she did, placing both hands flat on her thighs.

Her breasts were beautiful, not so large that they were pendulous, but perfectly shaped. Their nipples were long and tightly erect. He smiled, wondering if she were sensitive there.

She leaned on her left forearm, placing her right hand

beneath her right breast and offering it to him as if it were an apple, he thought, licking the tip. Perhaps the sages had it wrong. There was no apple in the Garden of Eden, only the bounteous fruit of Eve's body.

His tongue encircled her nipple before his mouth gripped it firmly. He pulled on it gently, watching as she closed her eyes, the delicate lashes fanning against her cheek like the soft brush of butterfly wings. His thumb continued to gently stroke her most private core, back and forth and then in a circular motion.

If he had no other incentive to gain the use of his hand, this was it. Touching Mary, stroking her with his fingers and his thumbs, probing the delicate, private places.

Heal me. It was a command he almost uttered aloud, but he was not so lost in passion that his senses had gone begging.

Suddenly, she leaned back, crossing her hands over her chest and holding herself so still that he knew every sensation was trapped where his thumb now pressed. Her lids clenched shut and she took a deep breath, exhaling it on a long, drawn-out sigh.

Her hands clutched her upper arms tightly, making him wonder if she would bruise herself. But her utter stillness fascinated him even as he felt the moisture dampen his fingers. Her head arched backward, and she bit her lip. Other than that, she made no movement, but he felt her shudder around him, gripping him with tiny internal muscles.

He reached up and extended his hand around to her back, pulling her to him. He welcomed her with a kiss, an openmouthed exploration of tongues, teeth, and breath even as he arched his hips and surged within her. Long moments later he heard her soft exclamation and smiled against her lips. His second explosion was less forceful than the first but no less sweet.

It might have been possible to believe, in that instant, that this was why he had been saved, for the sheer joy of living, encapsulated in this experience. He hooked his arm around her shoulders and held her close, unwilling to let her move.

He kissed her again, murmuring something in the aftermath, words that he would be hard-pressed to recount five minutes later. A grunt or a murmur, some sound to express to Mary his gracious and unending thanks.

She nuzzled close to him, and he moved, pulling her next to him so that their faces lay only an inch apart. They shared each other's breaths, an act as intimate as their joining a few moments earlier.

"I should leave," she murmured softly.

"No." He was indescribably weary, the weeks of fitful nights having taken their toll. Now he wanted to rest, to sleep the sleep of the sated, and know that when he woke, she would be there, guardian of his rest.

"If you're here, I won't dream," he said.

Her hand rested on the side of his face, a gentle benediction, a cool touch. How could she be so cool when he was still so heated?

"Did I please you?" A question he'd not asked since his first time with a woman.

She nodded, but he wanted her assent in a word, something that he could hear and acknowledge.

"Did I please you?" he asked again.

"Yes." She kissed the corner of his mouth, whispering softly. "Oh, yes."

Just that, no embellishment or ardor, only the simple

assent he'd requested. He found himself wanting to ask her for more, but discovered that even that thought was abruptly buried beneath a sudden and overwhelming fatigue.

"Stay with me," he said. He would explain to the others, Hamish thought, as sleep drifted over him.

Chapter 10

Mary watched as Hamish fell asleep, lying beside him and feeling strangely exhilarated. She'd never felt this way before, as if he'd filled her with his seed and his energy at the same time.

What had she done? Something wicked, wanton, and altogether wonderful. Who was to forbid her, after all? Not her long dead parents or her recently deceased husband. Her friends were far from here. She was in a strange place with a stranger who had just brought her delight and joy.

She pulled away from him a little, and moved to the edge of the bed. The light from the brazier cast flickering shadows around the room, but they suddenly didn't look so fearful. She left the bed and blew out the candles, returning to Hamish's side a moment later.

He was so large that he took up most of the bed. He looked like some sort of creature of the darkness, someone from the shadowy world of nightmares. A man turned into a beast by the cruelties of other men.

Her hand hovered over his chest as she traced a path in the air of the monster they'd created on his skin. Not a monster, but a god. Shiva. Creator and destroyer. In a way, Hamish had been that, both creating and destroying something within her. Destroying the loneliness and creating a need.

It's not love I want from you.

Still, she'd stood there, waiting, afraid that he might withdraw his offer, scandalous as it was, leaving her with only regret. She hadn't given him time to reconsider. She'd never been loved so sweetly, but it wasn't love, was it? Something sensual, passionate, forbidden, perhaps.

She would wait a few minutes and then return to her room. She was under no illusions that Brendan would remain ignorant of what had happened there. She shouldn't have agreed to meet Hamish in his room, but then, she'd been hoping for something like this.

There, the truth finally.

She would have to meet Brendan's eyes in the morning, but not, thankfully, Hester's or Micah's, since they'd chosen to sleep in the Great Hall. As for Brendan, she owed nothing to him, not even an explanation. However, having to account for her actions was a hard habit to break. Mary found herself conjuring up a dozen different excuses to explain why she would have lingered in Hamish's room so long. In the end, it probably didn't matter.

Would anyone be able to see her secret delight? If so, would they think the worst of her? Or simply understand that the need for touch was a hunger as sharp and painful as that for food?

"Stay with me," Hamish murmured, and she answered by whispering an assent.

Straightening out his left arm, she noted that the muscle felt tight. She thought that was a good sign but couldn't be sure. There might be so much damage that he would never regain the use of that limb.

Closing her eyes, she felt her face warm at the realization that she, Mary Gilly, was lying here naked beside Hamish. Her body was still reverberating with tiny little shocks in memory of their loving. Her lips curved in a smile.

Sitting up, she drew the blanket from the bottom of the bed to cover them, and lay beside Hamish. Just a few moments, she told herself.

When Mary awoke, the sun was streaming in through the window, and the air promised a temperate day.

Hamish was standing, fully dressed, in front of her, a smile on his face as he surveyed her.

Sitting up on one elbow, she pushed the hair out of her face and smiled ruefully at him. "I meant to be gone before dawn came." A glance at the sky told her that she was hours too late.

"There's no harm done, Mary," he said. "There's no one here who'd think the less of you for being with me."

"Do you lay claim to the thoughts of others so easily, Hamish? Or do you simply command the inhabitants of Castle Gloom to think as you do?"

His smile deepened. "Castle Gloom? Is that what you call it? I've named it Aonaranach."

"The Gaelic for lonely? It is that." She sat up on the edge of the bed, gathering the sheet around her.

"Do you speak it?" he asked, looking surprised.

"My parents did when they wanted to keep things from me. They never realized that their secrecy was a great inducement to learning the language." She stood, wrapping the sheet around her and tucking the ends beneath her arm.

His smile disappeared, and he looked at her intently. If he kissed her, she might tell him all the secrets in her life. If he whispered in her ear, she would probably acquiesce to any suggestion he might make. If he tossed her back on the bed, she doubted she'd protest all that much.

"I should dress," she said, when the silence between them had stretched to an uncomfortable length. "I need to get our breakfast."

"Brendan's already been here," he said, gesturing to a tray on the table. "He brought a breakfast tray."

She glanced at it, chagrined to discover that there were two cups and plates arranged there. A surge of warmth flooded her cheeks, but the embarrassment was not as deep as it should have been. Overlaying it was the memory of the night before, recollections that were powerful enough to banish any thought of propriety.

"The exact reason I should have left last night," she said. "I suppose Micah and Hester know where I slept last night as well?"

"I'm not entirely certain that Brendan will tell them."

"But you're not entirely certain he'll remain mute, either," she said.

"My brother is not the most reticent of men," he admitted.

"Are you certain you're brothers?" she asked. There was a faint resemblance between them, but Brendan had a slighter build and wasn't as tall as Hamish. The younger man's eyes were a hazel hue, while Hamish's were deeply brown. But it was in their natures that they were so dissimilar. Life seemed to have marked Hamish, while Brendan seemed so much younger in comparison.

"I remember asking my mother that question when I was small," he said, smiling. "She was very put out, as I recall."

She matched his smile, and once again silence stretched between them.

"I should dress," she said again. He nodded, but didn't move. She gathered up the clothing he'd folded into neat stacks and placed on the chair. The idea of him handling her intimate garments brought another rush of warmth to her face.

"Are you going to watch me?"

"May I?" His smile was teasing. "It seems a good way to start my morning."

"No," she said, smiling back at him.

He turned and faced in the direction of the open window, and she realized it was as much privacy as she was going to get.

She dropped the sheet and donned her shift. Her body felt sensitized, and the sheer linen slid over her skin like a lover's breath.

"Stay with me, Mary."

She stared at him, but he didn't turn.

"Stay with me," he said again. "Not for forever, but for a little while."

Sitting on the edge of the bed, she rolled one stocking up her leg and fastened her garter around it before repeating the action on the other leg. Standing, she fastened her stays, taking more time with the laces than the task required.

He glanced over his shoulder at her. She bent and retrieved her skirt, clutching the fabric in front of her.

"I cannot," she finally said when words returned to her once more. "There are those in Inverness who need my assistance."

He turned and faced toward the sea again, and she donned her skirt and then her bodice. Finally, she bent to find her shoes. On discovering them neatly arranged against the wall, she sat on the edge of the bed and began to put them on.

"I need you as well."

Her thumbs stilled, caught between her stockings and the heels of her shoe as she stared at his back. She'd never heard a man say those words before, not even her husband.

Hamish's pose was rigid, his back straight. She could imagine him standing on the deck of his ship staring at the horizon. He was a man with great strength of purpose, even now.

"Stay with me a few weeks, Mary."

For an instant, she allowed herself to pretend that it might be possible. She'd come to know him, to learn about the man who fascinated her. She knew his body; would his mind prove to be as captivating?

A foolish thought, and an even more foolish woman to be thinking it.

"I cannot even do that," she said with a reluctance that was all too genuine. "Charles would worry about me, and I have friends who would miss me."

"Send word to them. Tell them that you'll return in a matter of weeks. Stay with me."

Stay with me. It shouldn't have been such a temptation, that simple sentence. Three words, that was all, and she yearned to tell him yes. No one would know that she'd taken an interlude in her life, that she'd simply disappeared from all her responsibilities and roles and become someone new and different for a short time.

Her absence could, after all, be easily explained. She

was treating a patient out of town, someone important enough to justify her travel and time. No one would think any worse of her. Even in Inverness, she'd often spent the night at a patient's bedside if his condition warranted it. There was plenty of money in the household strongbox to take care of expenses for a while. Charles was no stranger to managing the accounts. He'd done the task before she and Gordon were wed.

There were only two people who might suspect the truth. Charles because he was too intrusive in her affairs, and Elspeth because she was a romantic at heart.

"I can't," she repeated, but this time the refusal was not as forceful as before. Almost as if she begged him silently to convince her otherwise.

He turned and went to his trunk, withdrew a small writing chest, and handed it to her. She took it with both hands and laid it on the bed beside her. Inside was a stack of thick vellum and a place for quills, a pot of ink, and stick of sealing wax.

"Write them, Mary. Tell them you'll return in a matter of weeks. Tell them that your patient requires your attention and your care."

"Do you?"

Instead of answering, he only reiterated that simple sentence. "Stay with me."

Dear heavens, she was tempted to. More than was wise.

"What do you have waiting for you in Inverness?"

"Mr. Marshall," she said, remembering the appointment that was so important to her. At least it had been before Hamish MacRae. "He's agreed to meet with me."

"Is he more of an inducement to tempt you from here than I am to entice you to stay?"

What a very difficult question to answer. "He can only add to my reputation, while I'm afraid you'll do nothing but take from it."

He nodded. "You're right, of course."

"He's an elderly man. He may never return to Inverness."

"I can only take your word for that."

"Meeting with him is a great honor."

"I'm certain that it is."

He walked to the window and faced outward again.

"If I remain," she said, the words startling her, "do you promise to do whatever I choose as a treatment?"

"Have I not already?"

He turned. His half smile was back in place as he studied her. His gaze was intent, as if he were trying to read her soul.

"What kind of treatments do you have in mind, Mary?"

"I want you to exercise your arm," she said. "And get some sun."

She shouldn't stay, of course. Patients called on her not only because of her reputation for healing successes but because she was generally well thought of throughout Inverness. Mothers considered her a suitable chaperone for younger girls, while the poor she treated considered her a kind and generous benefactor. Above all she was considered a proper matron.

There was never an untoward word spoken about her by the older women of Inverness. Even in her grief for Gordon, she'd done nothing but gather accolades from those whose sole duty seemed to be to approve or disapprove of her behavior. Sometimes Mary felt as if she were practicing for a role beside them. One day, she, too, might walk along the streets of Inverness with an eye on anyone who might be acting improperly. She would frown on laughter and signs of flirting and only nod her head in approval at a woman's demure, downcast looks.

She was being groomed for propriety when she didn't feel the least bit proper.

What would the citizens of Inverness do if they knew that her demure appearance hid a rebellious soul? Her actions of the night before were shocking, but they were only a shadow of her true self. She wanted something she'd never had. Adventure, not sameness. Delight and joy, perhaps. And passion, too. She wanted to be shocked and startled, delighted and dazed by life. Not saddened and depressed by the suffering she saw.

"Write them, Mary," he said. A moment later, he was at the door, his hand on the edge. He looked as if he would like to say something else, but he was gone in the next instant, leaving her alone with her conscience.

Staring at the writing desk, she wished he hadn't left. If he'd remained in the room, she would have found it easier to write her friends. Yet the decision must be hers alone, and he'd been wise to leave it to her.

How foolish she was. How unwise to jeopardize her standing in the community, to sully her good name. For what? A few days of pleasure. Mindless, delicious pleasure that made her limbs feel as if they were swimming in warmth. Pleasure that dulled her mind, and banished sadness or fear.

Hamish MacRae was a drug, as dangerous as the morphine she occasionally dispensed. Who would have ever thought that the Widow Gilly would be overcome with lust? Yet she didn't feel the least bit of shame or consternation, only a fevered anticipation of lying with him again.

Stay with me.

She would be a fool to do so, to risk even a chance that news of her behavior would reach Inverness. Still, she knew she was going to stay.

No one need know. Hamish certainly would not divulge the information, and Brendan would not be in Inverness. If she stayed a week or two, no one could accuse her of hedonism or sport.

It's not love I want from you. From the beginning, he'd been direct. Nor did she know him well enough to give her heart. Her body, however, might be loaned to him for this time, for the sole purpose of pleasure. Just as she would have the use of his.

She stared down at her hands, remembering the touch of his skin. Her palms tingled as if she could feel him now.

Pulling out a piece of vellum from the writing desk, she began to write, wondering if God would look askance at a prayer for guidance in this situation. However, she needed the proper words to write to Charles, something that would allay his suspicions while reassuring him as to her safety and well-being. He took too much upon himself, and it was beginning to grate on her nerves. Because Gordon had felt a fondness for him, however, she'd hidden her irritation all these many months.

Charles,

Circumstances are keeping me longer than I had originally planned. Rest assured that I am well. I will be remaining with my patient to ensure his well-being. If you need any assistance in the meantime, please contact my solicitor.

Mary

To Elspeth, she was a little more forthcoming.

My dear Elspeth,

I am staying at the most interesting place, a lonely looking castle perched at the edge of the loch and overlooking a desolate countryside. At night, I can almost envision shadows in the courtyard and think of them as the ghosts of the people who once lived here.

She hesitated, biting at the end of the quill, wondering how she could describe Hamish while keeping his privacy.

My patient is an unusual man who has selected to live here alone, shunning everyone. I have found myself curiously attuned to him, however. I will stay here, until I am certain he is well.

Her conscience pricked at her, but not enough to set down the quill or rework the letter.

Please be advised that I am well and shall return to Inverness as soon as possible and call upon you then.

Elspeth's family had agreed to host Mr. Marshall on his most recent trip to Inverness, and she had an inkling that Elspeth's father had been instrumental in encouraging the minister to meet with her. She should return to Inverness and keep her appointment if for no other reason than politeness.

Standing, Mary went to the window, wondering where

Hamish had gone. As if her wishes sought him out, she saw him standing on the rocky shore outside the curtain wall, only an arm's length from the loch. He wore no jacket, and the wind came from the north, ruffling his shirt, and hair. He stood there motionless, as if he were fighting the forces of nature, a solitary man. A lonely one.

Did he wait for her to rebuff him? She should do so kindly, with well-chosen words that would let him know that she wanted, very much, to accept his invitation, but that she was more concerned with her decency and respectability.

She smiled at herself, thinking that it was a bit late for that.

Returning to the bed, she finished the letter.

I realize that this decision will make it impossible to meet with Mr. Marshall. Please convey my most sincere apologies to him, but I cannot leave.

Your friend,
Mary

She sealed the letters and sat back on the bed, staring at them. How innocuous they looked. No one seeing them would know that they represented such a shocking decision. From this moment forward, she'd hold a secret inside, an interlude she'd never discuss with another soul. Only Hamish would ever know that she wasn't the proper widow, that she'd turned her back on the life and the person she'd always been. Only she would hold these memories inside, warmth against a cold future.

Remaining at Castle Gloom would be a bit of hedonism

in a well ordered and pleasant life. Or something else that she didn't quite want to admit, a curiosity about forbidden behavior, or simply a desire to plumb the depths of her own wildness.

One day, perhaps, the rebellious nature that she so adequately hid would be tamped down at last, and she'd truly become one of the proper matrons of Inverness. If, from time to time, she thought of her wayward nature, it would be with a faint longing, like the distant pealing of a faraway bell.

Not now, however. Not yet.

Chapter 11

❦

"Are you entirely certain this is wise?" Brendan asked, glancing at the letters in his hands.

Hamish didn't answer him, choosing instead to remain silent. There were some questions that should never be asked, a lesson that Brendan had yet to learn. There were times when he thought his brother would be forever young. He possessed the careless insouciance of an adolescent. The only place he didn't act with joyful abandon was on the bridge of his ship. From time to time, Hamish had the impression that being a ship's captain was a role Brendan donned like a large and uncomfortable cloak, almost too heavy for his younger brother to wear.

"I want you to take Micah and Hester with you."

"You'll need people to help you," Brendan said in protest.

"I require no help. I lived here well enough for three weeks before you arrived. We'll do so well enough after you leave."

"So you'll keep Mary prisoner?"

Hamish smiled at that thought. Mary Gilly would be no man's prisoner. Hadn't Brendan learned her well enough to know that?

"Leave two horses for us, I will see her safely to Inverness when the time comes."

"When will that be, Hamish?"

"When it's time," he said, more forcefully than he'd intended.

Brendan turned over the two letters in his hands once again, as if committing their addresses to memory.

"I know this one place; it's the goldsmith's shop. But the other?"

"A friend of Mary's. Surely you don't begrudge her communicating with a friend?"

"I only begrudge her making a mistake. Or your doing the same."

"Have you become the arbiter of our morals, then, Brendan? I don't need fatherly advice from you. Go back to Gilmuir and forget about us."

"You would never have done such a thing before India, Hamish."

Nothing could restore the past, or the man he'd been.

"What if Mary's friends question me? What am I supposed to say to them?"

"Silence would be the best answer, Brendan."

"The world is not your hermitage, Hamish." Brendan lifted his hand and gestured around the room as if to encompass the whole of the castle. "It's not an empty place like this deserted fortress. It's filled with people and opinions, reputations and words like honor and dignity."

"If you don't tell anyone, Brendan, then no one will

know what goes on here. So I place the ruination of Mary's reputation in your hands."

"And your honor, Hamish?"

Brendan looked so intent that he almost answered his brother. But Hamish knew that he could never explain how he truly felt, or translate what he'd gone through into words. Words sometimes weren't enough; a man had to live through an experience in order to understand.

Honor? Honor was a code of ethics, a way a man behaved in society. Dignity? Again, a way of behavior. A man did not take tea naked in the parlor, or appear drunk in the company of ladies. But to a prisoner, what did either word mean? He'd lost his honor the first time he'd screamed in agony, and his dignity had been stripped from him as he was led nearly naked from village to village.

He'd faced himself in those months in India, seen himself as he truly was, not as he wished to be. He'd tested each of the words he'd been reared to believe in, coming away with the knowledge that he'd strayed far from his upbringing. He'd faced, at the last, the true degradation of his spirit. Not from the acts of others, but from his own behavior.

That was something else he wouldn't tell Brendan.

Mary offered him a respite from himself, and he would greedily and gratefully accept the interlude. Perhaps she was unwise to agree to stay with him for however long he could convince her. However, he thanked Providence, or heaven, or whatever mankind wished to call it that had convinced her to do so. He'd been given a reprieve from his own shame and horror in the form of a gently smiling, forthright lover. He was not going to be so noble as to send her away.

Brendan's look darkened in the silence, as if he bit back

a hundred words. It was the first time in their lives that he could ever remember Brendan being so restrained. His brother turned and would have walked from the room, but hesitated on the threshold. He glanced over his shoulder at Hamish.

"India really did change you, didn't it? You told me that it had, but I refused to believe it. I told myself all this time that you were so different only because you were injured or simply lonely for home. I never realized that you weren't the same man I'd always known."

"You should have believed me," Hamish said gently. "I wouldn't lie to you."

"Then tell me the truth, Hamish. By keeping Mary here, won't you hurt her?"

"I don't know," Hamish said. "I only know I must."

"Is he gone?" Mary asked, walking into Hamish's tower room an hour later. She carried his lunch tray and gratefully set it down on the table beside the door. Climbing the stairs had not become easier with familiarity.

"He's crossing the bridge now," Hamish said, glancing over at her. "Hester and Micah are leaving also."

"I know," she said. "I've said my farewells."

"You're not going to try to convince me to let them stay, are you?"

"Should I?" Her friends would know that she was here with him, but there would be no one to tell that they were alone. She doubted if Brendan would divulge that information. Therefore, there would be no one to tell tales of her behavior, or look at her disapprovingly. Even so, Hester had made no secret of her disappointment, and Micah had not once looked in her direction. Mary had only known them a few days, and their opinions of her shouldn't matter, but oddly enough she found that they did.

Brendan had only looked at her across the courtyard and turned and walked in the other direction. Repudiation in a glance. It was practice for her, if anyone in Inverness ever learned of what she was doing.

She studied Hamish, framed as he was in the window, bared to the light. She'd known him even less time than Hester and Micah, and here she was, altering the very framework of her life to stay with him.

He turned his head and returned her stare, as if he knew every doubting thought that tumbled into her mind.

"They're barely over the bridge. If you hurry, you can catch up with them."

Her conscience was remarkably silent. Her heart didn't even speak. Her mind had no logic at all to offer.

"I know that I should," she said softly. "I can occupy myself very well in Inverness. There are probably patients to see even now."

"No doubt," he said dryly.

He turned and watched the empty wagon roll over the bridge.

"They left all their provisions here," Mary said. "We won't starve."

"When you're tired of jerky and smoked fish," he offered, not turning his head, "I can hunt."

"Are you a good hunter?"

"All the MacRaes are," he said offhandedly. His hands clutched the edge of the window frame tightly, belying his casual speech.

She should have been shy with him. Instead, it felt as if he were the dearest of companions, someone she'd known for most of her life.

She came and stood beside him, placing her left hand on his right arm, slowly caressing him from forearm to shoulder, a long smooth stroke. He glanced at her once, his smile summoning hers.

"Brendan looked very angry when he left," she said. "He doesn't approve of my staying with you, does he?"

He shook his head.

"We're both doomed to perdition, then."

"Do you care what the world says about you, Mary?"

"I should say that I don't, shouldn't I? The mark of a truly independent person. Like you. But I'm afraid that I do. Does that make me foolish in your eyes?"

He turned toward her. Her hand fell, and she clasped it with the other, standing in front of him, the object of his intense regard.

"Do you care about my opinion of you, Mary?"

"Yes," she said softly. "I find that I do."

His smile slipped. "You shouldn't, you know." He threaded his fingers through the hair at her temple. "I'm no one to judge another. I have sins beyond sins on my soul."

"Do you?" She placed her hand on his cheek, feeling the scars beneath her fingers, wondering why he should be handsome to her when he was so marked. There was something about him that was greater than all his scarred parts. "Then you and I have something in common. I can claim a multitude of sins, not the least of which is remaining here with you."

His smile was back in place, and this time, it was replicated in his eyes.

"You're the Angel of Inverness. What great sins can you have?"

"I question entirely too much," she said, dropping her hand to place it on his chest. His heart beat so steadily and loudly that it was oddly reassuring. "I used to wonder, if God did not wish me to question, why he'd given me a mind with which to do so."

"An appropriate curiosity. What did people say?"

"I learned not to mention my thoughts," she said, her fingers playing on the buttons of his shirt. They looked to be carved from bone, or perhaps ivory.

"I give you free rein to do so, at any time you wish."

She glanced up to find that his smile had disappeared again, and in its place a solemn look. One he might wear when giving his promise or granting a wish.

Too many times, she'd wanted to discuss what was on her mind and had no one with which to do so. At first, Gordon had been amused at her thoughts, but then she'd realized that for all his fondness of her, he would forever treat her like a gamboling kitten or a frolicking puppy. Nor could she speak of such things with Elspeth; the young woman looked to her as an example, for all that they were friends. How could she teach Elspeth to question all that society had taught her to believe? Why deliberately foment rebellion when there was no need?

She tested him, perhaps, by asking a question. "Why do men treat women as if they should be cosseted, while outside of the parlor, life itself does not treat them so gently? I've seen grown men pale at the sight of their wives giving birth."

"I don't know," he admitted, "but your thought has merit."

He trailed a path along her jaw, gently traced her bottom lip.

"Why are women considered more sinners than sinned against? Why do poor women and children seem to suffer more than men in a similar plight?"

"Because it's easier to blame the defenseless," Hamish said. "And those who have no one to speak for them."

She looked at him, startled at his quick answer.

"Will you talk to me of the places you've seen?" she asked. "Even if they're not considered proper?"

"When have we been entirely proper with each other?" he asked, amusement obvious in his sudden smile.

"Will you teach me shatranj?"

"So that you can win? I doubt you will."

There, that's what she wanted, his honesty.

"Will you tell me what happened in India?"

His face suddenly froze. Just as quickly as a thought, his smiling expression was gone, to be replaced by absolutely no expression at all. Yet she had the impression that she'd surprised him with her question.

"Have I not?"

She shook her head. "I suspect that more occurred than you've told anyone."

"Why would you think that?"

He half turned toward the window again, distancing himself from her. She took a step closer, wrapped her arms around his waist, and waited. Finally, he glanced down at her again.

"Because of the look in your eyes sometimes, Hamish," she said softly. "They seem to be haunted, as if you're keeping a secret that's poisoning you."

"Do I know your secrets, Mary?"

"No," she admitted, "you don't."

"Then it's hardly fair of you to ask for mine without divulging some of your own, don't you think?"

"Will we be that intimate?" She tilted back her head to study him. "I thought we were to be lovers, not friends."

He looked disconcerted at her bluntness. "Can't we be both?"

"It might be wiser to remain the former, and not strive for the latter."

"Why? Don't you wish to be my friend?"

No. She wanted to be able to leave him behind when the time came and not feel a loss.

She raised her hands and put them on his shoulders. Instead of answering him, she asked another question of her own. "Are you going kiss me?"

"Is that a request?"

"If we're to be lovers," she said softly, "perhaps we should begin immediately."

She linked her hands behind his neck, thinking that a man who had undergone such grievous injuries should not look so alluring. Nor should a healer be having such lascivious thoughts about her patient.

His friend? No, she wouldn't be his friend. That was only one short step removed from other, deeper emotions. Hamish MacRae would not give his heart easily, if at all, and she should guard hers with care.

Reaching out, she began to unfasten his shirt. Pulling it from his waistband, she placed her hands beneath the fabric, flat on his chest.

"I should treat your wounds," she said.

"You are." His smile was infinitely charming, with a touch of wickedness to it.

She shook her head at him, amused.

"I want you to undo your hair like you did last night, but I don't want you to take your hands from me. How can I accomplish both?"

She felt a surge of heat travel through her at his words.

How could he do such a thing to her with only a softly voiced sentence?

Withdrawing her hands, she hurriedly fumbled with her braid.

"You are so indescribably lovely," he said. "And I'm so ugly beside you."

She clutched at her hair with both hands, wishing that she didn't hear more in his words. She didn't want to be so attached to him that her heart ached at the hint of his regret. These days were for sensuality only, not for emotion.

"I am not," she said. "I am simply ordinary."

His smile broadened to become a grin, a boyish expression she'd not seen before. "Then if you're simply ordinary, what must I be in comparison?"

"Hamish. You are simply Hamish. Isn't that enough?"

There was that look again. Something lingered in his eyes, some horror he'd not yet articulated. So disturbing was the thought that she wanted to reach out her arms and enfold him in her embrace. She couldn't shield him from what he'd already endured, but she could help him forget.

"Hamish," she said gently, placing both her hands on his exposed chest. "Whatever they did to you is over. You needn't remember it again. Not ever." Just as quickly as it was there, the look was gone.

He reached out one hand and finished undoing her braid, spearing his fingers through her hair until it fell in coils around her shoulders.

The two of them were framed in the window, but she didn't seek the shadows. Instead, this sunlit moment seemed perfect to begin their forbidden relationship.

"Kiss me, Hamish." It was both a declaration and an order.

But he said nothing, nor did he react. His stillness was almost a dare. She'd been the darling of her older parents, having been their only surviving child. Being so well loved had given her a foundation of confidence, something she needed now as she extended her hands upward to cup either side of his face. Slowly, she pulled his head down and stood on tiptoe to press her lips against his.

As he'd taught her last night, she allowed her tongue to dart out and trace the seam of his lips, the fullness of his lower lip.

His arm went around her, holding her close. But even that touch was not enough. Her skin warmed in remembered passion, and dampness pooled in secret folds as her body readied itself for him. How odd that she should anticipate and welcome him with no more than a kiss.

The dress was one she'd worn the day before. Over it, she'd donned her treatment apron. Without being asked, she removed it, and then slowly began to unfasten the laces of her bodice.

He watched her, his eyes downcast, as if hiding his response from her. His silence made her shy, made her question why she was there and why she'd agreed to stay. It felt as if he tested her by standing there doing nothing but regarding her.

"You'll not urge me, will you?" she asked, understanding suddenly.

He lifted his eyes, and the strength of his gaze was startling. How could he convey so much in a simple look? "Does it need to be seduction, Mary? I've found that shared passion is more powerful."

Not seduction, perhaps, but it would most certainly be surrender.

She let her skirt fall to the floor. Removing the bodice and stays, she stood before him as she had the night before, clad only in her shift and stockings. Last night, there had been concealing shadows, and flickering candles that shielded and enhanced. Now there was the glare of the sun streaming in through the window. No artifice was allowed, no maidenly shyness, no reserve.

Slowly, she gripped the hem of her shift and pulled it over her head until she was clad only in her stockings and garters. She bent and untied her shoes, stepping out of them and standing before him almost naked.

His hand reached out and cupped her breast, his thumb playing with the tip of it. A small smile hovered over his lips as he watched it become tightly erect.

She closed her eyes, captured in the moment, feeling abandoned and wicked and adrift in a dozen emotions she couldn't describe.

"And you dared to call yourself ordinary," he murmured. "Nothing about you is ordinary, Mary. Not your smile or your body." His hand left her breast to spear through her hair.

He pulled her close. His kiss was openly carnal, and demanding. She stood on tiptoe again and wrapped her hands and arms around his neck. Impatient, she pulled the material of his shirt open until her breasts pressed against the wiry hair on his chest.

He turned her until his back was to the window, shielding her from the sun's glare.

Her eyes blinked open. There, beyond the land bridge even now being partially submerged by the incoming tide, was Brendan. Beside him stood Micah and Hester, all of them looking toward Castle Gloom, to where she and Hamish stood framed in the window.

"Did you want them to see us like this?" The choked whisper didn't sound like her voice.

He glanced over his shoulder. "No, but I'm not sorry for it. Are you?"

"No," she said, an indication of her wantonness, that she could so easily forget herself. He'd shielded her from their gaze, but they should have stepped away from the window. Instead, he bent to kiss her again, and she allowed it, or welcomed it, as well as the passion that swept through her at his touch.

She shivered as his hand swept down her body, his talented fingers searching out the heat of her.

"You're ready for me," he said, sounding too smug and pleased with himself.

"Yes," she admitted, conciliation in a single word. All he had to do was smile at her, and her body warmed. Or kiss her, and she was eager for him.

He led her to the bed, but this time she would not easily acquiesce to his plans for her.

Slowly, she began to undress him, uncovering every inch of his skin with great deliberation. When his shirt was removed, she bent and kissed his chest. His boots were next, and she was grateful they slipped easily from his feet.

Her hands reached down to his trousers and unbuttoned three of the buttons, feeling the mound of hard male flesh that strained against the material. It burst free and she cradled his erection between her hands. It was as hot as she felt inside. Heat seeking heat.

He'd not looked quite so large last night.

A few tiny shocks traveled through her at the sight of this magnificent erection, and the memory of last night.

Slowly, she trailed a path from the head to the base. A noise emerged from Hamish that was half groan, half laugh, and warned her that he might well stop this game before it began.

She was not, evidently, the only one ready at a moment's notice.

The rest of his clothing was soon stripped from him, and she pushed him until he sat. Standing over him, she felt both powerful and weak at the same time.

Lifting one foot, she planted it on the side of the bed, uncaring that the pose revealed the dampness on her inner thighs. She removed her garter and rolled down her stocking, being deliberately slow in the task. She did the same with the other leg, tossing the second stocking after the first.

Standing in front of him, one hand flat against her abdomen, the other fisted between her breasts, she studied him as he had her. "Are you certain you didn't mean for them to see me?"

He looked surprised, a point in his favor. Yet she would not have left this room even if he had admitted to the act. That confession made secretly and silently was an indication of how fascinated she was with him and her own response to him.

"No," he said softly. "I wouldn't have done that to you. Your body is mine alone to see."

There, a type of arrogance or selfishness she was coming to associate with him. Perhaps at its root was a supreme form of assurance, or maybe he simply knew his limits because they'd been breached time and time again. He was a complex man to understand, but she wanted to try, an even more dangerous impulse than friendship.

She moved closer to him until her knee touched his thigh. He reached out his hand, placing it on her inner thigh, moving upward until his thumb brushed the intimate curls.

"You're very responsive," he said, addressing the comment to her abdomen. He bent forward to brush a kiss across her knuckles where her hand still rested on her stomach. Her fingers curled into a fist, and then rubbed against his cheek. "Have you always been so?"

"Yes," she admitted. Passion was nothing new to her, but it was different with him.

His finger slipped past her intimate folds and inserted itself into her. She closed her eyes at the gentle stroking rhythm he began. She wanted him inside her, but she said nothing, only stood in front of him enduring the delicious torture for as long as he wanted to inflict it.

"Do you always make those little sounds at the back of your throat when you find your pleasure?"

She smiled, feeling heat travel through her. Her hand between her breasts spread out, her palm covered one nipple simply because it needed to be touched.

"No," she said smiling. "I've been known to scream, but only when I'm feeling abandoned."

He pressed the palm of his hand hard against her in a sudden upward movement that had her almost sinking to her knees. The pleasure was so intense that for a long moment she couldn't hear or feel anything else. She closed her eyes to savor it more intently.

"I've promised to take you back to Inverness when you're ready, Mary."

"Have you?" she said, feeling as if her blood was heavy and her heart was beating in a languid rhythm.

"However long or short a time that may be."

At the moment, she couldn't imagine ever leaving him. Not as long as his breath was against her stomach and his tongue licked out and traced a path from her navel to her hipbone. Not when his fingers were doing decadent and delicious things to her.

She needed this. She wanted it. She wanted him.

He inserted another finger into her, and she bit her lip to keep from crying out. She was being drugged with pleasure, and it was thrumming through her limbs, touching the tips of her toes and her fingers.

"I want be kissed," she demanded softly.

"You'll have to wait," he said.

"I don't want to wait," she said.

"Do you always get what you want, Mary?" he asked.

She opened her eyes to find his look intent, his eyes heated. There was a flush on his cheekbones, and his smile had disappeared.

"Yes," she admitted. "But I'm very good, and I should be rewarded for my patience."

He slowly inserted three fingers into her. But his fingers were no match for his erection, and she was suddenly nearly desperate for it.

She stepped back. Gently, she pushed him until he lay back on the cot. He swung his legs over, reaching up with one hand to draw her down atop him.

Slowly, she went, teasing them both. With her knees on either side of him, she kissed him. Moments later, her mouth left his, as she trailed tiny kisses along his jaw, delicately saluting one scar and then another. She kissed her way to his chin and then down his neck, where her teeth made a mark of their own at the base of his throat.

"Now," she said, her breath hot against his skin.

In a swift gesture, she was lowering herself on him, so crazed that she was certain if she didn't have him now, her life would end.

He entered her, stretching and filling her, so hard and large that she felt deliciously impaled. Her hand reached down to touch the base of his erection, marveling at his size.

His fingers touched her intimately, and she pressed them against her as she rose up slightly and then lowered herself again, feeling the friction with each subtle movement. She wanted it to last, but was afraid it would not. All she could do was close her eyes and concentrate on the feeling of him buried deeply inside her.

She heard a sound, an oath, a strangled laugh, an imploration, she wasn't sure which, but she ignored him, so enthralled with what she was feeling that pleasure suddenly became a singular and selfish thing.

Abruptly, his knees rose up, and he pulled her down even more firmly atop him. That was all she needed, just that little nudge of movement to send her catapulting somewhere, where pieces of her body splintered in the air. Her breath, harnessed by delight in these last moments, was finally released on a deep sigh. She thought she screamed, or whimpered, or cried, and then he was moving beneath her, pressing up and then surging down again and again and again.

She could feel the heat of his eruption inside her. Even that seemed to prolong the pleasure, deepen the sensation of losing herself.

Long moments later, she sank down atop him, her cheek pressed against his sweaty chest, her arms lying weakly on either side of him. His heartbeat was like a furious drum. Inside, her body echoed that rhythm, clenching repeatedly around him like a faint echo.

Stay with me. For how long? Would she survive it?

Brendan turned away from his view of the castle, deliberately not looking at either Micah or Hester where they sat on the wagon seat. The board of the empty wagon bed vibrated as it moved, sounding like thunder as the wheels struck the ruts on the road.

Part of him was glad that Hamish had an interest in something, even if it was only pleasure. The other part was feeling guilty. If he hadn't brought Mary there, she wouldn't be staying now. Nor would the three of them have been summarily banished from Castle Gloom because Hamish wanted to be alone with her.

The least he could do was protect her reputation. Brendan didn't intend to tell anyone what he'd seen, and before they reached Inverness, he'd convey the need for silence and discretion to both Micah and Hester.

Still, the vision of the two of them framed in the window remained in his mind. Brendan knew exactly what Hamish felt at that moment. His body had stirred in response, reminding him that he had been too long without a little feminine comfort of his own.

He pressed his hand against his chest where the letters rested. He'd first go to the goldsmith's shop, before seeing Mary's friend.

After that? He'd go back to Gilmuir, and rejoin his ship. He didn't anticipate seeing Alisdair, however. His oldest brother had a way of seeing through any tale.

It had been hard enough to get away from Gilmuir

without Alisdair following him. The only thing that had stopped him from doing just that had been Brendan's honesty.

"He didn't come to Gilmuir because of you. He doesn't want to see anyone, Alisdair."

His older brother had frowned at him, and a moment later he'd nodded.

"You'll let me know how he is?"

Brendan had agreed.

What would he tell Alisdair? That he wouldn't recognize Hamish? He'd changed, not simply in appearance, but in temperament. His easygoing brother had been transformed to a man who was curt and detached.

Sometimes, Brendan got the feeling that he hadn't heard the whole story, only bits and pieces that Hamish reluctantly divulged. He suspected that something terrible had happened to Hamish in India. But until Hamish wanted to tell him, there was nothing he could do.

Brendan had understood, ever since he was a boy, that there were certain things he couldn't change. He'd never be as tall as Alisdair or Hamish, or as handsome as James. He probably was the most affable of the MacRae brothers, but not the one that people remembered. He had little ambition other than to be a good man and a credit to his family. That, he reasoned, was a fair enough goal for any man.

The farther he got from Castle Gloom, the more relaxed he felt, a thought that propelled him to turn back and stare at the castle, now no more than a shadow on the landscape.

"It's a dour place," Hester said from her seat on the wagon.

He nodded.

"We can make good time to Inverness, without a full wagon," Micah said.

"That we will," Brendan agreed.

He glanced back at the castle once more, wondering if he were a fool to leave Mary behind. It was her choice, and one she'd made freely. He couldn't help but think, however, that it was a mistake.

Chapter 12

~~~◯~~~

"**A**re you certain I'm not hurting you?" Mary asked, dabbing at the deepest lines on Hamish's back. Even though there were ingredients in the salve that might prove caustic to his scarred skin, he didn't flinch. She regretted the fact that she might be causing him pain, or replicating, in any way, the actions of his captors.

"I can barely feel what you're doing."

They sat in the middle of the courtyard on a bench that they'd moved from the kitchen. She'd persuaded him to take off his shirt, and now the sunlight revealed a tracery of lines deeper than the pattern of Shiva carved on his flesh.

"What are these?" she asked, following the lines with her fingers.

"Lash marks," he said casually, as if he discussed the weather, or something equally mundane.

"Did they beat you, too?"

"It's over, Mary," he said gently, glancing over his

shoulder at her. "Someone recently told me that I needn't remember it again."

It was annoying to have her words turned around and used as weapons.

"The sun will help you heal further," she said, feeling a surge of protectiveness. "I wish that I were as talented as those in Inverness believe me to be," she said, placing both hands flat on his shoulders. "If so, I would erase these marks from your body."

"If you were indeed an angel from Inverness, I wouldn't be able to touch you," he said, turning and smiling at her. "I wouldn't want to trade that pleasure for anything."

"Not even being unscarred?"

"Does it matter so much to you, Mary?"

She shook her head, realizing it was true. The tattoos were a part of him, as much as his brown eyes or his hair.

"Why doesn't it matter more to you?" she asked him.

"Perhaps I deserve it," he said, a cryptic remark that he didn't explain.

She continued rubbing in the salve. When she finished, she wiped her hands and gently blotted the excess from his skin.

"It's a beautiful day," she said glancing up at the clear sky. The hint of winter was back in the air, but the warmth of the sun offset the cool breeze.

"That it is," he said. When he spoke conversationally, his voice sounded almost like a whisper. Only when he spoke louder, what might have been for another man a shout, did his voice seem to regain a normal pitch. She didn't ask why that was, preferring ignorance in certain things between them.

She sat on the edge of the well and watched him, sitting there with his face tilted back to the sun, that small half smile playing around his lips. She knew now that he used the expression as a shield, less amusement than simply a way of hiding whatever emotion he was experiencing.

"Will you play a game of shatranj with me this evening?" she said, capping the vial and placing it back in her medicine chest resting on the edge of the well.

He glanced over at her, his gaze intent and somber.

"What wager shall we make this time?"

"Must we make one?" she asked. "Isn't it enough to simply play for the joy of the game?"

He smiled again, his expression altering to become teasing. "I would much rather win something from you."

"You'll do the laundry if you lose, then."

He laughed, surprising her.

"I agree that that's a wager I'd prefer to win, but I have more interesting stakes in mind."

He winked at her, a slow and taunting gesture, one that shouldn't have escalated her heartbeat.

She carefully closed her medicine chest before moving it from the rim of the well. Once it was at her feet, she looked at him again.

"What, exactly, did you have in mind?"

"If I win, I will teach you something I learned in the Orient."

"A healing technique?"

"If you prefer to think of it as that," he said, smiling.

"Or is it something to do with cobras?"

He laughed.

It really was a strange occurrence, losing her breath around him. Still, it seemed wicked to discuss such things, and even twice as decadent to do so in the bright light of the sun. She could hear the waves lap up on the rocks, and the seabirds calling as if the sheer joy of life was too much to restrain.

She'd already betrayed herself as being a woman who was led by her impulses rather than her logic. If not, she would have left with Brendan, been in Inverness now, congratulating herself on her fortuitous escape. But what Hamish didn't know was that she'd never before acted in such a fashion. Only with him had she been so foolish. And brazen.

Instead of telling him that, she smiled back at him as he sat there, a satyr with his shirt unbuttoned and the pattern of a godless deity cavorting upon his chest.

Had he always been a man of wild wants? Someone who explored the world with a reckless disregard for what other people might say or think? Had he always done exactly as he wished and been an adventurer with a wicked gleam in his eye?

"Very well," she heard herself say. "I accept your wager."

He only smiled in response.

One thing she'd learned from ten years of marriage was how to gauge a man's moods. Gordon had sometimes been affable, yet she had known how to read his irritation, knew when it would subside or presage a greater anger. She was often the brunt of his annoyance, and she accepted both his outbursts and his later apologies, understanding that she was an easier target than the customer who'd angered him, the price of gold, or a dozen other reasons. However volatile his nature, Gordon never meant to be unkind.

Hamish MacRae had not once demonstrated or revealed any emotion at all, other than lust. Surely, however, he felt something other than understanding about his imprisonment and the torture he'd endured. Perhaps his true sentiments were buried too deep to surface easily.

She stood and walked to where he still sat. At her approach, he opened his eyes. When she drew near he stretched out his hand, resting it on her waist, his thumb brushing an arc beneath one breast.

Reaching out, she touched his face gently, trailing a path along his jaw. Pressing three fingers against his bottom lip, she leaned forward and whispered to him. "Hamish." That's all, just his name.

His smile slipped as he looked at her.

"I shouldn't have kept you here, Mary."

"Since it's too late for regrets, can we disallow them?" Remorse, she discovered, couldn't coexist side by side with joy. Her smile wouldn't subside, and her heart felt remarkably light.

"Then I'll have to ensure that you don't regret your decision," he said. A promise he sealed with a kiss.

Brendan said farewell to Micah and Hester at an inn on the outskirts of Inverness.

"If you ever need work," he said as they parted, "go to Gilmuir and tell my brother Alisdair that I recommended you."

"Won't you be there, sir?" Micah asked.

"Ships are for sailing," Brendan said with a smile. "I'm certain my crew is enjoying their unexpected holiday, but sooner or later they're bound to be restless."

He said goodbye and made arrangements for the horses before continuing into Inverness to fulfill his errand for Hamish.

Brendan entered the goldsmith's shop, hearing the bell's soft summons as he closed the door. A moment later, the apprentice appeared, wiping his hands dry on a towel. Brendan's nose wrinkled as he smelled a foul odor, something that clung to Charles like a cloud.

"It's a solution to purify gold," he said, frowning at Brendan. He looked behind him as if expecting Mary to magically appear. "Where is she?"

"She remained behind," Brendan said. He extended the letter to the other man. Charles took it without a word, breaking the seal with a snap, and scanning it quickly. He turned it over in his hands as if expecting more.

Charles Talbot was a young man with a narrow face and intense blue eyes. His eyebrows were bushy and his lips thin, giving him the appearance of a fox. Or some other feral forest creature.

"Is this all?"

The apprentice, Brendan thought, didn't look too happy about Mary's letter. In fact, he looked as if he would rather take a swing at him than force a smile to his face. The sentiment was equally shared. Brendan hadn't liked the man when he'd first met him. He'd been given directions by Iseabal, as well as a written introduction. Charles had been rude and dismissive before realizing that Brendan was Alisdair MacRae's brother. Evidently, the apprentice's manners were attached securely to his pocketbook.

"I've no other message from her if that's what you're asking."

"Your brother is no better?" The effort of forcing his tone to be pleasant was taking its toll, Brendan noted. One of Talbot's hands was clenched in a fist; the other trembled markedly as he held the letter.

"He's not as well as I would wish," Brendan said, which was not exactly a lie.

"What's the nature of his ailment?"

Brendan just stared at the man, irritated that the situation was forcing him to lie. He would, but only to an outsider. He'd tell the truth to a member of the family.

"He's been wounded," he said, hoping the man wouldn't press him.

"But not grievously," Charles said. "Otherwise, you wouldn't have left him."

"With Mary tending him, he doesn't need me."

"But he must be well enough and not at death's door," Charles insisted. "Otherwise, you would not have left him with a stranger."

They were hardly strangers by now, a thought he wouldn't convey to the narrow-eyed apprentice.

"I have another letter," he said, "one for an Elspeth Grant. Could I get directions from you to her house?"

Charles held out his hand. "Give it to me and I'll see that she gets it."

Giving the letter to the other man would save him the trouble of delivering it to her, and allow him to travel without delay to Gilmuir. But something in Charles's eyes made him doubt that the young woman would ever see Mary's words.

"I've promised Mary I would deliver it to Elspeth personally," he said. Another lie. "If you don't know the way to her house, I'll ask a passerby."

Charles gave him the directions grudgingly, and Brendan left the goldsmith's shop, feeling relief that his errand was nearly complete and irritation that Hamish had forced him into it in the first place.

* * *

Matthew Marshall had a voice that seemed to carry from the hilltop to the crowd arranged around at the bottom, yet he didn't appear to be shouting. For the most part, he exhorted those who'd come to hear him speak to live a more healthful, fulfilling life. He then began answering questions, the first leading to a very long commentary about his travels.

Elspeth Grant listened with half an ear, wishing that Mary were there. If nothing else, her friend could take away some of the boredom of this task. Shame filled her instantly at the idea of mentally criticizing Mr. Marshall. He was an exceptionally fine gentleman, and a man of the cloth.

But he did love to talk.

She and her brother, Jack, had been given the task of escorting Mr. Marshall to their home, where her parents would officially greet him as members of his extended congregation. Her father's gout precluded him from walking very far, and her mother had remained behind to see to last minute preparations.

She focused on Mr. Marshall's comments and realized he was still answering the first question posed to him.

"I find that I have the same strength now as I did thirty-five years ago. My sight is better now and my nerves firmer than they were in my youth. I am grateful to report that I have none of the infirmities of old age and have lost several that I had as a young man. I can only attribute my good health to my constant journeys, because I have not traveled less than five thousand miles a year for the last twenty years."

Mr. Marshall had a thick head of white hair that flowed nearly to his collar. His face, heavily lined and deeply tanned, was genial. His complexion was clear and smooth, his eyes bright and piercing.

If Mary were there, she'd hang on the man's every word. But Mary wasn't in Inverness, which was surprising in itself.

A few days ago, Elspeth had visited the goldsmith shop only to discover that her friend had left Inverness the afternoon before.

"But where has she gone?" she asked Charles.

"To treat the brother of an influential customer," Charles said, looking none too pleased with Mary's decision.

"It's not like her to leave Inverness."

"She'll not do so again, I can guarantee you that."

Elspeth hadn't said a word, but she hadn't liked the look in his eyes. Since Gordon's death, Charles had changed, becoming more vocal in his disapproval of Mary's actions.

"If you hear from her," she said, turning toward the door, "let her know that I asked about her." She slipped from the shop before allowing her discomfiture to show.

She forced herself to pay attention, listening as Mr. Marshall spoke of his clinics in London. She'd try to remember the details for Mary's sake, as well as all the information he'd passed on about his healing treatments.

It was with Mary that Elspeth experienced her greatest freedom. Because of her reputation, Mary was considered a proper companion. Her parents didn't know that there were times when Mary's laughter rang out so loud that the sound of it echoed back in the narrow Inverness streets. Or that people sometimes stopped what they were doing to determine the source of the merriment.

She doubted that anyone would suspect the secret thoughts that Mary had confessed upon occasion, walking back from church or shopping. There were times when

Mary surprised her, so much that Elspeth would stop in the middle of the street and stare at her friend, her mouth agape.

"You don't need to see the world to know human nature," Elspeth had argued one day when Mary had confessed she wanted to travel. "You know all that you need to now. I think that people are the same the whole world round, don't you?"

"Do you never want to see different places, or meet different people?" Mary had asked.

Elspeth shook her head vehemently. "Why should I? Everything I need to know of the world is right here in Inverness. If I want laces or linens or wools, I can find them here. As well as porcelain and silver and all manner of goods from London or even the continent. Or from the British East India Company. Even the Orient," she'd said, thinking of the beautiful blue and silver bowl that her mother had set aside for her.

When she wed, her life would be narrowed even further, but it was not a constraint against which she fought. True, there were times when being chaperoned by her mother and older sisters was burdensome, but she didn't want the greater freedom that Mary seemed to desire.

An unusual silence made her glance up to find Mr. Marshall surrounded by well-wishers. The speech was evidently finished.

Looking around for Jack, she spied him talking to a young boy his age. She nodded at him and he frowned back, but she was as familiar with his recalcitrance as she was her parents' doting on him. As the only boy in a family of seven daughters, he was lamentably spoiled. But he could be charming when he wished, flashing that grin at the object of his cajolery. Elspeth had often been the recipient of it, and found herself like as not acceding to Jack's wishes.

"Straighten your jacket," she whispered when he joined her. He frowned again but obeyed.

It wasn't the first time her parents had played host to a visiting dignitary. Their house, built for a large family, seemed cavernous now that six of her sisters were married and living in homes of their own.

"How long is he going to stay there talking?" Jack asked, watching as Mr. Marshall slowly made his way through the crowd.

"He doesn't come often to Inverness," she said. "As long as it takes, I imagine."

"I've other things I'd rather do," he said mutinously. Elspeth didn't bother correcting him. She would much rather be doing other things as well.

The crowd gradually thinned, enough that they could get closer to Mr. Marshall. Jack manfully stepped forward and introduced himself. "This is my sister, sir," he said, glancing at Elspeth. "We've come to escort you to our home. That is, if you're ready."

Mr. Marshall smiled kindly at both of them. "If you don't mind, I'll inform a few acquaintances that I'm ready to take my leave, and then accompany you."

"He's a talker, isn't he, Elspeth?" Jack said, as they watched the older man move through the crowd.

"I suppose he has to be," she replied. "After all, he's a well-known speaker on two continents."

"Do you think he's a speaker because he has to be or because he's a talker?" Jack asked.

She ruffled his hair, which she knew irritated him. He

was acting very grown up, and she was proud of him while at the same time wishing that he wouldn't hurry so to be an adult. It seemed to Elspeth that everything was racing past her, including her own youth.

Finally, Mr. Marshall was ready, and making his way back to them.

"Our parents are sorry that they couldn't be here," Elspeth told him. "My father suffers from gout, and it worsens from time to time."

"My arrival is not inopportune, I trust," he said, his eyes appearing concerned. "There are other families with whom I can stay."

"Not at all," Jack said. "They've spoken of nothing but your arrival, sir. The only thing is that my father cannot walk very far, but then he's not one for regular exercise."

"I've found it to be a good treatment for gout," Mr. Marshall said. "That, and a bland diet, with no ale or pork."

Elspeth smiled. "You sound like my friend Mary," she said. "She's a great devotee of your work, sir."

"Would you be speaking of Mrs. Gilly?" he asked. "I've been anticipating meeting with her."

"She's away from Inverness at present," Elspeth said, "but I anticipate her return momentarily."

They left the meadow, the crowd of people attending Mr. Marshall's sermon gradually fading away. Elspeth hoped sincerely that he wouldn't ask her what she thought of his words. Surprisingly, her parents were entertaining in the parlor, her father's boisterous laughter greeting them as they walked in the front door.

At their entrance, her mother smiled and stood, coming forward to greet Mr. Marshall with both hands outstretched. "I'm so very pleased to meet you, Mr. Marshall," she said, "and so glad that you're to be our guest." She turned, standing at his side.

"My husband, Horace," she said. Elspeth's father nodded cordially.

"Forgive me for not standing, sir," he said, "but I've been confined to my footstool for a few days."

"Not at all," Mr. Marshall said, eyeing the bandaged foot with some interest. "I trust you are abstaining from those foodstuffs that would only aggravate your condition?"

"Mary Gilly has insisted upon it," Horace said. "She's a great believer in your books."

"I am indeed sorry to hear that she's gone from Inverness," Marshall said.

"Nor is she apt to return any time soon," Mrs. Grant said, indicating the other man in the room.

Jack peered around Elspeth, and she didn't chastise him. For once, she had the same curiosity.

A stranger sat there. He was certainly the most handsome man she'd ever seen, dressed in his buff trousers and deep blue jacket. He was smiling, at least until he glanced at her. Abruptly, his smile faded, and the look in his hazel eyes grew more intense.

She'd never been the object of a man's undivided attention before, and she found it disconcerting.

He stood, bowing slightly to her, and it seemed to Elspeth that the conversation faded off into silence as they stared at each other. The oddest thought occurred to her then. Perhaps God was indeed favoring her for having attended Mr. Marshall's sermon. In payment for her patience, He'd brought this smiling young man to her house. A man who'd evidently earned the approbation of her father.

"Captain Brendan MacRae," her father said, his words dispelling the fog that seemed to surround her.

She made a small curtsy and tapped Jack on the shoulder so that he remembered his manners. He bowed impatiently, but ruined his effort at politeness with a rude outburst.

"You're a captain, sir?" he asked excitedly. "A sea captain?"

Captain MacRae nodded, but his attention was directed toward Elspeth. She knew because her gaze hadn't left him from the moment she'd entered the room.

The disappointment she felt was so powerful that Elspeth thought she might faint from it. A sea captain?

She wanted to tell him how sorry she was that he would be leaving them so soon, for places and destinations too far away from Inverness. Words, however, were suddenly beyond her, trapped at the base of her throat. She placed her fingers there as if to urge them forward, but not a sound emerged.

Her mother escorted Mr. Marshall to a chair, but the elderly gentleman hesitated until the women were seated. Elspeth took a seat on the settee, next to her mother, and directly across from Captain MacRae.

He didn't actually look like a ship's captain. He could as easily have been a solicitor, perhaps, or a clerk at her father's distillery. His hair was clubbed at the nape of his neck with a soft blue ribbon, and she wondered if a woman had helped him with it. More than once, she'd seen her mother assist in her father's dressing, teasing him as she patted the folds of his stock into place while he gave her a kiss on her forehead in payment for her solicitousness.

"Where's your ship?" Jack asked, only to receive a quelling look from their father.

"Some distance from here, I'm afraid," he said.

"Captain MacRae has brought word from Mary, dear," her mother was saying.

She glanced over at her mother and nodded, still feeling incapable of speech.

Captain MacRae held out a letter to her, and she took it, her fingers trembling. For a brief moment, the paper linked them together, and neither he nor she relinquished their grip. She glanced up to find him staring at her as intently as before.

"Thank you," she said, feeling the constriction in her throat.

He let go, withdrawing his hand and nodding, leaving her absurdly disappointed not to hear his voice.

They were all looking at her, and although she would have liked to take the letter to her room to read it, she opened it there. Her smile grew as she read Mary's words.

Glancing over at Captain MacRae, she asked him, "Are you acquainted with this patient of hers?"

"He's my brother. You have me to thank for her absence, I'm afraid," he said. "My older brother and his wife had heard of her reputation, and I coaxed her to treat Hamish."

His voice was lower than she'd expected. The kind of tone that resounded in a room, revealed an inner confidence.

"This castle sounds as if it's a fascinating place," she said. Mary seemed equally as charmed with her patient.

"It's a deserted fortress in the middle of nowhere."

If she hadn't been watching him so closely, she wouldn't have noticed the fact that his features stiffened almost imperceptibly. Had she offended him, or did talking about the castle disturb him in some way?

"What does she say, dear?" her mother said gently, and

Elspeth realized that she'd once again been unconsciously rude.

She didn't feel comfortable reading the letter aloud, but she explained the gist of it. "She says that she cannot leave her patient until he's well, and that she's especially disappointed not to be able to meet with you, Mr. Marshall."

"I do understand," Mr. Marshall said, nodding and smiling affably. "The well-being of a patient comes before all else, I'm afraid."

"Is he so very ill?" she asked Captain MacRae, feeling sorry for him to have such a grief to bear.

"I expect his complete recovery any day," he said, smiling at her.

"Will you be returning to the castle, then?" she asked, holding the letter firmly on her lap so that the vellum did not betray the tremulousness of her fingers. She concentrated her attention on it and not their visitor.

"I had planned on returning to my ship."

Elspeth felt a tiny pang, too small really to note, in the area of her heart. Even her breath seemed tight, and her chest felt as it had when she was ill last winter of a lingering cold. But she forced her smile to remain as it was, clinging fiercely to her lips. "Then I shall wish you a safe journey. Will you be leaving soon?"

"I don't know," he said.

She glanced over at him in surprise, to find him looking at her in an altogether strange way. Never had a man regarded her as intently as this young captain, and with such a somber expression on his face. He was studying her as if she held the answer to his plans.

"Perhaps you can join us for dinner," her mother said, standing. "In order to welcome Mr. Marshall to our home."

He replied courteously, the words slipping past Elspeth as if they were simply a faint breeze. She couldn't stop staring at him, even though she knew that what she was doing was hideously impolite. It seemed, however, as if her heartbeat were tied to his gaze, and the only way to calm it was to keep smiling at Captain MacRae.

She heard her mother saying something, and Jack murmuring a reluctant assent. Perhaps her father conversed with Mr. Marshall, or the maid responded to her mother's query. The world could have marched into their pleasant and cozy parlor at that moment, and Elspeth wouldn't have noticed.

Nor, did it seem, would Captain MacRae.

Chapter 13

Two small candles sat in the center of the kitchen table, illuminating the empty bowls and the loaf of bread. A small bowl of chopped green onion sat next to it. It was a simple meal but a hearty one, reminding Hamish that some of the greatest pleasures of life were uncomplicated and unadorned. Without speaking, Mary ladled the soup from the large pot where it simmered on the fire.

He sat opposite her, and they began to eat. A moment later, he looked over at her and smiled. "It's the first time I've shared a meal with anyone for over a month," he said.

"You needn't have been a hermit, you know."

He only smiled, thinking that if anyone could coax him from his lair, it would be Mary. What had she said when first approaching him? Something about dragon's toes.

"Shall we adjourn to my chamber, then?" he asked when their meal was finished.

"Wouldn't it be wiser for us to play here?" She looked around the well-lit room. He knew her thoughts as well as his own. In his tower room, the bed took up most of the space. How could he concentrate on their playing when he had a game of another sort on his mind?

"I won't touch you until the winner is certain, Mary. You have my word on that."

She only nodded, once, dependent so easily on his oath that it momentarily disturbed him.

He went to the well, drawing the water for her, and when she washed the dishes, straightened the table and chairs. Turning, he found her looking at him with a smile on her face.

"You're very appealing, Hamish MacRae," she said. For a moment they simply looked at each other.

"Is there a reason for your approval?" he asked.

She shook her head, still smiling.

He banked the kitchen fire and waited until she was at the door before extinguishing the lantern and the remainder of the candles. He crossed the courtyard with her hand in his, for all the world as if they were two sweethearts in a darkened garden.

Once in the tower, he followed her upstairs. Twice, she hesitated, no doubt due to her dislike of heights. The second time she did so, he came up beside her, placing his hand on the small of her back, leaning close as if they were two people in a crowded room and his words were directed to her ears alone.

"It's all right, Mary," he said. "You'll not fall. I won't let you."

She nodded, accepting his word without reservation once more. She began the ascent again.

"You shouldn't believe me quite so easily," he said, hearing the words echo back to him.

She looked surprised, or perhaps it was just the effect of the flickering candle in her hand.

"Is your word not to be trusted, Hamish?"

He smiled, thinking that she was his equal in bluntness. "It's not my word that concerns me as much as your trust. You grant it too easily."

Once, he, too, had believed the best of others, but he was no longer the fun-loving and open-to-adventure man with a ready smile.

She reached the landing and turned and looked at him, her eyes serious over the candle flame. "Should I not believe you, Hamish?"

He should tell her that he wasn't a man she should depend upon, that others had done so and they'd died. But he didn't, because saying the words would darken the look of expectation in her eyes and make her turn away. He wanted her hunger and her passion, needing them more than any softer emotions.

He led her inside his room, closing the door firmly behind them. Pulling up the chair, he stood behind her as she sat. He let his hand trail over her shoulder before loosening the end of her braid and watching as it fell down her back.

"I like your hair free," he said, pulling the pins loose. Her hands reached up to catch them, but she was too late. They'd already fallen to the floor in a shower of gold.

She looked abandoned and flushed, and they'd not yet begun to play.

Reaching out, he touched her cheek.

"Did you blush as much before you met me?" he asked. "If so, it must be a detriment to your healing career. Or did the citizens of Inverness call you Angel simply because you were so innocent?"

"I'm neither innocent nor maiden," she said. "You ought to know that better than anyone."

He knew only too well. Having lain with her twice, he was also disturbingly aware that it wouldn't be enough. He wanted her in the morning and in the evening, and perhaps instead of their noon meal as well.

"But no," she said, "I'm not known to blush."

Hamish didn't tell her that more than once he'd seen her cheek pinken, or her gaze fall to the floor is if she were afraid to reveal the look in her eyes.

He lit more candles, being improvident with the supply that Brendan had brought from Inverness. One day, he would need to replenish his store of provisions, but that time seemed too far away to matter to him now.

Mary said nothing as he rounded the table and sat opposite her, in a pose similar to the one they'd had as genial dinner companions. Here, in his tower room, the atmosphere was more charged. Even the air felt thicker. The wind was coming out of the north, and the room was a little chilled since he'd not yet lit the brazier. But he didn't move to do so, thinking that their heat would warm them.

Suddenly, he didn't want to play games with her, not with words and certainly not shatranj.

"Must we play?" he asked, feeling on the knife's edge of desperation, an abrupt and uncomfortable feeling.

She looked up from where she was arranging her pieces on the board and smiled softly, a teasing, almost haunting expression. "Yes, we must. Unless you're willing to concede to me."

"Then I concede."

She sat back in the chair and surveyed him. "That easily?"

"Some things are worth fighting for. Some aren't."

She played with the elephant piece, her fingers stroking it from tusk to tail in one tender movement of her finger. He would have preferred her hand on him instead.

Her cheeks were blossoming with color, but he didn't tease her about it. Instead, he reached out his hand and covered her wrist, feeling the pulse beat fast and heavy.

"I know how fleeting time is, Mary, and how fragile our own little worlds. Why should I waste time in pretense?"

She looked at him, that singular directness of her gaze that always surprised him. "We haven't, have we? We've both stated what we wanted in clear terms."

"Have you been unsatisfied with the bargain?"

She shook her head, stared down at the board. "We've been selfish, though, haven't we?"

"There are worse things, Mary," he said, his voice more grating than he wished.

"You act as if people each live in separate worlds, Hamish. That none of us ever touch another's life."

"Would that be so bad?"

"It would be lonely, wouldn't it? In that sort of world, there'd be no understanding, no kindness. No communion between people. We would all be independent, and alone."

He was unaccountably irritated with her. Standing, he walked to the window and opened the shutters wide, uncaring that he invited winter into the room. He turned his head and saw her rubbing her hands over her arms to warm herself.

"There are worse things than being alone," he said.

"You don't believe that. If you did, I wouldn't be here now."

"It's not for the state of my soul that you're here," he said, the words sounding base and crude.

She only smiled in response and stood, coming to his side.

"You've said that before. Once more, and I will begin to believe that you're trying to convince yourself more than me."

"You would have me be someone I'm not, Mary."

"While you would have me believe you're someone I doubt you are," she argued.

"Who do you think I am?" A question he probably should not have asked, but she stirred his curiosity.

"A man struggling to find his way," she said, startling him with her words. "Someone who's basically decent, but who doubts even that about himself. Someone who's trying to accept a horrible time in his life, to put it behind him, and go on."

"Is that who I am?" He didn't refute her words. He wasn't the tortured knight she portrayed him to be. But he didn't tell her the truth, even though the moment shouted for it.

Who was he? A man who asked himself eternal questions, none of which he could answer. Could he have done more? Could he have done something differently?

His hermitage had accomplished what companionship could not, allowing him to focus on the reality of what had happened and not allowing him to avoid or ignore it. Eventually, he'd come to accept the act he'd committed. Perhaps the one person he truly didn't trust was himself, an alarming realization to have at this moment.

"A man is not solely defined by his thoughts of himself," Mary said gently. "Other people help to flesh him out as well. A loved one, parents, siblings, and friends. You might have lost your sense of self, for however long you were a prisoner, but you were never truly alone. There were people who loved you even when they thought you dead."

"My father had a saying," he said, wondering why this particular errant memory had been buried until now. "He said that if you would truly know a man, talk to his friends."

She smiled at him almost approvingly. So much so that he almost hated to say the words that would dispel the myth she'd created about him.

"My family and my friends knew the man I was, Mary. Not the man I am now."

"Are they so different?"

As much as night was from day. He reached out and pulled her to him. To warm her, he told himself, but that would have been more easily accomplished by closing the window. To silence her, then. He wanted her passion, not her prose. Not her wickedly incisive way of pushing him to the brink of honesty.

"How long were you a prisoner?"

"Thirteen months." *Seventeen days, four hours.* He knew the time well.

"Can't you forgive yourself for having been captured?"

He pulled back and looked at her. Her eyes were swimming with compassion, a look that made him want to shield her eyes, cover them with his hand. Her tenderness was almost his undoing. But she wasn't done yet.

"I don't think it would be an easy thing for you to be prisoner. I don't doubt that you railed against it every day until your body simply gave out."

"Don't ascribe to me actions of a hero, Mary. I did what I had to do in order to survive." There, as close to the truth as he would come.

"You remind me of my husband's apprentice," she said surprisingly.

He turned, closing the window while keeping his back to her. It was the last thing he'd expected her to say. "Why?"

"Charles would always look at one of Gordon's chalices, something he'd worked on for months, and then place his own work beside it. He never noticed his own ability to fashion flowers and fruits so beautifully they looked real. He only saw that Gordon was so much better than he at carving rampant lions and doing delicate scrollwork. A man should not measure himself against other people's strengths without knowing his own."

He turned and faced her again, unwittingly amused. He didn't measure himself against others, but against himself. What he thought was right counted for more than a stranger's beliefs. That's why he'd had so much difficulty accepting what he'd done. He'd violated his own ethics.

"What do you think my strengths might be, Mary?"

"Your endurance," she said unhesitatingly. "Your ability to survive what would have killed a lesser man. Your capacity to simply be patient and wait for the propitious moment to escape. I've no doubt that you were planning it all along."

He nodded slowly, wondering how she knew. Walking back to the table, he touched a few of the pieces on the board.

"Are you certain you want to play?" he asked, deciding that the subject should be changed, and quickly, before he told her what had happened in India. He wanted absolution. Did Mary's compassion extend that far? He realized that he didn't want to put her to another test.

"Especially with the stakes you've laid out?" she asked,

smiling slightly as she walked toward him. "I would be wiser to say no. But I don't think I'm especially wise when it comes to you, Hamish. So yes, let's play."

She sat and arranged her pieces, an intent look in her eyes. Competition enlivened her, it seemed.

"Tell me about this apprentice of Gordon's," he said, sitting. "What happened to him after Gordon died?"

"He's still with me," she said, not looking up from the board. "Ever since Gordon died, he's become more and more interested in my activities. He fusses if I'm not back to the shop before dark, and looks fierce when I'm called to the bedside of a sick patient. It's a treat being here and not having to answer to Charles."

"How did you manage to escape him long enough to leave Inverness?"

"You're Alisdair MacRae's brother," she said, glancing at him with a smile. "Such an important customer could not be slighted."

"He sounds very possessive," Hamish said carefully, wondering why the thought annoyed him.

"He is," she agreed. "I've felt for many months now that I should talk to Charles, that we should make other living arrangements. Sometimes, he acts as if he inherited me along with Gordon's customers. It's very taxing."

"Have you given him any reason to think that there's more to your relationship than apprentice and widow?"

She looked up from the board. "Charles? Of course not. Gordon thought of him as his son. I've come to look on him almost as a stepson."

"But he was much younger than Gordon, as you are. Perhaps he thinks of you differently."

She shook her head, concentrating on the board, as if the game held momentous attraction for her.

She was a voluptuous woman with a lovely face and unforgettable figure. He could well imagine the dreams Charles had had, with her sleeping in the same house. Hamish could almost pity the man; he'd felt Mary's allure from the first moment they'd met.

After a moment, he spoke again. "I imagine that he won't be happy about your decision to remain with me."

"No," she said, looking at him once again. "But perhaps it's just as well. If he doesn't wish to buy me out, I'll simply close the shop and move to a smaller house with my maid, Betty."

That idea did not sit well with him, which was doubly strange since her future was none of his business.

It took him fifteen minutes to beat her at shatranj. He would have done it in less time had she not taken great deliberation with every move. In fact, he almost convinced himself to let her win again. Almost. However, he was feeling decadent and devilish. Satan in his tower. She was an angel who had been delivered to him for his delectation. In this place she called Castle Gloom, it was almost as if they were fighting the eternal struggle of good versus evil.

He wondered who would win that eventual battle even as he won the game. He moved a piece on the board and watched as she realized what he'd done.

"I can't move," she said, but still didn't look at him, as if she didn't want to admit defeat.

"No," he said calmly. "You can't."

"That didn't take any time at all," she said, staring at the board.

"I could have done it faster, but I decided it wouldn't be chivalrous of me."

She propped her chin on her hands and looked at him directly. The smile on her face wasn't the least bit innocent, but it did have a tinge of self-mockery to it.

"You're a very arrogant man, Hamish MacRae," she said.

"Do you think so?"

"Yes," she said calmly. "It's a pity that I'm not a better player. I might have at least lengthened the time between the beginning of the game and its end."

"You'll get better. All you need is practice. You already understand the rudiments, and beyond that you have the intellect, and if I may be so bold, the ability to smile at your opponent while trying to trounce him fiercely."

"Is that a requirement?"

"No, but it's certainly distracting."

"Do you think so?" she asked, mimicking his earlier question.

"Yes, I do," he said, wondering why he was so charmed by the competitive spirit she showed.

"I've lost, then."

"Yes, you have."

He leaned back in the chair and let his left hand fall to his lap, the better to cover his tumescence. However, he'd been hard for the last ten minutes, and it was foolish to pretend himself unaffected.

"Come here, Mary," he said softly. He pushed his chair back, extending his right arm to her. She took his hand, stood, and circled the table. Finally, she stood in front of him, as he deliberately widened his legs, pulling her even closer until her skirt covered his trousers.

Once again, he cursed his useless left hand. When he'd awakened that morning, he thought he'd felt some sensation, like a tingling, in his fingers, but he'd not yet gained any movement. Nor could he lift his arm.

He fumbled with the ties at her waist. A measure of his true arrogance, perhaps, that he didn't intend to ask for her help. Finally, he pulled her skirt from her, and pushed it to the floor. She stepped away from the garment delicately, balancing against his shoulder with one slender hand.

"I've been undressed in front of you more than I have been dressed, Hamish," she said. But her voice held no embarrassment or shame, for which he was profoundly grateful.

His hand flattened against her shift-covered body, feeling the curve of her buttocks and the slight flare of her hips. She was so essentially female. Pretty wasn't a good enough word for Mary. Beautiful was more apt, but if he labeled her that, the comparison between them would be so drastic that he'd be able to think of nothing else. So to equalize them, he lessened her beauty and mediated his own ugliness.

Once, however, he'd been known as a handsome man. Once, he'd winked at more than a few young girls, and they'd giggled in delight. Once, he'd been sought after for the fact that he was a MacRae, and for his own attractiveness.

How foolish to be concerned about his appearance, when he should be more concerned about his immortal soul. But the topic of souls was for moonless nights and lonely days, and nightmares that made him awake gasping, frozen with fear. Not for moments like these, poised on the edge of seduction, sensual, heady, and silent with too many pained breaths.

He reached up and unfastened her bodice, easing it off

her shoulders while she stood unprotesting in front of him. He'd never known a woman as acquiescent as she was. She was stubborn, and firm, and didactic in her insistence on treating him, but when it came to their mutual lust, she let him take the lead.

No more. Not after tonight. He wanted her to be his equal in this. They were not unevenly matched in life. She was a wealthy widow. His fortune had done nothing but multiply during his time in India until he was rich as well. Unlike his older brother Alisdair, Hamish bore no title. Neither did Mary. They were both unmarried.

But there were other things that separated them. Mary had a quest in life, a goal. He had none. For months, all he'd cared about was survival, never thinking beyond that fact. Now the years stretched out in front of him, empty and without purpose.

He missed the sea, his ship, and the men who'd sailed with him.

Mary had a past filled with love and affection. That was evident from the fond way she talked about her husband. All he had was his family, and he'd tried to distance himself from them.

Her life was richer, not beset with the doubts and the condemnation that accompanied him every hour. Her conscience was clean, unlike his.

Yet she was his equal in willingness and curiosity. Here, at least, they were the same.

He removed her stays, but left her adorned in her shift. The areolas of her breasts, large and dark, pressed against the fine material, nipples protruding. He touched one with a tender exploring finger, and it felt hot and hard.

She didn't look away when he glanced upward at her face, but her cheeks deepened in color once again.

"You're blushing, Mary," he said, placing his hand on her back. He pulled her forward, pressed his mouth against the material. Her nipple strained against his lips as if to find a way through the fabric. When he drew back, there was a circle of moisture there. He did the same to her other nipple, then sat back to survey his handiwork.

They looked at each other, the moments stretched out and waiting.

Finally, Mary spoke. "What do you want from me, Hamish?"

"You must kneel now," he said gently.

She knelt on the floor between his legs, reaching up to place her hands on each of his thighs, her thumbs pressing against the swelling of his erection behind the cloth.

He smiled at this sign of her eagerness.

"You must release me."

Unbuttoning his trousers, she freed him from the constriction of the fabric, brushing her fingers down his length. "Am I going to put my mouth on you, Hamish?"

His smiled broadened. "I fervently hope so. But first, make a ring of your thumb and forefinger and wrap it around me."

She did, slipping her fingers around the head of his penis, her thumb on the bottom of the underside ridge. But before he could give her any further instructions, she made another ring with her other hand and slipped it below the first. She slid her top hand up while the bottom one exerted pressure downward. The sensation was indescribable.

Her gaze was rapt as she studied him, and he felt himself lengthen in her grasp. He was fully dressed, his engorged erection being tantalized between her busy hands. She kept up a steady rhythm, smoothly driving him slightly insane.

He reached out and pulled her to her feet, but she didn't relinquish her grasp. Only when he pulled her atop him did she release him. Bracing herself with her hands on his shoulders, she lowered herself slowly over him. He entered her firmly and selfishly, grateful for the wet heat that welcomed him.

When she would have moved, he shook his head. When she would have kissed him, he pressed two fingers to her lips, and when she would have spoken, he kept them there.

He whispered something soft and comforting to her, closing his eyes at the feeling of being deeply in her. Slowly, he lifted her with one hand and removed himself from her.

Her eyes looked confused as he lowered her to her knees once again. Only then did he kiss her gently. Short, darting kisses that made her open her mouth for more. But he pulled back when she placed her arms around his neck.

He ran his fingers delicately over her hard nipples beneath the fabric of the shift.

"A taste," he said softly. "It must last us for a while."

"You intend to drive me wild," she said, her voice husky with passion. "Am I to beg you?"

"Never," he said firmly. "Not here and never between us."

She braced her forearms on each of his thighs and reached down and touched his erection again, her fingers smoothing up and down the shaft and pressing gently on the underside ridge.

Once more she made rings of her fingers, repeating a stroke upward and downward at the same time. Just when he decided that he was the one who would beg, she removed one hand, sliding it downward until she cupped him gently. One finger slid behind, pressing tiny circles while she kept up the stroking of her other hand.

"You never told me you were so talented," he said in a voice that sounded unlike his own.

"It's not something one boasts about," she said, so close that he could feel her breath on his stomach.

"My curiosity is vying with my self-preservation," he confessed. "I'd like to know what else you know, but I'm almost afraid to ask."

"Perhaps I should show you," she said.

"Will I survive the demonstration?"

"Perhaps you won't," she admitted, a small, teasing smile appearing on her lips.

"But then, perhaps we should wish to die in such a fashion. I can see the epitaph on my tombstone now. Here lies Hamish MacRae, the victim of a beautiful woman."

"But he died with a smile on his face?"

"As your husband did?"

She stood, so quickly that he was jarred by her movement. One moment, he was being teased by her talented fingers, entranced by her husky voice. In the next, she was standing on the other side of the room, her back to the wall, her gaze on him so cold and distant that he felt as if she'd turned into another person in a matter of seconds.

He felt uniquely vulnerable in the face of her rage. Perhaps because he recognized that he deserved it.

"Are you bereft of sense? How dare you bring my husband into this moment?"

"I agree, it was unwise of me."

He stood, tucking his recalcitrant member back into his pants with difficulty. It seemed to have a mind of its own, straining toward Mary as if it could erupt at the sound of her voice alone. How had delight turned to antipathy so quickly?

"Was he such a saint, Mary, that the very mention of him turns you grief-stricken?"

She didn't respond. Her arms were folded in front of her, and her gaze was directed not at him but at the floor.

"What is it, Mary?" he asked, taken aback by her sudden change of mood. In one moment, she was a siren. In the next, she was a flaming virago. Now she looked as if she might weep.

"What is it?" he asked again, cupping her face and lifting it until her eyes met his.

"Nothing."

"Hardly that," he said, irritated when she didn't confide in him. "Tell me."

"A command that I'm to obey, Hamish?" She pulled away from him, slid a few inches to the left on the curved wall.

"Please."

She studied him for long moments, her gaze peering into places he'd rather she not see. Dusty vaults of thought where remorse lingered in shadowy corners. Did she know that she was the only recipient of his pleas? Other than God, and He had been stoically silent in response. Hamish couldn't bear it if she remained mute as well.

"I should have loved him more," she said, the words hesitant and so obviously reluctant that he almost pressed his fingers against her lips to spare her the revelation.

"I doubt a man could have been loved more than you loved him," he said. "You always speak of him with fondness."

"I respected him," she said, turning her head and staring beyond him to the far wall. "I liked him. But I never felt the passion for him that I do for you." Her gaze turned to him. "Make of that what you will, Hamish. I've given you a weapon to use against me."

She'd never been held captive. She'd never escaped from imprisonment. Nor had she been guilty of a deed like the one that kept him awake. But the result was the same. She knew herself well, and knew him too quickly. In that fleeting moment, he resented the knowledge she had so easily gained of herself. He'd suffered for his.

"Do you know why I wanted to lie with you, Mary?"

She shook her head slowly from side to side.

"For forgetfulness. To be able to submerge thoughts and memories beneath pleasure."

"Has it worked?"

"So much so that it might well prove to be an addiction." There, he'd neutralized her figurative sword with a confession of his own.

"Then my epitaph might well read Mary Gilly, done in by her sins."

"Perhaps we should be buried side by side, exiles in the same churchyard. People will walk over our graves, and whisper about our decadence. He was a rogue, they'll say. And she was a wanton."

There, she finally smiled, and it was payment enough for his effort.

"Shall I tell you how much a rogue I truly am?" he said, picking up her hand, and bringing it to his lips to softly kiss her fingertips. They were talented hands, soft and delicate, capable of bringing him a great deal of pleasure.

He pressed her hand to the front of his trousers, where he swelled hard, stiff, and impatient.

"Make me forget, Mary. Can you do that?"

Her smile slipped. In its place was a look too somber for his mood. "I can," she said softly. "But I think we would be wiser if I returned to Inverness."

There, she had put into words his secret thoughts. She had an uncanny ability to do that.

Suddenly, he didn't want any more conversation. All he desired was the comfort she offered him in lust.

He pressed her hand harder against the bulge in his trousers, and she took on a rhythm of her own, stroking up and down with firm fingers. Unfastening his trousers, she inserted one hand inside, and he almost sighed in relief, needing her touch.

She was the one to lead him to the bed and remove her shift, baring her body in one swift movement while he undressed feverishly. But this time, she didn't remove her stockings, only draped herself over him like a half-clad nymph. She took his erection in her hand and rubbed it against her, teasing him by sliding it back and forth against her moisture. Finally, she guided him inside with one hand, before leaning forward and resting her hands on the bed.

At one point she straightened up and clasped her hands behind her, a position that thrust her breasts forward. Reaching up, he cupped one and then the other, his fingers gently pinching the nipples. She slowly lifted herself up and then down, then slowly from side to side. She rode him like a horse, and like a beast of burden he lay, letting her use him as she will. A fitting punishment, perhaps, for his earlier crudeness.

His body had once betrayed him, giving out when he needed strength. In India, his mind had refused to remain rational, sending him traveling through dark corridors of nightmares accompanied by the faint reverberation of his own screams. He had begged God toward the end, for them to kill him. The fact that the words were never uttered aloud was due more to the fact that he'd lost the ability to speak than to any remnant of courage he might have possessed. He'd waited for death to claim him, barely clinging to life, like a drowning man treading water.

Now, however, he gloried in his life, in this moment, in the sheer joy of feeling all the separate sensations flooding his body. When the end came, his gaze darkened as if it were death itself coming to claim him. Or a rapture so deep that his bones shook. He heard Mary cry out, and some errant thought matched the sound with an earlier comment, making him feel vindicated that he, too, had made her cry in release.

Chapter 14

When Mary entered the tower room, she found it empty. Hamish wasn't there. Nor had he been in the courtyard. Had he gone hunting, then, as he promised? A movement to her right captured her attention. Going to the window, she pushed open the shutters and stared in fascination at the sight that met her eyes.

Hamish was emerging from the sea, like a creature from a tale, half man, almost beast. His skin was colored so brightly that she could see the twisted shapes from there. But it wasn't the pattern of Shiva that she concentrated on as much as a look on his face. A bright and disarming smile, one whose origin was either amusement or enjoyment, altered his face, making it something youthful and carefree. In his right hand he carried something that looked like a spear.

Naked, he looked like one of the first warriors, a long ago ancestor of the people who'd lived in Scotland and fought against the Romans. Even in depths of her imagination, she could never have envisioned anyone like him.

As she watched, he tilted back his head, raised the spear as if challenging the world itself. She wondered if he'd always been this way, serenely himself. Not selfish as much as centered in himself. Confident and strong, certain in a way that most people are not. Or had this knowledge of himself been thrust upon him during his imprisonment? Either way, it didn't matter. He was who he was.

A little of his assurance must have rubbed off on her. The longer she remained at Castle Gloom, the less she cared about what other people thought. What, after all, could they say to her? Nothing that would, in any way, offset the sheer joy she felt.

She'd experienced physical pleasure before, but never to this magnitude. Nor had her mind ever been so free and her thoughts so unfettered. It was a heady mixture, a seduction of all her senses. She didn't care what she revealed to him, silly notions or incomplete wonderings, or secret musings that she'd never shared with another soul.

With each conversation, each laughing quip, each somber moment shared, he began to occupy a place in her mind as real and as uniquely his as if she'd invited him into her house and given him a room.

She was too honest with him, too giving of herself. This morning, she'd dressed in full view of him, asking for no privacy as he watched her. Until today, her body had simply been part of her, but as she had dressed with him watching her, she had the most curious sensation of being distant from herself, almost as if she hovered at the doorway, looking back on both of them.

That curious feeling of being detached had lasted as long as it had taken to dress. She'd watched herself stand

and don her shift, knowing that the garment offered no shield from his gaze. Then once more she'd sat, rolling up her stockings, patting them in place and securing them with her garters, all the while feeling him watching her.

He hadn't said a word and neither had she, and when she was dressed she'd gone to him and kissed him slowly. For long moments they'd simply stood there together, holding each other. She'd tasted new ale once, and it had peppered her nose. The feeling she'd had inside was similar, something effervescent and sparkling.

The day was a gray one, and Hamish the brightest object in it. The weather was too cold for him to be naked, and she didn't doubt that the water was near to freezing. Yet he stood on the rocky shore, his head tilted back, smiling at the sky as if God Himself grinned back at him.

Mary stepped away from a window before he could see her.

It was Elspeth's turn to go to market, and Brendan asked if he could accompany her.

"Of course you can," Mrs. Grant interjected, smiling broadly. "You can help Elspeth carry the parcels home. Take Jack with you as well."

He'd not yet left Inverness, finding a dozen or more excuses to remain in the city. The Grants had proven to be wonderful tour guides. A few days ago, they'd taken a carriage ride to visit the ruins of Craig Phadraig Hill, visible from their home. The walls of the fort, originally made of granite, had somehow become vitrified, a fact that mystified any visitor.

Yesterday, all six married sisters and their husbands

had accompanied them as they'd visited the Clava Cairns, just outside Culloden Moor.

"My grandfather fought at Culloden," Brendan said when they'd passed it. "As well as my father, although on opposite sides."

"You're part English, then?" Elspeth had asked, surprised.

"Does it make a difference to you if I am?"

"Of course it doesn't," she said, and he wondered at his relief.

Beyond those outings, he was fast running out of reasons to delay his departure. He'd called on Mr. Grant often, genuinely growing to like the older man. They'd engaged in many long conversations during which he sat on one of the settees in the parlor, Elspeth and her mother opposite him.

From time to time, she would look up and smile at him with those blue eyes of hers, and he'd lose his thoughts. Mr. Grant would only grin and nod, as if such stupidity on his part was to be expected. Neither he nor Mrs. Grant ever commented on the fact that Brendan had remained here long beyond his original plans. A good thing, because he didn't know what he would tell them if asked. He could understand why he was loath to return to Gilmuir, but he'd never before been so reluctant to go to sea.

The day was clear and bright, and in the distance Ben Wyvis sparkled with its cap of snow. They crossed the bridge spanning the River Ness, taking a moment to study the fast-moving water beneath them.

Jack pulled on Elspeth's sleeve. "Robbie's waiting for me," he said impatiently.

She nodded an assent, both of them watching as he ran off to join a companion.

The Inverness market was composed of rows of stalls separated by aisles. He and Elspeth walked together, one of them occasionally stopping to remark on an item.

"You'll be going back to sea soon, Captain MacRae?" she asked, toying with a selection of ribbons. He wanted to tell her that the dark blue would look best on her silvery blond hair, and match the shade of her eyes, but such a remark might be construed as too personal.

He nodded. "My crew is no doubt enjoying their holiday."

"And your brother? Will he sail with you?"

There was silence while he searched for an answer. "Hamish had his own ship, but it was lost in India."

She turned concerned eyes to him. "Was he badly injured? I hope not. I would hate for you to suffer any grief on his account."

He didn't want to lie to her; at the same time, he was constrained by propriety in what he actually said. "I would say that his recovery is nothing short of miraculous," he answered carefully.

"No doubt due to Mary," Elspeth said loyally. "Mary is quite an accomplished healer."

"Yes," he said.

They spent some time strolling through the stalls, until Elspeth turned and looked at him quizzically.

"What is your brother like, Captain MacRae?"

"What is he like?" Mary had asked him to describe Hamish, and he'd failed miserably at the task. What did he tell the young woman at his side?

She smiled, but it didn't ease his sudden feeling that he'd walked into a trap of words. "He must be a formidable man indeed, to keep Mary with him. Especially since I doubt he's very ill."

"Why would you think that?" he asked, surprised.

"You wouldn't have left him," she said simply. "Or, once your errand was done, you would have returned to his side."

He felt warmth rise to his cheeks and wondered if he'd ever before been as embarrassed as he was at that moment. Elspeth continued to look at him with her innocent wide eyes, the silence stretching out between them as she waited for him to speak.

"He's a complex man," he told Elspeth truthfully. "Although he's my brother there are times when we seem to be little more than strangers. His time in India changed him profoundly. He could, indeed, benefit from Mary's attentions."

"Is he a compelling man, Captain MacRae? Mary had planned for months to meet with Mr. Marshall. To miss that meeting would require a very good reason."

"Didn't you say she was an accomplished healer?" he asked, feeling as if he were floundering.

She slanted a look at him. "But she's never treated anyone this long."

He glanced at her and then away, trying to find a way to answer her so that she would no longer question him, while at the same time not speaking of things that were too indelicate for her ears. Unlike Mary, Elspeth was innocent.

She consulted her list, directing him to the butcher shop not far away. They entered, ducking beneath the lintel and into a small, smoky room where a multitude of meats hung from the rafters. Only then did she speak again.

"I've not seen as much of the world as you, Captain MacRae, but I do know that Mary is acting unlike herself. Is she in love with him? Women give their hearts easily while men only loan theirs." She turned troubled eyes to him.

He thought about the men in his family, how they'd altered their lives for the women they loved. But what Hamish felt was need, or lust, nothing more. Hadn't he as much as made that confession himself?

He was interrupted from having to answer her by the painful exclamation of a girl at the other end of the store.

"What am I to do with this?" she said. "I can't carry this back to the house. He bites!" She stood holding a squawking chicken by the neck, looking as if she were terrified of the fowl.

"You'll take it and be grateful you have food in your mouth."

Elspeth glanced at the two of them, speaking in an aside to Brendan. "It's Betty," she said. "Mary's maid."

He nodded, recognizing Charles Talbot from his earlier meeting with the man. Talbot hadn't improved with familiarity.

Striding forward, Elspeth spoke to the proprietor. "You need to crate the bird for her," she said. Taking the chicken from Betty, she calmly held it out to him.

Talbot looked as if he wanted to argue with her, but Brendan joined Elspeth, regarding the other man coolly. Without a word, he watched as the butcher took the chicken and disappeared into the back of his shop.

"That should solve the problem, Betty," Elspeth said, smiling at the girl. She ignored Talbot, speaking to the young maid. "How are you doing in Mary's absence?"

"It's been difficult without her, miss." She glanced at Talbot out of the corner of her eye, and Brendan couldn't help but wonder what she might have said if Charles hadn't been present.

"You must remember that Mary is your mistress," Elspeth said, glancing at Charles as she spoke. "Even if she's away from home."

"For too long," Charles said tightly. "Tell me, is your brother never going to get well or die?"

For a moment, Brendan only stared at Talbot. Elspeth put her hand on his arm and he glanced down at her, forcing a reassuring smile to his face.

"Mary's been gone entirely too long. She's not comporting herself as a proper widow. But, then, she never has."

Elspeth looked as if she would like to respond to Charles, but the man grabbed the cage the butcher proffered and moved toward the door, Betty following.

The young maid glanced over her shoulder, and just before Talbot whisked her out of the butcher shop, managed one last question. "Do you know when she'll return, miss?"

"Soon, I'm certain," Elspeth said. She sent a glance to Brendan, and he didn't contradict her. What could he say? That Mary had already remained at Castle Gloom far longer than she should? Or that he wasn't entirely certain that even respectability would move her from that place? He'd seen the looks between Mary and Hamish, had heard their muted conversations. Brendan hadn't been all that surprised when Hamish had asked her to stay and she'd acceded.

"She's a sweet girl," Elspeth said, staring after the two of them. "But Charles thinks himself the arbiter of Mary's behavior. He dislikes her work with the poor, and resents the fact that she tends the sick. I'm surprised he remains in her household with all her flaws."

"Shall we go see the dolphins in a few days?" he suggested in an effort to change the subject. Charles Talbot was not going to ruin the rest of his day. Nor did he want to discuss Mary and Hamish. That situation could not get better with the passage of time, and he wondered if the two of them realized it.

"What do you know of the dolphins?" Elspeth asked, smiling and evidently pleased at the suggestion.

"I've been told that they can be seen at Moray Firth."

She nodded. "Mother will be pleased; it's one of her favorite destinations."

One day, Brendan thought, he might be allowed to be with Elspeth without the whole of her family in attendance. Then it struck him that except for the errant Jack, who might appear at any moment, he and Elspeth were now alone. He banished Betty, Mary and Hamish, and any other concerns immediately from his mind.

"I'm not Mary, you know," Charles said to Betty once they were back at the house. "I don't think you're cute and clever and to be cosseted. You need to learn that things have changed around here. Or should I toss you out on your ear?"

There, he'd finally gotten her attention.

"I was only being polite to them, sir," she said.

"You'll talk when I give you leave to do so," he said, tightening his hand around the girl's arm.

Rage ran through him. He gripped the door handle so hard he could feel the pattern etch itself into his skin. They entered the house, and he tossed his hat atop the coat rack, uncaring that it fell or that Betty immediately picked it up and dusted it off.

He'd overheard their conversation so clearly that Elspeth and Brendan might have been speaking to him. *Is she in love with him?*

Betty put his hat on the sideboard with great care, looking at him out of the corner of her eye. "I didn't mean to anger you, sir."

She was almost to the door when she turned and looked at him again. "Miss Grant said I should remember that it was Mrs. Gilly who was my employer. Begging your pardon, sir, but I don't think I'm the only one who's forgotten that." The door closed behind her.

He stared after her, thinking that he should dismiss her after all. But Mary liked her, and for that reason he hadn't replaced the young maid.

Now he didn't care. He looked around the foyer of the house he'd come to think of as his.

Mary couldn't do this to him. Not after all this time. Not when he'd been so patient, telling himself that all he had to do was wait. His fury was like molten gold, pouring into hidden depressions and fissures, revealing previously concealed imperfections.

Charles realized that he could hate Mary now.

Chapter 15

❦

Mary smiled at Hamish, the firelight adding a golden hue to her skin and a sparkle to her eyes.

Hamish continued to whittle a long branch. Earlier that afternoon, he'd soaked it in a bucket of well water until it was supple. He'd already stripped the bark from it, and was now sharpening the point.

"What's the stick for?" she asked.

"To spear the fish I caught this morning," he said. Reaching over, he threaded the stick through the brace of fish, and then placed them in the fire.

Her curiosity evidently piqued, she watched him with interest while he prepared their dinner.

"The kitchen fire is larger," she said.

He glanced at her. "You're right, but I like the tower. It's big enough for our needs."

"Are you sure I can't help?"

"It's only fair that I do the cooking for one night, at

least. I didn't mean for you to wait on me like a servant, Mary. Consider it a reward for doing the laundry."

"But you lit the fire, carried the kettle, and emptied the buckets." The look in her eyes dared him to argue with her.

His smile was a gentle acknowledgment of her words.

"You never told me you knew how to cook."

"There have been many times in my life when I've had to eat," he said with a smile, "and there hasn't been a cook around to make me a meal. My mother wanted all of us to be self-sufficient, so she taught us enough of the rudiments that we'd never starve."

"How many MacRaes are there?" she asked.

"There are five brothers in all."

"Are any of them like you?"

He smiled at the thought of any of his brothers being compared to another. "We're all ourselves. My brother Alisdair is the oldest, and then James. Then me, followed by Brendan."

"Who's the youngest?"

"Douglas."

"I know Alisdair and Iseabal," she said, surprising him. "Gordon did several commissions for them in the last five years. But I've never met James."

"He doesn't live at Gilmuir," Hamish said. "Instead, he's chosen a little village called Ayleshire to make his home. He's become a farmer, something that surprises all of us."

"And Douglas?"

"Douglas was in school in France. Brendan told me that our father called him home. Douglas had evidently become fascinated with Paris, but my parents deemed it too unsafe with the political climate."

She nodded. "The demand for national elections for

the Estates-General," she said, startling him with her knowledge.

"You shouldn't look so surprised, Hamish."

"I don't know many women who are so conversant with political unrest."

"Then you'll have to expand your circle of female acquaintances," she said. "There are many of us interested in what's happening on the continent, for a variety of reasons. Not the least of which is the price of gold."

He grinned at her, pleased with this sign of her practicality. It wasn't the romance of rebellion that interested Mary as much as the commerce of it. In that, she was a woman after his own heart. The events of the day weighed heavily on a sea captain's mind. It became increasingly difficult to make a living trading between countries if they were forever at war. Neutral ships were often trapped in the middle of quarrelling nations.

"How long has it been since you've seen your family?"

"Years," he said. Talking about his family brought them vividly to mind. He'd not, in all the time in India, missed them as much as he did right at this moment. He wondered why that was, and then glanced at Mary again, thinking that she had something to do with it.

In India, he'd tried not to hate his imprisonment or his captors. He couldn't afford to be angry because any strong emotion stripped him of the energy he needed to live. After a while, he found himself almost adrift in nothingness, a kind of fog that was, perhaps, one of the reasons he'd survived.

With Mary's arrival, however, the numbness had begun to wear off. He'd begun to feel every emotion, those he'd expected and even a few that surprised him.

He turned the fish over, concentrating on his task.

"What is it, Hamish?" She stood and walked toward him.

He knew she was near the instant before she put her hand on his shoulder, being attuned to her in a way that he had never before been with anyone.

"Sometimes," she said softly, "you simply go away. Your eyes get a faraway cast to them, and I know you're thinking of India. One day, the memories will cease, and you'll only think back on that time with pride."

"Pride?" Amusement raced through him at her words. "What do I have to be proud of?"

"Surviving."

"I traded too much for it," he said. "I've given up parts of my soul in order to keep my body alive."

She dropped to his side on her knees, her hands on his arm.

"You mustn't say that, Hamish."

The look on her face was one of stricken horror, and he realized that she didn't hear the hints in his voice, had heard only the resignation in his tone. He hadn't truly wished to die. If he had, he wouldn't have done what he did.

He turned and grabbed a platter, putting the fish on it before setting it on the table. Then he stood and pulled her into his embrace, feeling her breath against his bare throat.

"Shall we make an agreement between us?" he said. "That we never talk of India again? It will be as if it never happened. Let's just say I was on an extended voyage."

"And the marks on your body were made by Chinese concubines," she said. He felt her smile against his skin and laughed.

"What would you know about Chinese concubines?"

"I have ears," she said, pulling back and smiling at him. "Inverness has its share of travelers."

"One of your patients?"

She raised one eyebrow at him. "I can assure you that all of my patients are proper citizens of Inverness." She looked away and then back at him, her cheeks deepening in color. "Not that you aren't as well, Hamish."

He grinned at her. "I think we can agree that I'm not."

"But, then, neither am I."

He wanted to ask her why she'd stayed with him. Lust had been at the base of his request. He'd wanted her to remain because he was hungry for a woman. He hadn't expected to like her, to be able to laugh with her. Nor had he known any woman quite like her, a confession that he didn't make aloud.

He bent and kissed her lightly.

"Have you always acted with scrupulous care and decency, Mary?" he asked, setting aside caution. "Is there nothing you've done which shames you?"

She looked at him and smiled. A dangerous woman, one of grace, charm, and infinite allure, someone who made him wish that he could alter his past. "Of course I have. I'm no saint. These days should have taught you that much."

"Have you ever committed an act that sickens you?"

She shook her head slowly from side to side. But he noticed that she didn't recoil from the question. He shouldn't test her. He'd asked her to stay because he'd wanted the comfort of her body. Yet now he discovered he wanted the absolution of her spirit, or at least for her to understand why he'd acted the way he had.

He'd known that it was unlikely that anyone would ever

truly comprehend what he'd done. Perhaps that's why he'd taken himself off from other people, isolating himself like a leper. In a sense, he felt diseased. How he craved three simple words: *You are forgiven*.

Absolution might never come to him.

"We should eat," he said, drawing back, turning to pull out a chair for her.

"It looks delicious," she said, glancing at him curiously but not questioning his sudden foul mood.

"It will do," he responded, hearing the curtness of his own reply and not ameliorating it. Anger suddenly suffused him, an emotion of protection. Over the past months, he'd grown increasingly self-reliant, a creature that lived within its habitat and needed only itself to survive. But he discovered that he needed her, and that realization didn't sit well at all.

She said nothing, watching his face with a curiously guarded expression. As if she knew that his anger wasn't directed inward, as it should have been, but at her. He was enraged by every decent individual he knew, even the members of his family. His brothers would have died rather than do what he did in the desert. Each of them would have clung to his principles, his honor, and his decency.

Instead, Hamish had chosen life, trading any hope of his peace of mind or a clear conscience for it. He'd wanted to breathe, to feel his heart beat, to know that years stretched out before him in some quasi-guaranteed span. He'd wanted to plan for his future, to father a child, feel himself age. He had wanted to see the faces of those beloved to him, to count the sunsets, to hunt once again, simple wishes that had kept him going even when it would have been easier to quit. Too many times he'd wanted to simply lie down in the sand and let the sun scorch him to death. But he'd carried on, one plodding foot after another.

With all the memories still left to him, and even with this enduring legacy of guilt, he knew he'd make the same choice again.

Suddenly, he didn't want to eat or talk. He wanted forgetfulness, the kind he could find only in the pleasure of Mary's abandon. His conscience would be silenced only when he was kissing her. He reached for her without apology, needing her in a way that was suddenly desperate and selfish.

She came, hands outstretched, resting on his shoulders, her smile understanding and so softly serene that it was almost his undoing.

He nearly told her then, his face pressed against the swell of her bodice, his eyes closed, and his hand against her back to keep her there, pinioned against him. He almost confessed as he had not to Brendan or to any of those who'd treated him, burned and incoherent from exposure. Only God knew, and He was not speaking, either to Hamish or to the world. The secret was, unbearably, his and his alone.

He sat and abruptly pulled her to him, reaching up beneath her skirt. A instant later, an eternity, he freed his erection and buried himself in her. He closed his eyes as she sank down on him, as her soft, sweet lips pressed against his throat and she murmured something in his ear.

Only then did he realize that she wasn't quite ready for him. "Forgive me," he said roughly. "Forgive me." He pulled out of her, gritting his teeth and summoning the will from some far off place where he'd stored it.

"Did I hurt you?" he whispered, placing soft kisses across the edge of her jaw. "Please, tell me if I hurt you."

He was nearly desperate with desire. Now panic blurred it, the confusion of his mind transferring to his body. His hand fumbled at her laces as he wondered when he'd lost sensation in his fingertips, or when they'd become so clumsy. Once again he cursed the fact that his left arm was useless. Suddenly, it enraged him that he couldn't be articulate and whole, instead of suffused with guilt and teetering on the edge of frenzy.

He wanted, suddenly, to offer her Hamish MacRae as he'd been before India, whole and confident. He was not quite ready, for all his surface acceptance, to embrace the man he was. This man was too scarred, had too many sins, had too many regrets, and was beset by too many demons.

He unfastened her bodice, finally, wanting to touch her skin with a feverishness he had never before felt. Even at his most frantic, he'd never felt this clawing need. He'd always felt that with her he could find peace, a respite from the voices, faint but insistent, of his conscience. Now, however, she was the source of his desperation.

"Forgive me." He cupped a breast in his hand and kissed it gently. "Forgive me," he murmured again, his lips on her collarbone, trailing a penitent's path between her breasts.

She placed both her hands on either side of his face, kissed his lips, then his cheeks, his chin. "It's all right, Hamish." Soft words that didn't free him from his regret.

He slowed himself, taking deep breaths and inhaling the scent of her. Something that smelled of camphor and the laundry soap she'd used earlier. Not provocative scents as much as ordinary ones. She was the one who'd altered them, changing them until they swirled around her in a bouquet of heady smells.

He wanted her naked, but there was no time. He cupped a breast and held it for his lips, his tongue teasing the tip of it before drawing it into his mouth and sucking. Her hand caressed his cheek, a sensuous and artless invitation to continue. Her other hand rested at the nape of his neck, her fingers trailing up and down softly.

She seemed so calm while he was delirious inside. Where was all his restraint now? Gone in the magic of Mary. He nuzzled at her other breast, all the while murmuring words that might have weakened him at another moment.

He must make her see that she was the last person in the world he would willingly harm. But he had, and he must make it up to her, even though she didn't speak a word of condemnation. As he reached up to pull her head down for a spiraling kiss, he prayed that she was as lost in the moment as he.

His fingers dug beneath layers of fabric that separated them, found her and teased her with his thumb.

He wanted her now, yet all the finesse that he'd once possessed as a lover deserted him. He was an untried youth once again, his fingers trembling on a woman's flesh. But he'd never before felt as he did it this moment.

He'd wept only a few times—as a boy. Impossibly, incredibly, horribly, Hamish felt as if he would weep now.

"Help me," he said, breathing against her throat.

Suddenly, her fingers were on him, and he was almost inarticulate with need.

"No, please," he said, and her fingers halted at the tip of his erection, yet he could feel fingers and thumb gently resting there as if to stroke him to bliss in the next second. He would erupt in her hands, the knife edge of pleasure so close now that it was not unlike pain.

She didn't move, and he was infinitely grateful. As if she read his mind, or divined his chaotic thoughts, she rose up, pressing her bare breasts against his face as she guided him into her.

A sound escaped him, a muted hosanna of gratitude as his eyes closed. A spearing bliss surged through him as Mary moved again, and he wanted to be over her, thrusting into her with the power of two arms supporting him.

He would hold himself at the entrance to her soft, heated sheath, poised there just for a moment until her head flung from side to side and she pleaded with him to continue. Only then would he enter her again. The man of that vision had more control and finesse.

Desire had become a maelstrom, the sensation centered where she enveloped him and drew him in and then lifted herself before plunging down. He had begun as the seducer and was now the beguiled. She led the pace and he only followed, grateful and humbled.

She stiffened in his arms, and once again, he wanted to say a prayer to the Almighty who made such things possible. Her release hadn't been due to any of his skill this time. It was a result of her wishes and his almost desperate wants. Because this was such an enchanted moment, created from fervent prayers, he followed an instant later, feeling such pleasure that he drew her head down for another kiss.

She laid her head on his shoulder, sighing against his throat, and he closed his eyes in muted wonder and thankfulness.

* * *

Elspeth knelt at her window, elbows on the sill, watching as the night lengthened. The moon was bright, casting bluish shadows on the buildings and the landscape. Her second-floor room looked out over Inverness, with a view of the river bridge in the distance. The water looked black and sparkling. The River Ness flowed out to the sea, where ships and sailors disappeared.

Not that far away was a town at the end of the promontory. Cormech, it was called, where oceangoing vessels berthed and huge cargoes were offloaded. She'd visited it once, years ago, with her parents and four of her six sisters in tow. The reason slipped her mind now, but it must have been something for her father's business, the only justification that could budge her father from Inverness.

She loved her home, never thinking that she might leave it. There were, after all, enough men in Inverness that she wouldn't have to go shopping for a husband. Her father's wealth guaranteed that she wouldn't be ignored.

Until this month, there had been only a few men who interested her. Though none of them had made her heart beat loudly or the breath falter in her chest. Nor had she acted the fool with them as she so easily did with Captain MacRae. Brendan.

For the first time, she began to understand Mary's craving for adventure. Yet she knew something that Mary had never discussed. It wasn't a change of scenery she wanted as much as the company of one man.

Was that why Mary remained at a lonely castle?

She'd not told her parents what she suspected, nor did she and Brendan discuss it again, but she often thought of Mary and her shocking behavior. Yet now, on this moonlit night, with Inverness sleeping outside her bedroom window, Elspeth could understand her friend only too well.

Every day she woke to wonder if this was the day she'd no longer see Brendan. Every day, when he appeared on their doorstep, she felt her whole body sigh in relief. Every morning, she dreaded hearing him say that he'd be leaving. Not yet, but soon.

What would she do then? How would she bear it?

"Please don't let him leave," she said, addressing the moon. The moon was silent, as was the world around her.

Sighing, she stood and went back to her bed, knowing that when she slept it would be to dream of Brendan.

Chapter 16

Mary was retrieving her medicine case from the chamber two floors below, and would join him shortly. Hamish propped open the door so that he'd know when she was on the staircase. He liked to stand on the landing as she came up the steps. He'd always engage her in conversation so that she'd forget about the height, directing her attention toward him and not the distance below her. Yet for all her fear, she didn't hesitate in joining him at the top of the tower.

More than three weeks had passed, and they'd existed in a timeless, shielded world of no interruptions. The only voices they heard belonged to the two of them, the only wishes they followed were theirs. Sometimes, he wondered if it was wise to be alone with Mary this long, to be immersed in her character. He grew to know her with each passing day, to note the habit she had of tapping her foot on the floor as she massaged his arm, as if she were keeping time to an inaudible tune. Sometimes, she surprised him with the wit of her response, or the knowledge she had of the world, for all that she'd never left Inverness.

He realized one morning that he'd been lured into her spell, and then smiled at himself. Witches, he suspected, were an invention of man to excuse his weakness around women.

She was bringing a sense of normalcy to his life, something that had been missing for too long. One day, as they were walking across the courtyard, she'd turned and glanced at him over her shoulder. He couldn't remember what she'd said, or why she was laughing, but he'd recall the sight of her until the moment he died. The sun was behind her, making a crown of gold light around her dark hair and bathing her face in shadow. Her lips were curved in a smile, her eyes sparkling with happiness.

Hamish realized that he'd be proud to introduce her to his brothers, knowing that she could be assimilated into his growing family without a ripple of discord. Her laughter would echo with those of his sisters-in-law, and he could almost envision standing with his brothers and watching the women, each of the MacRaes feeling a masculine pride.

Sometimes, when he awoke in the middle of the night, he wanted to wake her, to talk to her about his dream, or listen to her voice. Sometimes he'd be content simply to watch her sleep, feeling a warm protectiveness as he covered her in the blanket and worried about the chill.

During the day, if they chanced to be in different corners of the castle, he'd find excuses to share things with her. He'd show her the bird's nest that he'd seen balancing on the curtain wall or the sketch he'd made of a new hull design for a ship still in his mind. Once, they'd even shot at the pines with the cannon, Mary so excited when she'd actually hit something that she planted both hands on either side of his face and bussed him soundly. That response had led to other, equally effusive rewards.

He'd begun to listen to the sound of her voice. Not only her words, but also the resonance of her speech. When she spoke of Gordon, which was infrequently, her voice took on a sadness. When discussing her friends, he could almost hear her laughter, and when she teased him, seducing him with words, her voice sounded low and melodious.

Why, then, did he feel the stirrings of warning around her? Perhaps it was because she made him want to laugh. Too often in her company he found himself wishing to confide in her, to tell her of things he'd vowed never to speak aloud. Somehow, she'd burrowed past the barrier of his will with a gentle touch, a soft rejoinder, or the barest curve of her lips into a sweet and gentle smile.

He placed his hands on his cheeks, feeling the scars on either side of his face. Sometimes, his face twitched in remembered agony or his jaw ached from where the nails had been driven into the bone. Mary hadn't flinched from touching him, but had put her hands gently on his face, her thumbs brushing over the blackened marks.

She'd smiled when doing so, not in derision but in gentle comfort, as if she'd empathized or felt the pain. Even now, his face seemed to tingle where her fingers had rested. His back didn't ache as much, and even the tattoos on his body seemed oddly faded. But that could have been no more than wishful thinking. He would go to his grave with Shiva.

Yet he was beginning to sleep without nightmares. More than a few times, he'd awakened in the morning, blinking open his eyes to see Mary sleeping beside him, and realizing that she'd featured prominently in his dreams.

Gradually, he'd begun to anticipate the mornings, where once he'd craved the darkness because it so closely mirrored his state of mind. One day, perhaps, his mood might even replicate the daylight, and he'd be jocular and sunny.

Now he heard her footsteps on the stairs and went to the landing.

"You would think," she said, smiling up at him, "for as many times as I've made this journey, that I would become more comfortable with it."

"It hardly seems fair that you must tend to a hermit in a tower," he teased. "But this chamber is more pleasant than the others."

"And has a window to view the loch, and a cannon," she said, tapping the barrel of the weapon as she passed it on the landing.

"How are you?" he asked, even though it had been only an hour or so since he'd left her. He followed her into the room and closed the door behind them.

"Well. And you?" Her eyes scanned him as if to attest to his health. He'd left the window open and stood now in full sunlight.

"As well as when you saw me last." Better than he'd ever thought himself to be, but that was a comment he kept to himself.

"It's time to massage your arm."

"Again?"

"You promised. It's the only way you'll ever regain the use of it."

"You're very strict, Mary."

She smiled at him, but ignored his words. She placed

both hands on either side of his arm, her fingers stroking softly up and down. "Have you felt anything here?"

"Not yet, but my healer tells me that it's only a matter of time."

"She might be a bit optimistic."

"No doubt," he agreed. "But I have a tendency to believe her, nonetheless."

A flush suddenly appeared on her face. "Perhaps you're the one who trusts too easily, Hamish."

"Do you lie, Mary?"

"No, but I might hold out too much hope. As I recall, you warned me of doing that as well."

"I never expected a cure," he said, to ease her. "Will you think me less a man with one good arm?"

She looked surprised at the question, which was answer enough.

He reached out and drew her closer. Slowly, so that she could pull away if she wished. But she never did.

"Stay with me," he said abruptly, bluntly. "Don't go back to Inverness."

She looked shocked at his words. He wanted to tell her that he didn't mean it, of course, that he'd only been teasing. The end to this idyll must come sometime. He'd known that as well as she. But those were more words that didn't seem to be able to make it past his lips.

"For how long?" she said, her voice sounding tremulous and too faint to be hers.

"For as long as we both wish it," he said, an impulsive request and one that hinted at a future together.

She stepped away from him, deliberately distancing herself. "I cannot, Hamish. I've been foolish enough to remain here this long."

"Is that what you call it? Foolishness?" He waited for

her words, feeling a vulnerability unlike him. Even the Atavasi hadn't been able to make him feel this defenseless.

She didn't look at him. Instead, she closed one of the shutters, concentrating on the wood beneath her hands.

"Yes," she finally said, and he almost wished that she hadn't answered him at all. "What else would you call what I've done?" She glanced at him, the smile on her face containing little humor. "It's foolishness to remain here solely for the sake of pleasure."

He wanted to shake her. Or shout at her. But he shouldn't have been surprised at her words. Mary had always given him the truth, even when it was unpalatable.

"Was it only for pleasure?" What a fool he was to ask.

"I've never felt such delight, Hamish, nor wanted it more than with you."

He didn't say anything, stripped of a rejoinder by the directness of her words. It should have been enough, but oddly, it wasn't. He'd lived in silence for more than thirteen months. He'd not understood the language of his captors. Nor had the Atavasi bothered to attempt to communicate. He was told what to do and when at the point of a knife. He felt the same right now, as if he were being directed to the table with a sharp point at his spine.

She would never know it, but he'd opened his heart to her.

Suddenly, she was at his side, her hand on his arm.

"Stay with me," he said softly, pulling her to him. He breathed the words against her temple, into her hair, against the tender skin of her throat. Never before had he realized that he might need something so beyond his own capability to acquire it.

"I cannot, Hamish."

"Stay with me," he whispered once again.

This time, she didn't answer.

Alisdair MacRae circled the pedestal on which the bust rested. Without a doubt, it was a perfect likeness of him. Iseabal had worked diligently on it for months, followed by months more of polishing. Then she'd put it away, hiding it from his view until this very day.

She'd set it on a pedestal and had it placed at the very end of the newly restored corridor of their home, so that the sunlight struck it through the lacework of the curved bricks. It was the first thing that any visitor to Gilmuir would see.

The last five years had been devoted to the restoration of the castle, the ancestral fortress of the MacRaes. Only one solid wall of the ruin was left, now incorporated into what was the new clan hall. The color of the bricks was different, enough that even a casual visitor would note the great age of the old stone, and wonder at the structure that had stood there for four hundred years.

The undertaking had been a difficult one, and there were times when he and Iseabal had grown weary of the sound of chisels and hammers, if not the incessant dust. Through it all, however, they'd comforted themselves with notions of what Gilmuir would be like when it was completed.

Two years ago, the exterior had been finished, but it had taken an army of masons and other craftsmen to finish the interior to Alisdair's specifications.

"Your work is magnificent, of course," he said now. "But must I be here? It's all that anyone sees when entering Gilmuir."

Iseabal laughed gently. "As well they should, Alisdair. If it were not for you, Gilmuir would not be rebuilt at all."

He glanced over at her. "I think the stonemasons worked harder for you than they did for me."

Tilting his head back, he stared up at the broad beamed ceilings. The roof had been finished over two years ago, but he was still not used to the sight of it. For decades, Gilmuir had sat abandoned and neglected, open to the elements. Now, the inside walls were painted a pale yellow, the embrasures finished in blue with designs festooning the sides of the arches.

What he lacked was some of the treasures of the MacRaes, and he'd already sent word to Nova Scotia. By return ship, he expected to receive the pipes from his great uncle, and a few broadswords and claymores that had not been lost to the centuries. Whatever his clan could give up, he would gratefully mount on the new walls of Gilmuir.

A woman in the village was crafting a pennant based on a design he'd heard about in his childhood. Iseabal had given some thought to their own flag that would fly above Gilmuir. However, his wife's greatest talent was in creating masterpieces from stone, and never more so than his own face staring back at him in ebony marble.

"I had hoped you would have forgotten about it," he said honestly.

Again, she laughed. "You knew I would not. It's my best work."

"Perhaps I should be grateful you didn't wish to carve me whole and naked."

She smiled at him, and it seemed to him that it was a mischievous look she gave him. A year ago, they'd traveled to England, to oversee some of the properties he'd inherited. They'd remained, as they did when visiting

England, at Sherbourne Hall, where there was an impressive statue of a near naked man. He'd always thought his wife took too intense an interest in the techniques employed in its creation. From time to time, he'd seen her glance at him as if wanting to replicate his body in stone.

"Don't even be thinking it, Iseabal MacRae," he said, shaking his head at her.

She only continued to smile at him, a look that summoned him to her side. He bent and kissed her lightly, then stared at the bust again.

"I look very imperious. Is that my normal expression?"

She tilted her head, surveying both the bust and him. "I think," she said, after considering the matter, "that you are a very imperious looking man. But then, you're an earl, and I suppose earls are."

She was the only one who teased him about his rank. Other people were either in awe of it or contemptuous of the fact that in addition to being a MacRae, a laird, and lord of Gilmuir, he was an English earl.

Next week, they would have the ceremony blessing Gilmuir. A priest was coming from France to do the honors in the old religion, and a few days later, a Presbyterian minister would perform his own blessing. All they needed now was a Saracen, a Jew, and a Buddhist, and Gilmuir would be blessed from all four corners of the earth.

"Do you think Brendan and Hamish will be here in time for this ceremony?"

He shook his head. A few weeks ago Brendan had sailed into Loch Euliss, anchoring his ship and disappearing as quickly, giving them a disjointed explanation of Hamish's illness. Only by talking to Brendan's crew had Alisdair learned of what had truly befallen his brother in the years since he'd seen him last. It wasn't a pleasant tale, and what irritated him even more was the fact that Brendan hadn't divulged a word of it.

"You could go after them," Iseabal said.

"Perhaps at another time I would have," Alisdair said. "Not now. They're beyond my control, and I doubt they'd listen to my counsel. Besides, my place is here, at Gilmuir."

"You're still angry," Iseabal said, extending an arm around his waist.

He placed his arm around her shoulders and drew her closer. "I am, it's true. I expected more, perhaps. I hadn't seen either of them for three years."

"At least Brendan left his ship here," she said. "You know you'll see him again."

"But it's Hamish I'm concerned about," Alisdair said. "From what I've learned, the past years haven't been easy for him."

"Then we'll simply have to wait for him to come to us. And if that doesn't work," Iseabal said, "we'll go after him."

Alisdair smiled down at his wife, thinking that she had truly become a MacRae in the years since they'd wed.

Sir John Pettigrew adjusted his stock in the mirror. The last fold in place, he let his fingers rest on his chest, his thumbs hooked into his vest. His hair was thinning on the top, but full and curling on the sides. His face was full, a crease forming from midpoint at his nose to travel down his cheek to burrow into a fleshy chin. Another line led from the corner of his mouth to curve in a disapproving comma on his flesh. They were marks of somberness, a serious demeanor of a man who wielded great influence and power.

He looked every inch the sheriff, Charles thought.

"I summoned you to learn of the truth of these rumors I've been hearing," Sir John said, staring at himself in the mirror and appearing to approve of his image. "But the person I truly wished to examine was Mrs. Gilly herself."

"She is out of Inverness at the moment," Charles said. Part of his plan had already succeeded. The citizens of Inverness were a garrulous lot, and rumors spread quickly from one interested person to another. Adding to the fever pitch of the stories being spread was the fact that it involved a young, attractive woman and a great deal of money, twin inducements to gossip.

"That's what I've heard," the sheriff said, frowning. "What do you know of Gordon Gilly's death?"

"I believe that Mrs. Gilly is troubled," Charles said, lowering his voice as if he were reluctant to admit the truth. "At night, when she believes herself alone, I've heard her talking to her dead husband as if he's still in the room with her." The best lie was one made up of snippets of the truth. He'd often heard Mary converse with Gordon as if he were sitting in the chair in the corner.

"What does she say to him?"

"She begs him not to haunt her." He bent his head, staring at his interlaced fingers.

"The man has been dead more than a year. It concerns me that these stories are just now beginning to surface." Sir John seated himself at his desk and peered at Charles.

Charles sat up straighter in his chair. "Doesn't truth always have a way of surfacing, Sir John?"

"It would do no harm to investigate this matter," Sir John stated. "A woman cannot be allowed to get away with murder. Not even one whose conscience so obviously troubles her. More and more of the miscreants brought to my court are female. I'm not inclined to pity them for their sex. Even if a woman claims her belly, asking for a reprieve because she's pregnant, I ignore her plea and sentence her to the punishment befitting her crime."

He stood, surveying Charles. "How am I to keep Inverness safe otherwise?" Sir John reached behind him and jerked on a bell pull. "Where is she now? I'll send my men to detain her."

"Do you believe it important enough to seek her out?"

Sir John frowned at him. "If she's committed murder, then she should be punished for it. Surely you agree?"

"Of course," Charles said, standing and bowing slightly, and trying not to reveal how pleased he was at the sheriff's decision. Mary would be returned to Inverness in disgrace.

Then he would allow her to choose her fate.

Chapter 17

Mary came into the courtyard, looking for Hamish, but he was gone. For a moment, she thought he might have gone fishing again, but a quick, cursory glance around the courtyard showed her that was unlikely. One of the horses was missing from the lean-to that served as their stable. He'd gone hunting as he'd promised the night before.

Their provisions were dwindling. Soon they would have to go into Inverness, and she would no longer have an excuse to stay. Her mind slid from that thought, but the abrupt regret she felt made her realize the depth of her jeopardy. The longer she remained at Castle Gloom, the greater the grief she'd feel when she left. Giving up Hamish would be more of a loss than she'd initially imagined.

Dear, brave Mary Gilly. The words floated in the air, a reminder of all the times the matrons of Inverness had looked on her with pity. She wasn't the only woman to be married to a man of advanced years, but she'd been treated as if her circumstances were different. When Gordon had died, it was the same, kind looks sent in her direction and whispers following.

She wanted to be envied for her happiness, not pitied for her sorrow.

What would the good matrons of Inverness have to say to her now? She could only imagine. At least when she'd lost Gordon, her friends and acquaintances had looked on her with kindness. If she were sad from time to time, it was no less to be expected. No one would understand this grief. She could almost hear their words now. *It's what she deserves. Foolish woman. Didn't she think about what would happen?*

She had considered the cost, but the truth was that it hadn't mattered. She'd even considered the fact that she might have a child from this arrangement. Because of the risks, she'd begun using sponges soaked in vinegar after that first, and unexpected, coupling with Hamish. Nothing, however, was foolproof. A week from now she would know for certain. If she weren't with child, she'd leave Castle Gloom with all possible haste, return to her pious role of widow once again, and consider herself fortunate despite her foolishness.

And if she was? A fanciful notion, since she'd never had a child in ten years of marriage. A week's reprieve, then. Until that time she wouldn't share Hamish's bed. A helpless laugh escaped her at that foolish idea. She wanted him even now.

The castle felt so empty. A deserted structure made even more so by the absence of one man.

But he wasn't just any man. The longer she knew him, the more fascinated with him she became. All the warning bells that had pealed so ominously in her conscience had been muted by a stronger emotion. Not lust but something else entirely.

She'd gone from her parents' home to Gordon's. In the intervening years, her fondness for her husband had turned to love. At least she'd always thought so. But comparing that emotion against what she felt for Hamish MacRae was like comparing a gray, overcast sky to the sun.

Stay with me. A few days had passed since Hamish had made the suggestion, and he'd not mentioned it again. But she'd not been able to forget it.

Entering the kitchen, she stood, admiring the room. The place looked lived in, less orderly than when Hester had been in charge, but still a welcome place. All that was needed were a few pots of herbs on the windowsill, and perhaps a savory pie cooling on the table, and one or two children gamboling under foot. For a second, she could almost see them playing tag, being boisterous and in the way. Unbidden, she'd made herself part of the vision, as a mother of those children.

That scene brought her abruptly back to reality.

This interlude was only that, a time out of her life that she could recall with fondness and a smile. A secret that she would hold to herself, one that was hers alone. No one else would know that the oh-so-proper Mary Gilly had once been a wanton.

During these past weeks, she couldn't imagine leaving Castle Gloom, and consequently envisioned staying forever. Hamish's words didn't promise anything, just the same sort of impermanent arrangement they had now, living as children might in an abandoned fortress. She wanted to go home, yet she never wanted to leave him. She wanted propriety, but she wanted him.

Those wishes weren't compatible with each other.

She left the kitchen, walking back into the courtyard. The day was a sunny one, although the temperature had dropped in the past few days. She blew a breath and saw it smoke. Last night, she'd curled next to Hamish for warmth, and he'd laughed at the coldness of her feet, before getting up to light the brazier. When she'd awakened that morning, it had been to find him curled behind her, his front warming her back. She'd smiled in drowsy contemplation before going back to sleep.

She needed to leave. But how could she bear it?

Each night, they'd played a game of shatranj, the stakes more and more decadent. But there were times when the game ended in laughter, and the experiments did also. She'd never known delight so sharp that it had cascaded into joy. Nor had she thought that these days of abandon might give way to curiosity, and empathy, and feelings she'd never expected.

She'd learned of Hamish's childhood in Nova Scotia, of the good-natured rivalry among the five brothers. The year of his imprisonment was never discussed, but never forgotten. Every day she bathed his chest and back, applying a mixture of barley root and mustard to the deep scars.

They'd tortured his body, but they'd never degraded his spirit. When she'd said as much to him, he'd only smiled that half smile. "You wouldn't have thought so to see me during that year. I was little more than an animal."

She'd never known anyone who had been through what he'd had to endure. What would she have done, in his place? She wasn't entirely sure.

"You're amazingly brave," she'd said. He'd only focused on the game, giving her the impression that her words had embarrassed him. "Or are MacRaes always brave?" she asked, to lighten the moment.

He finally looked at her. "I had a remarkable will to live. It's elemental, and all creatures have it."

She didn't think it was that simple, but she'd not pressed the matter.

A noise at the land gate made her turn. She walked toward the opening with a smile on her face.

"Have you caught our dinner, then?" she asked. "Something easy to prepare, I hope."

To her surprise, it wasn't Hamish standing there, but two strangers. Her first thought was that these people were the actual owners of Castle Gloom, and they'd come to the castle demanding a reason for Mary and Hamish's trespass. Her second thought, following immediately on the heels of the first, was that they didn't belong there at all.

One of the men was short and stocky, with brown hair cropped so close that it made him look almost bald at first glance. The other man was of average height with a mane of black hair, cut in a bowl shape around his skull with bangs stopping just short of his eyebrows. Both were attired in dark-colored coats and breeches.

"Are you Mary Gilly?" the nearly bald man asked.

She frowned at him, surprised. "Why would you be wanting to know?" Pushing aside a growing sense of unease, she approached the men, both of whom were looking around them with interest.

"Are you alone here?"

She didn't answer them, instead broached a question of her own. "What do you want?"

"Are you Mary Gilly?" he asked again.

"I am," she said, pressing her clenched hands hard

against her midriff to still the quivering sensation in her stomach.

"We've come to arrest you, Mary Gilly," the bald man said. "For the murder of your husband."

When Hamish returned to the courtyard, he called out her name. Mary didn't respond; only silence answered him. He halted where he was and looked around him, all senses alert. He left his horse beside the well and went looking for her in the kitchen.

Mary, however, was nowhere to be found.

He strode through the remains of the castle, seeing where feminine touches had altered the old structure. It no longer seemed abandoned as much as waiting.

The dread he was feeling grew as he left the castle and crossed the courtyard. She had a habit of coming there in the morning, and sitting on the edge of the well. Sometimes, he watched her staring up at the sunrise as if she'd never seen it in Inverness. The sky over the loch exploded in color, streaks of yellow, pink, and blue, but in truth, it was no match for her loveliness.

Now, however, the well rim was empty, as was the courtyard. Only he and his horse occupied it, and Hamish could feel the silence fold in around him.

He headed for the tower, climbing the circular stairs, calling out her name. "Mary." The sound echoed up the steps, then faded to silence.

He entered his chamber, half expected to see her sitting on the bed teasing him with her smile.

"Did you miss me?" she'd say, and he'd want to shake her for worrying him. Instead, he'd kiss her soundly, a reward for being there.

She wasn't there, either.

He opened the window, feeling the bite of the winter wind off the loch. She wasn't in the castle. The place felt as empty as it had the day he'd left the longboat. He'd come here to live out his life, doing nothing to lengthen or shorten it himself. It was an agreement he'd made with God, a punishment he'd offered up for his sins.

Perhaps she'd gone out to gather leaves or herbs or roots for her medicines and gotten lost. Perhaps she'd injured herself and was waiting for him to come find her.

He retreated to the courtyard and mounted his horse again.

He looked for her until it became dark, and beyond. Calling out Mary's name, he rode in concentric circles away from the castle until he realized that she couldn't have walked that far. After dark, he exchanged his horse for Mary's. After hours of riding, he returned the horse to the castle, retracing his steps on foot. But she wasn't to be found. Dawn, when it came, found him bleary-eyed and tired, but determined to find her.

He mounted the stairs and entered the room she'd once called hers. It was only then that he realized her medicine chest was gone. She was never without her case. He recalled one time when she'd spread it open on the table, taking out each jar and holding it up to the light.

"What are you doing?"

"An inventory," she said. "It's not enough to heal; you must have the medicines with which to do so."

Curious, he'd come and watched her, picking up a few of the jars. "What's this?"

"Camphor oil," she said.

"You've a great many herbs," he said, noting the labels.

"The stock of any good healer." She held up a vial with a solid yellow substance inside. "Pork fat rendered with rosemary and distle weed. It's very soothing on a congested chest."

"You're missing a vial," he said, pointing to an empty opening.

She made a face. "It's my mercury distillation. I no longer use it," she said.

Glancing at him, she answered his unspoken question. "I have my doubts as to its efficacy. I gave it to Gordon when he was experiencing stomach pains, and I think it made his discomfort worse."

"You should talk to my older brother, Alisdair," he said. "He's been fascinated with Chinese medicines for years. In fact, Gilmuir has an apothecary of sorts, filled with all kinds of potions he's imported from China."

She looked entranced, as if he'd promised the jewels of the world to her.

"I've never known anyone who had such an interest," she admitted. "I've only studied Matthew Marshall," she said, handing him a dog-eared, much thumbed book.

He scanned it quickly, and then read the cover. *The Primitive Physick, a Practioner's Guide to Commonsense Medicine.*

"Although he's a minister, Mr. Marshall is very learned in medicine. I've found him a great source of advice."

After she'd taken her inventory, Mary had closed up her chest, rubbing the leather of the case with a clean cloth.

Now the case was gone, and her valise. He realized, finally, that she'd left him.

He hadn't wanted to be deviled by a healer from Inverness. Yet he had been, and equally so by the woman she'd revealed herself to be. Mary, whose laughter made him smile, and whose taunting words were the equal of his daring. He stood and left the room, closing the door firmly behind him. A moment later, he was in his lair, the home he'd made his for weeks before she'd entered his life.

The sun was coming up on the horizon, and it looked to be a changeling day. Toward the north, storm clouds announced that snow was coming.

He should rest, but he knew that despite the fact he'd spent the night searching for her, sleep would elude him. His nightmares would return. Or worse, dreams of her. He'd deliberately not thought of this moment, wishing it away rather than thinking of when she'd leave him.

Stay with me.

I cannot.

The sun's rays gleamed on the bronze form of Shiva dancing merrily within his crenelated circle. The statue was the embodiment of a tenuous belief that even good might come from bad circumstances. A lesson he'd learned not from his imprisonment, or the events afterward, but from his parents. They'd taught him that even despair and tragedy might eventually beget joy.

For most of his life, he'd believed in himself, had labored under the notion that anything he wanted could be had as a result of his efforts, timing, and perhaps luck. His family had shown him that survival was a matter of will, that he could, if he wished, surmount any difficulty. Yet his experiences in India had taught him that resolve was not enough. Pride, courage, endurance—none of these was enough. There were some circumstances he couldn't endure, just as there were some things he couldn't have.

Like Mary?

He grabbed the statue and flung it out the window, where it lay half submerged in the icy waters of the loch. There it would remain, he vowed, until hell itself claimed him.

He wasn't going to allow her to leave him. Not like this.
Not without a word spoken or an explanation proffered. If
she didn't want to remain with him, let her tell him to his
face. Let her try to walk away from what they shared. Let
her deny that it was important. Let her convince him that
she wouldn't miss it.

What if she wouldn't?

The thought sobered him. Perhaps what he'd thought
so unusual, so special, even rare, she considered commonplace. Had she experienced the same passion with her
aged husband?

*I have been known to scream, but only when I'm feeling
abandoned.*

He hated the dead Gordon Gilly, in all his aged splendor, hated the fact that he'd called Mary wife, that he was
uncomplicated and pure of thought and deed. A trades-
man, with no onerous sins plucking at his conscience like
the talons of a bird of prey. Not for him sleepless nights or
sweating nightmares. No, Gordon's only sin was to die
and leave behind a widow who genuinely mourned his
passing.

She must have gone back to Inverness, and without a
backward glance, no doubt. Had he bored her, or kept her
here so long that she sought an escape? He should thank
her for the kindness of her desertion. There would be no
scenes between them, no harsh words.

Except, of course, that this mute defection was unlike
her. He could conjure up a dozen instances when she'd
surprised him with her directness. He'd tested her with his
questions or his statements and she'd responded in kind, a
verbal daring. The Mary Gilly he knew would have come
to him and told him it was time.

"I'm leaving now, Hamish." He could almost hear her

words, spoken in her grave voice, a low, somber tone to match the seriousness of her speech.

"Must you?" He would be smiling, his attitude one of casual nonchalance, as if her departure mattered little.

"My life waits for me. It's time for me to leave."

"Are you certain there's something for you in Inverness, Mary?" Something more important than Castle Gloom, or the hermit who occupies it? Even in his imagination he came close to begging, and that would not do at all.

"There is my life," she would say, and he'd nod, carefully hiding any emotion from her.

"Very well," he'd respond, looking as if he were bored. "I promised I would take you back, and I will."

"There's no need."

But he would insist upon returning her to Inverness.

It made no sense. She would have come to him. There was only one thing to do, of course. He was going after her.

The coach that carried Mary back to Inverness wasn't luxurious. In fact, it was little more than a box on wheels. The journey was done in silence, her two jailers choosing not to speak other than a few softly voiced comments to each other. They'd searched the castle, taking her case, which now rested on the seat beside one of the men, and stuffing her clothing into her valise. She'd had no time to leave word for Hamish, and she hadn't told either man about him. The last thing she wanted was a confrontation between him and the men sent to arrest her.

"I'm not guilty," she said now, but neither of them looked at her. "Who has accused me?" Again, no answer.

She and Brendan had covered the distance between Inverness and Castle Gloom in a day. But then, they'd been traveling with a slower wagon. In a matter of hours, it seemed, they crossed the River Ness into Inverness.

A few minutes later, she was ushered into a building she knew well, but only from the outside. The jail was a red brick building set adjacent to the Sheriff's Court. Each man took an arm, and she was led through a series of hallways. They passed a dozen doors with small barred openings, slowing before one where a guard was seated at a small table.

"Is she the murderess?"

"The very one," the bald man said.

She remained silent as the guard opened the door, and the two of them followed her into the small room. The encroaching darkness dimmed the one barred window.

"Am I to be left here, then?"

Neither of them answered her.

"Until when? Can I not, at least, prove my innocence?"

"You'll come to trial eventually," the bald man said.

"When?"

"When the sheriff wishes, and not before."

They left her there, closing the door behind her.

Slowly, she looked around the room. In the past, she'd worked with the poor, visiting dwellings that seemed hardly able to act as shelter with their sagging roofs and dirt floors. But this place, although solidly built, offered less comfort than a rude cottage. The window had no shutters to block out the cold, and she could feel the chill of the stone floor seeping through the leather of her shoes. The only furnishing was a bucket, and it quite evidently served as a chamber pot.

She stood on tiptoe to look through the bars of the window at the view of a remarkably pretty courtyard.

"If it's the gallows you're looking for," a voice said,

"you'll not be finding them. Sir John doesn't believe in littering Scottish soil with corpses. Instead, he ships them off to other places to die. Or they perish at sea."

Mary turned to find a woman sitting almost at her feet, her back to the wall. She hadn't seen her in the shadows. Her clothes were wrinkled, the hem of her skirt edged with dirt, but otherwise, she was remarkably clean given the condition of their surroundings. Her brown hair was liberally sprinkled with gray and braided tightly. A dark crimson scarf covered half of the coronet of her hair and was tied at the nape of her neck. Her face, shadowed as it was, hinted at age, but her voice was that of a younger woman.

"I thought I was the only one here."

"Sir John rarely allows this cell to remain empty. What is your crime?"

Mary turned back to the window, wondering how to say the words. "They say I killed my husband," she said finally.

"Are they correct?"

She didn't turn, but addressed her remarks to the bars. They felt cold and rough to her hands. "I did not," she said firmly.

"Then I pity you doubly for your innocence. He will find you guilty despite your protestations. Our sheriff believes in rough justice."

"I'm not guilty," Mary said, feeling as if this experience was no more than a terrible dream, that the woman addressing her was a talking apparition whose tired-sounding voice foretold a terrible future.

"You don't have to be guilty to be punished in Sir John's court," the woman said. "If you have a brother or father, now is the time to solicit their aid on your behalf."

"I don't," Mary said faintly.

"Someone, then, who might speak a fair word for you?"

"What about you?" she asked, glancing over shoulder.

"If I had anyone I would not be sitting here, calmly waiting for my fate."

"What is to happen to you?"

"I'm to be transported. That is my sentence for stealing a few apples."

Mary had heard of Sir John, of course, but up until this moment had never considered that his form of justice might be wrong. For the most part, the good citizens of Inverness appreciated his strict sentences. He ensured that there was little crime in the city.

How could he believe that she'd murdered Gordon?

She'd expected to be judged for the sin she'd committed, for disregarding the rules of the society in which she'd lived, by spending delicious days with a man in a tower. She'd been willing to endure the censure, the talk, even criticism from those who'd once smiled on her in approval. However, she'd never thought to be accused of something as horrible as the death of her husband.

Ever since they'd taken her from Castle Gloom, she'd been afraid, but she'd been able to tamp it down, waiting for the moment when she could face her accuser.

Even that had been taken from her, and she'd never before been so alone or terrified.

Chapter 18

Hamish told himself that he was a fool, but censure didn't alter his course. Instead, he continued on toward Inverness, banishing his fatigue, intent on finding Mary.

If she was going to repudiate him, let it be to his face. Let her tell him exactly why she was leaving. Why? So that he might argue with her? Or attempt to change her mind? Perhaps. But at least he would know why she'd returned to Inverness without a word.

He might even kidnap her, take her back to Castle Gloom, and keep her a prisoner, as Brendan had once accused. He'd seduce her with pleasure until she'd never think of leaving him again.

The journey was surprisingly easy, the road one built by General Wade decades earlier. From time to time, he'd catch sight of an odd hamlet or village, but he skirted civilization, choosing instead to keep to the road.

The time reminded him of when he'd escaped from the

Atavasi. The last days, he'd been alone as well. His conscience had nagged at him so completely that it served as his companion. In the end, he'd pushed on toward the horizon, hoping that he'd find civilization. This journey was as filled with thoughts of his own culpability. He wondered what he'd done to cause Mary to leave him so precipitously.

Yesterday morning, he'd kissed her gently on the nose, almost changing his mind and joining her beneath the covers, rather than going hunting. But the larder was getting empty, and they needed fresh game.

He'd stood, realizing that if he'd retrieved the cot from the room below, he could lash it together with this one, thereby making the bed more spacious. The cannon had long since been moved to the landing, but he glanced around a room to see if there were other pieces of furniture that could be similarly disposed of to make room for a larger bed.

He'd begun to plan. Without being aware of it, the future had slipped into his mind.

He'd given some thought to the woman he'd eventually marry. She'd be as intelligent as Iseabal and as charming as Riona, thinking of his sisters-in-law. He'd never considered where she might live, what nationality she might be. Perhaps he'd thought of returning home to find his bride, selecting her from one of the many women who'd shared his childhood. He'd never thought that she might have loved before, or been a widow. That her nature would be one of stubbornness and pride, or that she might prove to be so fiercely independent.

Or that she might choose a life without him.

"My patients will be missing me," she'd said a few nights ago.

"They can wait," he'd said curtly.

"Can they? Perhaps I miss my friends as well."

He knew he was being arrogant, but he didn't care. He didn't like the idea of her choosing others over him. "Who?"

She'd only smiled at his churlishness. "There's Elspeth. I treat her father for his gout, and her mother for headaches. She's a good friend, and I've missed her. And there's Betty, my maid. She and Cook fuss if I'm not there."

Who did he expect she might enumerate? A suitor? A friend, someone she hadn't spoken of but would mention now? He'd not felt jealousy over a woman since . . . His thoughts ground to a halt. He couldn't remember ever feeling jealous before. In fact, he'd teased Alisdair one day, when one of the stonemasons at Gilmuir had regarded Iseabal with more favor than Alisdair thought proper.

"You look as if you'd like to throttle the man, Alisdair. All he's doing is smiling at your wife."

"Let him smile at some other woman," Alisdair had said. Hamish had shaken his head at his brother as Alisdair went to retrieve his wife, walking her away from the construction scene. He'd heard Iseabal laugh merrily, and seen Alisdair's thunderous look.

He wondered if he looked as foolish. After India, he simply didn't care what other people thought. With one exception, he thought now, guiding his horse around a fallen tree limb. He cared very much what Mary thought.

The sun was high in the sky by the time he entered Inverness. The city was larger than he remembered. Nor was he used to the noise of the wagons and the people in the street, a cacophony of sound that made him long for the serenity of his life at sea or his hermitage in Castle Gloom.

Hamish found the goldsmith's shop without much difficulty. The shop looked exceedingly prosperous, with several men milling in the front. He went to the rear, tethering the reins of his horse before knocking on the back door.

A short while later, he was greeted by a diminutive young girl wearing a smock of butternut yellow, her blond hair tucked into a black wool cap.

"Patrons are asked to use the front entrance, sir," she said, bobbing a little curtsy.

"I'm not a patron," he said. "I want to see Mrs. Gilly." He arranged his features in some sort of acceptable fashion. He wasn't, however, feeling especially amenable toward Mary at the moment.

"She isn't here," the young maid said politely. "She's been away from Inverness going on a month, sir."

"She's returned," he said curtly.

She looked surprised. "I'm sure you're mistaken, sir. She's not at home."

He studied her closely, trying to determine whether she lied. In the end, he believed her, not because of her youth or the fact that she looked guileless, but because of Mary. She wasn't the type of woman to hide behind her servants. Instead, she'd be just as apt to stand in the doorway, point a finger at him, and demand to know why he'd followed her to Inverness.

"She's off treating a patient, sir," the young maid offered in the silence. "She's a great healer, is Mrs. Gilly."

A shadow moved behind her, and then suddenly a man was there. Mary had never described him, but Hamish knew it was Charles. He was a short man with pale blue eyes. Hamish felt an instant and unreasonable antipathy.

"What do you want?"

"He's come to ask about Mrs. Gilly," Betty said.

Charles put his hand on the maid's shoulder and gave her a not too gentle shove. Hamish took a step forward, but before he could do anything, Betty had ducked beneath Charles's arm and disappeared from the doorway.

"Why would you be looking for her?" Charles said. "You don't look ill."

"The reason is none of your concern."

In his travels as the captain of his own ship, Hamish had had to learn to deal with men in diverse occupations and stations of life. He'd been surprised at the number of truly disagreeable people he'd encountered, but they'd been offset by genuinely pleasant individuals. As his experience had grown, he'd learned to restrain his comments, and guard his tongue. Now however, he realized that he'd evidently lost the patience for diplomacy.

"Where's Mary?" he asked again.

"She isn't here."

"Have you heard from her recently?"

Charles didn't answer.

Hamish stared at the apprentice, aware that he wasn't going to get any answers from the other man. The dislike he felt for the apprentice no doubt had its roots in jealousy. This was the man who'd shared so much of Mary's life, who had been there to offer comfort after Gordon's death.

"I'll be back tomorrow," he said.

"I doubt she'll be here," Charles said.

The thought occurred to him instantly. If Charles hadn't heard from Mary recently, he at least knew where she was. Hamish was certain of that.

"Tell her I'm here in Inverness."

"I don't even know who you are."

"Hamish MacRae."

The belligerent grin slipped from his mouth, and Charles's eyes blazed with a sudden fierce anger. The two of them stared at each other before Hamish turned, and walked back to his horse. He felt the other man's gaze on him, and had the distinct feeling that he'd just made an enemy. It was just as well; he didn't care for the apprentice, either.

He sought out an inn, finding the Rose and Crown along a cross street. His mind was fixed not on the accommodations he and the innkeeper arranged, but on one question.

Where was Mary?

He thanked the innkeeper, arranged for his horse to be tended, and went up to his room. Closing the door behind him, he tossed his valise onto the bed and went to the window overlooking the street.

If she'd planned to avoid him, she might not return to the goldsmith's shop. Then where would she go?

Elspeth heard the rumors first at the shop where she went to pick up a length of lace for her mother. Two women were talking, and she didn't want to eavesdrop on their conversation, but their voices weren't as muffled as they should have been.

"He's very strict, but fair, my husband says."

"As my Harold does. Because of him and other sheriffs like him, there's little crime in Inverness."

"But still, a woman of her reputation. Can it be true?"

"She's a wealthy widow now, isn't she?"

As Elspeth moved to one side of the room, they glanced at her, and moved away.

"Who are they talking about?" she asked the shop owner, and despite the fact that she'd known him for years, he looked at her as if she were a stranger.

"I've no idea," he said curtly.

Her errand done, she made her way to the market, but before she ever crossed the bridge, she overheard more troubling talk. "Wasting away, he was, and Gordon always such a vital man."

"But he was aged when he died, don't forget that."

"Who's to say it wasn't the effect of the poison?"

Inverness might be a bustling city, but at times it felt much smaller. Now it seemed as if everywhere she went she heard only talk, all of it about how, impossibly, Mary had poisoned her husband.

Horrified, Elspeth made her way to Mary's house. Her mother often said that some of the best news to be found in Inverness was not at the taverns, but at Gordon's shop. People had a tendency to congregate there, especially the wealthy and more prosperous citizens. Often, in the afternoon, there would be at least four or five gentlemen in the front of the store engaged in conversation. She doubted that their talk always centered on jewelry or the cost of gold.

The front door was closed and locked, and it was evident from the fact that there was no movement inside that Charles had closed the shop for the day. Undaunted, she went around to the back of the house.

"I told you she isn't here," he said, opening the door to her knock. "Forgive me, Miss Grant," he said an instant later. "I thought you were someone else."

He moved aside so that she could enter.

"Have you heard what they're saying about Mary?" she asked.

The foyer was decorated with French wallpaper in a narrow brown and beige stripe. The floors were always highly polished and the sideboards on either wall were dusted each day. Now, however, there was a general air of disuse. Dead flowers were standing stiffly in the crystal vase that Mary loved, and no one had thought to replenish them. The drapes at the window had not been opened, and no sunlight filtered into the foyer.

The room looked as cold and lifeless as Charles's smile.

Charles stood at the end of the hall as if to bar her from continuing farther into the house. From the look of the entranceway, Elspeth thought that was perhaps a good thing. She didn't want to see what he'd done to Mary's lovely home in her absence.

"Have you heard what they're saying about Mary?" she asked again. "It seems as if the entire city is talking about her and Gordon."

His expression didn't change, but she had the feeling that the news she conveyed wasn't a surprise to him.

Since Betty was nowhere about, and she was without a companion, being there was not a wise thing. She turned and would have left, but for Charles's hand clasped tightly on her shoulder. He spun her around so that she faced him again. Any comment that she would have made simply faded away at the expression on his face. She'd never seen him as enraged as he appeared now.

Up until Gordon's death, Charles had been little more than a shadow in the background of her life. She rarely had any dealings with him, and when Mary spoke of him, it was in an offhand, detached way. He'd only become more prominent since Gordon's death. Now, as he stood in front of her, in Mary's house, his lip curled in an expression of disdain, Elspeth realized how much she disliked him.

"She brought any trouble on herself."

"How can you say that? You know as well as I do that she loved Gordon. She would never have harmed him."

He didn't answer her.

Reaching behind her, she opened the door, turning to escape before he could grab her again. Once on the steps outside she rearranged her dress, looking back at the goldsmith's shop.

Something was terribly wrong, a feeling that only intensified as she stared at Mary's house. Determined to discover what it was, she made her way to the market.

Hamish consulted his pocket watch before deciding that there was enough left of the day to find where Elspeth Grant lived. An hour later, after having asked another person for directions, he found the place.

He stood in front of the house, a pleasant enough looking whitewashed dwelling. A series of windows faced the street, each equipped with flower boxes now empty for winter. A brisk wind swirled around the corner of the building as if in greeting.

Gripping the brass knocker mounted in the middle of the ebony door, he let it fall heavily.

The woman who answered the door a few minutes later was quite evidently not a maid. Her dress was in the style Mary had worn, the material as expensive. He'd transported silks halfway across the world; he could easily gauge their cost in a glance.

"My name is Hamish MacRae," he said, introducing himself.

"Brendan's brother?" she interjected, before he could finish.

He nodded.

She startled him by reaching out and gripping his sleeve and pulling him inside the house.

"I am Nan Grant, and Brendan has told me of you. But I'm surprised to see you here," she admitted. "Are you well enough to travel, then?" With a quick glance she surveyed him thoroughly, the way his mother or Mary would, seemingly to ascertain his health and his well-being.

"I am," he said, wondering exactly what Brendan had told her. Something to assuage her suspicions and guarantee Mary's reputation, no doubt. "I owe my good health to Mrs. Gilly," he said.

She smiled. "I owe my son Jack's as well to her. Did you know that she saved his life?"

Hamish nodded. Nan turned and walked through the hall, opening an interior door. She gestured to him. "Come in, Mr. MacRae, and welcome to our home."

The chamber he entered was a parlor whose walls were lined in a pale pink striped silk. A black iron mantel dominated a far wall, fronted by two settees, each upholstered in a green floral fabric and arranged so that they faced each other. Wealth was evident in the room, but comfort made it cozy. A needlework frame sat in front of one chair, and a pipe table adjacent to another. It looked to Hamish as if it was a chamber in which a family gathered, and often.

"Won't you sit?" she asked, taking a seat on the settee and looking at him expectantly.

"Thank you," he said, taking a place opposite her while she reached behind her to pull a bell rope.

"How is Mary?" she asked, that pleasant smile anchored in place. He didn't, however, miss the sharp look in her eye. Mrs. Grant was not to be fooled. He felt as if he trod atop the catacombs of Rome. One false step would send him tumbling into the depths below.

"I don't know," he said, deciding that honesty was the best approach.

She looked startled, but before she could speak, a young maid appeared in the doorway. Mrs. Grant directed her attention to her. "Bring us some tea, Bridget," she said. Turning to Hamish, she asked, "Would you like something to eat?"

Hamish shook his head.

"Bring some of Cook's cake anyway," she ordered. "Perhaps a few biscuits as well. Cook makes the most delectable shortbread," she added in an aside to Hamish.

The moment the maid left, she turned to him. "What do you mean, you don't know? Where is Mary?"

"Haven't you seen her lately?" he asked.

She shook her head.

"Has your daughter seen or talked to her recently?"

Mrs. Grant folded her hands, and leaned forward. "Why are you asking, Mr. MacRae?"

"Mary left a day ago. I thought she might have returned to Inverness."

"But she isn't here," she said. "Have you gone to her home?"

"Yes, but she isn't there, either," Hamish said.

Suddenly, she looked as worried as he felt.

"But that's not right," she said. "Have you talked to Charles? Has he heard from her?"

"I have, and he says not."

"Then where can she be?"

The door opened, and he heard Brendan's voice and that of an older man. Mrs. Grant stood, looking first toward him and then back at the door. A tall man with stooped shoulders entered, limping, followed by a boy and Brendan.

An instant after Brendan noticed him, his brother came forward, grinning at Hamish.

"What are you doing here, Hamish?" Brendan asked, clasping him on the arm. "Have you decided to leave your hermitage for good, then?"

"I might ask you the same, Brendan," Hamish said in a low tone. "I thought you were in a fever to get yourself back to Gilmuir and your ship."

"Go and ready yourself for luncheon," Mrs. Grant said to a young boy who entered the room. "Wash your hands well, Jack."

The boy nodded reluctantly, staring at Hamish as if he'd never seen a stranger in their parlor.

"My husband," she said, introducing Mr. Grant. Hamish stepped forward and greeted the other man. "Hamish MacRae, sir," he said.

Mr. Grant was a tall man with graying brown hair that ended in muttonchop sideburns. His face was pale, as if he'd spent his life inside a shadowed room, but his blue eyes were lively.

"Horace Grant, and I'm pleased to meet you, sir," he said, smiling easily at Hamish. He limped to the wing chair and placed his feet up on the ottoman. "You'll have to pardon my informality, sir, but we've just come from the distillery, and I've been on my feet for too long."

"As glad as I am to see you, Hamish," Brendan said, turning back to him, "I can't help but wonder why you're here."

"He's looking for Mary," Mrs. Grant interjected.

"She's not with you?" Brendan asked. His brother's

voice was carefully devoid of expression, but his eyes were concerned.

Hamish shook his head, repeating the facts he'd told Mrs. Grant.

"Where do you think she is?" Mr. Grant asked.

"I don't know," Hamish said. "My only alternative is to retrace her steps. Perhaps she decided to take a different road, or stopped to care for someone."

"Do you think that likely?" Brendan asked, looking doubtful.

"Anything is possible," Hamish said shortly. Especially since she'd left him. He hadn't expected that.

Mrs. Grant turned from the sideboard, where she'd poured three glasses. She passed Brendan and Hamish each a glass, and then frowned at her husband when he held his up to the light. His portion was half that of the others.

"I have a touch of gout," he explained, "and Mary and my wife think to make me well by refusing me one of life's pleasures."

"It's a very good whiskey," Hamish said, sipping from his drink.

"I was fortunate to inherit a prosperous distillery," Mr. Grant said, nodding his thanks.

"Which he has only made better," Mrs. Grant declared loyally. "There is no finer whiskey in Scotland than Black Wing."

"For all that I don't get to partake very often." Despite his words, Mr. Grant sent a fond smile toward his wife before addressing another remark to Hamish. "Have you talked with Charles?"

"I have. He says that he hasn't seen her."

"Do you think he was lying?" Hamish glanced at the

older man, who smiled. "Your expression is such that it makes me think you doubt his words."

"I'm not certain," Hamish said. He hesitated for a moment, and then spoke the rest of his thought. "I didn't like the man, and I think he knows more than he's telling."

Mr. Grant didn't appear discomfited by his honesty. He only smiled and continued to sip from his glass. "I must admit that the man disturbs me somewhat as well. He seems almost toadying in his behavior, but if you watch his eyes, you get a different feeling."

"Nor does her behavior sound like Mary," Mrs. Grant said. "Not at all. She wouldn't have people worry about her like this. She'd make certain we knew where she was."

He nodded, thinking the same. But had she, in an effort to escape him, put herself in jeopardy? Something was wrong, he was certain of it.

All three of them looked as worried as he felt.

"Did you speak with Betty?" Mrs. Grant asked.

"The maid? I did. She professed the same ignorance."

"Then I'm certain that's all she knows. Betty would find it very difficult to lie."

They heard the front door open, and Mrs. Grant stood. "That will be Mr. Marshall. Perhaps he will have some suggestions for our dilemma."

"Matthew Marshall?" Hamish asked.

She nodded. "Do you know of him?"

"Mary is very much taken with his teachings," Hamish said, remembering the dogeared book in her medicine chest.

"But of course she is. That's why we were so disappointed when she could not meet with him." Mrs. Grant stood and walked to the parlor door. "Do you think she returned to Inverness to see Mr. Marshall?"

"I don't know," Hamish said honestly. He was running out of places to look for Mary and ideas where next to go.

Mrs. Grant opened the door, greeting her visitor as he entered the room. Taking his hat and cloak, she waved him to the settee.

"Luncheon will be served in less than an hour, sir," she said, looking as anxious to please as Betty, the young maid, had been.

Mr. Marshall, a tall man dressed in severe black, nodded absently. "I hope that you've not gone to any trouble on my behalf, madam. I have simple needs."

She bustled around him, as Mr. Grant leaned across to Hamish. "He's been our guest for nearly a month now, and he says the same thing before every meal. It doesn't stop my wife from feeding him royally, or Mr. Marshall from partaking of our food as if he's starved himself for a fortnight."

The minister allowed Mrs. Grant to remove his coat and hang it on the coat rack beside the door. A moment later, he sat on the settee beside Brendan.

"I didn't know that you'd be staying in Inverness for so long," Hamish said, remembering the meeting Mary had given up in order to remain with him.

"Indeed, I did not plan to," Marshall said, smiling in an absentminded way. "But I've had the most wonderful luck with a Scottish inventor who's been working on advancements to my electrical machine."

Mr. Grant made a face and stood, murmuring some excuse. Mrs. Grant made to leave the room as well, giving Hamish the impression that the subject had been well discussed in the Grant household.

Just then the door opened once more, and a lovely young woman with large blue eyes and silvery blond hair entered.

"My daughter Elspeth," Mr. Grant said.

Brendan stood, the expectant expression on his face giving Hamish a hint as to why his brother was delaying his return to Gilmuir.

She halted at the sight of him. Hamish stood, bowed slightly.

"I'd like you to meet my brother, Elspeth," Brendan said. "Hamish is the patient Mary was treating."

She came forward to stand directly in front of Hamish.

"Have you seen Mary, Elspeth?" Brendan asked. "She seems to be missing."

"I know exactly where she is," she said, removing her bonnet. It was only then that Hamish realized Elspeth had been crying. As he watched, her eyes puddled with tears.

"She's in the jail, Mr. MacRae. She's been arrested. They say she murdered her husband."

Chapter 19

❦

The door opened so suddenly that it startled Mary. She turned to see Charles standing there, illuminated in the light from the guard's lantern. He was attired in his usual dark blue trousers and coat. The white stock at his neck was immaculate as usual, and the gold buttons on his cuffs were of his design.

He entered the cell and gestured behind him with one hand. Instead of closing the door, the guard simply walked away.

"Have you bribed him?" she asked.

"Sir John sent word that I was to be allowed to speak with you. The guard only realizes that I'm to be given my way."

She didn't feel a sense of camaraderie with her husband's apprentice. It had been a month since she'd seen him, and prior to that they had lived in the same house for eleven years. But the young man who faced her might as well be a stranger, his lean face set in solemn lines, his eyes narrowed as he looked at her.

"What have you come to say, Charles?"

"I'm to convince you to confess, no doubt." He came closer, near enough that if he reached out his hand, he would touch her. As a precaution, she took a step backward, and that gesture made a frozen mask of his face.

"Why would he think I'd do such a foolish thing?"

He shrugged. "I, for one, do not believe you could."

"You know as well as I that I did nothing to harm Gordon. I certainly didn't murder him."

He smiled, but the expression wasn't amused. "Perhaps I do. Or perhaps I have evidence that you are guilty of Gordon's death."

She placed her hand flat against her chest as if to calm her rapidly beating heart. "What do you mean?"

"I am prepared to testify against you, Mary. A sad duty, but one that I will force myself to perform. Or . . ."

She waited impatiently for him to complete his sentence.

"Or what?" she asked when it was obvious he wished to be coaxed.

"You'll marry me."

She had a sudden wish to laugh, but tamped it down. No man liked his declaration to be ridiculed. But how inappropriate of him to declare his intentions while she was standing shivering in a cell. And how wrong that he should even consider her.

"You were my husband's apprentice, Charles. He saw you as his son, and I came to view you as the same. What you're suggesting is wrong."

"There are no bonds of family between us, Mary, and only two years."

"But I never thought of you that way."

"You can come to accept me."

Now she did smile. "Is it me you want, Charles, or the fact that Gordon left me all his gold and silver? A rich widow is a better prize for a wife than a young dowered girl."

His eyes narrowed still further.

"You would rather go to the gallows than marry me?"

Aghast, she stared at him. "Are those my only choices?"

He tucked his hands into the greatcoat he wore and smiled thinly at her.

Before Castle Gloom, she might have been intimidated by how tall he suddenly seemed or the sudden unfriendly look on his face. But she had spent a month in the company of a man who had taught her the true meaning of courage.

Charles took one step closer until the toes of their shoes touched. His breath smelled of mint; he had recently shaved. A bridegroom come courting. Hadn't Hamish predicted this? His words came back to her now. *Perhaps he thinks of you differently.* How foolish she was not to have seen it earlier.

She tilted up her head and met his eyes unflinchingly. "Now is not the time for such a declaration," she said softly. "Nor are you the man."

"Then prepare to die, Mary," he said, his lips twisted in an oddly malevolent smile. "Because I, and I alone, can prove that you murdered Gordon."

"You know I didn't. Are you willing to lie to the magistrate?"

"It will not be a lie, Mary. I wouldn't be so foolish. I would only tell the truth, one that I might be convinced to forget if you gave me the right inducement."

"So my choice is to be you, Charles, or some evidence you think you have?"

Mary turned and walked to the window, staring out at the night.

She didn't like Charles, and it was a sudden and surprising revelation. She had tolerated him because of Gordon and Gordon's memory, feeling as if she'd owed her elderly husband a debt of gratitude. But she'd paid it back in full, had she not? The last few years had been nearly unbearable, but she had never uttered a word of complaint.

She was suddenly heartily tired of being a martyr.

Turning, she faced him. "Do what you will, Charles. I have nothing to fear from you. I did nothing wrong. I cared for Gordon as well as anyone could."

"Perhaps too much," he said cryptically.

She didn't ask him to explain his words. The silence stretched between them, awkward and uncomfortable.

"I came here to give you a choice, Mary. And you've made it. You'll soon learn what a disastrous mistake you've made. You would have been happy with me, happier than you ever were with Gordon."

She didn't tell him that she had had a month of happiness. Perhaps not enough to last her for the rest of her life, but enough to measure against his almost obscene proposition. She'd rather be Hamish MacRae's mistress than Charles's wife.

"Take your threats and leave, Charles," she told him, her voice as gentle as she could make it.

"They'll send you to Edinburgh," he said. "You'll die on the gallows, a murderess."

She wrapped her arms around herself and watched as he left the cell. The door clanked shut after him, leaving her in silence, alone except for the memory of that one word.

Murderess.

* * *

"The Scots are a fractious lot, Mr. MacRae. I discovered that in the past twenty years I've been coming here," Matthew Marshall said. "They'll believe what they want to believe when they wish to and not before. Nothing I or any other man can do can make them alter their minds. I doubt if Sir John is any different in that regard."

"I think," Hamish said tightly, "that you underestimate yourself."

He was pacing in the Grants' parlor, unable to sit still. Marshall had to agree to his request; otherwise, he'd no other way to get word to Mary.

At first, he hadn't believed Elspeth when she'd entered the parlor several days ago with word of Mary's arrest. However, her explanation had made a hideous situation real. She'd told of her own confrontation with Charles Talbot, and the feeling she'd had that something was desperately wrong.

"I left Mary's house determined to find out what I could. At the market, I stopped and asked someone, and they told me to read the notice myself."

"Notice?"

"On the door of the Sheriff's Court."

It wasn't until he'd read it himself that he'd begun to believe that Mary had actually been arrested. On a wall beside the entrance to the court was pinned a series of bulletins, all listing names and infractions ranging from vandalism to theft. At the bottom was a single notation. "Mary Gilly—Murder."

He was unable to get past the guard at the jail to see her. The one person who had the literal power of life and death over Mary was Sir John Pettigrew, and he wasn't disposed to grant any visitations.

It wasn't the first time that the MacRae name and fortune had been unsuccessful in solving a dilemma. In India, he'd initially hoped that the Atavasi were holding him for ransom. When it was evident that they cared nothing for his money, he'd been left with no hope for a quick solution to his capture, relying only on his wits to extricate him from the situation.

However, even his cunning couldn't get him past Sir John's door. He'd tried again today, just as he had the day before, and the day before that. Once again, he'd been denied a visit with Mary, and when he'd demanded to meet with the sheriff, the guard only shrugged and refused that as well.

"What do you mean, he won't see me?" Hamish said, staring at the man.

"If he doesn't wish to give you an audience, he's under no obligation to do so. Mrs. Gilly's hearing is scheduled and he'll be adjudicating it then, not before."

"When?" Hamish asked impatiently.

"I've no inkling of the magistrate's wishes, man. You'll know when the rest of us know, by a notice on the wall."

"I want to see her."

"That's not possible," the man said, smiling perfunctorily at Hamish. "The accused has no rights until the hearing. You can see her when she's sitting in the defendant's box." Without giving Hamish time to respond, he slammed the door in his face.

"I believe that Sir John would allow you to see her," Hamish said now to Matthew Marshall. "As a spiritual adviser, if nothing else."

"The Scottish church is a vibrant part of everyday life, Mr. MacRae. But it does not dictate the actions of its public officials. In fact, sometimes I am surprised that the

Scots are not barbarians all, even now. Besides, what could I possibly tell her?"

Marshall eyed at him blandly, but Hamish didn't miss the intelligence in the other man's eyes.

"You can tell her that she has friends who are concerned about her, that she shouldn't worry."

"I can, but I'm not entirely certain of the advisability of doing so. I believe that she has ample reason for worry, don't you?"

Unfortunately, Hamish did. He'd heard his own innkeeper discuss Mary as he'd passed through the taproom to his chamber.

"She was a pretty girl, and she's grown into a lovely woman," he'd said. "It made her marriage to Gordon all the more strange. Why would she have such an old man for a husband?"

"His money, of course," someone else had then said, laughing.

"Don't forget Charles," another voice offered. "She had the old man's money and the young man's affection."

Everywhere he went, Hamish heard the case being discussed. On his way to the Grants' home this afternoon, he'd passed a group of matrons excitedly talking about Mary.

"A wife should stay close to her husband's side, especially when he's ill."

"Well, she didn't, not even when he was wasting away. Gordon was always such a vital man."

"Do you think she killed him?" one woman said, her voice dropping to a whisper that still managed to be audible in the narrow streets.

"She's rich now, isn't she?"

"You have a great deal of fondness for her, do you

not?" Mr. Marshall asked, summoning Hamish back to the present.

He turned on his heel and looked at the man.

"Some might find it odd that a patient would be so devoted to a practitioner of the healing arts. You were her patient, were you not?"

"Is that important?"

"It may prove to be," Marshall said calmly. "Especially since the two of you were alone for some time."

How had the man discovered that? Had Brendan said something?

"You might consider whether your concern for Mrs. Gilly would be seen as wise at this moment. The very last thing she needs is to have more speculation attached to her name."

And the very last thing Hamish wanted was advice from Matthew Marshall, but he stifled that comment.

"Will you try to see her?" Hamish asked.

The other man stood finally. He regarded Hamish with an intense stare, and then nodded once. "I will, more for her sake than yours. But I would think about your intentions. What is it you want for Mrs. Gilly? Notoriety or safety?"

"Freedom," Hamish said curtly.

"Very well," Marshall responded. "I'll call upon Sir John in the morning. But do not expect him to agree."

Hamish thanked the other man and took his leave of the Grant home, bidding the family farewell. At the door, Brendan joined him. His brother had moved from his accommodations to the Rose and Crown a few days earlier. Together they walked back to the inn.

"What did you tell Marshall?" Hamish asked, willing himself to speak in a restrained tone of voice.

Brendan looked surprised. "About what?"

"About Mary being at Castle Gloom."

"Nothing." But he noted that Brendan didn't quite meet his eyes. "I might have said something to Elspeth," he admitted. "But to no one else."

Then she must have confided in the minister. It didn't seem to matter, despite Marshall's words. Being accused of murder was worse than being labeled a loose woman.

"Has Marshall agreed to call on Sir John?"

Hamish nodded. "Tomorrow."

Brendan glanced at him from time to time as they walked, as if he were garnering his courage for the question he finally asked. "You're acting as if she's more important to you than a simple companion, Hamish."

Hamish halted at the corner of the street, turned, and looked at Brendan. The lantern hanging outside the inn cast shadows around them, enough that he couldn't see his brother's expression.

When had his feelings turned from lust to something more? On the morning when he'd awakened and studied her in the faint light? She'd curled toward him for warmth, and he'd smiled at the effort she'd made to burrow beneath the covers. One moment she was a siren, the next an elf. She'd blinked open her eyes, and they'd looked at each other for a stretch of minutes, each moment softly punctuated by the pulse beat of his heart and his suddenly constricted breathing.

He'd known on that morning that he should send her away, but he hadn't banished her from his hermitage. Instead, he'd turned to her, and they'd spent hours loving each other. He'd pretended it was lust, but need had never before felt as tender.

Until he'd met Mary, he'd never truly wanted to know a

woman's mind, the strength of her character, the tone of
her spirit.

"She is," he said, answering Brendan's question.
"Much more important."

"Do you think she murdered her husband? Or would it
even matter to you if she did?" Brendan asked.

They crossed the street together, Hamish's mind circling around Brendan's questions. He recalled another
time with Mary. They'd spent the night in abandon, and
before he slept he reached to snuff out the flame, but she
restrained his hand.

"Could you leave the candle burning?"

"Are you afraid of the dark?" he'd teased, never thinking that she might answer in the affirmative.

"A little."

"Some people never outgrow their childish fears."

"I was never afraid of the dark as a child." She sat on
the edge of the bed, faintly lit by the lone candle. He'd
never noticed how beautiful the shape of a woman's back
could be until that moment. "It's only been since Gordon
died. Sometimes, I think if I turn quickly, I'll see him
standing there."

He'd placed his hand on her shoulder, a wordless gesture of comfort.

"Do you think that's the reason ghosts are rarely seen?"
she asked. "Because they know that the living would be
terrified? I wonder if they whisper among themselves
about rules against visitation. Such vigilance would explain why ministers speak of heaven with such fervor, and
yet there's little evidence of the soul's permanence."

"I've never lost anyone close to me," he said. "Other
than a great uncle as a child. But if I had, I would probably
want to see them, even in my mind's eye."

She shook her head vehemently from side to side. "I don't want to see Gordon. Not as he was toward the last. He was wasting away with that dreadful illness, and there was nothing I could do. When he died, he looked more skeleton than alive."

Had she given him something to make his death easier? Was a guilty conscience the reason she didn't want to see Gordon?

He would have known if she carried that sort of guilt. If nothing else, they would have recognized each other for the burden they shared.

"No, I wouldn't care," he answered honestly.

He was going to do everything he could to save a woman who might well be guilty of the deeds ascribed to her, because he knew something the sheriff and Brendan probably didn't. A good person could still perform a vile act.

Sir John Pettigrew did not appear to Matthew to be a man with whom one could reason. Or a man with any type of warmth in his heart, for that matter.

"You can have five minutes with her, no more, and that only because of your ministry, Mr. Marshall."

"I would need more time than that," Matthew said patiently, but the sheriff was not to be moved.

"No more. And I will not have you," the man continued, pointing one imperious finger at him, "bringing her foodstuffs or any other article from outside the prison walls."

"She has not yet been found guilty," he gently reminded the sheriff.

"I have no doubt that she will be," Sir John said, gazing at him with narrowed eyes. As if any compassion directed toward the prisoner was suspect.

"Very well, five minutes." There was, after all, no other choice. Either he capitulated or he would be forbidden to see Mary. Everyone else who'd petitioned the sheriff had been refused.

"I see myself as a fair man, Mr. Marshall, although I'm aware that others sometimes view me as unnecessarily harsh. What my critics do not realize is that I see criminals like rats entering a corn crib. If they are allowed to proliferate, the damage would be incalculable. By being severe with my punishment, I am guaranteeing safety for the greater population of Inverness."

Matthew couldn't think of a tactful rejoinder, so he remained silent.

"I'll have a man take you to her," the sheriff said.

"Thank you for your consideration."

Sir John nodded and remained seated as Matthew stood.

As he turned to leave, he dared to ask another question, one that had not yet been answered to anyone's satisfaction. "When will the hearing be held, Sir John?"

"Tomorrow," Sir John said, eyeing him impatiently. "I grow weary of petitions for visits from this woman's proponents. You, of all people, should be interested in what they say about her, Mr. Marshall. They extol her virtues as if she's a saint, and call Mary Gilly the Angel of Inverness."

"I myself have heard her addressed as such," Matthew said.

"It's a pity that heretics are not still burned."

Matthew had the distinct impression that Sir John would have liked to have been born a few hundred years earlier, so that he might have participated in such tribunals.

As he followed the guard through the labyrinth of corridors, Matthew realized that he couldn't fault the sheriff for the condition of his jail. It was clean and airy, and had none of the stench of places he'd seen in London. However, with the first snow having fallen a few nights ago, it felt colder inside the building than it did outside.

The guard who led him to Mrs. Gilly's cell looked to be warm enough, but he doubted the condition of the prisoners would be as comfortable. A thought struck him as they came to yet another hallway. There was little noise. The only sound was a metallic bang from time to time, or a whimper, but no conversation.

"Is this where the women are kept?"

"Sir John don't like many women in jail, sir. He prefers them to be shipped off as soon as their verdict is read."

"How many of them are pronounced innocent?"

The guard turned and looked at him, smiling crookedly. "All them's that's here are guilty, sir."

Matthew remained silent as the guard nodded to another man standing outside a door at the end of a corridor.

"A visitor for the woman. He's to be allowed five minutes, no more."

The second man nodded, fumbled with his key, and opened the door, standing aside.

Matthew thanked him and entered the room.

The room was bright with sunshine, but frigid. He bundled up his hands in his sleeves and wished he'd thought to bring his gloves. He would have given them to the woman he addressed now.

"Mrs. Gilly?"

She stepped forward, into a beam of light. Something about her instantly reminded Matthew of his wife, a younger Madeline before her frown was etched permanently between her eyebrows. Mrs. Gilly had obviously made some effort to remain clean and tidy, even in this barren place. She'd carefully braided her hair, but her clothing was wrinkled, and as he scanned the room, he realized, with some shock, that there was no place to sleep.

"Have you no blanket?" he asked. Her arms were folded around her midriff, less a stubborn stance than one designed to stave off the cold. Even from where he stood, he could feel the wintry wind coming in through the window.

He'd expected a much older woman, someone with less vulnerability in her eyes. Her head tilted to one side and she was so obviously attempting to recognize him that he hastened to introduce himself.

"We've never met, Mrs. Gilly," he said. "I'm Matthew Marshall."

Her face instantly changed, becoming even younger with delight. "Mr. Marshall. How pleased I am to meet you, sir. I've read your books from cover to cover. I consider you a great source of information about medicine and healing."

"I regret that we must meet under these conditions," he said. "I was greatly anticipating our talk."

She nodded, and he wondered if her smile would also remind him of Madeline's. There was little resemblance between the two women in actuality. Her hair was brown while Maddy's was lighter. Her eyes were brown as well, while his dear wife's were blue. What had recalled Madeline to mind? he wondered, and then realized what it was. She wore her hair in the same way, in a braid in a coronet, and her dress was likewise similar to what Maddy wore, a soft stripe with a contrasting colored scarf that crossed in front of the bodice.

"I will talk to Sir John about getting you a blanket," he

said, angered that the sheriff had provided nothing in the way of kindness to her.

"I would not be overly hopeful. Sir John does not seem to be responsive to my requests. I've petitioned him every day I've been here to know when I am to be tried, but I've heard nothing."

He had the information, but he wasn't entirely certain it was good news he brought her. "Your hearing begins in the morning, Mrs. Gilly."

She looked down at the floor, still hugging herself.

"There are a great many people who have rallied to your side, Mrs. Gilly. People who will do all that they can to ensure that you are proven innocent."

"That is very kind of them," she said. "But I don't know if it will be enough. The sheriff must be convinced."

What he'd seen of Sir John made him doubt the man would be easily persuaded of anyone's innocence.

"I must ask this question, and I pray that you will understand why. Is there any truth to the charges against you?"

"No," she said firmly. "Except, perhaps, for wishing Gordon free of agony. He was suffering so terribly toward the end. That's as close as I've ever come to wanting anyone dead."

He, too, had visited patients in extremis, and had known a fleeting hope that he might be able to do something to aid them. Occasionally, he'd prayed that a life might be ended quickly when it was all too evident that God had already chosen that path for the patient.

"I must keep this visit short, Mrs. Gilly, but I will return. I bring you several messages from people, and although I did not receive approval from Sir John to pass them to you, I can't think it that great a sin." He reached into his pocket and pulled out a sheaf of envelopes. "Perhaps you could destroy them after you've read them? Or hide them, at least."

She nodded again. "Thank you, Mr. Marshall." She smiled, and he halted, arrested in the act of placing the letters in her hand. He'd thought her young and unbearably fragile in this stark place, but he'd not realized until now that she was beautiful.

The guard peered in, and he quickly stood in front of her so that Mrs. Gilly could hide the letters from him.

"It's time, sir."

"I'm coming." He glanced at Mrs. Gilly. "Is there anything I can tell anyone for you?"

"Tell them to pray," she said softly.

Outside the Sheriff's Court, Hamish and the others waited for Marshall to emerge. Mr. Grant sat on one of the stone pediments that marked the boundaries of the square. His gout was troubling him, but it was a mark of his regard for Mary that he was nonetheless there. Brendan was smiling at something Elspeth was saying, the picture one of sweet courtship. Hamish realized that envy fueled his sudden, unexpected anger. Because of that, he looked away, his attention fixed on the door.

When it finally opened, Hamish strode toward Marshall. "What did he say?"

"I was allowed to see Mrs. Gilly."

"How is she?"

"As well as can be expected," Marshall said, adjusting his hat. "Given her conditions, that is. We must apply to Sir John for a blanket and a cot, however. And perhaps a candle or two."

"She's left in the dark? She hates the dark," Hamish said.

Marshall glanced at him. "The sooner she is cleared of the accusations against her, the sooner she will be freed of that place."

"She shouldn't be there at all," Hamish said tightly. He'd wanted to rescue her from the jail the moment he'd heard she'd been placed there, but the sheer number of guards proved that unwise.

"She won't be here long, if Sir John has his way," Mr. Grant said.

Hamish turned at the older man's words.

"The Sheriff's Court has jurisdiction over some crimes, but not murder. If there's enough evidence against Mary, Sir John will send her to be tried by the High Court of Justiciary in Edinburgh."

"When is this damnable hearing to take place?" Hamish asked.

"Tomorrow," Marshall said.

The five of them turned and began making their way back to the Grants' home.

"He can't believe that Mary actually killed Gordon?" Elspeth asked.

"I believe Sir John is intent upon seeing himself as the arbiter of justice in Inverness," Marshall said, seeming to choose his words carefully. "If there's a hint of murder, he will ferret out the truth, even if he must create it to satisfy himself."

"What evidence do they have against her?"

"I'm not entirely certain," Marshall admitted. "Sir John was not very forthcoming. But I imagine we'll discover that tomorrow."

"I'll not just sit by and let them lead her to the gallows," Hamish said, icy cold fear settling in the bottom of his stomach.

Elspeth turned and looked at him, her expression one of horror. Not one person spoke.

After Mr. Marshall left her, Mary returned to the corner Annie had once made hers. The older woman had been taken from the cell days earlier, leaving Mary alone. From time to time, an occasional female prisoner would be led into the cell, but she never stayed long. Mary had begun to keep track of the elapsed time by scratching a mark on the wall. By this method, she knew that four days had passed since she'd been taken from Castle Gloom.

What a silly name to call such an enchanted place. This was gloom, this horrid cell with its long shadows. She remembered thinking, once, that she should remain alone in the dark until she lost her antipathy for it. After all this time, she still hated the sunset and the promise of hours and hours of darkness.

Now, however, the sun gleamed brightly, almost warming the space.

She withdrew the packet of letters from below her scarf. The handwriting of the first one was unfamiliar to her. Bold strokes of black ink proclaimed her name. Mary. Just that, and it seemed as if she could almost hear his voice. Her heart pounding, she inserted her nail beneath the seal, and scanned the signature. Hamish.

He was here.

She held the letter to her chest, pressing both palms on it. How many times had she dreamed that he might come? A hundred? A thousand? Her thoughts had not gone further than that.

For an instant, she imagined what he might say. Perhaps he'd set to paper words he'd once spoken to her. *I would have you stay with me, for as long as you wish.* He'd asked nothing from her, but he'd promised little as well. She discovered that she wanted demands placed on her. Give me your heart, he might say, and she'd tell him that he'd had it for a very long time.

There were only three sentences in his letter, but they took up most of the page in his large handwriting.

Mary,

We will find a way to get you released. I tried to see you but was not allowed. My thoughts are with you, always.

Hamish

A simple letter, not revealing much to a casual reader, but she heard the words he hadn't written. He'd tried to see her. He'd come to Inverness in search of her, leaving his hermitage. Dear Hamish. Dearest Hamish. Dear Love. Her fingers pressed against the inked words as if she could feel him through the strokes of the quill.

One tear fell on the back of her hand, slid over her knuckles to wet the page, dampening his signature.

In all this time, she'd not cried, even being as afraid as she was. Tears would weaken her and give Sir John a victory over her before they ever met face-to-face.

How had Hamish borne his imprisonment? Hers had been only days, while his had been more than a year. Nor had she been tortured as he'd been. His words came back to her. *I found that I very much wanted to live.* However poor her conditions, they would never equal the deprivations he had endured.

She held grief at bay, pushing it from her behind a wall of tears. If she didn't cry, she wouldn't mourn. If she wept, everything would overwhelm her until there was nothing left of the Mary Gilly she'd always known.

She missed him. How could she not? What would the sheriff say to know that she, a proper widow, felt this loss so acutely? That she grieved not for her husband but for her lover?

Hamish. His name was an invocation, a whisper of yearning.

One by one, she opened the other letters, brushing her tears away as she read the words of support and encouragement from Elspeth and her family. Tucking the letters back into her bodice, she returned to her corner, sitting on the stone floor and wrapping her scarf around her in a futile attempt to get warm.

Her hearing was tomorrow. The truth would come out then, and she could go home. Please God, let her go home.

She laid her head against the wall and pretended she was at Castle Gloom again, standing in the tower room. Closing her eyes, she could almost feel Hamish's arms around her, his cheek against her temple, remembering one particular moment.

"What are you staring at so assiduously, Mary?"

"The horizon, the loch," she said.

"To what purpose? To mark the boundaries of the world or to extend them?"

"Simply to marvel that the water is so many different shades, Hamish. Green, to dark blue, to almost lavender."

"You've not seen the Mediterranean. Or the Caribbean.

Sometimes, it's like sailing over amethysts or sapphires, the water is so clear and perfectly colored."

"Do you miss the sea?"

He'd hesitated, and then answered. "I do. My older brothers have been able to give up their ships without a backward glance, but I find myself thinking of mine, instead. Or a ship I'd commission Alisdair to build for me."

"Perhaps one day you'll return to the sea." Strange, how those words had pained her.

"Perhaps," he'd said.

"How could they leave this place?" she'd asked, speaking of the former inhabitants of Castle Gloom. "How could they simply abandon its beauty?"

"Sometimes the most beautiful sites are the most inhospitable. It's a lonely place. Perhaps some who lived here died out, and the rest simply wanted the company of other people."

Mary blinked open her eyes, the image of Hamish, Castle Gloom, and the loch fading from her view.

She wanted to be anywhere but here, someplace safe, and warm with a fire and a view of the sea.

Chapter 20

The Sheriff's Court was held in a building that looked to predate Inverness itself. The walls, made of pink harl, were two feet thick, and the broad doors leading into the courtroom itself were ten feet high and thickly carved.

Hamish wondered if the structure had once been a church before Scotland's reformation. If so, then it was not a setting for Sir John's brand of justice. He had no liking for the sheriff, even though he'd never met the man. His actions alone dictated his character.

He and Brendan found seats beside Mr. Marshall in the first row. They'd come early, suspecting that the hearing would be well attended. Less than an hour later, the room was filled with spectators. The gallery, located above the main floor, and surrounding the chamber on three sides, was likewise fully occupied.

The space in front of him appeared almost like an empty stage waiting for a performance to begin. To the left was a high desk set up on a pedestal, no doubt so that

Sir John could look down on the accused and the audience. To the right was a paneled box five feet high and surrounding a chair on three sides. A guard moved to stand on either side of the box, making him certain that that was where Mary would sit. In the center, again on a pedestal, was a large chair with a high back upholstered in green leather. Here was where the witnesses would give their testimony, beneath the disapproving gaze of Sir John.

Because of the high ceilings, sound carried very well. Whispers, laughter, and joking remarks from the crowd behind him made it seem as if this were an occasion for merriment.

As if Marshall suspected his growing rage, the older man leaned over and whispered to him. "It's unlawful to print court proceedings. Therefore, anyone who truly wants to know what has occurred must attend. It's curiosity for them, Hamish, and nothing more personal."

He nodded, more to silence Marshall than in agreement. How could it not be personal? Sir John had set into motion actions that could end Mary's life.

He hadn't slept well the night before, his nightmares propelling him awake. He no longer dreamed of the desert. Now he saw the gallows, and Mary being led to them, a determined smile on her face.

The door to the left opened, and Sir John strode to his desk. At his entrance, the atmosphere in the court abruptly changed. As the sheriff frowned at the audience, speech subsided and laughter vanished.

He was dressed in severe black, not unlike Mr. Marshall. Whereas the minister's face always appeared genial, even when unsmiling, Sir John's expression could only be deemed somber below his wig of sausagelike white curls.

A moment ago, Hamish had wished an end to the levity in the room. Now, he wanted it back. The sheriff's expression banished any hope that this might be a formality, an excuse to find Mary innocent and thereby quell the rumors.

When they led her into the courtroom, an audible gasp emerged from the crowd. Brendan clamped his hand down on Hamish's shoulder, hard, to keep him in place.

"You cannot help her if you're thrown out of court," Brendan whispered to him.

"Look at what they've done to her."

Marshall looked at him in concern as Sir John frowned in their direction.

There were deep circles beneath Mary's eyes. Her lips were nearly bloodless in her pale face. She looked almost frail in appearance, and she'd lost weight since he'd seen her last.

She'd braided her hair, and the plaits were tucked into a bun at the nape of her neck. Her scarf was neatly arranged across her bodice, her hands pressed at her waist. A sound escaped him when he realized the pose was necessary because her wrists were bound. But he forced himself not to move, and a moment later shook off Brendan's hand.

A woman escorted Mary to the chair before stepping back and disappearing out of sight, leaving her to be guarded by the two men on either side of the box. Hardly necessary, Hamish thought, especially since she looked as if she might faint at any moment.

Sir John did not make an opening remark to the court. Instead, he called the first witness.

The man who took the witness chair was stocky, with a broad face; a direct, almost bulldoglike stare, and black hair that fell nearly to his eyes. He looked directly at the court rather than at Sir John.

"State your name and your relationship to the accused."

"My name is Archibald Smyth. I am the Sheriff Substitute of Inverness Shire. I know Mary Gilly as a prisoner that I procured from Castle Starn on the thirtieth of October of this year."

He pointed his finger toward Mary, and she stared back at him without flinching.

"Did you have any conversation with the accused?"

"I did," the man said, nodding. "She stated that she did not kill her husband, that she did not believe her husband had been murdered. That she did not, despite her skill as a healer, have any notion of why her husband died."

"Did she say anything else?"

"No, sir. But her statement was freely given and not coerced."

A moment later, the man stepped down.

The next witness stared hard at Mary before he sat. The look he continued to give her was filled with antipathy.

Before being prompted by Sir John, he began to speak. "My name is Hugh Grampian. I am a physician in Inverness. I knew the late Mr. Gordon Gilly for fully twenty years. He consulted me from time to time, but after his marriage eleven years ago, I'd not seen the man professionally for years. Three months prior to his death, he consulted me at my offices on James Street, on the condition that I not mention his visits to his wife."

Hamish glanced over at Mary, wondering if her stoic expression was helping or hurting with the sheriff. Sir John stared at her just as dispassionately, his expression impossible to decipher.

"It seems she was considered a healer, with an unwarranted reputation. She evidently could not see that her husband was ill. He complained of fever and nausea, mentioned that he had been purging. I took his complaint to be a difficulty in his bowels and prescribed a draught containing magnesia and soda. Two weeks later, he returned to see me, stating that the pain was getting worse in his stomach. I prescribed some powders containing rhubarb, soda, chalk, and mercury."

"Did he improve?"

"On the contrary. But he would only come to see me when his wife was away, treating patients I believe." He glanced out at the assembled crowd. "People shouldn't be foolish enough to ignore their physician's advice and then listen to anyone who will tell them what they wish to hear."

"Would you say that Mr. Gilly's condition grew worse?"

"Without a doubt," the doctor said. "He was growing frailer with each passing week. Over the course of our treatments, I noticed that he became more and more irritable. I would even venture to say that he was somewhat delusional. There were times in which he believed that I was his father, and then the son he never had. On one occasion, Mr. Gilly even commented that I had the whiskers of a neighbor's cat." At the audience's titters, the physician frowned. The sheriff cleared his throat and the sound subsided. "His gait grew so unstable," Dr. Grampian continued, "that it was difficult for him to leave his home. Finally, he grew so weak that he was restrained to his bed. When I last called upon him in August, he urged me to stay away, stating that he did not want his wife to be hurt by my presence."

He turned and looked at Mary again. "He seemed certain that anything I would do to assist him would be looked upon with disfavor by that woman."

Mary looked down at her folded hands, and it seemed to Hamish that she trembled under the regard of the physician.

"When did you last see Mr. Gilly?"

"On the morning of the twenty-third of September, I called upon Mr. Gilly, only to be informed that he was dead. I asked to see the body so that I could give any opinion as to the cause of death. Mrs. Gilly looked surprised that I would ask, stating that her husband died of old age, with complications, perhaps, of a stomach tumor.

"I told her at the time and I will tell you now that such diseases do not often happen in the way they did with Mr. Gilly. A healthy man is not normally struck down with pains in the stomach and bowels, nor does his mind disintegrate in the way Mr. Gilly's did without a reason."

"Then you were not able to examine Mr. Gilly after his death?"

"On the contrary, I presumed upon the apprentice, when Mrs. Gilly was otherwise occupied. The body was laid out on a bier in the dining room, already dressed in his grave clothes. The skin had a slightly jaundiced hue. I examined the body as well as I could and noted that over the region of the heart the sound seemed normal while over the liver the sound was dull.

"I left the house, conferred with some of my colleagues, then returned to the house in the afternoon. I requested from Mrs. Gilly permission to perform a postmortem on the body. She refused."

"She refused the post-mortem?"

"She did. I found it odd that a woman with such a reputation for being a healer would be so adamant about not wishing to learn more about her husband's death."

"But you did not press her on it?"

For the first time during his testimony the physician looked a little uncomfortable. "She was within her rights not to agree, of course," he said. But Sir John was not content with his answer.

"But you might have convinced her, had you tried to do so?"

"Perhaps," Dr. Grampian answered.

"Why didn't you?"

The doctor fingered his stock, adjusted the row of buttons on his waistcoat, toyed with the lace on his wrists. "You must understand, Sir John, that Mr. Gilly was an influential man. His death was a great loss to the citizens of Inverness."

Sir John sat back and surveyed the doctor with the first hint of disfavor. "And you did not wish to be linked to his death, Dr. Grampian?"

"He was not my patient when he expired."

"But he might have been considered so had you insisted upon a post-mortem?"

"He might have been," Dr. Grampian reluctantly admitted.

"And so, you simply guessed at the cause of his death?"

"Indeed not!" the doctor exclaimed, sitting erect in the witness chair. "It was mismanagement, of a surety. That woman, who calls herself a healer, is solely responsible."

"You do not believe Mrs. Gilly possesses any healing powers?"

"I believe that she's capable of reading books and parroting instructions, or that she could serve as a midwife. I do not think she has sufficient learning or training to be of true assistance. She seems to have adopted a unique way of treating people, which leads them to believe that she's giving them helpful advice. They would be better served," he said, looking out over the crowd, "to heed their physician's instructions."

"If you have so much antipathy for Mrs. Gilly, Dr. Grampian, why have you not come forward before now?" the sheriff asked.

The entire courtroom silenced to hear the doctor's answer.

The physician only stared at the magistrate, his features fixed in a stern look, one that might have precluded further questioning. But Sir John evidently feared no man.

"Is it because she treats the poor, Dr. Grampian, and offers no interference to your business?"

Dr. Grampian didn't answer. The words lingered in the air even as the physician was dismissed and Charles Talbot took his place in the witness chair.

"Please state your name and your relationship to the accused."

"My name is Charles Talbot, and I was the late Gordon Gilly's apprentice."

"For how long did you work in that capacity, Mr. Talbot?"

"For twelve years."

"So you came to be in his employ before his marriage to his wife, is that not correct?"

"It is, sir. I was in the household when Mrs. Gilly married her husband."

"Did you think it odd that he chose to marry a woman so much younger than himself?"

"I thought he was a fortunate man," Charles said. "Or maybe just a wealthy one."

Laughter erupted in the courtroom.

Sir John didn't look at the miscreants, simply addressed his comments to Charles.

"Are you aware that Mr. Gilly had the opportunity to consult a physician several months prior to his death?"

"Yes," Charles responded. "I was. He didn't actually tell me, but I had seen him taking a medicine twice a day. When I asked what it was, he admitted it was something that the physician had given him."

"Did you discuss his illness with Mr. Gilly?"

"I did not wish to ask any inopportune questions, sir. Mr. Gilly didn't have any use for illness, and disliked feeling bad. I believe that he subscribed to the same philosophy as his wife that the less said about something unpleasant, the better."

"But he continued to be treated by his wife?"

Charles nodded. "He was. We had a habit of sitting in the parlor after dinner, and it was then that Mrs. Gilly would give him the drink she prepared."

"And he took it with no reluctance?"

Charles seemed to hesitate. Sir John frowned at him, and he continued, looking reluctant. "He didn't want to drink the mixture some nights, but she insisted."

The crowd behind Hamish began to stir, individual voices that began as murmurs picking up and becoming words that he could discern only too well. The sentiment was turning against Mary. She sat immobile in her box, paying no attention to the audience in the courtroom, no expression on her face. Both Brendan and Marshall glanced at him, but Hamish didn't move.

"What did she do on those nights?"

Charles glanced quickly at Mary and then away, the impression that of a man who was forced by necessity to tell the truth, but who didn't wish to betray a woman.

Mary might have been carved from marble.

"She would plead with him to drink the medicine, saying that it was for his own good, that she wouldn't be able to sleep unless she knew he'd taken it. Sometimes, she'd weep."

Mary looked up, staring at Charles. Her gaze was intent, but not revealing. Hamish, however, had the impression that the young man lied.

"Did you ever see Mr. Gilly become ill after taking one of these potions?"

Charles murmured something, his head bent and his gaze on the floor. Hamish didn't believe the pose of reluctant accuser one moment.

"I cannot hear you, Mr. Talbot."

Charles raised his head and stared directly at the sheriff. "Yes," he said, loudly enough to be heard in the back of the courtroom. "He was ill almost every night after she gave him the drink."

The murmurs were growing louder. Sir John leveled a gaze on the assembled people in the chamber and the gallery until the voices once again subsided.

"What was in this potion she gave him?"

Charles shook his head. "She never told me, although I saw her mix it once. After Mr. Gilly's death, I began to investigate." He glanced at the sheriff, and Sir John nodded. "I found this in Mr. Gilly's room."

Withdrawing something from an inside vest pocket, he began to unwrap it from a linen handkerchief. Hamish could feel the tension in the room as people around him leaned forward to get a better look. When the unwrapping was complete, Charles held a small vial with a frosted glass top up to the light. Hamish had seen many similar ones in Mary's chest.

"This was one of the ingredients in the mixture she prepared."

"Can you identify the contents?"

"As you can see, sir, it's clearly labeled." He stood and walked the short distance to the sheriff's desk, reached up, and placed it in front of Sir John.

The sheriff peered at the container and read the label aloud. "Mercury."

For the first time, Mary's eyes met Hamish's before quickly sliding away. So, she'd known he was there all along. The look on her face was dispassionate now, but he'd seen her flinch as Charles gave his testimony.

The sheriff surprised him and the rest of the courtroom by recalling the physician.

"Is mercury used for the treatment of disease?" Sir John asked.

"Frequently it is, but only under the care of a trained physician. Mercury is efficacious for several diseases, some of which would not be wise to mention in mixed company, sir." He glanced at several of the women in the gallery. "However, it should be treated with caution."

"So it might it be possible to give a fatal dose to a patient?"

"Indeed it could."

Dead silence filled the room, and hundreds of pairs of eyes looked at Mary.

Next, Sir John called the young maid, Betty. She walked to the chair looking as if it were the gallows, instead. Her hands clutched a handkerchief with a punishing grip as she sat and looked at Sir John. She kept pressing her lips together and alternately licking them. When he asked her to identify herself, she jumped at the sound of his voice.

"My name is Betty Carmichael."

"State your relationship to the accused."

The young girl looked first at the sheriff and then at Mary. "I am maid to Mrs. Gilly, and to the late Gordon Gilly."

"You had occasion to tend to Mr. Gilly prior to his death, did you not?"

"Well, I do what I'm told, sir. If Mr. Gilly wanted a bowl of soup, I fetched it. Or if his linens needed changing, I did that, too." She bowed her head, and Hamish didn't doubt she would have made a small curtsy if she hadn't been seated in the chair.

"He was a very kind man, sir. He was forever saying thank you and please, and he never forgot the smallest kindness. He often gave me a few coins for the market, and told me to bring back a pretty ribbon for my hair or a sweetmeat for me and Cook to share."

"Have you ever seen him ingest any substance that would knowingly do him harm?"

Betty looked confused. "I'm not sure what you mean, sir. Mr. Gilly was very careful about what he ate. For the longest time, he had a problem with his bowels, and he couldn't eat more than a few oats in the morning or some toast in the afternoon."

"For how long was he ill?"

"Oh, I wouldn't say he was ill, sir. He was old."

Again, that hint of laughter, this time from the gallery.

"He was losing a lot of weight because of it," she said, her head bobbing up and down. "There were times he wouldn't eat anything at all but Mrs. Gilly's drink."

"She was the only one to feed him, then?"

"Not really, sir. It were a bunch of herbs all ground up with some ale to give it a taste. She would mix it up for him in the evening and he'd drink it."

The courtroom had grown hushed.

"For how long did she give him this potion?"

"Well, a few months, sir. But she was forever giving him tonics, at least while I was with them." She glanced over at Mary and smiled wanly.

"How long have you been with the accused?"

Betty looked at Mary again. "Nearly five years, sir. Since I was twelve. She took me home when my mother died. I learned my numbers from her, and how to read. She taught me how to be a maid so that I could always have a job."

"I only asked you how long you'd been with the accused, Miss Carmichael, not a description of each day that passed since you entered her employ." Sir John scowled at Betty, but she didn't wilt under his censure. Instead, she tilted her head back and looked up at him with a frown on her face. A chick facing down a hawk.

"Did he take the drink up until the night he died?"

"No, sir. He couldn't eat anything by then, or hardly drink anything at all."

Mary stared straight ahead, looking as if none of what was happening had anything to do with her. Hamish wondered if she were maintaining that aloof demeanor in order to endure what was happening to her. He'd looked the same, he was certain, as he was being tortured.

"Did you ever see him become ill after he drank this potion?"

The young girl shook her head vehemently from side to side. "No sir, if anything he seemed better after he drank it. But like I said, he didn't have any for nearly a week before he died."

She looked over at Mary again. "Sometimes, I'd see Mrs. Gilly at his bedside at night. I'd look in on her just before I retired to see if she needed anything, and she'd be sitting with him. Toward the end, the poor man was losing his mind. He was raving, thinking he saw things like animals and things. He said that he had insects crawling all over his body and scratching at his eyes. Then he started screaming that he was on fire. Cook and I used to sit in the kitchen and look at each other and pray that the poor man would just die."

"How, exactly, did he die?"

"He just went to sleep, sir. A blessed release, I call it. He just went to sleep, and he never woke up again."

"What was Mrs. Gilly's reaction to his death?"

"I found her, sir, on the floor, next to the bed. She had her face against the sheet, her cheek next to Mr. Gilly's hand. There were tears all over her face, like she had been crying for hours."

Hamish glanced at Mary, thinking that there were secrets between them even now. Even though she'd spoken of Gordon, she'd never alluded to how he'd died or what she'd gone through in those last days. Mary was not a woman who sought pity, but he couldn't help but wonder where she'd found her strength.

"How much longer will this take?" Hamish asked, but neither Brendan nor Marshall answered him.

"I beg leave to address the court."

Hamish turned to see Marshall standing.

The minister was dressed in his customary black suit and white stock. His shoulder length silvery gray hair was brushed back from his forehead and tucked behind his ears. His face was serene, as it always appeared, but his dark eyes were filled with resolve. In his left hand he clutched the Bible; his right was fisted and resting on his hip as he stared at Sir John. It was, Hamish realized, a duel of wills between the sheriff and the church. In this case, the church won.

Sir John nodded, and Marshall came forward. Betty left the witness chair, and Marshall took her place, resting the Bible on his lap as he sat.

"I come to give my evidence not as a minister, but as a man who's studied medicine for some thirty years. I've detailed my experience in various books on the subject."

"We would certainly welcome any expertise, Mr. Marshall," Sir John said, his expression belying his words.

"Mercury poisoning is a terrible way to die, but it's my opinion that the entire vial should not have been enough to cause Mr. Gilly's death." He sent a sharp look to the container still resting on the Sheriff's desk.

"By itself, perhaps. But have you considered that the physician administered mercury as well?"

Once again, the courtroom was solemnly quiet as Marshall and Sir John looked at each other. Finally, the magistrate looked into the audience, seeking out the physician.

"Dr. Grampian, how much mercury did you give Mr. Gilly?"

The physician stood. "A scant spoonful in a mixture of other ingredients."

"Administered how often?"

Dr. Grampian hesitated for a moment. "Every day for a matter of weeks."

The sheriff turned to Marshall once again. "Coupled with the dosage Mrs. Gilly administered, would that have been enough to kill?"

Marshall nodded, evidently unhappy to be forced to concede the point.

Hamish was growing increasingly concerned about

Mary. He'd thought her pale before, but now she was almost ashen. She stared at Mr. Marshall with wide eyes as if she'd received a shock.

"So, Mrs. Gilly could have poisoned her husband without knowing what she was doing?"

Marshall once again nodded.

"But because she labels herself a healer, it is my belief she should have known," Sir John said, staring at Mary.

The sheriff didn't seem to be willing to consider Mary innocent. Nor did Hamish believe that the physician would be called to the witness stand again to account for his actions.

Mary was plainly going to be the one to be made responsible for Gordon's death.

Why are women considered more sinners than sinned against? Mary had asked him that question weeks ago.

A moment later, the minister left the witness chair, to be replaced by a series of people, all of whom had requested time to speak. They told how Mary had saved a family member or themselves. Mr. Grant testified as well, his story touching, and revealing more about Mary than her treatments.

"Jack was only five at the time. He contracted what we thought was a cold, but it seemed to settle around his chest. His fever mounted, and it grew more and more difficult for him to breathe. We fetched the physician, and he prescribed several tonics for him, but none seemed to work. I didn't think my youngest child would survive the night," he said, his voice hoarse. "My wife was beside herself. The physician counseled that we should simply remain at Jack's bedside and be prepared for death by morning."

His eyes searched and found the physician sitting on

the other side of the courtroom. Hamish hadn't been in Mr. Grant's presence often, but he'd never seen the older man look as angry as he did now.

"I confess to being of a stubborn nature," Mr. Grant continued as his wife smiled faintly and dabbed at her eyes. "I was not willing to lose Jack without a battle. So, when Elspeth told me that she'd heard of a woman who was treating the poor with some success, I agreed to summon her."

"I take it your son did not die?" the Sheriff said.

"No, he didn't. Mary came and sat on the edge of his bed, asking a dozen questions or more about his symptoms and his treatment to date. She did some things that I thought odd at the time, but the longer I've known of her methods, the more respect I have for them."

"What did she do that you found odd?"

"Dr. Grampian told us to burn several pots filled with camphor. She extinguished them, and had us open the window a little. The room was stifling, and I feared that the change of temperature would worsen Jack's condition. But his fever decreased over the next hour, especially after she began bathing him in cool water."

"Did she ever give him mercury?"

"No. Nor did she ever discuss it. In fact, I don't recall Mary giving Jack any medications at all. She said later that the body has a way of healing itself if obstacles are removed from it."

Marshall nodded vehemently, and Hamish glanced at him, thinking that, at another time, Mary would be pleased at his approval.

"Mary elevated Jack on the pillows, and used a reed to eliminate the obstruction in his throat. She said that it would aid him in breathing easier. Toward dawn, his color was better, and she was right, he didn't sound as if he were laboring as much. By the next day, his fever was down, and by week's end, he was almost back to his normal self."

"You're saying that Mrs. Gilly was responsible for the boy's cure?"

"I saw the proof of it with my own eyes."

Sir John waved away Mr. Grant's words as if he considered them of little value.

Elspeth was next on the list, and she took her place in the witness chair with a soft smile to her father.

"Have you seen Mrs. Gilly involved in any miraculous healings?" Sir John asked.

"I don't consider them miracles, Sir John," Elspeth said. "Nor does Mary. She takes a great store from the teachings of others and has tried to do good in all her dealings with people."

Elspeth smiled at Mary, who smiled back, the first emotion she'd willingly demonstrated since taking her seat hours earlier.

"There was the Lambeth baby," Elspeth continued. "He had the croup so bad that he wouldn't eat. The poor thing was nearly a skeleton before Mary happened upon a cure. And old Mr. Parkinson who had rheumatism. But he died last year of old age, so he wouldn't be a good witness."

An interruption of laughter made Elspeth frown and look down at her hands. Brendan half rose from his chair, but Hamish pressed him down again in his seat.

"I'm all for grand gestures as well," he told his brother, "but now is not the time." As much as he would like to go and rescue Mary, the sheriff's men aligned around the courtroom made that thought as impractical as Brendan's rushing to Elspeth's aid. He would do nothing more than complicate the situation.

"Have you any further information that you can provide this court that would assist in rendering a verdict in this matter?"

Elspeth looked directly at Sir John. "No, I don't. Only that I do not think Mary could harm Gordon. I would trust her with my life."

"It seemed as if her husband felt the same way," Sir John said, and the courtroom fell silent at that remark.

"It being now two in the afternoon, the court is adjourned. Tomorrow we will hear from the accused." He peered down his fleshy nose at Mary. "Will you be ready to give testimony, Mrs. Gilly?"

She stood. "Yes," she said simply.

A female warder stood in front of Mary and pulled her unceremoniously from the chair by her bound wrists. She lifted her eyes, and for a moment, her gaze met Hamish's. She looked away, releasing him, deliberately rebuffing him. Nevertheless, the hopelessness in her eyes made him want to rescue her now.

Be brave. Would she hear him? Was there a way to communicate with her in just his thoughts? If so, he'd send his courage to her, the tattered remnants of his optimism, something that would aid her now.

She was led from the room as Hamish watched.

Not once did Mary glance in his direction.

Chapter 21

❝It's not going well for her," Hamish said, pacing the length of the taproom in the inn he and Brendan had called home for the past few days. His brother watched him from a table where he ate his evening meal. Beside him sat Marshall, acting as if he had a more positive outlook about these proceedings than Hamish.

"Mrs. Gilly has not yet given her testimony," Marshall said calmly, finishing off his pint of ale. The innkeeper looked at them from time to time, frowning. Their appearance had dampened his trade somewhat. Although the taproom was normally a crowded place in the evening, it was sparsely occupied now, and Hamish wondered if it was because Marshall was a minister. Or was it due more to the fact that the three of them were solidly on Mary's side?

"People are beginning to believe her guilty," Hamish said, finally sitting.

"I'm afraid that is my fault," Marshall admitted. "I should not have asked to address the court."

"You only wished to help," Brendan said.

"Do you think Gilly was murdered?" Hamish asked Marshall.

"Mercury poisoning is a terrible way to die. But it's just as possible that he could have had a tumor, or some other digestive disruption of the bowel. It's not uncommon, especially in a man his age." He stared off into the distance. "I would have liked to see his liver and intestines," Marshall said, sounding entranced at the idea.

"But she didn't know Gordon was getting treatment from the physician," Hamish said.

"So she says," Brendan said, a comment that caused Hamish to stare at him. "I am only voicing what other people will be thinking, Hamish."

"She didn't know."

"Your loyalty to Mrs. Gilly is commendable," Marshall said. "But you have no proof that she didn't poison him."

"She didn't," he said firmly.

Hadn't they seen the look in her eyes, the expression of dawning horror when she realized what had happened? He'd been watching her carefully and knew the moment it had occurred to her that she might have accidentally contributed to Gordon's death.

"The responsibility of another man's death is a heavy burden to bear," Marshall said. "Only God can absolve her of it."

Hamish nodded, wondering if the good minister was about to launch into a sermon. Thankfully, Marshall focused his attention on Hamish's arm.

"Is your lame arm the injury you sustained during your imprisonment?" Matthews asked.

Hamish wondered if Brendan had told Marshall of his

time in India. What else had his brother divulged? He nodded, deciding not to clarify that torture had been responsible for the damage to his arm.

"May I examine you?" Marshall asked.

"Here?" Hamish glanced around the snug taproom. Although the room was deserted except for the three of them, it was hardly an appropriate place.

"I only ask you to roll up your sleeve, Hamish," Marshall chided.

Hamish would much rather that Mary treated him, but he didn't demur. He stood, removed his coat, and rolled up his sleeve before sitting again.

"Have you any movement in it?" Marshall asked, after examining the scars on his arm.

"No, but I've begun to feel tingling in my fingers. I owe it to Mary's assiduous treatments, I think. She insists that I massage it with a salve three times a day."

"Have you done so?"

"Not recently," he said wryly. "There have been other things on my mind."

"You will never get better unless you do," Marshall pronounced.

Hamish took another sip of his whiskey. "Mary thinks that a few applications of your electrical machine might help."

Marshall looked delighted. "She truly has studied my experiments, then." He immediately launched into a description of how the stimulation might render the muscles fit again.

Hamish listened with half an ear, his thoughts on Mary. He couldn't forget the look on her face as Charles had given his testimony. She'd looked stunned at the information the apprentice had divulged.

"Charles knew," Hamish said abruptly.

The two men turned to look at him. "Charles said that he watched Gordon take the medicine from the physician, at the same time Mary was giving Gordon his nightly drinks."

"And he said nothing?" Brendan asked.

"Indeed," Marshall said. "Why?"

"He benefited by Gordon's death," Hamish said. "It was easy for him to simply sit back and allow Gordon to be poisoned. His hands were clean. Should anyone suspect foul play in Gilly death, he can claim ignorance."

"A fact that does not make him guilty of anything in the eyes of the law," Marshall said. "Or the physician."

"Mary is equally as innocent."

"But I'm very much afraid Mary will be the one punished, whether it's proper or not."

Hamish remained silent, having already come to that conclusion. He consulted his pocket watch again, and wondered how long until he could put his plan into motion.

Ian MacRae held his wife tight to him as he stood on the bow of his flagship, the *Ionis*. After all these years, he still preferred solid ground beneath his feet.

"Did you ever think, love," he asked softly, "that we would come back to Scotland again?"

She pulled back and looked at him, smiling. "I suspected that we might one day, especially after Alisdair decided to settle here."

"We were different people then," he said.

She laughed gaily. "Oh, I think we're the same people now, Ian, only much, much older."

"Do not remind me," he said crossly, and then smiled to

mitigate the effect. "My bones ache in the morning, and I've a shoulder that can tell the weather."

"I will not recite a litany of my complaints to you, my dearest," Leitis said. "Otherwise, you might cast your eye toward a much younger wife."

It was his turn to laugh. As if he would ever want anyone other than this woman who had shared his life for more than thirty years. True, there had been times when they'd not spoken to each other for days on end. Occasionally, they'd shouted at each other, and once he'd even taken a chair, lifted it, and put it down on the floor so hard that a leg had snapped.

Leitis MacRae infuriated him at times. She was opinionated, strong, and determined. She was also his best friend and dearest companion, and the one person he respected and trusted above all others.

The sky was gray with storm clouds, and he thanked Providence that he had an experienced captain aboard. He might design and build ships, but he still didn't like to sail them, a fact that amused his five sons.

It had been a busy voyage, one beset by bad weather. He'd been a fool to travel so late in the season, but it seemed an ideal time to return to Scotland. Alisdair had sent word that Gilmuir was nearly complete, and that any memento a member of the MacRae clan would like to send back to Scotland would be gratefully accepted and held in a place of honor in the clan hall. The request seemed like a call for them to return to Gilmuir. Here they were, all these years later, sailing along the coast of Scotland in the *Ionis,* sails half furled.

"We should be entering Loch Euliss in a day or so," he said, having just returned from a briefing with the captain and first mate. "We'll see Gilmuir in a few days."

"And Alisdair," Leitis said. "It's been so long. We have grandchildren to meet, Ian. Does it seem possible?"

He studied her in the faint light of the afternoon sun. Her hair had whitened at the temples, and there were streaks of gray through its thickness. A few creases surrounded her eyes, and a few more were visible around her mouth, but otherwise, she didn't look her age. Or perhaps it was simply because she was Leitis, the woman who'd been in his heart since he was a boy.

"You'll never look older to me than you did on the day I met you," he said. "I was nine, I believe." He bent to kiss her gently, touched by her tender look.

He'd expected his return to Gilmuir to be filled with memory, and that it was. He'd also expected to feel a soft, reminiscent sadness, but right at the moment, all he felt was joy. He'd lived the life he wanted with the woman he adored, and now he was returning to the place of his childhood, a fortress his eldest son had restored and made whole again.

"We should have sent word of our coming," Ian said.

"As I recall," Leitis teased, "you were intent on getting here."

"Intent on getting the voyage over, you mean."

Out of habit, he looked around for Douglas, and seeing him standing talking with the first mate, he felt somewhat reassured. Of all the MacRae sons, Douglas was most difficult. He'd wanted his own way since he was born. Nor had the events of the past months made it easier to deal with him.

Barely seventeen, he was well on his way to becoming a man. He'd proven that he was as virile as any MacRae.

Frowning at that thought, Ian determinedly put his youngest son out of his mind and turned back to his wife.

* * *

Mary heard the muffled sound of voices outside her cell. Night after night the guard and his cronies drank and wagered on a toss of a coin, activities she doubted would please Sir John if he knew. Their drunken jests had been her lullaby many nights, the sound of their companionship oddly comforting, however.

She walked to the window, placed her palms on the high sill, and braced her forehead against them. She didn't want to remember Gordon and how horribly he'd died, didn't want to feel the surge of guilt that accompanied each recollection.

Sometime later, she heard the bar in front of the door slide back and tensed in response. Slowly, she turned to face her visitor, hoping that she had the courage to refuse Charles. But the figure that gained shape and substance as he came forward, a lantern in his hand, wasn't Charles or Mr. Marshall, but the one person in the world she didn't wish to see.

Hamish seemed to know it as well. He closed the door and put the lantern on the floor. Reaching out, he placed a hand on her shoulders, let it fall when she stepped back.

"Did Sir John send you? Or Mr. Marshall?"

"Neither," he said, his voice one she'd longed to hear all these lonely days. "The guard, I've found, has a predilection for Mr. Grant's whiskey. In exchange for a cask, I get five minutes with you."

In the faint glow of the lantern, she watched his face. She'd always thought him a master of control. Rarely did he reveal his emotions, but it was different now. His brown eyes sparkled, and there was a faint smile on his lips, as if he were certain of being welcomed.

"Why are you here, Hamish?"

Instead of answering her, he moved his hand to her cheek. He was warm where she was frigid, her skin feeling as if she were made of ice.

Stepping back once more, she looked at his left arm. "Are you doing the exercises I gave you? You must massage your arm every day so that the gains you made aren't lost."

"Mary," he said, "I didn't come here to talk of treatments."

She frowned at him. "Then tell me why you're here."

"Have you forgotten those weeks at Castle Gloom?" he asked.

She was tired, and frightened, and so chilled that it felt as if she'd never be warm again. She told him a truth that might have been wiser to keep hidden.

"I'll never forget those weeks," she admitted in a voice barely more than a whisper.

"And me? Have you forgotten me?"

A more dangerous question, and one she'd be wiser not to answer. "No," she said simply.

"Then why wouldn't you meet my eyes all day, Mary? And why won't you look at me now?"

"Haven't you heard what they're saying about me, Hamish?"

"Do you think I care what anyone says about you?"

"You should, but then hermits don't care what other people think, do they?"

"Do you?"

"I find, oddly enough," she told him, "that I do." To know that anyone could so easily believe her guilty of murder was painful. She had looked out at the sea of faces and only a few had smiled back at her. Elspeth, and her family, Betty, Cook, and a few others, but not as many as she had tried to heal. She felt almost like a stranger among her neighbors, or someone who'd been labeled an enemy.

She turned and walked back toward the cot.

"Did you know?"

There was no point in pretending to misunderstand him.

"That Gordon was taking the doctor's potion as well as mine? Of course I didn't."

"There, I've asked and you answered. As far as I'm concerned, you're innocent."

She whirled and faced him again. "What makes you believe me so much more easily than anyone else?"

"Because I know you," Hamish said, the hint of his smile disappearing. "Or did you think the only thing we shared at Castle Gloom was our bodies?"

She wanted to go to him and put her hand in his, let him pull her into his arms. She wanted to be told that this nightmare wasn't real, but of course it was. She was too ashamed, too deeply shamed, even to look at him. However much she wanted to remake the past, she couldn't.

She heard him move behind her and prayed that he wasn't coming close. Or if he did, that he wouldn't touch her. Now she needed to be strong, as stoic as he had been during his captivity. She couldn't afford to think of good memories, or feel any regrets.

"I won't let anything harm you, Mary."

"It's too late for that," she said listlessly.

The door opened, and the guard stood there glowering at both of them. Hamish turned and made his way to the man's side.

"You'll remember your promise, then?" the guard asked. "Another cask of the same whiskey tomorrow?"

"I'll bring it myself," Hamish said, "as long as nothing of this meeting gets back to Sir John."

The guard grinned. "He'll not hear a word of it from my lips."

Hamish turned to look back at Mary. Without speaking further, he removed his cloak and returned to her, draping it over her shoulders.

"I won't let anything harm you, Mary," he said again.

Suddenly, he was striding to the door and gone, leaving only the cloak still warm with the heat from his body. For the first time since she'd entered this cell, she felt warm.

Slowly, she sat on the edge of the cot and buried her face in her hands. Only then did she cry, for the future, in fear, but most of all for the loss of Hamish.

Chapter 22

A lone woman escorted Mary into the courtroom but led her to the witness chair instead of the accused's box.

"Are you ready to give testimony?" Sir John asked, staring down at Mary.

She looked at him squarely, her expression somber. "I am," she said clearly.

If she was afraid, it didn't show in her voice or her manner as she sat.

"Identify yourself."

"My name is Mary Margaret McKee Gilly. I'm a life-long resident of Inverness. For years I resided with my parents at number seventeen Ashley Street until my parents died. At that time, I married Gordon Gilly."

"Your husband was a goldsmith, was he not?"

"He was." She folded her unbound hands on her lap and stared out at the crowd, but Hamish wondered how many people she actually saw. Her lips were pale, as was her face, and she appeared exhausted. His chest ached in sympathy for the ordeal she was enduring.

"You inherited his shop and his inventory?" the sheriff asked.

"I did."

"So, you were a prosperous wife and became an even more prosperous widow."

Mary glanced up at him. "Losing my husband offset any wealth I may have inherited," she said dismissively.

"Yet surely you must have known your husband would predecease you. Was he not much older than you?"

"He was," she agreed.

"There are those who say you married him only for his money."

"There are those who will say a great many things, Sir John," she said, looking at him again. "But that does not mean their words have any truth to them. If a person speaks nonsense firmly enough, some fool will believe him."

"Are you saying that such was not the case with you? Did you not marry your husband for his wealth?"

"Why else are marriages arranged, if not for the protection of one party and the comfort of another? I would be foolish not to align myself with someone who could bring me security. It's a cruel world for a woman alone." She looked around the courtroom as if to illustrate her point.

Sir John, no doubt feeling as if he were losing ground, became even more strident in his questioning. "Did you ever administer to your husband any substance that would prove injurious to him?"

Mary hesitated. After a long pause, she finally spoke again. "There are a great many substances that, if taken to the extreme, will prove injurious, Sir John. Water, itself, is one of these. A glassful is beneficial, but a man can still drown, given enough."

"You know what I'm asking, Mrs. Gilly," the sheriff admonished. "Did you administer to your husband any substance that might prove injurious to him?"

Again, she hesitated. When she spoke, however, her voice was clear and audible. "I prepared a drink for my husband, some herbs in ale that I believed would aid his digestive problems. However, when it became apparent that it was not helping, I discontinued it."

"Did you give your husband this drink every evening, Mrs. Gilly?"

"I did," she said, seemingly unaware that the entire courtroom had subsided. Hamish could hear his own breathing, it had grown so quiet.

"What else did you put in this drink?"

Hamish leaned forward, noticing that several other people were doing the same.

Mary looked out over the assembled crowd, as if knowing that everyone was hanging on to each faint word.

"Mercury."

A murmur began in the courtroom again, and this time the judge's frown could not silence it. He stood finally and looked out over the assembled townspeople. Only by asking Mary another question was he able to quiet the crowd, who moderated their conversation to hear Mary's answer.

"Did you know that your husband was also being treated by Dr. Grampian at this time?"

"No, I did not."

"Would that have changed your treatment?"

"Yes," she said, her voice ringing through the courtroom. "I've consulted the very best texts on medicine. I know the dangers inherent in the dosages of certain medications. A tiny amount of foxglove, for instance, will aid the beating of a damaged heart, but too much will cause it to falter. Mercury is one of those substances to be administered with a great deal of care. A little will aid digestion and eliminate obstruction. Too much will kill."

Sir John said nothing in response.

A moment later, Mary was led back to the accused's box. Sir John sat frowning at the vial in front of him. It was all too evident to Hamish that he'd made up his mind, and that the next words were going to be those that would send Mary to Edinburgh to stand trial for murder.

"Why now?" Hamish asked, standing.

The sheriff glanced up, frowning. "Do you have something to say to this court, sir?"

Hamish studied the sheriff with narrowed eyes. "Why, after all this time, were charges brought against Mrs. Gilly?"

"Who are you, sir?"

"My name is Hamish MacRae," he said. "I was the captain of the *Sherbourne* until last year. A trading vessel under the flag of the MacRae Shipping Company."

"Why do you question this court?"

"Because you do not see fit to seek the truth, Sir John."

The two guards on either side of Mary looked in his direction, and Hamish couldn't help but wonder if he were about to be arrested. Not before he spoke the truth, he vowed.

"Question Charles Talbot again," he said, looking directly at the apprentice. "Ask him why he has the vial of mercury."

The crowd around him was beginning to pay attention, a fact that evidently didn't please the sheriff.

Hamish turned and took Marshall's Bible from him,

holding it aloft toward Sir John. "Ask him to swear upon a holy book that Mrs. Gilly knew Gordon was being treated by a physician." When the sheriff made no move to do so, Hamish only smiled derisively.

Hamish sought out Charles again, and the two locked gazes across the courtroom.

"The physician would have Mrs. Gilly portrayed as too feebleminded to treat the ill and injured, yet you would have Mrs. Gilly seen as a deliberate murderess. Charles Talbot would have us all believe that Mrs. Gilly treated her husband on one hand and poisoned him knowingly on the other." He glanced toward Betty. "Her maid says she wept for her husband. Her patients attested to her care.

"I was Mrs. Gilly's patient for the last month." That revelation only seemed to intensify the whispers, but he continued. "She treated the injuries I sustained while in India," he said. "But I've had plenty of opportunity to study her, and to get to know her well. It is my belief that she could never have murdered her husband."

"What makes you so certain of that, Mr. MacRae?" Sir John asked.

"A variety of reasons. First, she loved him. She always spoke of him with fondness and friendship."

"But you've no proof that she is innocent of such an act?"

The words were so close to Marshall's that Hamish felt a surge of irritation. "Nor do you have proof that she's guilty, Sir John. Why would a woman who takes great pride in healing the ill administer poison to her husband?"

"That, I believe, is the decision I must make," Sir John said coldly. "Have you any other reason to believe her innocent?"

Hamish turned and looked at Mary finally, and she was staring at him, a look on her face that he'd never forget. As if he were water and she was thirsting.

"A man comes to know a woman he admires," he said slowly. "Mary Gilly doesn't have it in her to kill. I know that better than most, because the world would call me a murderer."

The whispers intensified, but Hamish didn't look away from her. He couldn't.

"She doesn't hate," he said, "but hatred isn't necessarily a requirement for being a murderer. A man can kill someone he doesn't even know well, if that man gets between him and something he desperately wants."

Was this to be the punishment for his sin after all? To bare his soul in front of a packed courtroom of interested spectators, none of whom knew him, but all of whom would judge him in the next few minutes?

"I spent a year in India, imprisoned, taken from village to village and put on display for the natives. I realized early on that I wanted very much to live. I woke in the morning and thought about staying alive. It was my last thought at night."

There was no sound in the courtroom, and even the sheriff looked sufficiently intrigued to remain silent.

"When the opportunity presented itself, I escaped with two other men. One of the men, a man named Thompson, was injured, but we bound up his leg wound and headed across the tip of the southern desert, one of the most inhospitable places on earth." He stood up straighter, never moving his gaze from Mary. "On the third day we ran out of water."

The courtroom had grown so quiet that Hamish thought he could hear the wind outside the building. Her eyes hadn't left him, and he drew a curious strength from her intense look.

"We found an oasis two days later, and remained there until we regained some strength. One of the things we'd not considered was that being in our cages for so long might have made walking long distances difficult. We made or gathered what we could to hold water and began our trek again. Harrison died four days later."

Hamish could remember the instant he'd turned to see the man facedown in the sand and scrub. He'd been stunned to find him dead, and then angry. He'd yelled at the man, he remembered, so infuriated that after so long Harrison had simply given up and died.

"Thompson became ill with fever and began having deliriums three days after that. He could no longer walk because of the wound in his leg, so I carried him as long as I could. Finally, my own strength was giving out, so I laid him down. He burrowed into the sand, thinking that it was a warm blanket, and that he was home in Surrey in the dead of winter. I left him there to die so that I could live."

In the silence, Hamish took a deep breath and continued. "I know what it's like to consider another human being's life less important than your own. Mary Gilly does not have that type of heart or damaged soul. Her spirit is generous and loving. She would never have killed her husband."

For a long time, there was silence in the courtroom, and then the sheriff spoke again. "I have taken into consideration all that has been said here." His words, however, didn't ease Hamish's increasing sense of dread. Hamish knew, in that instant, that Mary wasn't going to escape the sheriff's punishment.

Sir John stood, an imposing man in his somber attire.

Anyone who saw him could easily recognize that he was a man of power and influence. There was no compassion in his eyes, however, and no softness in his tone. Only a note of finality that made Hamish doubt Mary would ever be set free.

"Despite the accused's reputation, I believe her culpable in the death of her husband. There is sufficient cause for her to be bound over to Edinburgh for trial." He hesitated for a moment before speaking again. "God have mercy on your soul, Mrs. Gilly."

The hours ticked by slowly, as if the minutes were carried on the back of a turtle. Mary stood, then sat on her fragile cot, then stood again to pace the cell. She knew its dimensions well—a week of residence had acquainted her with every stone, each bar in the window, all the flagstones beneath her feet. Fourteen steps to the far wall, and ten from the window to the door. A mausoleum of a cell, it seemed even colder than normal tonight, as if even the stones knew her fate and retained no warmth for her.

She was going to die. Dear God, she was going to die. She hadn't been able to get the magistrate's voice out of her mind for the last four hours, his words ringing in her ears as if they echoed back on themselves. *God have mercy on your soul.*

A man comes to know a woman he admires. A better voice to remember, a revelation that had made her heart stutter. Hamish hadn't glanced away, but met her gaze unflinchingly, his courage in evidence again. Dearest Hamish.

If she cried, it would be because she'd never see him again, because her life would never again be enlivened by his presence. He'd never make her smile again, or touch her in tenderness and passion. They wouldn't have hours to talk or laugh or plumb each other's minds.

Murderess.

Voices outside her cell made her stop and listen. A few moments later, a burst of laughter split the silence. She began to walk again, knowing that sleep wouldn't come tonight. Should she count the hours until dawn, measure the time until she was taken to the coach that would take her to Edinburgh? How many days were left to her?

Thank God for Castle Gloom. Thank God that she'd ignored every tenet of her upbringing to lust and love. Thank God for those weeks of hedonism and laughter. She would cling to those memories until the moment death came to her.

She was cold, but not from the wintry winds. Tonight, she wore the cloak Hamish had left for her, but it was no comfort against the chill that started deep inside, accompanied by one word. Murderess.

Would he come again tonight? Would it be wrong to pray for such a thing? She wanted desperately to see him again.

"You'll wear a path in the stone, Mary."

Turning, she stared at him. She'd wanted Hamish to be real so fervently that for a moment she didn't comprehend that he was actually standing in the doorway, attired in a dark greatcoat.

"God granted my prayer," she said softly. "I so wanted to see you one more time."

Smiling, he shook his head. "I've come to take you out of here," he said.

"It's much too dangerous," she said, feeling a bite of regret. "I won't have you hurt."

"It might well be," he said, nodding. "But I prefer it to

the alternative. I haven't a taste for Edinburgh, Mary. Do you?"

"I've never been," she said, feeling an absurd wish to giggle.

"Then let's see other places in the world instead. I've been charting a few in my mind."

Her heart seemed to stop and then race ahead.

"Where are we going?"

"For now, out of here. We'll choose our destination later."

Gently, he placed his hand on the small of her back and urged her toward the door.

"What did you do to the guards?" she asked as they left the cell. Two men were sprawled facedown over the table.

"I didn't poison them, if that's what you're thinking," he said, amusement lacing his voice. "A little of Mr. Grant's excellent whiskey, laced with a sleeping draught."

"Will they be all right?"

"In the morning," Hamish assured her.

They slipped down the hall, following a labyrinth of corridors Hamish seemed to know quite well. When she would have said as much, he shook his head and put his finger to his lips. She remained silent.

Finally, they were out a door, but instead of taking the path to the road, he pulled her into the bushes outside the building.

"What are you waiting for?" she whispered.

"Scream."

"What?" She wished there was enough light to see his face.

"Scream, Mary. We need to attract attention."

Aghast, she stared at him. "Shouldn't we be more concerned about escaping?"

"Do you trust me?" He held her hand in his, brought it to his mouth, and brushed a kiss across her knuckles.

"Of course I do," she answered softly.

"Then scream."

Her first effort was a puny sound. She tried again, and this sound was less of a warble. The third scream was loud and strong, summoning the guards to the front door. In a matter of moments, it seemed that all the magistrate's men were pouring out of the building.

"They'll find us," she said, panic making her want to turn and run.

"Wait," Hamish answered, a thread of amusement in his voice. Before she could tell him that now was not the time for such lighthearted emotion, two riders came out of the darkness.

The lanterns in front of the building were not bright enough to illuminate their faces. The woman's hood was drawn down over her face and hair; her companion's cloak was equally as concealing. They circled the square, chased by three guards on foot. They easily outstripped the runners and disappeared into the darkness again, the echo of their horses' hooves a goad to the sheriff's men.

Hamish placed the back of his arm over Mary's chest, keeping her pinned against the building. A whisper was enough to silence her when she would have asked another question.

Commands were yelled, horses were saddled, and a force of ten or more guards soon followed the duo into the darkness.

"Who were they?" Mary asked when Hamish released her. They waited for several minutes in the silence before slipping to the edge of the building, and crossing the road.

"A couple you know," he said, surprisingly. "Micah and Hester."

"Hester is masquerading as me? Does she know the danger of her ruse, Hamish? The sheriff will not rest until he's found me." Sir John's zeal for justice had been adequately proven these past days.

"He'll have to find her first," Hamish answered. "They're on their way to Nova Scotia, a journey I doubt Sir John will make in search of you."

"Have you been planning this for long?" she asked, stopping at a corner. He placed his hand around her elbow and urged her forward. The hour was late, the night streets nearly deserted, but he was evidently not taking any chances that they might be seen. They kept to the shadows, away from the light emitted by doorways and windows.

"Did you expect me to leave you there, Mary?"

"You might have been wiser to do so."

"When have we been wise with each other?" The shadows seemed to accentuate the boyish charm of his smile.

Never. Not from the beginning, and certainly not now, slipping through the silent streets of Inverness hand-in-hand, his cloak around her shoulders.

"How can anyone become a criminal?" she asked breathlessly, as they slowed a few streets away. They began to walk, more sedate now that they encountered a few late-night citizens of Inverness. "I haven't the nerves for it. I'm terrified that someone will see us and know what we've done."

"I doubt anyone would think you lacking in courage, Mary," Hamish said.

She didn't tell him that there were plenty of times when

she'd emulated him, hoping for the same type of stoicism that Hamish demonstrated.

A few minutes later, they entered the back of the Grants' property. There a carriage, lamps extinguished, stood waiting.

"Where are we going? To Castle Gloom?"

"No, they'll look for us there. To Gilmuir," he said. "We'll go there first."

She grabbed his hand again and entwined her fingers with his.

"You shouldn't be burdened with the responsibility of my future."

Whatever he might have said in response was interrupted by the scullery door suddenly opening. Mr. and Mrs. Grant emerged from the house, followed by Elspeth and Brendan. Mary was immediately enfolded in a series of hugs, while Hamish stood apart.

"We have to leave," he said a few minutes later, his voice sounding loud in the darkness. "Any delay will only jeopardize all of you."

Hamish went to the carriage and opened the door. He was pulling down the steps when another voice rang out, his orator's tone startling all of them.

"No."

Mary turned, staring at Matthew Marshall. He stood at the head of the horses, his face illuminated by the lantern he held. He raised it high and stared at them.

"I'm afraid I cannot let you leave."

Chapter 23

For a terrifying moment, Mary expected the sheriff's men to appear out of the shadows.

"It's one thing to live together as man and wife without benefit of clergy, but quite another to expect me to condone it. Although you've done so once, I can't allow you to do so again."

Brendan looked startled. Elspeth, surprisingly, looked fascinated by the discussion, while Mr. and Mrs. Grant were edging both of them closer to the scullery door, leaving Mary and Hamish alone with Mr. Marshall.

"Who told you?" Hamish asked, staring at Brendan's back.

"No one," Mr. Marshall said. "I am, however, an observant man, and I simply added the various pieces together to make a whole."

Hamish didn't respond, and Mary felt too dumbstruck to comment.

"While I have taken it upon myself," Mr. Marshall continued, "to look the other way in certain proceedings, Mr. MacRae, I cannot countenance sin." He fixed a long and penetrating look at Mary. She didn't flinch when returning his stare, but inwardly she was more than a little cowed. Matthew Marshall, incensed, could be very intimidating. "I cannot allow you to continue living in harlotry." Now he stared at Hamish. "You must marry."

From not far away a dog barked, and one of the horses stamped its feet in response, as if the animals were having a laugh over the idea of Hamish MacRae and Mary Gilly married.

"I'd never thought to marry again, Mr. Marshall," she said calmly.

"It seems to me," Marshall said, his voice sounding kind, "that you should have given some thought to it, especially in view of your actions."

"You think marriage is the answer for our sins?" Hamish asked dryly.

"I think that you both need to cease irritating God," Marshall said firmly.

He turned once more to Mary. "Can you say with some certainty that, given the opportunity, you would not lie with Hamish again, Mary?"

Mary felt the heat rise to her face. She looked at Hamish and smiled faintly.

"Or you, Hamish?"

He didn't answer. Instead, he stared at Mr. Marshall, his anger banked but still evident.

"I'll give you a moment to talk between yourselves," Mr. Marshall said, looking smug. "I'll be waiting in the parlor to conduct the ceremony."

"And if we decide to simply leave Inverness as we'd planned?" Hamish asked in a clipped voice.

"Then I shall have no choice but to report the Grants' participation in your escape."

He left them alone. Mary walked some distance away and then returned, folding her arms around herself inside Hamish's cloak.

"I don't believe for a moment that he'll turn the Grants over to the sheriff," she said.

"I myself am not willing to test him," Hamish said easily. A milder response than she'd expected. She glanced at him, wishing she could see his expression more clearly.

"Marriage seems a harsh punishment for a few weeks of pleasure," she said carefully.

"You've not looked at this in the proper manner, Mary. We've proven we can share pleasure, and have some measure of regard for each other. Most couples don't have such an auspicious beginning. Didn't you once tell me that your married patients are happier than those who are not?"

"Hermits aren't married."

"My hermitage was of short duration in any event, Mary," he said, his voice again sounding amused. "I was finding it difficult to be without the sound of conversation or the presence of other people."

"We can simply ignore Mr. Marshall and leave Inverness," she suggested. "There isn't any reason for our marriage, other than that of propriety. Let them call me a harlot. They've already labeled me a murderer."

"But he's right, you know. The two of us have enough in our past that we should be trying to get into the Almighty's good graces."

He came toward her and drew her into the light. The better to see the truth of her expression? Or to witness the peppering of tears in her eyes?

"So you would marry me to make me proper, Hamish?" she asked, smiling slightly.

Hamish was willing to sacrifice himself for her, but she didn't want a martyr for a husband. She wanted them to be companions who could discuss any subject, friends who could share laughter, lovers. In Hamish's company at Castle Gloom, she'd allowed herself to feel vulnerable. With him, she didn't have to be strong all the time.

He continued looking at her with that expressionless gaze, the night darkening his eyes until they were no more than two coals in his face. She reached up and touched his cheek, her fingers smoothing over the stubble on his face. How beloved he was to her.

When had she known that she'd loved him? From that first moment, or later, when he introduced her to a world she'd never known? One of passion, freedom of thought, action, and will.

She wanted to be loved, not because it was the right thing to do or because Hamish was concerned about his immortal soul, but because he couldn't help himself. She wanted him to marry her because of all the women in the entire world, he would be the happiest with her.

"There's no way you can go back to your former life, Mary," he said gently. "You can't remain here."

She only nodded. Until today, she'd never before been faced with the dilemma of having to hide how she felt. Sitting in the accused's box had been excruciating. All those hours, she'd endeavored not to show her anger, and certainly not her fear. She'd made a mask of her face until not one emotion shone through. Could she hide her love for Hamish for an entire lifetime?

In exchange for a life with him? Oh yes.

* * *

"We must give some consideration to the causes for which matrimony was ordained," Mr. Marshall solemnly intoned. "One was for the procreation of children. Secondly, it was ordained for remedy against sin, and to avoid fornication, that such persons as have not the gift of restraint might marry." He stared fixedly at Mary before looking at Hamish. They were both being chastised, but it didn't disturb Mary one whit.

"Thirdly, for the mutual society, help, and comfort that one ought to have of the other, both in prosperity and adversity." He hesitated for a minute, as if to recognize the fact that they were facing adversity, especially since she and Hamish would be fleeing this cozy home in a matter of moments.

She glanced out of the corner of her eye to see Hamish smiling slightly. He caught her look, and slowly and deliberately winked at her, catching her off-guard. The room in which they stood was very familiar to her. Here, in the Grants' parlor, there were lovely velvet draperies on the window, a wing chair sitting by the fire with the iron surround. Beside the settee was a knitting table, a thread of wool peeping out from the hole on the side. It was a homey room, one where strangers were welcome as well as friends. How many times had she sat in this room, talking with the Grants? None of those times, however, had been as poignant or as meaningful as now.

The window revealed her like a black mirror. She'd been bathed, powdered, and buttoned into a dress of Elspeth's in less than fifteen minutes. She looked entirely too pale, but that was due to fatigue rather than her mood. Hamish, standing straight and tall beside her, looked both determined and impatient.

He had a look in his eyes that she'd never seen in another man. Perhaps it was an understanding of himself. He'd been tested by life, the evidence there in his gaze. There was a sharpness to his jaw that warned he was stubborn and determined. Yet, no matter how tumultuous the world might become, she suspected that Hamish would always remain upright in the middle of it.

At the conclusion of the vows, Hamish extended his arm around her, holding her against him. She leaned her head against his shoulder, extending her arms around his back. He bent and kissed her lightly, a proper kiss in front of her friends.

"Later," he whispered against her ear before pulling back. He smiled at the flush mounting on her cheeks, tracing its passage with his thumb.

Mr. Marshall gave them his felicitations, and together they accepted the good wishes of those who witnessed their wedding. She and Elspeth hugged, and then she was enfolded in Mrs. Grant's arms, feeling as if the older woman stood proxy for her own long-dead mother at that moment. Jack hugged her next before Mr. Grant kissed her on the cheek.

"I'll never be able to repay you for what you've done for me, Mary. Be happy."

She nodded, realizing that she would never be able to return to Inverness. She'd never see the Grants again, or the River Ness, the goldsmith's shop, or a hundred other sights she'd grown to love. Everything she'd been, known, and seen would need to be put aside. Her very identity had changed.

She glanced at Hamish. She was no longer a widow, but a wife. Not a healer as much as a helpmate. They exchanged a somber look that seemed even more poignant than their vows.

Finally, she looked at Brendan. She'd traveled with him, shared numerous conversations with him, and was now related by marriage. Yet in so many ways, he seemed almost a stranger. Unspoken constraint still stretched between them as she remembered his disapproval of her actions. He'd not wanted her to remain with Hamish. She'd been a harlot in his eyes. What did he think now?

"Welcome to the family, Mary," he said gruffly, opening his arms.

She walked into them, hugging him in return, and feeling tears welling in her eyes. How strange, that after so many days of being stoic, she now felt like weeping incessantly.

"We should be going," Hamish said. She nodded, understanding that they'd wasted too much time already. She needed to be away from the city before Sir John and his men returned to Inverness. Every moment she delayed was another moment that she brought danger to her friends.

Together, they left by the rear door, followed by the Grants, Mr. Marshall, and Brendan. The only belongings she'd take with her were those given her by Elspeth and Mrs. Grant. There was no time, and it was too unsafe to return to the home she'd known for eleven years.

"Will we ever see each other again?" Elspeth asked as Hamish opened the door, unfurled the steps.

Mary turned to her friend as Mr. Grant called Hamish to the rear of the coach. "I don't know," she said honestly. "I hope so." She hesitated and then asked one last favor of Mrs. Grant. "You've already done so much for me, but could you do one thing more?"

"If I can."

"Could you take Betty in? Charles won't be kind to her after her testimony at the hearing."

Mrs. Grant nodded, smiling. "Of course, and Cook as well, if she'd like to come."

"I shall miss you dreadfully," Elspeth said when her mother stepped back. "Who will know my secrets now?" She slanted a glance toward Brendan. Mary smiled in response.

"I shall miss you as well," she said. "But you must write me as often as you wish. When I have an address, send me all your letters, and I'll do the same."

Elspeth sent a look in Hamish's direction. "I doubt you'll have time to write, Mary," she whispered, smiling.

They hugged one last time, and Mary got into the carriage, pushing her skirts aside, and waiting for Hamish.

"If you have a moment," Marshall said from behind Hamish. "I've a gift for you." In his arms, he carried a leather chest. For a moment, Hamish thought it a duplicate of the case Mary had used for her medicines, but then realized there were clasps around the top to allow the sides to drop down.

Marshall lowered it until it rested in the back of the carriage.

"I've been working on a new design of my electrical machine, but I would like you to have this one."

He opened the case to reveal an apparatus consisting of a hollow glass cylinder supported on two wooden cradles. On the outside of the cylinder, midpoint, was a metal bar with a handle. Against the length of the glass was a piece of black leather attached to a rectangle of crimson silk. Behind the cylinder was a thin rod topped with a metal ball.

"The practitioner cranks the handle while the patient grips the ball," Marshall instructed. "You'll get a shock. Not enough to kill," he said, in an obvious attempt to reassure Hamish, "but more than sufficient to cause some stimulus to the damaged nerves."

"Mary will be overjoyed," Hamish said, hoping to mask his own, less enthusiastic, response. "Thank you."

"Use it for your good health, Hamish. A way of apology for my earlier forcefulness."

Hamish smiled. "If I'd not wanted to marry, Marshall, no threats of heaven or hell would have swayed me. Even those against the Grants."

Marshall studied him for a moment, then nodded once. "Yet you would never have allowed them to be harmed, I think."

"No," Hamish agreed.

Marshall stepped back, and Hamish thanked them all again.

"Where will you go?" Brendan asked.

Hamish stepped away from the rear of the carriage. The lantern was extinguished, and the courtyard plunged into darkness.

"To Gilmuir," Hamish told him.

It was too dark to see his brother's face, but surprise was evident in Brendan's voice. "Is that wise? Do you really want to bring trouble down on Alisdair and Iseabal?"

"We won't be there that long," Hamish said. "Only long enough to buy a ship from Alisdair."

"You're going back to sea?"

Hamish nodded, thinking that he should confide in Mary before Brendan.

The two brothers looked at each other, the darkness easing the farewell. For the first time since India, Hamish felt close to Brendan. Or perhaps loving Mary made him feel as if he belonged to the world again.

"Will you go back to Castle Gloom and gather up my belongings?"

"I will," Brendan promised.

"Be careful," Hamish said. "As soon as word of Mary's escape is discovered, I'm certain we'll fall under suspicion."

"I'm a MacRae. I'll be fine, as you will," Brendan said, the echoes of childhood daring in his pronouncement. "You should have told me about India, Hamish."

Hamish nodded. "I think perhaps I should have," he agreed. But he'd had to begin to accept his own actions first, before he could share them with another soul. It was strange, however, how much lighter he felt after his confession in a crowded courtroom. He'd never forget Thompson, or that singular moment when he'd made his decision to live, but Hamish no longer hated himself for refusing to die like those around him.

The farewells done, Hamish climbed into the carriage. The door closed, the signal was given to the driver, and the coach began to move.

Chapter 24

Hamish settled into the seat beside her. Slowly, they made their way out of the Grants' courtyard, bound for freedom and even more adventure.

She turned and looked at Hamish. "What happened to Thompson?" she asked gently.

He glanced at her, and for a moment she thought he wasn't going to answer. When he did his voice was low and hesitant. "When I was rescued, my first thought was to go back and find him. It was too late; he was already dead."

"Was there suppuration in his wound?" she asked.

"Some."

"Any discoloration?"

"There were red streaks leading from it to his thigh, and down to his foot."

"Smell?"

He nodded. "Are you determining the degree of his injury, Mary? If so, I can tell you that he probably would not have survived his wound."

"But you still blame yourself."

He said nothing, and she was suddenly reminded of those moments in the courtroom when their gazes had locked and he'd told her the story of his escape. It hadn't seemed important that there were people all around, rapt and entranced by his tale. He'd spoken directly to her, telling her what all those nights and days and conversations between them had only hinted at. Now she understood the agony of his soul more completely.

"He was alive, and because of me, he died," he said gently, cupping her face in his hand.

She understood, at that moment, exactly what kind of man he was. Because he accepted the responsibility for his actions, he was also branded by them. But if he'd been another type of man, she wouldn't have been so captivated by him. She never would have remained at Castle Gloom for all those weeks, and her heart would not be touched now by his unvoiced pain.

She had a confession of her own.

"Have you ever noticed that when you stub your toe and concentrate on the pain that it seems much worse? Whereas if you stub your toe and think of other things, the pain disappears within moments?"

"There must be a reason for such a question," he said, amused.

"I've never told you about Gordon. Not truly. I preferred not to think about him."

"So the pain would go away?"

She looked away, fingering the curtain and staring out as if she could view Gordon from there. All she witnessed were the sights of a town in which she'd lived all her life. A place that felt alien to her now. "Not the way you mean. Perhaps more my guilt. I was grateful to my husband for more than one reason. He was kind to my mother, and helped settle my father's debts. At first, it wasn't difficult to love him."

He remained silent, listening.

"A few years later, his mind began to wander. He would accuse me of not feeding him immediately after our evening meal. He said that Charles stole his gold, and the neighbors were laughing at him. He began to forget things. Once, I came into his workroom and found him just sitting there, holding one of his tools. When I asked him if anything was wrong, he looked at me as if I were a stranger. He wanted to know if he worked with the tools and what he did. I wanted to cry. A few minutes later, however, he was working again."

"He was an older man, and sometimes the old lose their way."

She shook her head. "It was more than that. I should have investigated it further." She turned to face him. "I began to spend less and less time with Gordon. I'd find any excuse to leave the house, and when we were there together, I was always in my workroom. If I'd been the kind of wife he deserved, perhaps I would have noticed his condition.

"I'm not innocent, Hamish," she said, speaking the hideous truth. "I want to be, but I'm not." Accident or not, she'd urged Gordon to drink the medication that might have killed him.

"Neither am I," he said gently. "Leave innocence to babies and saints, Mary. People are flawed, incomplete, and occasionally simply wrong. Even Gordon deserves his share of blame."

"How can you say that?"

"Because he didn't tell you he was also taking Grampian's potions. Does that not reveal a lack of trust on his part?"

She considered that point for a moment. "Will we always feel guilty, Hamish?" She should have chosen a better time to ask, perhaps, but there might never be a more intimate moment. They were alone with the rest of the world sleeping around them. Their whispers were carried on the night wind, the chill of the evening evident in the puffs of smoke that coated each word.

"I think so," he said after a moment of silence. "Some guilt is not an altogether bad thing, Mary. It keeps us from repeating our actions, makes us hone our souls."

A philosophy she'd never before considered. "What will happen to Charles? He, too, knew what was happening, but chose to tell no one."

"Perhaps nothing right now. Or not that we can witness."

She glanced at him, surprised.

"Unfortunately, some wicked people escape justice and good people pay for crimes they didn't commit. Life is occasionally not fair." He sat back against the seat and reached for her as the horses rounded a corner. "The Hindus believe that a man will ultimately pay for his crimes. If not in this life, then in the next."

"Is that a philosophy you espouse?"

He chuckled. "It begins to make perfect sense if one can believe in a universal justice."

"He should be made to pay for his actions, Hamish. If he'd only spoken sooner, Gordon would not have died in such agony."

"One thing that my time at Castle Gloom taught me was that I didn't want to waste the joy of my days on hatred and anger. You helped me realize that, Mary."

"I did?" She smiled, realizing that, like Charles, he offered her a choice. But this one was so much more palatable. To be bitter or happy. "I say we should consign Charles to the past, Hamish. Along with Sir John."

He bent his head to kiss her, taking her from this chilled and shadowed place into one filled with warmth and delight. Suddenly, her cheek was pressed against his chest, her arms were under his, her hands pressed flat against his back. He was there, solid and real, not simply a man she'd dreamed to fill in her nights. She clutched his shirt, not wanting to move.

Days of being subjected to Sir John's imprisonment, the hearing, and her own sense of sorrow for failing Gordon conspired to overwhelm her. Because of her fatigue, her grief, and her longing, she wasn't wise, or restrained, or mindful of her pride.

"I love you, Hamish," she said, no doubt startling him with her declaration. She'd thought of him in the morning when she'd awakened to visions of his smile, and replayed all the memories of their loving at night to keep her company.

She wrapped her arms around him as far as they would go, pressed her cheek against his chest, and closed her eyes. Tears fell now, dampening her cheeks and his shirt.

When he would have pulled away, she held on tighter, not allowing him to move or see her crying.

"Mary," he said tenderly. Just that and no more.

"You'll come to love me," she promised him rashly.

"Do you think I don't now?" he asked, extricating himself from her grip and pulling back to look down into her face. "Or do you suppose I go about betraying my secrets, rescuing prisoners, and proposing marriage to any woman?"

"You didn't exactly propose," she corrected, blinking

up at him. "I believe we were cowering under some sort of theological threat."

He smiled at her and gently wiped the tears from her face with one thumb. "I do not cower," he said.

Mary pulled back and studied his face, wondering at the delightful sense of buoyancy she was beginning to feel. A bubble of excitement was opening up inside her and spreading from her toes to her fingertips.

"Besides, you had to marry me," he said.

"I did?"

"Yes, to save my reputation."

He kissed her again, and she felt his smile.

The carriage left Inverness with all possible speed, but not so much that their flight would attract attention. Less than an hour had passed since they'd left the jail, but there was still the possibility that the ruse with Hester and Micah hadn't worked.

A little while later, Mary fell asleep beside him and Hamish extended his arm around her. Gently, he untied her bonnet and slipped the ribbon free before tossing the offending headgear to the other side of the carriage.

He propped up his feet on the opposite seat so that he might make himself a bed for his wife. He eased her head down until her cheek was pillowed on his thigh. She made a soft sigh as if she fell into a deeper sleep. He hoped her dreams were sweet ones.

All that time at Castle Gloom, she'd never complained, never made herself out to be a long-suffering spouse to garner attention or sympathy. She'd commented on Gordon's good qualities and remained silent about the rest.

How long would it take him to know her, and would the

journey prove to be as fascinating as the introduction to Mary had been?

They drove onward into the night, the moonlight illuminating the road. Twice, Hamish thought he heard the sound of hooves thundering behind them, but it was only the hills and valleys carrying back the sound of the speeding carriage.

They were little more than shadows, an occasional silhouette thrown down onto the surface of the road by the moon to their left. He leaned back against the seat, allowing his eyes to close, hearing the rhythm of the shod hooves of the four horses.

With any luck, there would be a ship available at Gilmuir, one that Hamish could purchase from Alisdair. It would be a difficult bargain. Alisdair would want to give the ship to him, but the shipyards at Gilmuir were his brother's future, and he wouldn't jeopardize it. Besides, a MacRae ship was worth the price. Sleek and fast as a swan coming to rest on the water, one of Alisdair's ships would take them from Scotland with all possible speed.

His mind cataloged all the places they might go. Florence, first of all, where he would commission the finest Italian leather case for the medicines Mary would begin to collect again. Then to Rome, perhaps. Anywhere but India. Not that the country had a monopoly on cruelty. There were too many other places in the world where the recent British incursion had angered the natives, making them want to rebel as fiercely as the Atavasi.

He would never put his wife in danger.

His wife. Words that held a tinge of justifiable possessiveness. He knew so much more about her now, and her allure had only deepened. He'd thought to want only one thing from this woman, and discovered that loving her physically was not enough. He wanted to plumb her mind and test the dimensions of her soul.

Her smile always possessed an edge of sadness, and her eyes, sometimes sparkling with mischief, sometimes sober and intent, had always seemed a little weary of the world. He'd known of her ability to heal, but now suspected that she did so as a way to fight loneliness.

Sitting in the courtroom today, he'd finally pieced it together, understanding that what he saw in her was what he'd also felt in himself, an apartness, an aloofness that separated him from other people. He recognized a kindred soul in her.

The woman he'd bedded had merged with the woman who fascinated him. The two became one, an amalgam of charm, physical grace, intelligence, and more. He found himself wanting to know why she thought certain things, what her childhood had been like. What her dreams were, her favorite color, all answers he might have known if he'd courted her properly.

Once, he might have been a proper suitor, but he'd returned from India a different man, the idea of indulging in courtship far from his mind. Yet somehow, Fate or Providence had brought Mary into his life. A reward, perhaps, for his stoic refusal to die?

His mind wandered to those days in the desert. For months, he'd not wanted to think about Thompson. Hamish found himself reliving the scene as if he were not simply involved in it, but as if he also stood apart, watching the man he'd been.

His clothes were in tatters and his skin burned to blisters by the sun. His lips were white with sores as he knelt beside Thompson.

"Get up," he'd commanded, his throat feeling as if he'd

swallowed burning hot sand. Months of screams had cracked his voice. "Get up, damn you."

Thompson hadn't moved for a long while. Finally, he'd opened his eyes, staring full-faced into the sun. "Susan? Is that you? Oh, my dearest girl, I've dreamed of you."

"Get up, Thompson."

The other man shivered, burying himself deeper into the sand until only his chest and head showed. "It's cold in Surrey in winter," he said to no one in particular.

Hamish stood, his reserves nearly gone. It would be so easy to simply join him, lie down in the sand and pretend himself home. He shook himself and stared off toward the far horizon. Only a day more. He repeated that to Thompson, but the man didn't answer. "Damn it!" he shouted. "Do you want to die?"

Again, no response.

"Susan, close the window, it's cold in the room."

Thompson crossed his arms over his chest as his body bowed, his entire frame shaking. He, like Hamish, had lost so much weight over the past months that it wasn't difficult to imagine his skull through the thin layer of flesh and muscle. His grin wasn't humor but a muscle spasm.

"Thompson!"

The longer he stood there, fatigue leaching the last of his resolve, the more the sun seared into him. Thompson was dying, just as Hamish would if he didn't find shelter.

He looked toward the far horizon once more before bending and picking up Thompson's water jug. He poured half of it into his own container, and tried once more to rouse him. When Thompson didn't answer, Hamish turned and staggered toward the horizon. If he found help, he'd come back for the man.

When the search party found him, Thompson was dead, looking so utterly peaceful that he might have fallen asleep in his bed in Surrey.

Hamish found himself now uttering a profound and fervent silent plea for forgiveness to Thompson. In his vision, the other man opened his eyes, looking at him directly as if he saw the future Hamish. Then he simply smiled and disappeared.

Suddenly, that time at Castle Gloom seemed foolish, the act of a man mired in pity for himself. Up until this moment, he'd not realized the extent of his self absorption. In addition to learning to forgive the Atavasi, he needed to forgive himself. If he could.

Perhaps the way he lived his life from this point forward was the only way he could make reparations for his past actions. He could be a better son to his parents, a better brother. In time, he would be a good father, the pattern for his behavior already laid down by his own father, Ian MacRae. Above all, he would be a good husband.

Those attributes might help to balance out his sins.

How odd that his past evaporated and his future began in that instant. How strange, too, that in this shadowed and chilled carriage, Hamish experienced the first hope and exhilaration he'd felt in years.

Mary stirred restlessly in her sleep, and he reached out with his hand to smooth the hair back from her cheek. Her hand reached up and cupped his knee, patting him gently in her sleep as if he were a pillow.

He shouldn't have felt a surge of lust. The position reminded him of other times, when she teased him with her mouth and hands. Predictably, he grew hard, a not uncommon occurrence around Mary.

Burrowing his right hand beneath her skirts, he allowed his fingers to trail up one stockinged leg and flatten against her hip. Beneath the shift her skin was warm, enticing. A moment later, she sighed again, moving a little. He let his fingers smooth against her delectably curved bottom. Her hand cupped his knee, slid down his calf and then upward again. Not the actions of a sleeper, unaware.

Glancing down, he caught the edge of her moonlight-dusted smile.

He moved his hand slowly up one thigh, to slip between her legs. Three fingers found her heat, gently pressing against soft folds even now moistening.

Her face was a monochrome in the moonlight. Passing beneath the trees gave the night a lacy pattern. Her fingers brushed against her own lips, and she moved again, separating her legs to give him greater access.

He slipped a finger into her slowly, penetrating her with great delicacy. She made a sound in the back of her throat, one of welcome or yearning, he thought. He knew she was no longer asleep, but experiencing the feeling of gentle arousal. Tenderly, he pressed his remaining fingers against her, feeling the rhythm of the wheels against the surface of the road, and wondering if the sensation added to her pleasure.

She pressed back against his hand, answering the question. He removed his finger slowly, and her movement stopped. A moment later, he inserted his finger again, mimicking his possession of her in the actions of his hand.

He wanted to tongue her nipples, kiss her neck, and stroke that spot just above her knees where she was especially sensitive. But he restrained himself. Anyone, seeing them, would think they presented an idyllic picture. She, innocent and demure, asleep on his lap. He, awake and watchful, the guardian of her rest. No one would know, to look at them, that his finger was buried deep inside her or that she was heated and trembling.

Her fingernail scratched against his breeches, and he smiled.

"You've always been a demanding lover," he said tenderly.

She blinked open her eyes, gave him a soft and sleepy smile. "I was asleep," she said. "Dreaming of you."

"Were you?" He moved his finger just the slightest bit, and she closed her eyes again, making a sound deep in her throat.

He moved the tip of one finger slightly forward, stroking it up and then down through her swollen folds. When he went faster, she shivered. Slower, and she made that sound again. He deliberately lengthened the movement, and when her hand cupped his knee, her wrist half shielding her face from view, he deepened the penetration.

There was no hurry. No one to see them, no one to know. Feeling her was an aphrodisiac, touching her was a wish granted. He could stroke her for hours, keeping himself on a pinnacle of need and want, making the times he was satiated all the more wondrous.

Or would he ever get his fill of her?

She moaned softly, arching her hips to the side, and pressing against his hand. He closed his eyes as he felt her erupt around him, tiny little tremors milking his finger and making a mockery of his restraint.

He hoped to God that they'd reach an inn soon.

Mary didn't look at him when she exited the coach. She couldn't. Her body was still trembling inside, and her clothes felt rough, abrasive to her skin. Without truly trying, he could make her forget circumstances and place. He always had been able to do so.

How delightful and delicious to be married to such a conjurer.

She waited while he made arrangements with the owner, and followed a young girl up the stairs.

"It's our best room," she was saying. "I put the bed warmer between the sheets just an hour ago." She opened the door. "I put a little bouquet of flowers there," she said, pointing to the circular table on the other side of the room.

Mary glanced to where she indicated. Sitting in a milk vase in the middle of the table was a profusion of greenery, small flowers branching off a network of tiny vines, looking like clusters of stars.

"It's too late in the year for flowers, of course, but the white blooms have a scent of their own, something spicy that tickles the nose."

The chamber was large, roughly the same size as the tavern downstairs.

To the left, dominating one wall, was a large red brick fireplace. To the right was a wardrobe and screened-off area. Sitting in the middle of the room, in front of the fire, was a very large, very imposing four-poster bed.

It would be the first time that they had slept together in such a magnificent bed.

Suddenly, Hamish was there, thanking the maid and closing the door behind her.

She tried to remember her wedding night with Gordon, and then recalled that he'd taken a nap early in the evening. But this husband was not elderly. Not at all.

Neither would this marriage be anything like her union with Gordon.

Removing her cloak, she hung it on the peg by the door.

She moved to Hamish's side in front of the armoire and watched him hang up his coat, then his vest before unfastening the buttons of his shirt. Slowly, she removed her long jacket, then her scarf, hanging them both beside his shirt. A marriage of their clothing.

She couldn't help but glance at him out of the corner of her eye. The tattoos on his body seemed particularly vibrant tonight, as if the flickering candlelight in the wall sconces gave life to Shiva.

They'd not spoken since entering the room, but the silence seemed charged with emotion.

Turning, she placed her hands between the base of his throat and his navel, feeling the ripple of muscle beneath the skin.

"You're beautiful," she said softly.

He frowned at her, and she smiled at his expression.

"I'm grotesque, but I thank you for your generosity."

"Silly man, you aren't the least ugly, and the tattoos aren't deforming. They're evidence of what they tried to do to you. Being in prison gave me a taste of what you endured. It was less than a week, Hamish, and yet it nearly drove me mad. But I kept telling myself that if you had been strong enough, I could at least try to be brave."

He stood there now in the flickering candlelight, strong, virile, and handsome. Despite what he said, he was beautiful to her.

Her other hand came up to cover a nipple. She stroked it gently, and the nipple constricted until it was tight and hard. She did the same with the other nipple, and watched in fascination at his response to her.

"Am I that responsive to your touch?" she asked him, already knowing the answer. He only smiled.

"Thank you for rescuing me," she said.

"Thank you for marrying me," he said.

She smiled. Unfastening his trousers, she plunged both hands inside, hungry for the feel of him.

An indrawn breath was his response when she found him hard. She stroked the length of his erection, her attention focused on him growing at her touch.

"It's like magic," she said, fascinated. "It always gets large so quickly."

"Any time you're around."

Her smile deepened at this evidence of his tact. It wouldn't do for him to admit that he was like this with any other woman.

She didn't think that she could tolerate the idea of his loving anyone else. Pushing the thought away before her imagination could conjure up too many details, she grasped him with both hands. "You're mine now."

"Am I a possession, then, Mary?"

"Oh yes," she said, the answer breathless and trembling.

She pushed his trousers down until they were at his hips, uncaring when he took over his own undressing. He removed his boots, then stepped free of his clothing. She'd not yet relinquished his erection, as if it were a prize she'd captured.

Even now, wetness pooled in secret crevices as her body rushed to welcome him. He was naked, and she was ready. But there were too many layers of clothing still between them.

She sat on the floor in a cloud of billowing skirts, reaching up to pull him down to her.

With a quizzical expression, he sat. "We've a bed, Mary," he said, but his smile didn't reach his eyes. His gaze was as hungry as she felt.

"Later," she said, pushing him down to the floor. She

was grateful that a rug lay beneath him since she wouldn't want him to get splinters on that beautiful backside of his. Once he was prone, she stepped over him, lowering herself onto his body. Her bodice was still fastened and her skirts covered him nearly to his chin, billowing out behind her to reach his knees and beyond. But inside, he was hard and hot and filling her.

She leaned back the tiniest bit, to more fully savor the sensation. Streaks of pleasure traveled from where they joined to the tips of her fingers and toes. Slowly, she began to unbutton her bodice. Hamish's hand was helping her, and she brushed it away, taking more time at the task than he would have. He arched up beneath her impatiently, and she bent forward to press her fingers to his lips.

"No," she said softly, chastisement in a word. "Slowly."

"You don't know what you're asking."

She only smiled in response.

He was swelling, lengthening inside her, and suddenly her fingers lost the ability to unfasten her buttons. She dropped her hands to her sides, and for long moments sat motionless, her bodice half opened and her eyes closed. Twice, she bit her lip rather than make a sound. Nothing must disturb this mindless descent into sheer, abandoned pleasure.

Hamish opened her bodice, tearing her shift. She heard the sound of the cloth ripping, but didn't open her eyes. Finally, his hand was on her, and she sighed aloud as he lifted first one breast, then the other from their tight restraint. They sat high above her stays, plumped into position by the constraint of them. He pressed his thumb and forefinger around a nipple until she opened her eyes.

A spear of desire shot through her at the sight of his tanned hand against her white breast. He plucked at a nipple, elongating it, trapping it between two of his fingers.

"You've beautiful breasts."

"Thank you." Ever polite. "You've a beautiful erection."

"Do you think so?"

"Indeed," she said, smiling at him.

He lifted his hips below her again, and this time she didn't try to restrain him, but rode down the feeling, closing her eyes at this sudden intense sensation. She wanted to experience that delicious sensation she'd felt only a few moments earlier. Or draw out the pleasure until she felt nothing else, until the memory of this feeling would always be with her. She'd close her eyes in the midst of a mundane chore and pull it to her, or before sleep and feel herself drowning in it.

"No," he said.

She glanced down at him.

"No," he repeated. "We'll use the bed."

"Must we?" She smiled at him, feeling deliciously wicked. He was deep inside her, and they were conversing as decorously as if they were in a parlor. "I don't want to move."

"You must."

"Must I?" She closed her eyes, ignoring him. "I've missed you," she told him. "I've missed this. I really don't want to move."

"If you don't, I won't pleasure you."

She opened her eyes, staring down into his flushed face. "You won't be able to help yourself," she said kindly.

"Would you like to wager on it?"

His eyes sparkled at her. His cheeks deepened in color, and his mouth thinned in determination. This was the man who'd faced down the Atavasi, who'd walked out of a desert. A lover with the soul of a lion.

"Should I care?" she asked, perfectly selfish at that moment. "I can have a great deal of enjoyment without your participation."

He smiled, a particularly leonine expression. "I won't move, then."

"That's an interesting threat, Hamish," she said softly. She rose just slightly and then lowered herself on him. The feeling was wondrous. "Perhaps if you stay just as you are?" she suggested.

His hand was suddenly there below her thigh, raising her. She slipped out of him, and was catapulted in a flurry of skirts to the floor. He stood, his erection throbbing at her, and pulled her to her feet, leading her to the bed.

She didn't have a chance to protest before he'd pushed her gently backward. She lay there, outwardly clothed, with him naked and masculine and very virile standing in front of her.

The bed was high, coming to Hamish's waist, just the right elevation. He gathered up her skirts and spread her legs.

"Put your legs around my waist," he said. She should refuse him, but he was very convincing, and she felt so very empty at the moment.

An instant later, she wrapped her legs around him, and he was slipping into her again, feeling harder and larger than he ever had before.

She gasped, being deliciously invaded, and enervated. Suddenly, it was too much effort to hold on to his shoulders. Her grasp weakened, and her arms fell back on the bed. He surged into her, and she wondered if she could die of pleasure.

"We've never done this before," she said breathlessly.

She tightened her legs around him, hung on as his strokes lengthened.

"We've never had a real bed before."

"You should have told me what we were missing," she said, finding the energy to curl her arms around his neck and bury her face in his shoulder.

"I wanted to show you."

Oh, and he did. Again, and again. She could do this forever. And feel this forever. She heard nothing but an indrawn gasp, and then suddenly her mind went blank and dark. Her body stilled, then shattered, trembling inside. The moment, silent, and terrifying, was transformed into one of pure joy that marked itself in her consciousness forever.

She welcomed him as he lay on top of her, wrapping her arms around his shoulders. He turned his head and kissed her, and she smiled against his lips.

"Such a wonderful bed," she said, her eyes closed.

"You should see what I can do with a bath," he teased, nuzzling her neck.

"Have they one here?" She peered over his shoulder, wondering what was behind the screen.

"In a moment," he said, laughing.

Her life in Inverness had been content, a warm sort of existence she'd made for herself, filled with routine and purpose. These moments, however filled with passion and laughter, were the ones she would always remember. Although she was escaping for her life, without money or possessions, she'd never felt more alive, happy, or in love.

Chapter 25

Mr. Grant entered the house stiffly, closing the door softly behind him. He limped to his favorite chair in the parlor, smiling his thanks to Elspeth, who hurriedly arranged the ottoman for him.

Brendan stood and greeted the older man, waiting patiently for him to be settled.

"I believe, daughter," Mr. Grant said finally, "that Brendan would like to speak with me."

Elspeth sent a flushed look in Brendan's direction and hurriedly excused herself.

"She'll be lonely without Mary," Mr. Grant said. There was an expectant expression on his face as he waited for Brendan to speak.

The timing could be worse, Brendan supposed. Of course, he could wait until he returned from Gilmuir, but that would leave him uncertain and wondering. Better to get a thing over with. He cleared his throat and straightened his shoulders, trying not to notice Mr. Grant's smile.

"I come from a very old family, Mr. Grant, with a very proud name. I've made my fortune at sea, but I've been thinking, for some time, of settling down."

"In Inverness?" the older man asked, sipping his forbidden whiskey. His gout was worsening, but Mr. Grant refused to abstain.

"Yes," Brendan said.

"Have you ever considered the distillery business, Brendan? It's an old and honorable trade."

"Perhaps I should," Brendan said, beginning to feel a little less panicked. The collar of his jacket felt as if it were strangling him. And his knees were knocking.

"I'd be pleased to have a junior partner. It'll be several years before Jack is old enough to join me, and none of my sons-in-law have expressed an interest in whiskey. Sometimes, I think they're not quite Scots."

Brendan smiled, thinking that he would have liked the older man even if he had never met Elspeth.

"Would you be as pleased to have me call upon your daughter?" he asked, summoning his courage. He stood with his legs braced apart, clasping his sweaty hands behind him.

Mr. Grant suddenly smiled. "I would at that, lad."

Only then did Brendan take a deep breath.

They celebrated over a glass of whiskey, and a few moments later, Brendan stood and began his farewells. Before he could start his future, he had to go to Castle Gloom and on to Gilmuir.

Elspeth was nowhere to be seen, and for a moment, he thought that he'd have to leave without bidding her farewell. But she was waiting for him in the courtyard, beside his horse. This morning, he'd given up his accommodations at the inn in preparation for this very journey.

"You're leaving for Gilmuir," Elspeth said.

Brendan nodded.

"Will you be gone long?" She stepped closer. "I'll miss you," Elspeth said, clasping her hands in front of her. The words were said in a soft, almost wistful tone.

He'd wanted to say what he felt in a more auspicious setting. Not standing a few feet away from the stable, with a horse's head between them. The sky overhead was a leaden gray, promising rain. The air was cold, and remnants of snow still clung to the ground. It was an ugly day for such a declaration. He wanted spring, and flowers, and words that had been rehearsed. Brendan moved away from his mount, gripping the reins in his right hand. Standing in front of Elspeth, he studied her. Today, she was dressed in blue, something that reminded him of sunny and warm summer days. Always before, being around her had brightened his mood. Now, however, he was all too conscious of his departure.

"I'll miss you as well," he said. Talking to her father was easier, he discovered than telling Elspeth how he felt. "But in addition to doing an errand for Hamish, I need to make arrangements for my ship."

She didn't look at him, and he knew, then, that she hadn't understood his subtle hint.

"I'll not be going back to sea."

Her head whipped up. She looked astonished, he thought, with her wide eyes and her mouth half open.

"I've always wanted to try my hands at another occupation," he said. Only a little falsehood. In actuality, he'd not given much thought to staying on land until he'd come to Inverness. No, he corrected himself, until he'd met Elspeth Grant.

But he'd already made his fortune; he could afford to

simply enjoy whatever venture he chose next, even that of making whiskey.

"Where will you live, Brendan? At Gilmuir?"

He shook his head. "In Inverness," he said, thinking that this business of divulging his heart was even more difficult than it had appeared at first.

Elspeth seemed to take a deep, relieved sigh. "Would you welcome me back?" There, the question he meant to ask all this time.

"I would, Brendan," she said breathlessly.

"I'll try to make the journey as fast as possible, Elspeth." He looked around, and seeing no one there, did a most forbidden thing. Hamish was not the only MacRae with a touch of wickedness to him. He bent and kissed her lightly on the lips, then stepped back before temptation proved too difficult to overcome. Elspeth's face blossomed with color, and her eyes sparkled merrily.

"Hurry and leave, then," she said. "The sooner you're gone, the sooner you'll return."

The afternoon was well advanced by the time the *Ionis* approached the end of Loch Euliss.

"Scotland hasn't changed," Ian said, hearing the sound of footsteps behind him and correctly identifying his wife. He glanced over his shoulder as Leitis joined him.

"It's an old country; the passage of a few decades makes no difference."

"Whereas Nova Scotia seems to be growing more crowded every year."

She sent him a fond look. "You don't like the English getting closer, Ian."

He smiled in agreement. "We'll be seeing Gilmuir

soon." He glanced around the deck. "Has Douglas found something more important to do?"

"He's talking with the captain, negotiating with him for a chance to pilot the ship out of the firth." She laughed, leaned her head against his shoulder. "Don't look so surprised. He's a MacRae."

"He's been adamant about never going to sea. Isn't that the reason we sent him to France?"

She nodded.

"What the blazes was he studying, anyway?"

"Philosophy."

"And women," Ian added in an annoyed tone.

"A MacRae trait," his wife said, trying and failing to stifle her smile.

"I'd rather he cultivated an interest in the sea than some French noble's daughter."

Her face abruptly sobered, and Ian wished he hadn't commented about Douglas's newest scandal.

"We have to do something about that, Ian."

He agreed, but he didn't know what could be done. Trust his youngest son to attempt to disgrace the family. "Did we spoil him?"

"Undoubtedly," she said, sighing. "The other boys were so much older when he was born. It would have been helpful to have them around when he was growing up."

"They would have kept him in line."

"It can't have been easy for him, though, being the youngest MacRae."

Ian sent her a look that summoned another smile.

"Very well," she admitted, "you're right. He is very securely himself."

"Being the youngest has never been Douglas's problem," his father said. "In fact, I would have preferred a little more reticence in his nature, at least where females are concerned."

"Do you know that I had a stream of visitors before we left? All young and all female, and every one of them concerned as to the length of the voyage. They didn't even have the tact to claim it was out of worry for us, either."

"Missing Douglas already?"

She nodded.

"With any luck, all the females at Gilmuir will be happily married or too young to be affected."

It was Leitis's turn to chastise him with her expression. He grinned. An instant later, his smile slipped as he looked past her.

"Dear Almighty God," he said, awed.

The ruins that had been Gilmuir had disappeared. The English fort that had stood beside the ancient castle was likewise gone. In its place was a tall, multiturreted structure of golden brick.

This new, imposing Gilmuir stretched the width of the promontory, two towers on either side seeming to rise up from the sheer cliff face. The sun's bright rays illuminated the fortress, causing the stones to appear golden and the high set windows like inlays of dark jewels. Perched on the edge, looking out over Loch Euliss, was the priory, with its fabled arches and pillars stretching the length of the castle.

"He's replaced the priory windows with stained glass," Leitis said, her voice sounding as astonished as Ian felt.

"But otherwise, it looks as it must have four hundred years ago," he said.

"Only larger."

Alisdair's accomplishment nearly overwhelmed him.

He felt pride, both as a MacRae and as the father of the man who'd created this miracle.

"We need the sound of the pipes in the background," Leitis said. "Something proper to welcome us back to Scotland."

"Pipes, hell," Ian said, grinning. He turned and shouted for the captain. "Peter," he said, when the man appeared, "break out the cannon."

"The cannon, sir?"

The *Ionis* was a trading vessel designed for ocean voyages. As such, she was equipped for any eventuality, including ten small cannon.

"Yes, cannon," Ian said. "We're going to announce our arrival in Scotland. The MacRaes have come home."

"Did you hear that noise?" Mary pulled back, but Hamish only murmured something deep in his throat and kissed her again. For ten minutes, he'd been kissing her like this, deeply, thrillingly. She felt warm all over, a delicious feeling like being drugged spreading through her body. She barely noticed the coach, or the sometimes steep incline. If asked, Mary would have said that the roads were like heaven only because she never felt any discomfort.

"Kissing you to Gilmuir is a wonderful way to travel," she said long moments later. She laid her head on his shoulder, lazily kissing his neck. His skin felt hot to the touch.

She entwined her fingers with his, realizing, suddenly, that they were moving. Surprised, she gripped his left hand. This morning, she'd insisted upon massaging his arm. But this was the first time she'd seen any change in his condition.

"I've been having some sensation," he admitted. "Like a tingling."

"Can you move your arm?" she asked, excited.

He shook his head. "No. Just the fingers and only a little."

"Still, it's more than you had," she said, smiling at him. "This is the very best news, Hamish," she said, bending to press a kiss to his palm.

He raised her head and kissed her mouth. She surrendered without much protest, wrapping her arms around his neck.

There it was again.

"Don't you hear that?" she asked, pulling back. "Like thunder, but the sky is clear."

She glanced out the window, staring at the sight before her eyes.

"Is that Gilmuir?" she asked, finding it difficult to swallow.

Hamish followed her look, and nodded. "Not quite as I remember," he admitted. "But yes, that's Gilmuir."

She had imagined it to be large, and it was. But she'd never realized that it might dominate the land on which it sat, or envisioned the blue loch that surrounded it on three sides. The glen rose from the land bridge, became hills that were nevertheless dwarfed by the magnificence of Gilmuir.

Hamish tapped on the top of the coach, a signal for the driver to stop. The horses slowed and then halted, the coach wheels rolling backward and then finally stopping.

Opening the door, he unfurled the steps and turned to help Mary down from the carriage.

"My father used to stop in this very place every year," he said. "His mother was a MacRae, but she married an

English earl. One of the conditions she arranged before their marriage was that she return every summer to Gilmuir with her son."

Mary didn't say a word, looking as awed as he felt.

He hadn't seen Gilmuir for three years, but it might have been a century. Alisdair had expanded the old castle until it took up most of the promontory. No one, seeing the behemoth of a building his brother had created, would be able to remember the ruins that had once stood on this spot. Most of the scaffolding was gone, and in its place was a four-towered structure that dominated the countryside.

In the middle of the new Gilmuir was a huge courtyard, spanned by an arch and framing the view of the loch. Hamish wondered if the staircase to the secret cove still existed or if Alisdair had built another way down to what was now his shipyard. They'd find out shortly.

"Well, Mary MacRae, shall we go home to Gilmuir?"

She looked momentarily disconcerted.

"Your new name sounds right," Hamish said, smiling at her.

"It feels right," she said, returning the smile.

They both got into the carriage again for the descent through the glen.

A circular drive curved in front of a wide flight of steps. At the top were two broad, heavily carved oak doors, flanked by a pair of lanterns mounted on tall iron poles. Similar lanterns lined the road from the glen. At night, the approach to Gilmuir would be both dramatic and welcoming.

Hamish opened the door before the driver could dismount, and helped Mary from the carriage. Taking his hand, she held her skirts with the other and mounted the steps to Gilmuir beside him.

A moment later, she heard the booming sound once again.

"What's that noise?"

"Cannon," Hamish said, identifying the sound. He descended the steps and stood in the courtyard staring out at the loch. There, on the horizon, was a ship, and from the puffs of smoke dissipating as it drew near, it was also clearly the source of the noise.

Mary joined him, shading her eyes from the bright sun.

"Why are they firing on us?" Mary asked, wondering where the inhabitants of Gilmuir were and why they weren't alarmed by the noise.

"They're not," he said, bemused. "They're signaling."

"But why?"

"To announce their arrival."

"Who?"

"My father." He turned to Mary. "You're about to meet my parents," he said, beginning to smile.

"There were times I despaired of ever seeing you again," a voice said from behind him. Hamish turned and greeted his oldest brother; the first time he'd seen him for three years.

Alisdair surveyed his face in silence.

"I'd heard you'd been tortured. Is that true?"

Hamish's smile faded. "Did Brendan tell you that?"

"Our brother has been suspiciously silent, Hamish. But his crew has not."

"What you heard was true enough, Alisdair."

A little girl followed by a toddler came running from the castle. Their feet flew over the grass, and Hamish was reminded of tales his mother had told, of growing up at Gilmuir as a child.

They ran to Alisdair, and he greeted them with a laugh as each gripped one of his legs. Both had silky black hair, and their features marked them as Alisdair's children, just as the intense blue eyes of the youngest child decreed him a MacRae.

"Aislin you'll remember," Alisdair said, ruffling the hair of his daughter. "And this little lad is Robert."

Hamish knelt until he was eye-level with both children.

"Well," he said smiling at the little girl, "I knew about you. In fact, I was here not long after you were born. But I had no idea about Robert."

"We call him Robbie," Aislin offered.

"I can talk," Robbie said indignantly.

That was, however, the extent of their conversation.

Hamish glanced over his shoulder, realizing he'd been rude. Standing, he drew Mary forward, placing his arm around her while he introduced her to his brother.

"I'd like you to meet my wife, Mary," he said.

Alisdair looked as surprised as Hamish had been at the sight of his brother's children. However, he hid it faster.

"You're the Angel of Inverness," he said.

"She doesn't like to be called that," Hamish said protectively.

Alisdair didn't even spare him a glance.

"Welcome," Alisdair said, extending both hands to Mary. She placed hers in his. "You're welcome to Gilmuir and to the family," he said warmly.

"Did you know they were coming?" Hamish asked, glancing out to sea once more. The vessel was the *Ionis;* the flag it flew identified it as the flagship of their merchant fleet. Only one man was entitled to fly that pennant, and his father did so rarely, since he disliked being at sea.

"I didn't," Alisdair said, turning to look at the loch. "But I'm glad of it. I never thought that they'd come home to Scotland."

"Nor I."

"They'll need to dock on the other side of the necklace of rocks and come around by land. We've hours until they arrive. Why don't we go inside, and you can greet Iseabal. I expect James today or tomorrow."

Hamish must have looked surprised, because Alisdair smiled. "We've been watching their ship since it entered the firth," he said. "What about Brendan?"

"He's on his way," Hamish said. "He's doing an errand for me."

All day, he had tried to keep Mary's thoughts from the verdict, and he knew he'd been only partially successful. When Alisdair looked quizzical, Hamish realized he'd have to tell his older brother the story.

Mary slipped her hand in his. He clasped it tightly, and together they walked toward Gilmuir.

Chapter 26

Three massive crystal chandeliers imported from France illuminated Gilmuir's clan hall. Cunning lanterns in the embrasures banished the shroud of shadows from the corners. The walls, painted a pale yellow, seemed to reflect the light, and acted as a perfect foil for the multicolored banners draped from the ceiling.

The table was long and wide, stretching the length of the room. What space wasn't occupied by platters of food was taken up with crystal, silver, and more candles. The guests sat on chairs with high backs, richly upholstered in tapestry.

Mary's past merged with her present in an odd way. Only Alisdair and Iseabal knew that the silver goblets they used came from Inverness, or that Gordon had fashioned them. Mary had seen them before, having marveled at Gordon's artistry as he'd packed a dozen of them in their specially designed wooden case.

Each chalice was seven inches tall and set with a leopard agate in the stem. Around the top was an ornate design of thistle and heather blossoms. Three main panels depicted scenes no doubt from the MacRaes' history: a tonsured monk painting on the wall of a cave, a woman bent over the neck of a horse clearing a hedge, a ship in full sail.

The room was filled with conversation. Occasionally, someone would exclaim aloud, or a burst of laughter would erupt from the end of the table.

Mary's silence wasn't because of the splendor of her surroundings. Her own home in Inverness had been filled with treasures. If anything kept her mute, it was the fascination with which she viewed her new in-laws.

She'd never met anyone like the MacRaes.

Ian was tall and broad shouldered, his temples rendered silver with age. His face was lined, true, but other than that, he appeared as youthful as his sons. Leitis, the matriarch of the clan, had more wrinkles, and she hesitated somewhat in rising and walking, but she had a youthful laugh. Her surprising blue eyes, young and now lit with laughter, were replicated in the faces of her two older sons.

It was their nature, however, that Mary marveled at more than their appearance. From the moment they'd met, Leitis had enfolded Mary in her arms. Ian had done so as well, welcoming her to the family.

Then there was Alisdair, who had rebuilt Gilmuir but insisted on sharing the praise with his wife, Iseabal.

"She's the one who saw Gilmuir finished," he said, smiling at her down the length of the table. "My only discontent with her is that she insists upon sculpting my face from time to time. There are better subjects for her talent."

"I concur," James said, raising his goblet. He and his wife, Riona, had arrived only an hour earlier.

The remaining MacRae was as different from Hamish as her husband was from Alisdair. Douglas had the curious aloofness she'd noted in Hamish upon first meeting him, and she wondered if it were caused by the same type of deep emotion. He'd met her eyes twice during the dinner, and twice looked away. Yet when addressed, he answered quickly enough, and his smile was often in place. Nevertheless, Mary had the thought that he was far from there. Not at Gilmuir at all, but some other location.

A loud banging on the massive oak and iron-banded door interrupted what Leitis was saying.

Alisdair stood, excusing himself, a grin on his face.

"He looks very pleased," Mary said, watching him.

Hamish turned and smiled at her. "He has a surprise for our mother."

A moment later, a giant of a man with bright red hair and a large grin entered the great hall in a limping gait. Leitis stood and stared at him, fisting her hands in her skirt. Mary couldn't decide who was the more fascinating to watch, Leitis, the stranger, or the rest of the MacRaes.

"Well, sister," he roared, "it's not a ghost you're looking at. Have you no greeting?"

Leitis began to smile, crossing the room to be enfolded in a bear hug. The two clung to each other as the rest of the MacRaes watched.

"It's her brother, Fergus," Hamish explained. "They haven't seen each other for over thirty years. Until Alisdair came back to Scotland, neither knew the other was alive."

There were more introductions as Fergus brought his wife forward. Mary learned that they had been sweethearts as young people but had not been reunited until a few years ago. There was also a bond of kinship; the woman she met was Iseabal's mother.

Room was made for them easily at the table. Aislin and Robbie had been put to bed hours ago, but Riona's baby was passed around to be greeted and kissed. As she watched them, Mary could feel herself becoming part of a large and warm family.

Gilmuir was as wondrous a place as she'd always heard, but not simply because of its magnificent architecture. The MacRaes lent it life.

"You must tell me how Hamish truly is," Leitis said, interrupting her reverie. She spoke under cover of another burst of laughter. "You know men; they rarely tell the truth if they think it might upset us."

Mary nodded, understanding only too well. "He's better now than he was," she admitted. "There's some movement in his fingers, and it's my hope that he regains the use of his arm. But it will take time, I'm afraid." She couldn't wait to try the electrical machine on his arm. All she had to do was convince Hamish. He'd looked decidedly unenthusiastic from the moment he'd unveiled Mr. Marshall's surprise gift.

"And you," Leitis said, patting her on the wrist. "I suspect you have a great deal to do with it."

Hamish was seated on the other side of her. Every few moments, he'd glance in her direction as if he weren't quite sure she was real. These hours at Gilmuir felt like time in an imaginary land. Hamish was laughing, sharing memories with his family. She was welcomed as she'd never thought to be. The verdict two days ago seemed very far away as was the realization that she could never return to Inverness again.

Or remain in Scotland.

She exchanged a look with Hamish and forced a smile to her face, determined to forget for a while at least.

Leitis was given the baby once again, and she cradled the infant in her arms. Ian leaned over and smoothed his finger across his wife's cheek.

"If you continue to cry on them," he said, "they'll forever think of you as their weeping grandmother."

"I can't help it," Leitis said. "Babies make me cry." She smiled down at James's son, born last August. "We're soon to have another grandchild as well," she said softly.

Douglas abruptly stood and left the room.

Riona only laughed when James looked at her.

Iseabal held up both hands when Alisdair's interested gaze fell on her. "I've no news to tell you," she said. "I swear."

Hamish sent an even more inquiring look at Mary. She smiled and shook her head.

"Douglas is the father," Leitis said.

"Douglas?" Each of the MacRae sons intoned their youngest brother's name in shock.

Hamish set down his goblet and stared at his father. The older man was nodding soberly, and didn't look at all pleased.

"He's too young to be married," Hamish said.

"On that, I agree," his father said. "But it hasn't stopped him from becoming a father."

"What about the girl?"

"Won't have a thing to do with him," his mother said.

"She's some damn count's daughter," Ian said tightly, "with an inflated view of herself, evidently. Sort of a noblesse oblige attitude the French are so famous for."

Hamish sat back in his chair. "This just keeps getting worse. She's French?"

Alisdair sent him an amused look. "At least she's not English."

"She's taken herself off, and the count refuses to tell us where she is. We don't know what's to become of the child."

There was only silence as they all looked at one another. An unwanted child could easily disappear.

Another clanging sound from the door knocker made Alisdair stand. He left the room to return a few minutes later, Brendan at his side looking worn and tired. After being greeted by his parents, he pulled away and nodded at Hamish and Mary.

"Now are you going to tell me what secrets you're hiding?" Ian looked at his sons, and then Mary.

At their silence, he stared at Hamish. "Well?"

Hamish smiled and reached for Mary's hand. "What makes you think we're hiding anything?"

Ian gave an exasperated sigh and looked at Leitis. "Your son seems to think I've no sense at all."

Hamish smiled, and reached for Mary's hand. "It isn't my tale," he said, "but Mary's."

For a moment, she didn't want to say anything. Doing so would jeopardize her new standing in this family. They'd welcomed her without reservation. The story might cause them to as easily repudiate her. Who, after all, would want a murderess in their midst? Even an accidental one?

She glanced at Hamish. He nodded once, smiling, and she realized it didn't matter what anyone but Hamish thought of her. She told them everything, omitting only her time with Hamish at Castle Gloom. Those memories were for them alone, and didn't warrant the scrutiny of others.

She didn't know what she expected of the MacRaes, but each of them only nodded when she finished.

"I've had a taste of justice," Alisdair said, "when I first came back to Scotland. Magnus Drummond owned MacRae land, and threatened me with the courts. I doubt I would have been able to get my rightful land back. They dispensed an English kind of justice."

Hamish made room for Brendan to sit beside him. "The Grants and Mr. Marshall? Are they safe?"

Brendan nodded. "Mr. Marshall is on his way to London, and the Grants haven't been implicated in Mary's disappearance. What about your plans? Does Alisdair have a ship?"

Hamish and Alisdair exchanged a glance. "The new ship won't be ready for months," Alisdair said.

"All the better," Brendan said. "I've one you can use."

Hamish studied his brother. Slowly, he began to smile. "You're giving up the sea?"

"Inverness has a great many attractions," Brendan said. Alisdair passed him a goblet and a plate and he began to eat.

"Is one of them a blond-haired girl by the name of Elspeth?" Mary asked.

"It is," Brendan said, smiling.

"Does she know?"

He nodded. "And her father, as well."

Mary smiled, pleased.

Brendan turned to Hamish. "You need a ship, and I need to make arrangements for mine. You'll be doing me a favor if you take the *Moira MacRae*."

"Are you certain of this, Brendan?"

"I am," he said. "It's time I settled down, found my land legs. Inverness will suit me well." He grinned at Hamish. "Besides, it will do me good to be a thorn in Charles Talbot's side." He sobered, regarding his brother with earnest eyes. "I was all for convincing you to stay at sea when you wanted to do the same. I was wrong then, Hamish."

"If I had," Hamish said, "I never would have met Mary."

"One of these days, you'll be thanking me for that. Without my intervention, you wouldn't have met her at all."

"Without your interference, you mean."

Brendan grinned again. "Perhaps."

"Have I nothing to say about that?" Mary asked, her gaze veering from one MacRae brother to the other. "If I hadn't agreed to treat Hamish, we never would have met."

There, that silenced both of them.

"Will your crew agree to sail with me?" Hamish asked. "I've lost a ship and all my men."

"Not through any act of your own," Brendan said loyally.

"You know as well as I how superstitious sailors are."

"Take Daniel on as first mate," Ian said, from across the table. He'd been listening to his sons' conversation, but hadn't commented. "Daniel's aboard my ship," he said. "He's driving me insane with his superstitions. He'll sail with you because you're a MacRae. Take him with you. And all his cats. He's got three now, and I sneezed all the way across the Atlantic. No sailor would ever think you unlucky with Daniel and his cats."

Hamish grinned his acceptance.

Ian looked down at his plate, then over at Leitis. "You'll do me a favor, Hamish, if you'll take Douglas with you as well."

Hamish and his father exchanged a look.

"He wants to learn about the sea," Leitis said. "Besides, the change will do him good."

Hamish nodded.

In the buzz of conversation, Hamish turned to Mary, grabbed her hand, and brushed a kiss across her knuckles.

"You should see Brendan's ship. The *Moira MacRae* is long and sleek and built for long ocean voyages."

"Who's Daniel?"

"A cantankerous first mate who'll fill your days with one superstition after another. He's a trial and a nuisance, but we think highly of him nonetheless."

"You never said you wanted to go back to sea."

"I'd like to show you the world, Mary MacRae."

She felt a smile building up from her toes. "I've always wanted an adventure, Hamish. Wherever you wish to take me, I'll go."

"I've our voyages all planned in my mind. We'll do some trading, but we'll travel for the love of it. You can see the world, Mary, and study medicine as well."

"I doubt if I'll have the courage to treat another patient," she said, offering him the truth. He stood and took her hand. Together they walked some distance from the table.

"Why would you say that?" To his credit, he looked genuinely surprised.

"Look what happened."

He pressed a kiss to her forehead, and then pulled back.

"My father wishes that he'd never fought the Scots as he once did. There are scores of deaths at his hands, no doubt. Iseabal would probably wish to have treated her father differently. Fergus would have come back to Gilmuir after Culloden. Each member of my family has his own regrets. Yet they're all decent people, all good people."

He tilted up her chin with one finger. "I would willingly put my life in your hands. If I have faith in you, you must as well."

"As simple as that?"

"As simple as that," he said, smiling.

Impossibly, it was. His gaze was clear, his emotions visible for anyone to see. There was no doubt that he meant what he said, and that he loved her, truly, deeply, completely.

She blinked away her tears, feeling as if they were simply a release for all the happiness she felt bubbling up inside. How could she contain all this joy?

"I've never been to sea before," she said, placing her hands on his chest, feeling his heart beat loud and strong beneath her palms.

"If you're not a good sailor," Hamish said, "we'll have to find a remedy for you."

"A dose of Hamish, at least once a day," she teased, making him laugh.

Bending, he kissed her lightly.

"Will you miss Scotland?" he asked sometime later.

"I've never left before," she said smiling, "so I don't know. But with you at my side, it will be a grand adventure, I think. Under those circumstances, how can I regret anything?"

He smiled at her, and Mary felt her heart stutter.

She was reminded of when she'd first seen him, standing on the steps, his face in shadow. She'd thought, then, that he had a great force of presence. Now, she knew exactly who he was, and her initial impression had been correct. Yet he was also vulnerable, thoughtful, and had a sense of humor that always amused her.

He was a survivor, most definitely. A man with a past, who had done some acts he would always regret. Hamish MacRae wasn't a paragon without sins. Ah, but neither was she.

But together, they were perfect.

Epilogue

"**I**'m not as young as I once was," Leitis said, "and I feel it in every single bone in my body. It's not fair that you look so hale and hearty in return." The hill in front of them looked a great deal steeper than it had when they'd begun this walk.

Ian only grinned at her and held her hand more tightly. "I remember you as a child, running over these hills," he said. "You beat me at every foot race, I remember."

"That was a very long time ago."

"It seems like just yesterday, though, doesn't it?"

She smiled. "I don't feel one year older inside, Ian. It's outside where I've changed."

"You look the same to me, my love."

She stopped and studied him, thinking that he was the one who appeared unchanged by time. Aging suited him somehow. His face had mellowed with the years, but if she narrowed her eyes just so, she wouldn't think him any different from the English colonel who'd once captivated her heart. Or the boy she'd loved even as he bedeviled her.

They walked in silence up to the cairn stones. He found the one he wanted unerringly, as if decades hadn't separated the visits. A three-sided stone structure protected a shard of wood in front of the grave. As a boy, he'd carved the cross for his mother, but now there was little left to it.

Kneeling, he paid his respects, and she turned, granting him the privacy to do so. She looked out over the landscape. In front of them was Gilmuir, restored to its former glory. No, she thought looking at it with a mother's pride, better than it had been before. Alisdair had created a monument.

Below, Hamish unerringly led the sleek and beautiful *Moira MacRae* into the firth. He'd looked so happy to be going to sea again, and Mary appeared filled with awe as they'd rowed out to the ship. Even Douglas had lost his remote expression, showing an interest in something for the first time in months. What would become of him? She sighed, thinking of the untenable situation he'd left in France. She watched the ship for a while, sails full-bellied, eager for the ocean and the rest of the world.

A song she hadn't heard in years occurred to her as she stood there. The MacRae Lament.

> *We are an island, a people of pride.*
> *We are a past never to die.*
> *In good times or bad we'll always endure*
> *In the home of our hearts—Gilmuir.*

She knew something now that she hadn't known as a girl. Gilmuir would always link them, but love would bind them together.

"Are you weeping?" Ian said, coming to stand at her side. "I thought you were done with that."

"I thought I was," she admitted.

"They'll be fine," he said, extending his arms around her. "Hamish is an exemplary captain, and Douglas could have no better mentor."

"I know." She nodded against his chest. "I like Mary, too. She'll be a good influence."

"On both of them," Ian said, smiling.

"I like all their wives. I didn't expect to, isn't that strange? But I would have them as friends, each and every one of them."

"It's a good thing you feel that way," Ian said, amusement coloring his voice. "I doubt any of our sons would give his wife up because you disapproved."

"They love as fiercely as their father, I think." She pulled back and smiled up at him.

"Or their mother," he countered.

The sun was low on the horizon, casting shadows over the hills. In a few hours, night would come to Gilmuir once again. But there would be no sadness in the darkness. Only the sound of laughter as candles were lit and voices rose in teasing toasts. The wind would blow across the headland and carry the scent of the sea over the hills, ruffling the grasses and sighing through the pines.

If ghosts were disturbed, they would be temperate ones. Their heads might turn in the direction of the old fortress made new again. Some might momentarily grieve that they were no longer living and couldn't participate in earthly joy. But most would smile in remembrance, and feel a last, lingering pride in their descendants before slipping away into eternity.

Author's Note

Matthew Marshall is loosely based on John Wesley, the eighteenth-century traveling minister. Wesley, too, was fascinated with medicine, especially the electrical machine. In 1767, the Middlesex Hospital in London purchased an electrical machine to treat its patients. Iron deficiency, anemia, Raynaud's Syndrome, tuberculosis, and goiter were some of the diseases treated with the apparatus.

Medicine was practiced by two groups in the eighteenth century—those few individuals who were academically trained or who learned what they needed to know as apprentices of physicians who had attended university, and wise women and men, including clergymen, who practiced an irregular type of medicine. Although there was a gulf of differences between the academics and empirics (those who used a trial-and-error method of treating patients), there were several beliefs they shared in common. The idea of obstruction was one of the major tenets of eighteenth-century medicine. Mercury was considered one of the meritorious elements to aid in relieving obstructions since it is fourteen times heavier than water. Not until the twentieth century did practitioners come to understand how lethal mercury is.

Several localized rebellions occurred in India in the late eighteenth century as the native populations protested the British presence in their country. These rebellions were always suppressed, at least until the nineteenth century.

There were several deserted castles along the coast of Scotland in the last two hundred years. One, Castle Stalker near Oban, was the model for Castle Gloom, in size and location. My imagination, however, furnished the rest.

The Heritable Jurisdictions Act in 1747 abolished the clan laird system of justice in Scotland. Because this act also breached the Treaty of Union, a judicial vacuum was formed, creating the Scottish sheriff. The Sheriff's Courts had jurisdiction over most crimes, except cases of murder, which were always sent to a higher court.

The origin of chess is still a point of contention in many circles. Some believed it began in China, others in India. There are at least three different ways of spelling shatranj, which is considered the second known variant of chess. I've chosen the easiest to pronounce.

The word Atavasi appeared during my early research on India and then disappeared among my copious notes. Although I've never been able to define the word, I've taken it to mean the native peoples of India, especially those who resented the British incursion into their land, their culture, and their way of life.

In September, let the ladies of Avon Books bring you
the romance of a lifetime!

TAMING THE SCOTSMAN by Kinley MacGregor
An Avon Romantic Treasure

Nora is a woman with a mission. Rather than be forced
into a loveless marriage, she decides to leave home and head
for England. And the best guide to take her there is Ewan
MacAllister. Yet from the moment she meets Ewan, she sees
through his rough and tumble exterior and yearns to tame
the proud Highlander who protects his wounded heart.

OFF LIMITS by Michele Albert
An Avon Contemporary Romance

Emma knows there are certain men she should avoid—and
"bad boy" detective Bobby Halloran is a prime example.
But now she's teamed up with the heartbreaker, and everyone in the station house is making bets on how long Emma
will be able to resist him. With Bobby turning on the charm,
Emma wonders if it's true what they say—some rules are
meant to be broken.

Also available in September,
two beautifully repackaged
classic Julia Quinn love stories

SPLENDID
&
EVERYTHING AND THE MOON

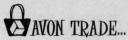